Prepare to fall in love.
JULIA QUINN

D0051727

USA TODAY BESTSELLER

Tessa Dare

A Week to Be Wicked

Enjoy another
Spindle Cove seduction
from romance master

Tessa Dare

Dare to Seek
Romance

"I don't believe you."

"You should. Others would."

"You've been mercilessly teasing me for months now. No one would forget that."

"All part of the infatuation. Don't you know? A man might engage in flirtation with disinterest, even disdain. But he never teases without affection."

He placed his hands on her shoulders. His gaze swept her body from boots to unbound hair, then back. "I could have them all believing I'm consumed by a savage, visceral passion for this enchantress with raven's-wing hair and sultry lips. That I admire her fierce loyalty to her sisters and her brave, resourceful spirit. That I'm driven wild by hints of a deep, hidden passion that escapes her sometimes, when she ventures out of her shell."

His strong hands moved to frame her face. His Bristol diamond eyes held hers. "That I see in her a rare, wild beauty that's been overlooked, somehow, by other men. And I want it. Desperately. All for myself. Oh, I could have them believing it all."

By Tessa Dare

A Week to Be Wicked
A Night to Surrender
Three Nights with a Scoundrel
Twice Tempted by a Rogue
One Dance with a Duke
A Lady of Persuasion
Surrender of a Siren
Goddess of the Hunt

Coming Soon

A Lady by Midnight

Tessa Dare

A Week to Be Wicked

AVON

An Imprint of HarperCollins*Publishers*

AVON BOOKS
An Imprint of HarperCollins*Publishers*
10 East 53rd Street
New York, New York 10022-5299

Copyright © 2012 by Eve Ortega
Excerpt from *A Lady by Midnight* copyright © 2012 by Eve Ortega
ISBN 978-0-06-204987-2
www.avonromance.com

First Avon Books mass market printing: April 2012

Avon Trademark Reg. U.S. Pat. Off. and in Other Countries, Marca Registrada, Hecho en U.S.A.
HarperCollins ® is a registered trademark of HarperCollins Publishers.

Printed in the U.S.A.

10 9 8 7 6 5 4 3 2 1

For all the girls who walk and read at the same time.

Acknowledgments

Many thanks to Tessa Woodward, Helen Breitwieser, Martha Trachtenberg, Ellen Leach, Pam Spengler-Jaffee, Jessie Edwards, and Kim Castillo, for their expertise and assistance. And much gratitude to my husband and family, for their love and patience.

Researching and writing this book made me so grateful to be a part of the romance community today. Romance authors and readers are a brilliant, diverse, inspiring group. We are doctors, lawyers, businesswomen, scholars, scientists, soldiers, and much, much more. And to interact with this vibrant, enriching community of women (and a few good men), I needn't travel any further than my laptop. This, to me, is a tremendous blessing. I am thankful every day.

So my thanks to the online romance community: the authors, the editors, the agents, the booksellers, the librarians, the bloggers, the reviewers . . . and the readers, most of all! Thanks to the many e-mail loops that keep me laughing and teach me something new every day: they include the Two Geniuses, the Vanettes, The Morning Juice, my fellow Ballroom Bloggers, the Avon Authors, and the Loop That Shall Not Be Named. Thank you, Twitter.

And thank you, Ada Lovelace.

Chapter One

hen a girl trudged through the rain at midnight to knock at the Devil's door, the Devil should at least have the depravity—if not the decency—to answer.

Minerva gathered the edges of her cloak with one hand, weathering another cold, stinging blast of wind. She stared in desperation at the closed door, then pounded it with the flat of her fist.

"Lord Payne," she shouted, hoping her voice would carry through the thick oak planks. "Do come to the door! It's Miss Highwood." After a moment's pause, she clarified, "Miss Minerva Highwood."

Rather nonsensical, that she needed to state just *which* Miss Highwood she was. From Minerva's view, it ought to be obvious. Her younger sister, Charlotte, was an exuberant yet tender fifteen years of age. And the eldest of the family, Diana, possessed not only angelic beauty, but the disposition to match. Neither of them were at all the sort to slip from bed at night, steal down the back stairs of the rooming house, and rendezvous with an infamous rake.

But Minerva was different. She'd always been different.

Of the three Highwood sisters, she was the only dark-haired one, the only bespectacled one, the only one who preferred sturdy lace-up boots to silk slippers, and the only one who cared one whit about the difference between sedimentary and metamorphic rocks.

The only one with no prospects, no reputation to protect.

Diana and Charlotte will do well for themselves, but Minerva? Plain, bookish, distracted, awkward with gentlemen. In a word, hopeless.

The words of her own mother, in a recent letter to their cousin. To make it worse, Minerva hadn't discovered this description by snooping through private correspondence. Oh, no. She'd transcribed the words herself, penning them at Mama's dictation.

Truly. Her own *mother.*

The wind caught her hood and whisked it back. Cold rain pelted her neck, adding injury to insult.

Swiping aside the hair matted to her cheek, Minerva stared up at the ancient stone turret—one of four that comprised the Rycliff Castle keep. Smoke curled from the topmost vent.

She raised her fist again, pounding at the door with renewed force. "Lord Payne, I know you're in there."

Vile, teasing man.

Minerva would root herself to this spot until he let her in, even if this cold spring rain soaked her to the very marrow. She hadn't climbed all this distance from the village to the castle, slipping over mossy outcroppings and tracing muddy rills in the dark, just to trudge the same way back home, defeated.

However, after a solid minute of knocking to no avail, the fatigue of her journey set in, knotting her calf muscles and softening her spine. Minerva slumped forward. Her forehead met wood with a dull *thunk*. She kept her fist lifted overhead, beating on the door in an even, stubborn rhythm. She might very well be plain, bookish, distracted, and awkward—but she was determined. Determined to be acknowledged, determined to be heard.

Determined to protect her sister, at any cost.

Open, she willed. *Open. Open. Op—*

The door opened. Swiftly, with a brisk, unforgiving *whoosh*.

"For the love of tits, Thorne. Can't it wait for—"

"Ack." Caught off balance, Minerva stumbled forward. Her fist rapped smartly against—not the door, but a chest.

Lord Payne's chest. His masculine, muscled, shirtless chest, which proved only slightly less solid than a plank of oak. Her blow landed square on his flat, male nipple, as though it were the Devil's own door-knocker.

At least this time, the Devil answered.

"Well." The dark word resonated through her arm. "You're not Thorne."

"Y-you're not clothed." *And I'm touching your bare chest. Oh . . . Lord.*

The mortifying thought occurred to her that he might not be wearing trousers either. She righted herself. As she removed her spectacles with chilled, trembling fingers, she caught a reassuring smudge of dark wool below the flesh-colored blur of his torso. She huffed a breath on each of the two glass discs connected by brass, wiped the mist from them with a dry fold of her cloak lining, and then replaced them on her face.

He was still half naked. And now, in perfect focus. Devious tongues of firelight licked over every feature of his handsome face, defining him.

"Come in, if you mean to." He winced at a blast of frost-tipped wind. "I'm shutting the door, either way."

She stepped forward. The door closed behind her with a heavy, finite sound. Minerva swallowed hard.

"I must say, Melinda. This is rather a surprise."

"My name's Minerva."

"Yes, of course." He cocked his head. "I didn't recognize your face without the book in front of it."

She exhaled, letting her patience stretch. And stretch. Until it expanded just enough to accommodate a teasing rake with a sieve-like memory. And stunningly well-defined shoulders.

"I'll admit," he said, "this is hardly the first time I've answered the door in the middle of night and found a woman waiting on the other side. But you're certainly the least expected one yet." He sent her lower half an assessing look. "And the most muddy."

She ruefully surveyed her mud-caked boots and bedraggled hem. A midnight seductress she was not. "This isn't *that* kind of visit."

"Give me a moment to absorb the disappointment."

"I'd rather give you a moment to dress." Minerva crossed the round chamber of windowless stone and went straight for the hearth. She took her time tugging loose the velvet ties of her cloak, then draped it over the room's only armchair.

Payne hadn't wasted the entirety of his months here in Spindle Cove, it seemed. Someone had put a great deal of work into transforming this stone silo into a warm, almost comfortable home. The original stone hearth had been cleaned and restored to working order. In it blazed a fire large and fierce enough to do a Norman warrior proud. In addition to the upholstered armchair, the circular room contained a wooden table and stools. Simple, but well made.

No bed.

Strange. She swiveled her gaze. Didn't an infamous rake need a bed?

Finally, she looked up. The answer hovered overhead. He'd fashioned a sort of sleeping loft, accessible by a ladder.

Rich drapes concealed what she assumed to be his bed. Above that, the stone walls spiraled into black, cavernous nothingness.

Minerva decided she'd given him ample time to find a shirt and make himself presentable. She cleared her throat and slowly turned. "I've come to ask—"

He was still half naked.

He had not used the time to make himself presentable. He'd taken the chance to pour a drink. He stood in profile, making scrunched faces into a wineglass to assess its cleanliness.

"Wine?" he asked.

She shook her head. Thanks to his indecent display, a ferocious blush was already burning its way over her skin. Up her throat, over her cheeks, up to her hairline. She hardly needed to throw wine on the flames.

As he poured a glass for himself, she couldn't help but stare at his leanly muscled torso, so helpfully limned by firelight. She'd been used to thinking him a devil, but he had the body of a god. A lesser one. His wasn't the physique of a hulking, over-muscled Zeus or Poseidon, but rather a lean, athletic Apollo or Mercury. A body built not to bludgeon, but to hunt. Not to lumber, but to race. Not to overpower unsuspecting naiads where they bathed, but to . . .

Seduce.

He glanced up. She looked away.

"I'm sorry to wake you," she said.

"You didn't wake me."

"Truly?" She frowned at him. "Then . . . for as long as it took you to answer the door, you might have put on some clothes."

With a devilish grin, he indicated his trousers. "I did."

Well. Now her cheeks all but caught fire. She dropped into the armchair, wishing she could disappear into its seams.

For God's sake, Minerva, take hold of yourself. Diana's future is at stake.

Setting the wine on the table, he moved to some wooden shelves that seemed to serve as his wardrobe. To the side, a row of hooks supported his outerwear. A red officer's coat, for the local militia he led in the Earl of Rycliff's absence. A few finely tailored, outrageously expensive-looking topcoats from Town. A greatcoat in charcoal-gray wool.

He passed over all these, grabbed a simple lawn shirt, and yanked it over his head. Once he'd thrust his arms through the sleeves, he held them out to either side for her appraisal. "Better?"

Not really. The gaping collar still displayed a wide view of his chest—only with a lascivious wink instead of a frank stare. If anything, he looked more indecent. Less of an untouchable, chiseled god and more of a raffish pirate king.

"Here." He took the greatcoat from its hook and brought it to her. "It's dry, at least."

Once he'd settled the coat over her lap, he pressed the glass of wine into her hand. A signet ring flashed on his little finger, shooting gold through the glass's stem.

"No arguments. You're shivering so hard, I can hear your teeth chatter. The fire and coat help, but they can't warm you inside."

Minerva accepted the glass and took a careful sip. Her fingers did tremble, but not entirely from the cold.

He pulled up a stool, sat on it, and fixed her with an expectant look. "So."

"So," she echoed, stupidly.

Her mother was right in this respect. Minerva considered herself a reasonably intelligent person, but good heavens . . . handsome men made her stupid. She grew so flustered around them, never knew where to look or what to say. The reply meant to be witty and clever would come out sounding bitter or lame. Sometimes a teasing remark from Lord Payne's quarter quelled her into dumb silence altogether. Only days later, while she was banging away at a cliff face with a rock hammer, would the perfect retort spring to mind.

Remarkable. The longer she stared at him now, the more she could actually feel her intelligence waning. A day's growth of whiskers only emphasized the strong cut of his jaw. His mussed brown hair had just a hint of roguish wave. And his eyes . . . he had eyes like Bristol diamonds. Small round geodes, halved and polished to a gleam. An outer ring of flinty hazel enclosed cool flashes of quartz. A hundred crystalline shades of amber and gray.

She squeezed her eyes shut. *Enough dithering.* "Do you mean to marry my sister?"

Seconds passed. "Which one?"

"Diana," she exclaimed. "Diana, of course. Charlotte being all of fifteen."

He shrugged. "Some men like a young bride."

"Some men have sworn off marriage entirely. You told me you were one of them."

"I told *you* that? When?"

"Surely you remember. That night."

He stared at her, obviously nonplussed. "We had 'a night'?"

"Not how you're thinking." Months ago now, she'd confronted him in the Summerfield gardens about his scandalous indiscretions and his intentions toward her sister. They'd clashed. Then they'd somehow *tangled*—bodily— until a few cutting insults severed the knot.

Curse her scientific nature, so relentlessly observant. Minerva resented the details she'd gleaned in those moments. She did not need to know that his bottom waistcoat button was exactly in line with her fifth vertebra, or that he smelled faintly of leather and cloves. But even now, months later, she couldn't seem to jettison the information.

Especially not when she sat huddled in his greatcoat, embraced by borrowed warmth and the same spicy, masculine scent.

Naturally, he'd forgotten the encounter entirely. No surprise. Most days, he couldn't even remember Minerva's name. If he spoke to her at all, it was only to tease.

"Last summer," she reminded him, "you told me you had no intentions of proposing to Diana. Or anyone. But today, gossip in the village says different."

"Does it?" He twisted his signet ring. "Well, your sister is lovely and elegant. And your mother's made no secret that she'd welcome the match."

Minerva curled her toes in her boots. "That's putting it mildly."

Last year, the Highwoods had come to this seaside village for a summer holiday. The sea air was supposed to improve Diana's health. Well, Diana's health had long been improved and summer was long gone, yet the Highwoods remained—all because of Mama's hopes for a match between Diana and this charming viscount. So long as Lord Payne was in Spindle Cove, Mama would not hear of returning home. She'd even developed an uncharacteristic streak of optimism—each morning declaring as she stirred her chocolate, "I feel it, girls. Today is the day he proposes."

And though Minerva knew Lord Payne to be the worst sort of man, she had never found it in herself to object. Because she loved it here. She didn't want to leave. In Spindle Cove, she finally . . . belonged.

Here, in her own personal paradise, she explored the rocky, fossil-studded coast free from care or censure, cataloging findings that could set England's scientific community on its ear. The only thing that kept her from being completely happy was Lord Payne's presence—and through one of life's strange ironies, his presence was the very reason she was able to stay.

There'd seemed no harm in allowing Mama to nurse hopes of a proposal from his lordship's quarter. Minerva had known for certain a proposal wasn't coming.

Until this morning, when her certainty crumbled.

"This morning, I was in the All Things shop," she began. "I usually ignore Sally Bright's gossip, but today . . ." She met his gaze. "She said you'd given directions for your mail to be forwarded to London, after next week. She thinks you're leaving Spindle Cove."

"And you concluded that this means I'll marry your sister."

"Well, everyone knows your situation. If you had two shillings to rub together, you'd have left months ago. You're stranded here until your fortune's released from trust on your birthday, unless . . ." She swallowed hard. "Unless you marry first."

"That's all true."

She leaned forward in her chair. "I'll leave in a heartbeat, if you'll only repeat your words to me from last summer. That you have no intentions toward Diana."

"But that was last summer. It's April now. Is it so inconceivable that I might have changed my mind?"

"*Yes.*"

"Why?" He snapped his fingers. "I know. You think I don't possess a mind to change. Is that the sticking point?"

She sat forward in her chair. "You can't change your mind, because you haven't *changed*. You're a deceitful, insincere rake who flirts with unsuspecting ladies by day, then takes up with other men's wives by night."

He sighed. "Listen, Miranda. Since Fiona Lange left the village, I haven't—"

Minerva held up a hand. She didn't want to hear about

his *affaire* with Mrs. Lange. She'd heard more than enough from the woman herself, who'd fancied herself a poetess. Minerva wished she could scrub her mind of those poems. Ribald, rhapsodic odes that exhausted every possible rhyme for "quiver" and "bliss."

"You can't marry my sister," she told him, willing firmness to her voice. "I simply won't allow it."

As their mother was so fond of telling anyone who'd listen, Diana Highwood was exactly the sort of young lady who could set her cap for a handsome lord. But Diana's external beauty dulled in comparison to her sweet, generous nature and the quiet courage with which she'd braved illness all her life.

Certainly, Diana *could* catch a viscount. But she *shouldn't* marry this one.

"You don't deserve her," she told Lord Payne.

"True enough. But none of us get what we truly deserve in this life. Where would God's sport be in that?" He took the glass from her hand and drew a leisurely sip of wine.

"She doesn't love you."

"She doesn't dislike me. Love's hardly required." Leaning forward, he propped an arm on his knee. "Diana would be too polite to refuse. Your mother would be overjoyed. My cousin would send the special license in a trice. We could be married this week. You could be calling me 'brother' by Sunday."

No. Her whole body shouted the rejection. Every last corpuscle.

Throwing off the borrowed greatcoat, she leaped to her feet and began pacing the carpet. The wet folds of her skirt tangled as she strode. "This can't happen. It cannot. It *will* not." A little growl forced its way through her clenched teeth.

She balled her hands in fists. "I have twenty-two pounds saved from my pin money. That, and some change. It's yours, all of it, if you promise to leave Diana alone."

"Twenty-two pounds?" He shook his head. "Your sisterly sacrifice is touching. But that amount wouldn't keep me in London a week. Not the way I live."

She bit her lip. She'd expected as much, but she'd reasoned it couldn't hurt to try a bribe first. It would have been so much easier.

She took a deep breath and lifted her chin. This was it— her last chance to dissuade him. "Then run away with me instead."

After a moment's stunned pause, he broke into hearty laughter.

She let the derisive sounds wash over her and simply waited, arms crossed. Until his laughter dwindled, ending with a choked cough.

"Good God," he said. "You're serious?"

"Perfectly serious. Leave Diana alone, and run away with me."

He drained the wineglass and set it aside. Then he cleared his throat and began, "That is brave of you, pet. Offering to wed me in your sister's stead. But truly, I—"

"My name is Minerva. I'm not your pet. And you're deranged if you think I'd ever marry you."

"But I thought you just said—"

"Run away with you, yes. Marry you?" She made an incredulous noise in her throat. "Please."

He blinked at her.

"I can see you're baffled."

"Oh, good. I would have admitted as much, but I know what pleasure you take in pointing out my intellectual shortcomings."

Rummaging through the inside pockets of her cloak, she located her copy of the scientific journal. She opened it to the announcement page and held it out for his examination. "There's to be a meeting of the Royal Geological Society at the end of this month. A symposium. If you'll agree to come with me, my savings should be enough to fund our journey."

"A geology symposium." He flicked a glance at the journal. "This is your scandalous midnight proposal. The one you trudged through the cold, wet dark to make. You're inviting me to a geology symposium, if I leave your sister alone."

"What were you expecting me to offer? Seven nights of wicked, carnal pleasure in your bed?"

She'd meant it as a joke, but he didn't laugh. Instead, he eyed her sodden frock.

Minerva went lobster red beneath it. Curse it. She was forever saying the wrong thing.

"I'd have found that offer more tempting," he said.

Truly? She bit her tongue to keep from saying it aloud. How lowering, to admit how much his offhand comment thrilled her. *I'd prefer your carnal pleasures to a lecture about dirt.* High compliment indeed.

"A geology symposium," he repeated to himself. "I should have known there'd be rocks at the bottom of this."

"There are rocks at the bottom of everything. That's why we geologists find them so interesting. At any rate, I'm not tempting you with the symposium itself. I'm tempting you with the promise of five hundred guineas."

Now she had his attention. His gaze sharpened. "Five hundred guineas?"

"Yes. That's the prize for the best presentation. If you take me there and help present my findings to the Society, you can keep it all. Five hundred guineas would be sufficient to keep you drunk and debauched in London until your birthday, I should hope?"

He nodded. "With a bit of judicious budgeting. I might have to hold off on new boots, but one must make some sacrifices." He came to his feet, confronting her face-to-face.

"Here's the wrinkle, however. How could you be certain of winning the prize?"

"I'll win. I could explain my findings to you in detail, but a great many polysyllabic words would be involved. I'm not sure you're up to them just now. Suffice it to say, I'm certain."

He gave her a searching look, and Minerva marshaled the strength to hold it. Level, confident, unblinking.

After a moment, his eyes warmed with an unfamiliar glimmer. Here was an emotion she'd never seen from him before.

She thought it might be . . . respect.

"Well," he said. "Certainty becomes you."

Her heart gave a queer flutter. It was the nicest thing he'd ever said to her. She thought it might be the nicest thing *anyone* had ever said to her.

Certainty becomes you.

And suddenly, things were different. The ounce of wine she'd swallowed unfurled in her belly, warming and relaxing her. Melting away her awkwardness. She felt comfortable in her surroundings, and more than a little worldly. As though this were the most natural thing in the world, to be having a midnight conversation in a turret with a half-dressed rake.

She settled languidly into the armchair and raised her hands to her hair, finding and plucking loose her few remaining pins. With slow, dreamy motions, she finger-combed the wet locks and arranged them about her shoulders, the better to dry evenly.

He stood and watched her for a moment. Then he went to pour more wine.

A sensuous ribbon of claret swirled into the glass. "Mind, I'm not agreeing to this scheme. Not by any stretch of the imagination. But just for the sake of argument, how did you see this proceeding, exactly? One morning, we'd just up and leave for London together?"

"No, not London. The symposium is in Edinburgh."

"Edinburgh." Bottle met table with a *clunk*. "The Edinburgh in Scotland."

She nodded.

"I thought you said this was the Royal Geological Society."

"It is." She waved the journal at him. "The Royal Geological Society of Scotland. Didn't you know? Edinburgh's where all the most interesting scholarship happens."

Crossing back to her, he peered at the journal. "For God's sake, this takes place less than a fortnight from now. Marietta, don't you realize what a journey to Scotland entails? You're talking about two weeks' travel, at the minimum."

"It's four days from London on the mail coach. I've checked."

"The *mail* coach? Pet, a viscount does not travel on the mail coach." He shook his head, sitting across from her. "And how is your dear mother going to take this news, when she finds you've absconded to Scotland with a scandalous lord?"

"Oh, she'll be thrilled. So long as one of her daughters marries you, she won't be particular." Minerva eased her feet from her wet, muddy boots and drew her legs up beneath her skirts, tucking her chilled heels under her backside. "It's perfect, don't you see? We'll stage it as an elopement. My mother won't raise any protest, and neither will Lord Rycliff. He'll be only too happy to think you're marrying at last. We'll travel to Scotland, present my findings, collect the prize. Then we'll tell everyone it simply didn't work out."

The more she explained her ideas, the easier the words sprang to her lips and the more excited she grew. This could work. It could really, truly work.

"So you'll just return to Spindle Cove unmarried, after weeks of travel with me? Don't you realize you'd be . . ."

"Ruined in good society? I know." She looked into the

roaring fire. "I'm willing to accept that fate. I had no desire for a society marriage, anyhow." No *hopes* of one, to put it finely. She didn't relish the thought of scandal and gossip. But could it really be so much worse to be cut off from fashionable society than to feel forever squeezed to its margins?

"But what of your sisters? They'll be tainted by association."

His remark gave her pause. It wasn't that she hadn't thought about this possibility. To the contrary, she'd considered it very carefully.

"Charlotte has years before her debut," she said. "She can weather a bit of scandal. And as for Diana . . . sometimes I think the kindest thing I could do for my sister is ruin her chances of making a 'good' marriage. Then she might make a loving one."

He sipped his wine thoughtfully. "Well, I'm glad you've worked all this out to your satisfaction. You have no compunction ruining your reputation, nor those of your sisters. But have you given a moment's thought to mine?"

"To your what? Your reputation?" She laughed. "But your reputation is terrible."

His cheeks colored, slightly. "I don't know that it's *terrible*."

She put her left forefinger to her right thumb. "Point the first. You're a shameless rake."

"Yes." He drew out the word.

She touched her index finger. "Point the second. Your name is synonymous with destruction. Bar fights, scandals . . . literal explosions. Wherever you go, mayhem follows."

"I don't really try at that part. It just . . . happens." He rubbed a hand over his face.

"And yet you worry this scheme would tarnish your reputation?"

"Of course." He leaned forward and braced his elbows on his knees. He gestured with the hand holding the wineglass. "I'm a lover of women, yes." Then he lifted his empty hand.

"And yes, I seem to break everything I touch. But thus far I've succeeded in keeping the two proclivities separate, you see. I sleep with women and I ruin things, but I've never yet ruined an innocent woman."

"Seems like a mere oversight on your part."

He chuckled. "Perhaps. But it's not one I mean to remedy."

His eyes met hers, unguarded and earnest. And a strange thing happened. Minerva believed him. This was one snag she never would have considered. That he might object on *principle*. She hadn't dreamed he possessed a scruple to offend.

But he did, evidently. And he was baring it to *her*, in an attitude of confidence. As though they were friends, and he trusted her to understand.

Something had changed between them, in the ten minutes since she'd pounded on his door.

She sat back in the chair, regarding him. "You are a different person at night."

"I am," he agreed simply. "But then, so are you."

She shook her head. "I'm always this person, inside. It's just . . ." *Somehow, I can never manage to be this person with you. The harder I try, the more I get in my own way.*

"Listen, I'm honored by your invitation, but this excursion you suggest can't happen. I'd return looking like the worst sort of seducer and cad. And justly so. Having absconded with, then callously discarded, an innocent young lady?"

"Why couldn't I be the one to discard you?"

A little chuckle escaped him. "But who would ever believe—"

He cut off his reply. A moment too late.

"Who would ever believe that," she finished for him. "Who indeed."

Cursing, he set aside the wineglass. "Come now. Don't take offense."

Ten minutes ago, she would have expected him to laugh. She would have been prepared for his derision, and she wouldn't have allowed him to see how it hurt. But things had changed. She'd accepted his coat and his wine. More than that, his honesty. She'd let down her guard. And now this.

It cut her deep.

Her eyes stung. "It's unthinkable. I know that's what you're saying. What everyone would say. It's inconceivable that a man like you could be in—" She swallowed. "Could be taken with a girl like me."

"I didn't mean it that way."

"Of course you did. It's preposterous. Laughable. The idea that you might want me, and I might spurn you? I'm plain. Bookish, distracted, awkward. Hopeless." Her voice broke. "In a geologic age, no one would believe it."

She wriggled her feet into her boots. Then she pushed to her feet and reached for her cloak.

He rose and reached for her hand. She pulled away, but not fast enough. His fingers closed around her wrist.

"They would believe it," he said. "I could make them believe it."

"You horrid, teasing man. You can't even remember my name." She wrestled his grip.

He tightened it. "*Minerva.*"

Her body went still. Her breath burned in her lungs, as though she'd been fighting her way through waist-deep snow.

"Listen to me now," he said, smooth and low. "I could make them believe it. I'm not *going* to do so, because I think this scheme of yours is a spectacularly bad idea. But I could. If I chose, I could have all Spindle Cove—all *England*—convinced that I'm utterly besotted with you."

She sniffed. "Please."

He smiled. "No, truly. It would be so easy. I'd begin by studying you, when you aren't aware of it. Stealing glances when you're lost in thought, or when your head's bent over a book. Admiring the way that dark, wild hair always manages to escapes its pins, tumbling down your neck." With his free hand, he caught a damp strand of her hair in his fingertips and smoothed it behind her ear. Then he brushed a light touch over her cheek. "Noting the warm glow of your skin, where the sun has kissed it. And these lips. Damn. I think I'd have to develop quite a fascination with your lips."

His thumb hovered over her mouth, teasing her with possibilities. She ached for his touch, until she was miserable with it. This . . . unwanted *wanting*.

"It wouldn't take long. Soon everyone around us would take note of my interest," he said. "They'd believe my attraction to you."

"You've been mercilessly teasing me for months now. No one would forget that."

"All part of the infatuation. Don't you know? A man might engage in flirtation with disinterest, even disdain. But he never teases without affection."

"I don't believe you."

"You should. Others would." He placed his hands on her shoulders. His gaze swept her body from boots to unbound hair. "I could have them all believing I'm consumed by a savage, visceral passion for this enchantress with raven's-wing hair and sultry lips. That I admire her fierce loyalty to her sisters, and her brave, resourceful spirit. That I'm driven wild by hints of a deep, hidden passion that escape her sometimes, when she ventures out of her shell. " His strong hands moved to frame her face. His Bristol-diamond eyes held hers. "That I see in her a rare, wild beauty that's been overlooked, somehow, by other men. And I want it. Desperately. All for myself. Oh, I could have them believing it all."

The rich, deep flow of words had worked some kind of

spell on her. She stood transfixed, unable to move or speak.

It's not real, she reminded herself. *None of these words mean a thing.*

But his caress was real. Real, and warm, and tender. It could mean too much, if she let it. Caution told her to pull away.

Instead, she placed a light, trembling touch to his shoulder. Foolish hand. Foolish fingers.

"If I wished," he murmured, drawing her close and tilting her face to his, "I could convince everyone that the true reason I've remained in Spindle Cove—months past what should have been my breaking point—has nothing to do with my cousin or my finances." His voice went husky. "That it's simply you, Minerva." He caressed her cheek, so sweetly her heart ached. "That it's always been you."

His eyes were sincere, unguarded. No hint of irony in his voice. He almost seemed to have convinced himself.

Her heart pounded in her chest with violent force. That mad, hammering beat was all she could hear.

Until another sound intruded.

Laughter. A woman's laughter. Trickling down from above, like a cascade of freezing water. A brisk, dousing shock.

Oh God.

"Bloody hell." He looked up, to the sleeping loft.

Minerva followed his gaze. From behind the draped bed hangings, the unseen woman laughed again. Laughed at *her*.

Oh God. Oh God.

How could she have been so stupid? Naturally, he wasn't alone. He'd all but told her as much. He'd taken forever to open the door, but he hadn't been sleeping. He'd paused first to . . .

To put on trousers.

Oh God oh God oh God.

The whole time. Whoever she was up there, she'd been listening the whole time.

Minerva groped numbly for her cloak, jerking it on with shaking fingers. The fire's smoky heat was suddenly cloying and thick. Suffocating. She had to leave this place. She was going to be ill.

"Wait," he said, following her to the door. "It's not how it looks."

She cut him a freezing glare.

"Very well, it's mostly how it looks. But I swear, I'd forgotten she was even here."

She ceased struggling with the door latch. "And that's supposed to make me think better of you?"

"No." He sighed. "It's supposed to make you think better of *you*. That's all I meant. To make you feel better."

Amazing, then, how with that one remark, he made a mortifying situation thirteen times worse.

"I see. Normally you reserve the insincere compliments for your lovers. But you thought to take on a charity case." He started to reply, but she cut him off. She glanced up at the loft. "Who is she?"

"Does it matter?"

"Does it *matter*?" She wrenched the door open. "Good Lord. Are women so interchangeable and faceless to you? You just . . . lose track of them under the bed cushions, like pennies? I can't believe I—"

A hot tear spilled down her cheek. She hated that tear. Hated that he'd seen it. A man like this wasn't worth weeping over. It was just . . . for that moment by the fire, after years of being overlooked, she'd finally felt *noticed*. Appreciated.

Wanted.

And it had all been a lie. A ridiculous, laughable joke.

He pulled on his greatcoat. "Let me see you home, at least."

"Stay back. Don't come near me, or my sister." She held him off with a hand as she backed through the door. "You are the most deceitful, horrid, shameless, contemptible man I have ever had the displeasure to know. How do you sleep at night?"

His reply came just as she banged the door closed.

"I don't."

Chapter Two

He didn't sleep that night.

After Minerva Highwood stormed off into the rain, even a dissolute, soulless rake like Colin couldn't simply continue where he'd left off. He roused the widow from his bed, put her in her clothes, and saw her back to the village. Once he'd satisfied himself that Minerva had made it home safe—by glimpsing her muddied boots outside the rear door of the rooming house—he returned to his quarters at the castle and uncorked a new bottle of wine.

But he didn't sleep a wink.

He never did. Not at night, not alone.

God, he hated the country. All the sunshine and sea air in Sussex couldn't make up for the dark, quiet nights. Lately, Colin thought he'd give his left nipple—bollocks were never up for negotiation—for a decent night's sleep. Ever since Fiona Lange had left the village, at best he'd been able to cobble together a few hours in the early dawn. For most of the winter, he'd taken to drinking himself into a nightly stupor. But his body, already taxed from lack of rest, was beginning to fray from the volume of liquor required. If he wasn't careful, he'd become a habitual drunk. He was too young for that, damn it.

So he'd finally given in and accepted the clear invitation Mrs. Ginny Watson's smiles and cocked hips had been making for some time. He'd resisted the young widow for months now, not wanting to entangle himself with a village resident. But he'd be leaving in a matter of days. Why not make his last few nights bearable? Who could it possibly hurt?

Who, indeed.

In his mind's eye, he saw Minerva Highwood. That single tear streaking down her face.

Poorly done, Payne. Poorly done.

He should have sent her away at once. He had no intention of marrying Diana Highwood, never had. But Minerva had been cold and wet, in need of some time before the fire. And he'd found it perversely amusing, teasing out her little chain of conclusions to its wild, illogical end.

Of all the mad schemes to propose . . . a fake elopement to win a geology prize? She'd never win any points on elegance. But Colin had to admit, that kind of girl didn't knock on his door every night.

The worst of it was, that seductive claptrap he'd spooned her . . . it hadn't *all* been lies. She wasn't without her peculiar brand of allure. Her dark hair, when unbound and spilling in heavy waves to her waist, was seduction itself. And her mouth truly did fascinate him. For a sharp-tongued bluestocking, she had the most full, ripe, sultry lips he'd ever seen. Lips copied from some Renaissance master's Aphrodite. Dark red at the edges, and a paler hue toward the center—like two slices of a ripe plum. Sometimes she caught her lower lip beneath her teeth and worried it, as though savoring some hidden sweetness.

Was it any wonder then, that for several minutes, he truly *had* forgotten Ginny Watson upstairs?

Minerva had paid the price for his thoughtlessness.

This was why he *needed* to be back in London. There, habitual debauchery kept him out of this sort of trouble. He and his friends roved from club to club like a pack of nocturnal beasts. And when he tired of the revelry, he had no problem finding worldly, willing women to share his bed. He gave them exquisite physical pleasure, they gave him some much-needed solace . . . everyone parted ways satisfied.

Tonight, he'd left two women profoundly dissatisfied. And he kept vigil with that old, familiar bitch, regret.

At least his days here were numbered. Bram was set to arrive at the castle tomorrow. Ostensibly, he was making the trip to inspect his militia after several months' absence. However, Colin knew from his cousin's express—he had other business in mind. After long months, Colin would have his reprieve.

Farewell, stone-cold quarters.

Farewell, torturous country nights.

In a matter of days, he would be gone.

"What do you mean, I'm staying here?" Colin stared at his cousin, feeling as though he'd just taken a punch to the gut. "I don't understand."

"I'll explain." Bram gestured mildly. "This is the normal way with birthdays, see? Amazingly enough, they arrive on the same day, every year. And yours is still two months away. Until then, I'm trustee of your fortune. I control your every last ha'penny, and you'll stay here."

Colin shook his head. "This makes no sense. He's surrendered. You just announced it to the whole village. The war is over."

They stood in front of the Bull and Blossom, Spindle

Cove's one and only tavern. After overseeing the afternoon militia drill, Bram had invited all the volunteers to gather for a pint. There he'd announced the latest word from France, sure to blaze across every broadsheet in England tomorrow morning. Napoleon Bonaparte had renounced the throne, and now it was merely a matter of paperwork.

Victory was theirs.

Jubilation shook the tavern to its timber frame. Children ran to St. Ursula's to ring the church bell. The first pint quickly became two, then three. As afternoon faded to twilight, wives and sweethearts filtered in from the village lanes, carrying with them dishes of food. Someone brought out a fiddle. Before long, the dancing would begin. All Spindle Cove—all *England*—had reason to celebrate.

By all rights, Colin ought to be rejoicing, too.

Instead, he felt dead inside. It was an all-too-familiar sensation.

"Bram, you needed me to oversee the militia in your absence, and I've done that duty." *At no small cost to my sanity.* "I've even looked out for your damn pet sheep. But if the war is over, there's no further need."

"Whether there's a need or not, the militia remains embodied until the Crown decrees otherwise. I can't just disband it when the whim strikes."

"Then Thorne can oversee it."

"Where is Thorne, anyway?" Bram scanned the environs for his corporal.

Colin gestured vaguely. "Off doing whatever it is he does. Shaving with a rusted field scythe. Skinning eels with his bare hands, perhaps. *He* actually likes this place."

"Ah," said Bram. "But you *need* this place."

Colin scrubbed his face with both hands. He knew Bram *meant* well. His cousin truly believed stranding Colin penniless in the Sussex countryside to oversee a local militia was his best chance at redeeming a dissolute existence. What Bram didn't understand was that they were different kinds of men. Military discipline and rural life may have tamed Bram's demons, but they were only feeding Colin's.

There was no way to explain that in terms Bram could understand. And what was Colin supposed to say, anyhow? *Thank you very much for giving a damn, but I'd rather you didn't?* Bram was his only family now. Over the past year, they'd forged a tenuous bond of brotherly affection, and Colin didn't want to muck that up.

"Colin, if you want to leave Spindle Cove, you have options. You know the trust ends if you marry. The right wife could be good for you."

He quietly groaned. Again and again, he'd witnessed this phenomenon with his friends. They got married. They were happy in that sated, grateful way of infrequently pleasured men with a now-steady source of coitus. Then they went about crowing as if they'd invented the institution of matrimony and stood to earn a profit for every bachelor they could convert.

"Bram, I'm happy that you're happy with Susanna and the babe on the way. But that doesn't mean marriage is a good thing for me. In fact, I think it would be a very bad thing for the woman I happened to marry." He tapped his fist against the building. "Listen, I need to go to Town. I made a promise to Finn."

"You promised Finn what, precisely?" Bram looked through the window, scanning the assembled militiamen for the fifteen-year-old drummer boy.

"I lost a bet to him, see. At stake was a pair of boots. I'd hand over my own Hobys, but they're several sizes too large yet. So I said I'd take him to London for a new custom pair. And then I figured we'd make some trips to schools, so we can have that sorted out before autumn term begins."

Bram shook his head. "I've already found Finn a school here in Sussex. Flintridge School for Boys."

"Flintridge? What about Eton? We told his mother we'd give him the best."

"The best for Finn. Flintridge offers an excellent education, closer to home. Besides, the Brights own a dry-goods shop, and you want to send him to Eton? You know he'd feel out of place."

Colin knew all about Eton and feeling out of place. He'd arrived there a young tragedy at the age of eight. Freshly orphaned, still reeling from the loss of his parents. At that time, small for his age. He would have been a favorite target even without the nightmares. The nightmares just added verbal taunts to the bullies' arsenal. He could still hear their mocking falsetto.

"*Mother!*" they'd squawk down the corridors. "*Mother, wake!*"

The first year had been torture. But he'd done well in the end.

"I know the adjustment won't be easy," Colin said. "But I can teach Finn how to hold his own. He needs to see a bit more of the world, lose that wide-eyed country wonder. He should have a tutor, so he's not lagging behind in his studies. And if I outfit him with a fine pair of Hobys and take him round to the boxing club, he can dazzle the impressionable boys and kick the obstinate ones in the arse."

Colin stared through the window of the Bull and Blossom, to where Finn Bright leaned against the wall, grazing elbows with his twin brother, Rufus. From their shocks of white-blond hair to their gangly arms and mischievous smiles, the Bright twins were identical. Or at least they had been, until last summer—when an artillery blast had taken Finn's left foot.

"It was an accident," Bram said, reading his thoughts.

"One I might have prevented."

"I could have prevented it, too."

Colin tapped a finger against the window. "Look at him. He's healed, but he's restless. The weather's growing warm. He sees the rest of the youths his age all running off to play cricket, work the fields, chase the girls . . . It's sinking in, for the first time, what this means. What it *will* mean, for the rest of his life. I know you have to understand."

Bram had taken a shot to the knee in Spain, over a year ago now. He'd kept the leg, but he still walked with a limp, and the injury had ended his career in field command. One would think his resistance to the idea should soften.

One would be wrong. Bram's expression looked every bit as soft as granite.

"Colin, you shouldn't have made the boy such promises. You're always doing this. I've no doubt you meant well, but your good intentions land like mortar shells. Again and again, you fire off that mouth of yours, and the innocents around you get hurt."

Colin winced, thinking of Minerva Highwood last night. That single tear streaking down her face.

"This is precisely why I can't release you any funds," Bram went on. "You'll spin a fine tale about wholesome days spent mentoring Finn, and by night I know you'll end right back in the clubs and hells."

"Damn it, how I spend my nights is my own concern. I can't stay in this place, Bram. You have no idea."

"Oh, but I do. I have a very good idea." Bram stepped closer and lowered his voice. "I've commanded regiments in battle. Do you think I don't know what witnessing death and bloodshed does to a man? The nightmares, the restlessness. The drinking. The shadow that lingers years, even decades later. I've known many a battle-shocked soldier."

As he absorbed his cousin's meaning, Colin's pulse

pounded. Naturally, Bram knew about the accident. Almost everyone in his social circle knew about the accident. But the rest were well-mannered enough to understand—Colin didn't discuss it. Ever.

He said, "I'm not one of your battle-shocked soldiers."

"No. You're my family. Can't you understand? I want to see you move past this."

"Move past it?" Colin laughed bitterly. "Why hadn't I ever thought of that?" He slapped his forehead. "I'll simply move past it. What a bloody brilliant idea. Here's one for you, Bram. Just straighten up and stop limping. And Finn . . . well, Finn can just grow a new foot."

Bram sighed. "I won't pretend to know exactly what it is you need," he said, "but I know you won't find it in the gaming hells and opera houses. These next months are my last chance to turn you around. After your birthday, the accounts, properties, Riverchase . . . they'll all be yours for the keeping. Or for the losing."

Colin sobered, instantly. "I would never risk Riverchase. Never."

"You haven't even been there in years."

"I've no wish to go." He shrugged. "Too quiet. Too remote." *Too many memories.*

"You'll need to manage the place," Bram said.

Colin countered, "The land stewards have managed it well enough for years. They don't need me there. And I'm happy living in Town."

"That debauched, aimless existence you had in Town . . . You call that 'happy'?" Bram frowned. "Christ, man. You can't even be honest with yourself."

Colin made a fist and checked the urge to use it.

He lowered his voice as Finn emerged from the tavern. "The boy has his things all packed, Bram. You can't disappoint him."

"Oh, *I* won't disappoint him. I'll leave that to you."

Ouch.

Finn crutched his way over to join them. "Well, my lords?"

Colin could tell the youth was struggling not to look too hopeful. That was Finn. Whether he'd lost a game of darts or his whole left foot, he always put a brave face on disappointment. He was stronger than he let on, had more ambition than anyone guessed. This boy would truly be someone, someday. And he deserved better than bloody Flintridge School for Boys.

"Finn, there's been a change of plans. We won't be going to London this week."

"W-we won't?"

"No," Colin said. "You'll be going to Town with Lord Rycliff instead."

Bram turned to him, stunned. "What?"

"As we agreed would be best." Colin shot his cousin a pointed look.

In return, Bram threw him a gaze that would pulverize walnuts in their shells.

"But . . . I thought I'd be staying with you, Lord Payne." Finn looked to Colin, confused. "We were going to set up bachelors' lodgings in Covent Garden."

"Yes, well. My cousin and I agree you need a wholesome family environment. For a while, at least. Isn't that right, Bram?"

Come on, man. You can't refuse. Don't be an ass.

His cousin finally relented. "We've just moved into the new town house, Finn. Susanna will be glad to have her first houseguest."

Colin drew Finn aside. "I'll be along this summer, don't worry. Just in time for boating on the Thames." He leaned in to murmur, "And the boxing, never you fear. There are tickets to a prize match in your future, if I hear good reports from your tutors."

The youth smiled. "All right then."

Bram said, "Get your things, Finn. Meet me at the mews, and we'll see them stowed in the carriage. We leave at dawn." The two of them walked off together, making plans that didn't include Colin.

He tried to tell himself it had all worked out for the best. If he'd taken Finn to London himself, Colin would have found some way to cock it up. Bram was right. Every time he tried to do something good, it had a way of going bad.

Strolling away from the tavern and onto the green, Colin brought out the flask from his breast pocket. He uncapped it and tossed back a quick draught. It burned going down—as did the knowledge that it would be the first drink of many. Already, night was drawing her purple spangled veil over the cove. How he'd survive the next few months without pickling his brain, he didn't know.

A group of ladies approached, walking across the green on the path that led from the Queen's Ruby to the tavern. No surprise that the rooming-house residents would be enticed by the strains of dancing music. Colin faded into the shadows of the chestnut tree, feeling unequal to polite conversation at the moment.

As the ladies drew closer, he recognized them.

The Highwoods. The widowed matron took the fore, and her three daughters followed. First Charlotte, then Diana . . . finally, the lagging Minerva, her face predictably buried in a book. The evening breeze flirted with their skirts and shawls.

If he wanted to leave Spindle Cove, he did have options. Here came two of them now.

He could marry Diana.

Or he could run away to Scotland with Minerva.

Fine options, those. Would he prefer to destroy one sister's reputation, or ruin the other's future happiness? To be sure, he wanted to leave this place. But he'd rather do so with some shred of decency intact.

Colin tossed back another swallow of liquor.

Diana Highwood *would* make some man a lovely bride. She was beautiful, elegant, refined, good-hearted. She could hold her own in the *ton*, no question, and she'd tolerate Colin's excesses better than most. Which meant her sharp-tongued, bespectacled sister was absolutely right.

Diana deserved better.

As for the bespectacled sister in question . . . As he stared at the group crossing the green, Colin scarcely recognized her as the girl who'd visited him last night. The bold, witty young woman who'd let down her hair by his hearth and spoken with such captivating self-assurance. Where had that girl been, all these months?

More to the point, where was that girl now? The sprigged muslin gown she wore was neither flattering nor hideous. It could best be described as wholly unremarkable. As she walked, her shoulders were hunched, as though she could curl into herself. Taken together with the book shielding her face, she'd done her level best to disappear.

Mrs. Highwood barked, "Minerva! Posture."

Colin shook his head. Considering the constant abuse she took from her mother, was it any wonder she wanted to hide?

Last night, she'd ventured out of that shell. She'd slogged all the way to the castle in the rain, pounded on his door until he let her in, and then offered to ruin herself to protect her sister. And what reward did she get for her pains? Humiliation. Derision. And more scolding from her mother.

He'd never dreamed he'd say this about the bluestocking

who'd spent the past several months skewering him with sharp glances and cutting remarks. But it was true.

Minerva deserved better.

Colin capped his flask and jammed it in his pocket. He might have to wait a few months to make his amends to Finn Bright. And even then, he'd never be able to replace the youth's foot.

But he was going to settle this business with the Highwoods.

Tonight.

Chapter Three

When Minerva lost herself in a book, her late father had once remarked, a man needed hounds and a search party to pull her back out.

Alternatively, a low-hanging tree branch could do the trick. *Thwack.*

"Ouch." Pulling up short, Minerva rubbed her smarting temple and adjusted her spectacles with one hand. With the other, she kept her page marked.

Charlotte gave her a pitying tilt of the head. "Oh, Min. Really."

"Are you injured?" Diana asked, concerned.

Ahead of them, their mother wheeled and gave a despairing sigh. "Minerva Rose Highwood. For all your unnatural love of education, you can be remarkably stupid." She walked over and grasped Minerva by the elbow, tugging her across the village green. "I will never understand how you came into being."

No, Mama, Minerva thought, trudging her way along the path. *I doubt you ever will.*

Most people didn't understand her. Even before last night's humiliation, she'd long reconciled herself to the fact. Lately, it seemed the one who best understood Minerva wasn't a person at all, but a place. Spindle Cove, this seaside resort for young ladies of gentle breeding and, well, *interesting* character. Whether sickly, scholarly, or scandalous—the young women here were all misfits of one kind or another. The villagers didn't care if Minerva dug in the dirt, or wandered down the country paths with the breeze whipping through her hair and an open book before her face.

She'd felt so at home here, so comfortable. Until tonight.

The closer they drew to the tavern and the revelry within, the more her sense of dread increased. "Mama, can't we go back to the rooming house? The weather's so dire."

"It's mild, compared to last week's rain."

"Think of Diana's health. She's just recovered from a cold."

"Pish. That was weeks ago now."

"But, Mama . . ." Desperate, Minerva cast about for some other excuse. "What of propriety?"

"Propriety?" Mama held up Minerva's ungloved hand, displaying the earth embedded under her fingernails. "*You* would speak to me of propriety?"

"Yes, well. It's one thing to frequent the Bull and Blossom in the afternoon, when it's a ladies tea shop. But after dark, it's a tavern." Minerva wouldn't mention where *she'd* been last night.

"I don't care if it's an opium den. It's the only hope of dancing in ten miles," her mother replied. "And Payne is certain to be there. We'll have a proposal tonight. I feel it in my bones."

Perhaps Mama felt it in her bones, but Minerva's reaction was more visceral. Her heart and stomach switched places, jostling inside her.

As they approached the tavern door, Minerva buried her face in her book. Be they novels or histories or scientific treatises, books were frequently her refuge. Tonight, the book was her literal shield, her only barrier against the world. She didn't dare leave Diana alone tonight, but she didn't know how she could bear to face Lord Payne again. Not to mention the hidden lover who'd laughed at Minerva's foolish hopes. His "friend" could have been any woman in this crowded room. And whoever she was, she might have already related the story to everyone else.

As they entered the establishment and made their way through the throng, Minerva was certain she heard someone laughing.

Laughing at *her*.

This was the worst result of that disastrous midnight visit. For months now, Spindle Cove had been Minerva's safe haven. Now she'd never feel comfortable here again. The echo of that cruel laughter would follow her down every country path and cobbled lane. He'd ruined this place for her.

Now he threatened to ruin the rest of their lives.

You could be calling me "brother" by Sunday.

No. She couldn't let it happen. She wouldn't. She'd stop it *somehow*, even if she had to hurl her book at the man's head.

"Oh, he's not here."

Charlotte's plaintive comment gave her hope. Minerva lowered her book and scanned the crowd. The militia volunteers filled the establishment, splashing bright red and gold against the lime-washed walls. She dipped her chin and peered over the lenses, focusing on the distant side of the room, where men and women crowded at the bar.

No Lord Payne.

Her breath came easier. She pushed the spectacles back up her nose, and she felt the corners of her mouth relax into some semblance of a smile. Perhaps he'd experienced an attack of conscience. More likely, he'd stayed behind in his turret to entertain his easily amused lady friend. It hardly mattered where he was, so long as he wasn't here.

"Oh, there," Mama said, swiveling. "There he is. He's just come in the back way."

Drat.

Minerva's heart sank when she caught her first glimpse of him. He did not look like a man who'd experienced an attack of conscience. He looked dark and more dangerous than ever. Though he'd only just come through the door, he'd instantly changed the room's atmosphere. A palpable, restless energy radiated from his quarter, and everyone could feel it. The whole tavern went on alert. An unspoken message relayed from body to body.

Something is about to happen.

The musicians struck up the prelude to a country dance. Around the room, couples began pairing off.

Lord Payne, however, was in no hurry. He raised a flask to his mouth and tipped it. Minerva swallowed instinctively, as though she could feel the liquor burning down her own throat.

He lowered the flask. Capped it. Replaced it in his pocket. And then his gaze settled, hot and unwavering, on the Highwoods.

The little hairs on the back of her neck stood on end.

"He's looking at you, Diana," their mother murmured with excitement. "He's sure to ask you to dance."

"Diana shouldn't dance," Minerva said, unable to take her eyes off him. "Not a reel like this. Her asthma."

"Pish. The sea air has worked its benefit. She hasn't had an attack in months now."

"No. But the last one was brought on by dancing." She shook her head. "Why must I always be the one to look out for Diana's well-being?"

"Because I'm looking out for yours. Ungrateful thing."

Mama's gaze pierced her. As a girl, Minerva had envied her mother's blue eyes. They'd seemed the color of tropical oceans and cloudless skies. But their color had faded over the years since Papa's death. Now their blue was the hue of dyed cambric worn three seasons. Or brittle middle-class china.

The color of patience nearly worn through.

"There are four of us, Minerva. All women. No husband, father, or brother in the portrait. We may not be destitute, but we lack true security. Diana has the chance to catch a wealthy, handsome viscount, and I won't allow you to stand in her way. Who else is going to save this family? *You*?" She laughed bitterly.

Minerva couldn't even summon a response.

"Oh, he's coming," Charlotte squeaked. "He's coming this way."

Panic fluttered in Minerva's breast. Did Payne truly mean to propose tonight? Any man with sense would. Diana was always beautiful, but tonight she looked radiant, dressed in an emerald silk gown with ivory lace trim. Her flaxen hair glowed incandescent in the candlelight, and her ethereal composure gave her the air of a lady.

She looked like a viscountess.

And Lord Payne looked every inch the powerful lord. The man strode across the room toward them, cutting his way through the crowd in a straight, unswerving path. People leaped out of his way, like startled crickets. His gaze was intent, determined, focused on . . .

On *her*. On Minerva.

Don't be a ninny.

It couldn't be. Surely it was just a trick of her spectacles. He was coming for Diana, naturally. Obviously. And she hated him for it. He was a horrid, horrid man.

But her heart would not stop pounding. Heat gathered between her breasts. She'd always wondered what it would feel like to stand on one end of a ballroom and watch a handsome, powerful man make his way to her. This was as close as she'd ever come to it, she supposed. Standing at Diana's side. Imagining.

Suddenly anxious, she looked to the floor. Then the ceiling. Then she chided herself for her cowardice and forced herself to look at him.

He drew to a halt and bowed, then offered a hand. "May I have this dance?"

Minerva's heart stalled. The book slipped from her hand and fell to the floor.

"Diana, pass me your reticule," Mama whispered. "Quickly now. I'll hold it while you dance."

"I don't believe that will be necessary," Diana answered.

"Of course it's necessary. You can't dance with that bulky reticule dangling from your wrist."

"I'm not going to dance at all. Lord Payne has invited Minerva."

"Invited Minerva. Of all the ideas." Mama made a disbelieving, indelicate snort. Which became a strangled gasp, when the woman looked up and finally noticed that Lord Payne's hand was indeed outstretched to Minerva. "But . . . why?"

He said simply, "Because I choose her."

"Truly?"

Oh God. Truly? As in, had Minerva *truly* just said that aloud?

At least she'd stopped herself from voicing the rest of the thoughts running through her addled brain, which went something like, *Truly? That whole determined, dangerous saunter across the room was for* me*? In that case, would you mind going back and doing it all over again? Slowly this time, and with feeling.*

"Miss Minerva," he said, in a voice smooth and dark as obsidian, "may I have this dance?"

She watched, mute and entranced, as his ungloved hand clasped hers. His grip was warm and strong.

She held her breath, feeling the eyes of the whole village on them.

Please. Please, don't let anyone laugh.

"Thank you," she forced herself to say. "I would be most . . . relieved."

He led her to the floor, where they queued up for the country dance.

"Relieved?" he murmured with amusement. "Ladies usually find themselves 'delighted' or 'honored' to dance with me. Even 'thrilled.'"

She shrugged helplessly. "It was the first word that came to mind."

And it had been honest, at the time. Though as she took her place across from him and the first bars of the music began, her relief evaporated. Fear took its place.

"I can't dance," she confessed, stepping forward.

He took her hands and twirled her round. "But you're already dancing."

"Not very well."

His eyebrow quirked. "This is true."

Minerva curtseyed to the wrong corner, colliding with the lady her to her left. Offering the woman a breathless apology, she overcorrected—and stomped on Lord Payne's foot.

"Good God," he said through gritted teeth, holding her close to his side as they moved forward and back. "You weren't exaggerating."

"I never exaggerate. I'm hopeless."

"You're not hopeless. Stop trying so hard. If we're going to manage this, you must let me lead."

The dance parted them, and Minerva was left reeling. She

tried to convince herself this meant he'd agreed to her plan. He would take her to Scotland, because he chose her. He chose *her* over Diana. Why else would he offer to dance with her, but to create the impression of some attraction between them? But her thoughts were quickly plowed under by thunderous footfalls and wild fiddling.

She bumbled her way through another series of steps. Then came a lovely few measures where she didn't need to do anything but stand still and clap.

Then it was forward again. To him.

He pulled her close. Indecently close.

"Say ouch," he murmured.

She blinked up at him. *What?*

He pinched the tender underside of her arm, hard.

"Ouch!" she exclaimed. "Why would you—"

He slid an arm around her waist. Then flexed it, causing her to stumble. Her spectacles went askew.

"What's that, Miss Highwood?" he said loudly, theatrically. "You've turned your ankle? What a pity."

A few moments later, he had her stumbling through the Bull and Blossom's red-painted front door. They made it a few steps away from the entrance. He rushed her so, her slipper caught on a rock and she tripped in earnest.

He caught her just before her knee hit the turf.

"Are you hurt?"

She shook her head. "Nothing bruised but my pride."

He helped her steady herself. But he didn't release her. "That didn't go as I planned. I didn't realize your . . . difficulty with dancing. Had I known, I would have—"

"No, this is fine. This is good. The dance, our leaving it. You . . . embracing me in plain view." She swallowed hard. "It's all good."

"It is?"

She nodded. "Yes."

His arms felt good indeed, wreathed about her waist. And the complex, fiery warmth in his hazel eyes was swiftly melting her intelligence to slag. One more minute of this, and she'd be a certifiable simpleton.

She cast a glance at the door. Surely someone would follow them. Or peep out the window, at least. Weren't they the least bit concerned for her reputation? Or her ankle, if nothing else? Someone needed to see them together, if they were going to make a convincing elopement. Otherwise, this dangerous, confusing embrace would be for nothing.

"Why?" she asked, unable to help herself. "You could have Diana."

"I suppose I could. And if I decided marry her, you could not stop me."

Her heart pounded so fiercely in her chest, she was sure he must feel it. "But you chose me tonight. Why?"

An ironic smile tugged at his mouth. "You want me to explain it?"

"Yes. And do it honestly, not . . ." *Not like last night.*

"Honestly." He mused on the word. "Honestly, your sister is lovely, elegant, demure, kind. It's easy for a man to look at her and imagine a whole lifetime stretched out before him. Wedding, house, china, children. It's not an unappealing prospect. But it all looks very settled and fixed."

"And when you look at me? What do you see then?"

"Honestly? When I look at you . . ." His thumb stroked her lower back. "I think to myself something like this: God only knows what trials lie down that path."

She twisted in his embrace, pushing against his arm. "Let me go."

"Why?"

"So I can hit you."

"You asked for honesty." He chuckled, but kept her close. "This . . . this struggle is precisely my point. No, you don't fit the beautiful, elegant, predictable mold. But take heart, Marissa. Some men like to be surprised."

Marissa?

She stared at him, horrified. And thrilled. And horrified at being thrilled. "You. Are. *The*m ost—"

A bell jingled. The Bull and Blossom's door swung open, and a handful of giggling village girls tumbled forth, riding a wave of music and warmth. Minerva's breath caught. If the girls turned this way, she and Payne would be seen. Together.

"Surprise," she whispered.

Then she pressed her lips to his.

Chapter Four

Surprise, she said.

Surprise indeed.

Sweetness. That was the first surprise. He'd heard so many tart words from these lips . . . but her kiss was sweet. Cool and sweet, with a hint of true decadence beneath. Like a sun-ripened plum at the height of summer. Ready to fall into his hand at the slightest inducement.

The falling. That was surprise the second. As she leaned into the kiss, she fell into *him*. He tightened his arms around her waist, pulling her close.

Their bodies met.

But that wasn't the right word. Their bodies had "met" some months ago, that night in the Summerfield gardens. Now their bodies renewed the acquaintance. The sense of intimacy was immediate, startling. The jasmine scent of her hair cocked a trigger, deep inside him. A memory stored not in his mind, but in his blood.

Which brought him to surprise the third.

Pleasure. Triumph. Damn, he'd been *wanting* this. He hadn't known it. Would have gone to his grave before admitting it. But a part of him had been wanting this. Badly, and for quite some time. He wasn't learning her through this kiss, so much as confirming long-suspected truths. That for all her unfeminine interests and education, she was pure woman beneath. That she didn't feel prickly and stubborn in his arms, but warm and pliant, her curves molding to his strength.

That he could make her melt. Sigh. Tremble.

That one taste of her wouldn't be enough.

He ran his tongue over her closed lips, seeking more. It had been ages since he'd kissed a girl simply for kissing's sake, and he'd forgotten what a pure, heady pleasure it could be. He wanted to sink into that cool sweetness. Get drunk on it, bathe in it. Utterly lose himself in a fathoms-deep kiss.

Open. Open for me.

A little sound escaped her. Something like a squeak. Her lips remained sealed under his.

He tried again, lightly dragging his tongue toward the corner of her mouth. Slowly, reverently—the way he knew a woman enjoyed being licked, just about anywhere.

Finally, her lips parted. He swept his tongue between them, tasting her. God, she was so sweet and fresh. But utterly still. Unmoving. Unbreathing. He paused to sip at her plump lower lip before trying again. He pressed a little deeper this time, swirling his tongue before retreating.

The sweet sigh of her breath whispered against his cheek. It was a confession, that sigh. It told him two things.

First, she had no earthly idea how to kiss him back.

But, secondly? She wanted to. She'd been waiting for this, too.

As they broke apart, a sense of mutual disbelief wavered in the air.

"Why—?" Her hands pressed flat against her belly. For a moment, she looked everywhere *but* at him. Then she lowered her voice and asked, "Whyever would you *do* that?"

"What do you mean?" he asked, chuckling. "You kissed *me.*"

"Yes, but why would you do . . ." Her face twisted. "The rest of it."

Colin paused. "Because . . . that's the way a grown man kisses a woman?"

She stared at him.

For God's sake, she couldn't be that naïve.

"I know you can't have had much experience, but surely someone's explained the natural way of things between the sexes?" He held out his hands in an attitude of illustration and cleared his throat. "It's like this, you see. When a man cares for a woman very, very much . . ."

She buffeted his shoulder with her fist, once. Then barely restrained herself from a second blow. "That's not what I mean, and you know it." She lowered her voice and slid a glance toward the group of girls, who were now disappearing into the rooming house, still absorbed in their own conversation. "Why would you do that with *me*? A simple kiss was enough. What could you be thinking?"

"What indeed." He pushed a hand through his hair, more than a little offended at her accusatory tone. "I'm male. You rubbed your . . . femaleness all over me. I didn't think. I reacted."

"You *reacted*."

"Yes."

"To . . ." She shifted her weight from one foot to the other. "To me."

"It is a natural response. Aren't you a scientist? Then you should understand. Any red-blooded man would react to such stimulus."

She stepped back. She dipped her chin and peered at him over her spectacles. "So you find me stimulating."

"That's not what I—" He bit off the rest of that sentence. The only way to end a nonsensical conversation was to simply cease talking.

Colin drew a deep breath and squared his shoulders. He closed his eyes briefly. And then he opened them and looked at her. Really *looked* at her, as though for the first time. He saw thick, dark hair a man could gather by the fistful. Prim spectacles, perched on a gently sloped nose. Behind the lenses, wide-set eyes—dark and intelligent. And that mouth. That ripe, pouting, sensual mouth.

He let his gaze drift down her form. There was a wicked thrill to knowing lushness smoldered beneath that modest sprigged muslin gown. To having *felt* her shape, scouting and charting her body with all the nerve endings of his own.

Their bodies had *met*. More than that. They'd grown acquainted.

Nothing more would come from it, of course. Colin had rules for himself, and as for her . . . she didn't even like him, or pretend to. But she showed up in the middle of the night, hatching schemes that skirted the line between academic logic and reckless adventure. She started kisses she had no notion how to continue.

Taken all together, she was simply . . .

A surprise. A fresh, bracing gust of the unexpected, for good or ill.

"Perhaps," he said cautiously, "I *do* find you stimulating."

Suspicion narrowed her gaze. "I don't know that I should take that as a compliment."

"Take it how you will."

She stared in the direction of the Queen's Ruby. The group of girls had disappeared. "Drat. I'm not sure anyone even noticed the kiss."

"I noticed it." He rubbed his mouth with the side of his hand. The taste of ripe plums still lingered on his lips. He found himself unaccountably thirsty.

"So when do we leave?" she asked.

"Leave for where?"

"Scotland, of course."

"Scotland?" He laughed, surprised. "I'm not taking you to Scotland."

"But . . ." She blinked furiously. "But just now, inside. You said you chose me."

"To dance with. I chose you as my dancing partner."

"Yes. Precisely. You chose to dance with me, in front of all those people. To pull me outside and hold me improperly close. To kiss me, in the middle of the lane. Why would you do all that if you didn't mean to elope?"

"For the last time, you kissed *me*. As for the rest . . . I regretted that scene last night in my quarters. I felt I owed you some apology."

"Oh. Oh no." She pressed a hand to her chest. "You're telling me it was a pity dance? A pity kiss?"

"No, no." He sighed. "Not entirely. I just thought you deserved to feel appreciated and admired. In front of everyone."

"And now, for a second time in as many nights, you're revealing that it was all deceit. So I can feel rejected and humiliated. In front of everyone." Red rimmed her eyes. "You can't be doing this to me again."

Oh, for the love of tits. How did this happen to him? He had the best of intentions, and then somehow . . .

Your good intentions have the impact of mortar shells.

"That's it," she said, balling her hands in fists. "I'm not letting you out of it this time. I insist that you take me to Scotland. I demand you ruin me. As a point of honor."

The bell on the tavern door jingled. They jumped back from each other a pace.

The party had outgrown the tavern, it seemed. Merrymakers spilled out from the Bull and Blossom, taking to the green.

Sniffing, Minerva crossed her arms over her chest.

"Listen," he said low. "Is there some time and place we can talk? Someplace that's not my quarters at midnight."

After a pause, she straightened her spectacles. "Meet me at the head of the beach path tomorrow morning, just before dawn."

"*Before* dawn?"

"Too early for you?"

"Oh no," he replied. "I'm a very early riser."

"You're late," she said, the next morning. The first rays of dawn glinted off her spectacles. "I've been waiting."

"Good morning to you too, Marianna." Colin rubbed his bleary eyes, then his unshaven jaw. "I had to bid my cousin farewell."

His gaze slid over her frock—a murky, shapeless abomination of gray fabric, buttoned to the hollow of her throat.

"What on earth are you wearing? Did you take orders in a convent since we spoke last? Little Sisters of the Drab and Homely?"

"I thought about it," she said dryly. "It probably would have been the wise course of action. But no. This is my bathing costume." She raked him with a look. "I don't suppose you have one."

He laughed. "I don't suppose I do."

"You'll just have to strip partway, I suppose. Come along, then."

He followed her down the rocky path to the cove, bemused but undeniably intrigued. "If I'd known disrobing would be involved, I would have been more punctual."

"Quickly, now. We must hurry, or the fishermen will see us."

They reached the beach. The air whipping off the sea had a bracing, sobering effect, clearing some of the cobwebs from his brain. The world began to take on crisper edges.

He stopped at the water's edge. The sea lapped at his boots. He took a long moment to inhale deeply, then surveyed the boulder-studded cove in the misty dawn. He'd never appreciated this view before, at this hour of morning.

It looked timeless. Almost mystical.

Seawater splashed him in the face.

"Wake up," she said, removing her spectacles and placing them into a small oilcloth pouch looped over her wrist. She strode past him into the gentle waves. "Time's wasting."

He watched, incredulous, as the stark raving mad girl sank into the water. Knee-deep. Then waist-deep. Then all the way to her neck.

"Come out of there," he said, sounding distressingly like a nursemaid, even to his own ears. "This instant."

"Why?"

"Because it's April. And freezing." *And because I'm suddenly curious to see you wet, without the mud. I didn't have a chance to appreciate the view the other night.*

Her shoulders lifted in a shrug. "It's not so bad, once you grow used to it."

For God's sake, look at the girl. Teeth chattering, lips turning blue. Beneath that horrid garment, her nipples were probably freezing to little icicles. And she seriously expected him to join her? Him, and all his precious, highly-susceptible-to-extreme-temperatures bits?

"Listen, Madeline. There's been some misunderstanding. I'm not here for a swim. We need to talk."

"And I need to show you an inlet, around those rocks. There's no other way to get there but to swim. We'll talk when we arrive." She cocked her head. "You're not frightened, are you?"

Frightened. Ha. What was that he heard, splashing into the water? Must have been a gauntlet.

"No."

Colin pried off his boots. He laid aside his coat. Then he rolled up his trouser legs, cuffing them at the knees, and likewise turned up his sleeves to the elbow.

He girded his loins.

"Very well. Here I come." He winced, plowing into the frigid depths. When the waterline reached his navel, he swore aloud. "This is true valor, I hope you know. Legends have sprung from less. All Lancelot did was paddle about in a balmy lake."

She smiled. "Lancelot was a knight. You're a viscount. The bar is higher."

He gave a raspy chuckle, breathless from the cold. "Why is it," he asked, nearing her, "that you only display that delightfully wicked sense of humor when you're chilled and wet through?"

"I . . ." Her eyelashes fluttered so fast and so hard, she might have been trying to take flight with them. "I don't know."

Even though she was submerged in icy water, she blushed crimson. All her invisible barriers went back up, instantly. So odd. Most women of his acquaintance relied on physical beauty and charm to mask their less-pleasant traits. This girl did the opposite, hiding everything interesting about herself behind a prim, plain façade.

What other surprises was she concealing?

"Let's keep moving," she said. "Follow me."

Swimming in easy, unhurried strokes, she led him around an archipelago of boulders, into a small inlet bounded by steep cliffs.

Colin craned his neck, looking up at the rocky bluffs. And he knew, right then, that so long as he lived, he would never understand what made a man—or woman—look at a stone wall and think, *I believe I'd enjoy attending a symposium on these.*

"So, what are we looking at?"

"Not up there," she said. "Down here."

"Down where?" He looked around him. He saw nothing but water.

"There's a cave. The entrance is hidden at high tide. I'll show you. Hold my arm."

She extended her arm, and he clasped it above the elbow. She clasped his arm in similar fashion.

She said, "Now take a deep breath."

"Wait. What are we—"

He never took that deep breath she'd suggested. Down she went, before he had any chance. Colin found himself being dragged by his arm, completely submerged beneath the water's surface. She propelled them forward, kicking her feet like little fins.

They'd entered some sort of tunnel, it seemed.

He felt rock scrape against his back. He kicked, and bashed rock with his foot. He reached up, where the water's surface ought to be.

Rock there, too. He was trapped.

He opened his eyes underwater. All was dark. Nothing to see. Murky as pitch. Walled in by stone. No air. No air, only water.

He tried to swim back. She pulled him forward. Then they stopped altogether, trapped in that narrow passage of rock. His lungs burned. His limbs tingled. His ears filled with the roar of water and the frantic pounding of his heart, trapped and thrashing against his ribs.

He could die here.

Perversely, his greatest fear was that he wouldn't. That his lungs would somehow learn to do without air, and he would simply remain down here—trapped in an endless, dark, watery silence. Reliving that hellish night forever.

This is death. I am alone.

But he wasn't alone. Her grip locked around his arm, like

a manacle. Her other hand closed around his wrist, and she gave a hard pull. He shot through the remainder of the rock tunnel and surfaced, gasping, on the other side.

More darkness greeted him. There was air to breathe, but he had to work for it.

"It's all right," she said. "You're through."

"Jesus," he finally managed, pushing water off his face. "Jesus Christ and John the Baptist. For that matter, Matthew, Mark, Luke, John." Still not enough. He needed to reach back to the Old Testament for this. "Obadiah. Nebuchadnezzar. Methuselah and Job."

"Be calm," she said, taking him by the shoulders. "Be calm. And there *are* women in the Bible, you know."

"Yes. As I recall it, they were trouble, every last one. What is this place? I can't see a bloody thing."

"There's light. Give it a moment, and you'll see."

He tilted his head. Light shone through a few lacy openings in the rock overhead. Meager white pinpricks against a blanket of jet.

She grasped his chin and swiveled his face away from the light, down to meet hers. "Don't look directly at it, or your eyes will never adjust. Just focus on me and take slow breaths. That's it. In . . . and out."

She spoke in a calm, soothing voice. Likely the same tone she employed to soothe her sister through a breathing crisis. Colin's pride bristled. He didn't need coddling. But he quite enjoyed the smoky, entrancing quality of her voice and her tender touch against his cheek. His pounding heart began to slow.

Eventually the white specks overhead diffused to a faint, milky glow that illuminated her features. Soft, dark calf eyes with inky lashes. Rounded cheeks and pale skin. Those lips, wet with seawater.

"You see me now?" she whispered.

He nodded. And it was surely that brush with death coloring his perception, or perhaps the dim light—but he found her lovely.

"I see you." Sliding his arms around her waist, he pulled her close.

"What happened? Did you lose your bearings underwater?" She pushed a damp strand of hair from his brow. "Should I be worried about you?"

What a question, asked in such a sweet, husky voice. Something made him delay answering.

"No." He dropped a firm kiss on her brow. "No, pet. Don't spare a moment's concern for me."

He released her then, and she drifted away.

"This way, then." She led him to a shelf of rock, and he gave her a boost as she struggled onto it. It felt good to retake the strong, manly role. It also felt good to cup her thigh.

Once they'd both pulled themselves onto the ledge, she felt her way along the cave's wall and reached into a high niche to withdraw some sort of box. From it, she took a candle and tinderbox. The flare of warm, waxy light revealed the cave, letting him know that it was just as small and suffocating as he'd suspected. But that candle's glow also created a small, intimate space within its golden circumference. Colin thought he would be content to stay within its borders for the foreseeable future.

Shadows played over her face as she retrieved and put on her spectacles. She held the candle up to the rocky wall at his back.

"So what is this place?

"A cave of wonders. Look. The entire exposed surface is a compressed layer of fossilized marine life." She skipped her fingertips over the rugged surface. "I've spent hours making casts and rubbings and drawing sketches. Chipping away specimens where I can. Here's an echinoid, see? Next to it, a trilobite. And just a few inches over, this is a fossilized sea sponge. Look."

Colin looked. He saw rocks, bumps, and bumpy rocks. "Fascinating. So this is the topic of your paper for the symposium? Echy-things and troglodytes. Hard to see how they'd be worth five hundred guineas."

"They're not, not on their own. But *this* is truly priceless."

She crawled sideways back into the cave, some half-dozen feet. Because she seemed to expect it, he followed. The farther back they went, the more the cave shrank around him, constricting his lungs. Even though he was dripping with seawater, a fine sheen of sweat pressed to his brow.

"See here?" she asked, lifting the candle. "This depression in the stone?"

He focused on it, glad for any distraction. "I suppose."

"It's a footprint," she said, in a hushed, reverent tone. "Untold ages ago, some creature walked in the mud here. And the print was preserved, compressed into stone."

"I see. And this excites you because . . . footprints are rare?"

"Fossilized footprints are rare. And no one's ever recorded a footprint like this one before. There are three toes spread wide, see?"

Colin did see. His entire boot could have fit in any one of the individual "toe" impressions.

"It's like a lizard's foot," she said.

"With a footprint that size, that deep? That would have to be one bloody large lizard."

"Precisely." Even in the dark, her eyes gleamed with excitement. "Don't you see? Mr. James Parkinson has published three volumes of fossil plates, from vegetables to vertebrates. He's documented dozens of larger animals, including an ancient alligator and a primeval elephant. But this footprint doesn't meet any description found in his volumes. This is evidence of an entirely new creature, unknown to modern science until now. A giant prehistoric lizard."

Colin blinked. "Well. That is most . . . remarkable."

A giant prehistoric lizard. *This* was the great scientific discovery that was guaranteed to win five hundred guineas. She wanted to travel all the way to Edinburgh to argue the existence of dragons. No scientists in their right minds would award a prize for that.

"This footprint," she said excitedly, "changes everything. *Everything.*"

He could only stare at her.

"Don't you see?" she asked.

"Not . . . really."

Unable to take the closeness any longer, he made his way back to the larger mouth of the cavern. He sat near the shelf's edge. Black water lapped at his fingertips.

He looked up. "Is there some other way out of here?"

Dropping to sit across from him, she exhaled. "I should have known this wouldn't work. You're right, the whole elopement business was a stupid idea. I thought maybe if you had a chance to see it, you'd understand the implications. And you'd see how certain you are to take home five hundred guineas. But apparently, you're incapable of grasping the scientific significance."

He made a conscious decision to let the insult slide. "Apparently I am."

"Not to mention, I expected you'd contribute something to the journey other than snide commentary. But I see I was wrong on that score, too."

"How do you mean?

"You know. Brawn, if not brains. Protection. Strength. But after that situation with the tunnel . . . I can't be dragging you kicking and flailing all the way to Scotland."

"Now wait just a moment," he interrupted. He cleared his

throat and lowered his voice a half octave. "I have strength of all sorts in abundance. I box. I fence. I ride. I shoot. I am the first lieutenant of a small yet plucky militia. I'm certain I could bodily lift this giant lizard of yours and toss him off the nearest balcony. I just don't have any patience for underwater tunnels."

"Or caves." To his offended silence, she replied, "Don't deny it. I can tell how hard you're breathing."

"I'm not—"

"For heaven's sake. You're fogging my spectacles from here. Do you have a fear of small spaces?"

"Not a *fear* of them," he said.

Her silence communicated skepticism.

He muttered, "A dislike. I dislike small, dark spaces."

"You should have mentioned this before we entered a cave."

"Well, you didn't give me much opportunity."

"Shall we go back out the way we came?"

"No." In this larger chamber, with the benefit of candles, the cave wasn't so bad. But he was *not* swimming through that tomb of a tunnel again. "You say the entrance is above water at low tide? Then I'll wait for low tide."

"That could be hours. People will wonder what's become of us."

He marveled at the "us" in that sentence—that it hadn't even occurred to her she might swim back and leave him there alone. He'd noticed this about her, over the months. She couldn't even contemplate the idea of disloyalty. Which was why she so disdained *him*, he supposed.

She pinched the bridge of her nose. "Oh dear. We'll have to go to Scotland now. If anyone notices we've disappeared together this morning . . . if anyone saw us kiss last night . . . if your lover decides to gossip . . ." She lowered her hand. "Separately, those things might go unobserved, but all three of them? In all likelihood, I'm already ruined."

"That's an extreme conclusion," he said, ignoring that each separate event looked rather damning. "Let's take this one crisis at a time. How many candles do you have?

"This, and one other."

Colin did a swift mental estimate. Three, four hours of light, perhaps. More than enough. A violent shiver wracked his body. "Are you chilled?" He could think of worse ways to pass a few hours than huddling with a woman for warmth.

She reached into a rocky niche. "I keep a blanket here." Crouching beside him, she shook it out and draped it over them both. She kept a buffer of several inches between their bodies.

The warmth seeped through his wet clothing. "I don't suppose you keep any whiskey here?"

"No."

"Pity. But still—candles, blanket. You must spend a great deal of time in this . . . place," he said, after fumbling several moments for a more diplomatic word than "hellhole."

He felt her shoulders lift in a shrug. "Geology is my life's work. Some scientists have a laboratory. I have a cave."

A dozen mocking rejoinders jostled for prominence in Colin's mind, but he sensed that teasing her on this point would leave him too vulnerable. She was a scientist. She had a cave. And he was an aimless aristocrat who had . . . nothing.

She said, "I had it all sorted out. There's a stagecoach that runs between Eastbourne and Rye. It passes by on Tuesdays and Fridays, just around six. If we walked to the main road, we could flag the coach down. Take it to the next town, and from there go north. We'd reach London tomorrow night."

Ah, to be in London tomorrow night. Bustle. Commerce. Society. Clubs. Glittering balls and gilded opera houses. Skies choked with coal dust. Lamps shining in the darkened streets.

"From there," she said, "we'd catch the mail coach."

"No, no, no. I told you the other night, a viscount doesn't travel on the mail coach. And this particular viscount doesn't travel in any coach."

"Hold a moment." The candle bobbed. "How did you think we'd be traveling to Edinburgh, if not by public coach?"

He shrugged. "We're not traveling to Edinburgh at all. But if we were, we'd have find some other conveyance."

"Such as what? A magic carpet?"

"Such as a private post-chaise, with hired postilions. You'd ride in, and I'd ride out on horseback."

"That would cost a fortune."

He shrugged. "When it comes to travel, I have conditions. I don't ride in coaches, and I don't travel by night."

"No night travel either? But the fastest coaches all travel by night. The journey would take us twice as long."

"Then it's a good thing we're not going, isn't it?"

She lifted the candle and peered into his face. "You're just making excuses. You want out of our agreement—"

"What agreement? There was never any agreement."

"—so you're plucking these ridiculous 'conditions' out of the air." She ticked items off on one hand. "No closed carriages. No travel by night. What kind of grown man has such rules?"

"One who narrowly survived a carriage accident," he said testily. "At night. That's what kind."

Her face softened. So did her voice. "Oh."

Colin drummed his fingers on the stone. He'd forgotten that she wouldn't know this. In London, everyone knew. The story passed around ballrooms and gaming hells every season. Skipped from matron to debutante, gambler to opera singer—always in mournful whispers. *Have you heard about poor Lord Payne. . . .*

"Was this recent?" she asked.

"No, long ago."

"What happened?"

Sighing roughly, he rested his head against the uneven, clammy stone. "I was a boy, traveling with my parents. An axle snapped, and the coach overturned. I survived the accident largely unharmed. But my mother and father weren't so fortunate."

"They were injured?"

"They died. There, in the carriage, right in front of me. My father went almost instantly. My mother, slowly and in tremendous agony." He paused. "I couldn't get out, you see. The way the carriage had landed on its side, the door was barred shut. I couldn't run for help, couldn't escape. I lay trapped there, all night long. Alone. A passing farmer found me the next morning."

There. That would teach her to press him for honesty.

"Oh." She gripped his arm. "Oh *God*. I'm so sorry. I can see why you'd be afra— er, why you would dislike dark, enclosed spaces. How dreadful."

"It was. Exceedingly." He rubbed his temple. "Suffice it to say, I've no desire to relive such a situation. So I have a few simple rules. I don't travel at night. I don't ride in enclosed carriages. Oh, and I don't sleep alone." A grimace tugged his mouth sideways. "That last is less of a rule and more a statement of fact."

"How do you mean?"

Colin hesitated briefly. He'd revealed this much. There seemed no point in denying the rest. "I simply don't sleep alone. If I don't have a bed companion, I lie awake all night."

He nudged toward the soft heat of her body and gathered the blanket close around them. "So you may want to rethink your plans, pet. If we did undertake this journey . . . I'd need you in my bed."

Chapter Five

Somewhere in the back of the cave, a drip counted out Minerva's stunned silence.

One, two, three . . .

. . . ten, eleven, twelve . . .

He needed *her*? In his *bed*? It was too much to be believed. She reminded herself it wasn't *her* he needed. Apparently, any woman would do.

"So you're telling me that this accident . . . this tragic night in your youth . . . is the reason for your libertine ways?"

"Yes. This is my curse." He gave a deep, resonant sigh. A sigh clearly meant to pluck at her heartstrings.

And it worked. It really *worked*.

"Sweet heaven." She swallowed back a lump in her throat. "You must do this all the time. Night after night, you tell women your tale of woe . . ."

"Not really. The tale of woe precedes me."

" . . . and then they just open their arms and lift their skirts for you. 'Come, you poor, sweet man, let me hold you' and so forth. Don't they?"

He hedged. "Sometimes."

Minerva knew they did. They must. She felt it happening

to *her*. As he'd related his story, a veritable fount of emotion had welled in her chest. Sadness, sympathy. Her womb somehow became involved, sending nurturing impulses coursing through her veins. Everything feminine in her responded to the call.

Then came the lies. Her heart told her *lies*. Wicked, insidious falsehoods, resounding with every beat.

He's a broken man.

He needs you.

You can heal him.

Rationally, she knew better. Untold numbers of women had already tried their hands—among other body parts—at "healing his broken soul," with no success.

And yet . . . although her mind knew it to be foolishness, her body ached with the desire to hold him. Soothe him.

"I can't believe this," she breathed, mostly to herself. "I can't believe you're working this spell on *me*."

"I'm not working any spell. I'm giving you the facts. Aren't you fond of those? If you're harboring any thought of compelling me to make this journey, you should know my conditions. I don't ride in coaches, which means I'd be on horseback all day. I can't ride on horseback all day unless I'm sleeping well at night. And I don't sleep alone. Ergo, you'd have to share my bed. Unless you'd prefer me to search out random serving girls at each coaching inn."

A wave of nausea rocked her. "Ugh."

"Honestly, I don't relish the thought either. Bedding my way along the Great North Road might have sounded like a grand time five years ago. Not so much, anymore." He cleared his throat. "Nowadays, it's more the rest I'm after. I don't even bed half the women I sleep with. If that makes sense."

"If that makes *sense*? Nothing about this makes sense."

"You don't have to understand it. God knows, I don't."

She sat next to him, reclining against the wall. Beneath the blanket, their arms touched. Even through that slight contact, she could sense the restlessness in his body. He was struggling to conceal his unease, but after years of vigilance with an asthmatic sister, Minerva was acutely attuned to small signs of distress. She couldn't ignore the raspy quality of his breathing, nor the way his muscles hummed with a desperate wish to be quit of the place.

And when presented with a complexity, she wasn't the sort to give up on understanding it. She was a scientist, after all.

"Is it just the cave?" she asked. "Or is it like this every night?"

He didn't answer.

"You say it's persisted since childhood. Is it getting better or worse with time?"

"I'd rather not discuss it."

"Oh. All right."

How sad, that he suffered so. How pathetic, that he turned to an endless chain of women to ameliorate his suffering. The idea made her nauseous. Irrationally envious. And just a little flushed, beneath her bathing costume.

A question burned inside her. She couldn't help but ask. "Who was she, the other night? It wouldn't matter, except . . ." *Except whoever she was, she has the power to make my life utter misery.*

After a moment, he reluctantly answered. "Ginny Watson."

"Oh." Minerva knew the cheery young widow. She took in washing from the rooming-house residents. Apparently, she took in washing—and other things—from the castle residents, too. But she didn't seem the sort to spread tales.

"It didn't mean anything," he said.

"But don't you see? That's the worst part." She moved away from the wall and turned to face him. The wet fabric of her bathing costume scraped over the rough stone. "Insomnia isn't an uncommon condition, you know. Surely there must be some solution. If you can't sleep at night, why don't you light some lamps? Read some books. Warm some milk. See a doctor for a sleeping powder."

"Those aren't new ideas. I've tried them all, and then some."

"And nothing works?"

Those drips counted the silence again. *One, two, three . . .*

He trailed a light touch up her arm. Then—slowly—he leaned forward.

And whispered in her ear, "One thing works."

His lips brushed her cheek.

Minerva stiffened. Her every nerve ending jumped to attention. She didn't know whether to be appalled or thrilled that he would make her another link in his amatory chain.

Appalled, she told herself. She ought to be appalled.

"You are shameless," she whispered. "I can't believe this."

"It's rather a shock to me, too." His lips grazed her jaw. "But you are a most surprising girl."

"You're being opportunistic."

"I won't deny it. Why don't you seize the opportunity, as well? I want to kiss you. And you need kissing, desperately."

She put a hand to his shoulder and pushed him away. The cave filled with her affronted silence. "Why would you suggest such a thing?"

"Because last night you wanted to kiss me back. But you didn't know how."

Her heart jumped into her throat. So mortifying. How could he tell?

Wordlessly, he removed the spectacles from her face, folded them, and set them aside.

"I can't believe this," she breathed.

"So you keep saying." He inched closer, eliminating the distance between them. "But you know, Matilda, what you haven't said?"

"What's that?"

"You haven't said no."

He reached for her in the dark, skimming a touch over her cheek, sliding down to cup her chin. With his hand anchored there, he stroked his thumb in ever-widening circles, until he grazed her bottom lip.

"You have a mouth made for kissing," he murmured, angling her to face him. "Did you know that?"

She shook her head.

"So soft and generous." Leaning in, he tipped her chin with the heel of his hand. "Sweet."

"No man's ever called me sweet."

"Has any other man kissed you?"

Again, she gave a little shake of the head.

"Well, then. That's why." He brushed his lips over hers, just lightly, sending pure sensation fizzing through her veins. He hummed with satisfaction. "You taste of ripe plums."

She couldn't help it. She laughed. "Now that's just absurd."

"Why?"

"Because it's too early in the year for ripe plums."

His husky chuckle shook them both. "You're entirely too logical for your own good. A thorough kissing can mend that."

"I don't want mending."

"Perhaps not. But I think you do want kissing." He nuzzled the curve of her cheek, and his voice dropped to a sensual whisper. "Don't you?"

She did. Oh, she did.

She couldn't deny it. Not when he touched her like this. She wanted to be kissed, and to kiss him in return. She wanted to touch him, stroke him, hold him tight. All those tender, nurturing impulses still pulsed within her, despite all her efforts to reason them away. Her heart kept pumping those lies through her body.

He needs you.

You can heal him.

She had feminine warmth in abundance, and he needed comfort right now. In return, she could glimpse what it felt like to be needed. To be kissed. To be called sweet, and compared to a ripened plum.

To be desired by a desirable man.

"Just this once?" she breathed.

"Just this once."

So long as they both knew it was all mere diversion . . . a harmless way to pass the time . . . It couldn't hurt to pretend, could it? Not in secret, in the dark.

Here, there was no one to laugh.

Her breath caught as he pressed a chaste kiss to her forehead. Then her cheek. Then her jaw.

Then her lips.

He pressed the tip of his tongue to that vulnerable hinge at the corner of her mouth, coaxing her lips to part. She gasped a little, and he took advantage of the moment, sweeping his tongue inside her mouth.

She froze instantly, pressing her hand flush against his chest. Then she pushed him away. "I don't understand." She made a fist, clutching his wet shirtfront. "I don't understand why you do that. I don't understand what I'm supposed to do in return."

"Shush." He stroked her hair, dragging his fingers through the heavy, damp strands to untangle them. "Kissing's like any skill. It takes a bit of practice. Think of it . . . think of it like dancing." He paused to kiss her neck, her earlobe. "Just surrender to the rhythm of it. Follow my lead."

They tried again. This time, he sucked her upper lip between his and worried it a little. Then he repeated the attentions with her lower lip.

And then he swept his tongue between the two.

His tongue rubbed over hers. She cautiously stroked back with her own, earning a little growl of approval. A thrill chased over her skin. Heat built between their bodies, melting away some of her anxiety.

He tilted his head, exploring her mouth from a new angle.

She understood now why he'd compared kissing to dancing. He had *moves*. A great many of them. Not just thrusting his tongue in and out, but swirling and toying and subtle coaxing. And just as she always did on a dance floor, Minerva quickly grew faint, dizzy. She felt overwhelmed and out of her depth. Always a step behind.

Once again, she broke away.

"This won't work," she said, wilting inside. "I'm hopeless at dancing. It simply won't work."

"No, don't say that." His labored breaths raced hers. "It was a bad example on my part. Don't think of it like dancing. Kissing's nothing like dancing. Think of it as you would . . ." He flicked a glance to the fossil-studded cave wall. "An excavation."

"An excavation?"

"Yes. A proper kiss is like an excavation. When you're digging up your little troglodytes, you don't just go plunging your shovel into the soil higgledy-piggledy, do you?"

"No." Her wariness stretched the word.

"Of course not. A proper excavation takes time and care. And very close attention to detail. Slowly sifting through the layers. Unearthing surprises as you go."

That sounded much more promising. After a long moment's reflection, she asked, "So who is excavating whom?"

"Ideally, it's a bit of both. We sort of . . . take turns."

She was silent for a long moment. Something about the air around them changed. Heated.

She swallowed hard. "May I go first?"

* * *

Colin struggled to suppress his triumphant grin. It would have ruined everything. He made his voice solemn. "But of course."

She rose up to sit on her knees, positioning herself to face him. The dim glow allowed him to see her in silhouette. Just an enticing hourglass of shadow with a halo of curling hair. He wanted to reach for her, pull her close again. Give his pulse some better reason to pound. Ease his soul with the warm, human contact he craved. At times like these, patience came at a premium.

But its reward was great. Her hand reached out to him, swimming through the dark to caress his face.

God, she was such a surprise.

Her curiosity marked her apart from other girls. She didn't concentrate on the features one would suppose—eyebrows, cheekbones, lips, the line of his nose. All the features that comprised "a face" in a schoolgirl's sketch. No, her touch was thorough, indiscriminate, searching out every detail. The flat of her palm scraped over his unshaven jaw. She smoothed a narrow furrow between his brows and stroked a light caress under his eyes, where the sleepless nights weighed heavy. He found himself nuzzling into the touch. He exhaled until his lungs were empty.

She brushed the fringe of his eyelashes with one fingertip, and a delicate cascade of pleasure rippled through him. What a revelation that was. He'd have to add eyelash caresses to his own repertoire.

When her fingers pushed into his hair, he moaned. Women always loved his wavy hair, and he always loved the attention they paid it. Pleasant sensations raced over his scalp as she sifted through the wet locks, teasing them back from his forehead. Her fingertip found his scar and traced it—the thin, pale ridge that began at his temple and curved back over his ear. His only physical souvenir of the carriage accident, it was undetectable to the casual observer.

But she found it, easily. Because finding buried things was what she did best, he supposed. A proper excavation left no secret hidden.

He began to wonder about the wisdom of this exercise.

"We're supposed to be kissing," he said.

"I'm getting to it." Her voice betrayed a hint of nerves. She moved closer, drawing her knees between his splayed thighs. Leaning forward, she brushed her lips over his.

The blissful shock of it rattled his very bones. But as she receded, he kept his tone glib. "You can do better."

She took the challenge and kissed him again, more firmly this time. Her tongue flicked out, nimble and curious. And all too fleeting. "Better?"

"Better." Almost *too* good.

"Hmm. You taste of spirits here." Her tongue traced the edge of his lip. "But here"—she dipped her head to nuzzle the underside of his jaw—"you smell of spice. Cloves."

Bloody hell. Colin's eyes went wide in the dark as she sipped at his skin, over and over, tracing the curve of his throat. When she reached the center, she brushed her lips over his Adam's apple. His breath was a painful rasp in his throat. He couldn't take much more of this.

"You still haven't properly kissed me," he said. "Are you afraid?"

She lifted her head. "No."

"I think you are." *I think I might be, too, just a little.*

And for good reason. Her mouth found his, and her parted lips pressed against his own. And there they stayed. Soft, sweet. Warming in the heat of their mingled breath. All the while, a snarling, feral need clawed him from the inside out, fighting its leash of gentlemanly restraint. He'd lose the battle if she didn't move soon.

This was more than an excavation. She was turning him inside out. Exposing the base, desperate needs studded in the deepest layer of his being. Until he felt not merely naked before her, but stripped bare. Cold and shivering and defenseless in the dark.

Kiss me, he willed, underscoring the message with a flex of his knee against her thigh. *Kiss me now, or suffer the consequences.*

At last. Her fingers twisted in his hair, drawing him close. Her teeth skimmed the ridge of his lower lip. And then she slid her tongue into his mouth. Just a shallow, teasing pass the first time. Then a bit deeper, on the second attempt. Then deeper still, again and again, by slow, tantalizing degrees.

She sighed into the kiss, just a little. The faint sound blazed through him, kindling his every nerve ending like a fuse.

Her fingers left his hair, and he worried for a moment that this all might stop.

Don't stop. God, don't stop.

But then she braced her hands on the cave wall, bracketing his shoulders, and pressed him against the rocky surface. With her *breasts*. So soft and round against his chest, tipped with the deliciously hard darts of her chilled nipples. She pinned him to the wall, using the leverage to make the kiss deeper, stroking deep with her tongue.

And just like that, his control was gone.

He reached for her, gripping her by the thighs. Holding her close and tight as she plundered his mouth with bold, innocent abandon. With her kiss, his whole body came alive. Not just his body. Something stirred in the region of his heart, as well.

Jesus. Jesus Christ and Mary Magdalene. Delilah, Jezebel, Salome, Judith, Eve. Trouble, every last one. Add Minerva Highwood to the list.

A woman like this could ruin him. If he didn't ruin her first.

"What do I call you?" Her breath came hot against his ear. "When . . . when we're doing this, what do I call you?"

He fisted his hands in the fabric at the small of her back. "You must call me by my Christian name. Colin."

"Colin," she whispered, tentative at first. Then with feeling, as she pressed an openmouthed kiss to his temple. "Oh, *Colin*."

Oh God. He could hear her moan his name a hundred times, and it wouldn't be enough.

As they kissed, he rubbed his hands up and down her back. Keeping her close. Warming them both. But after several passes traveling the length of her spine, he couldn't help but venture further. She still owed him his chance to explore.

He had to get to her. He had to get to the soft, secret part of her, the way she was getting to him.

He slid a palm down her hip, cupping her backside and giving it a brief squeeze. Then he brushed the same hand up her side, slowly dragging his touch over the curve of her hip, the indentation of her waist, the endless ridges of her ribs . . . he could have sworn he counted thirty-four or so . . . and then, at *last*, the soft, round swell of her breast.

"*Colin*." Her gasp told him he'd gone too far.

"Min, I . . ." He rested his brow against hers. He didn't know how to apologize. He wasn't sorry for any of it. Not in the least.

She pulled away, blinking at him. "Colin. I can *see* you."

The way she spoke the words, in such an awestruck tone, made him wonder for a moment if their kiss had actually cured her weak eyes. That would have been quite a miracle, but he'd be inclined to believe it. He felt rather changed by that kiss, himself.

"It's light in here," she said. "I can see you now." She moved away, reaching for her spectacles.

And he instantly understood what she meant. Without her silhouette blocking his view, he too could see that the tide had receded. Enough so the apex of the underwater entrance was revealed. A beam of sunlight shot through, like gold floss threading the eye of a needle—stabbing Colin straight in the eyes.

"Ah." He lifted his hand, shielding his eyes from the piercing dawn.

Now that he had a proper look at his surroundings, he could judge that the black, "endless" underwater tunnel he'd been so certain he'd die inside was actually . . . no more than three feet long.

Good God. He rolled his eyes at his own ridiculousness. No wonder she'd doubted his mettle.

"We'll be able to leave soon," she said, already up and bustling about. She pursed her lips and blew out the candle. "It's better that we waited, anyhow. Now I don't have to trust the oilcloth to keep my notes and papers dry."

As Colin watched her go about her preparations, he reeled with the strangest emotion. Disappointment. A forceful pang of it.

That made no sense. Light had made its way into the cave. The space was no longer dark. He was going to leave this cramped, miserable hole in the earth in a just a few minutes' time. And he was disappointed. Disappointed that he couldn't stay here and kiss her a few hours longer.

"I'll be damned," he muttered.

"Most likely." She folded the blanket with efficient snaps. "And I may be joining you, after what we just did."

"Don't be so hard on yourself. We were merely kissing." Though he knew there was nothing "mere" about it.

"Well, it can't happen again."

Colin pressed a hand to his solar plexus. There it went. That sharp pang of disappointment. This cave was just full of surprises.

She stared at the footprint and her notes. Then she looked up at him, deftly winding her hair into a knot.

"We'll leave tomorrow," she said, speaking around a mouthful of hairpins. "We must, if we're to have any hope of reaching Edinburgh in time."

He shook his head. "Pet, I thought I'd made myself understood. I—"

"I agree to your conditions. All of them. You can ride out. We won't travel at night. And the part about the bed . . . ?" A faint wash of pink touched her cheeks. "That too. But we'll need to leave tomorrow, if we're going to make the symposium."

He swallowed hard. The part about the bed . . . ? He really wished she hadn't said that.

Colin had rules for himself where women were concerned. So far he'd always followed them, and his remaining self-respect dangled on that slim cord. But this was different. *She* was different, in ways he couldn't yet define. He usually didn't find innocence so alluring, but in her case it was sweetened by bold, unabashed curiosity. Given the opportunity, he wasn't sure he could resist. And weeks of travel would present many, many opportunities.

Right this moment, he was entertaining a quite vivid fantasy of unwinding that knot in her hair, stripping that drab linen from her body, peeling away any layers of modesty beneath . . . and leaving those spectacles on. So she'd see him. So she'd know just who was making her twist and pant and moan with pleasure. So she'd watch each and every wince of pleasure on his face as he pushed into—

"Don't come for me at the rooming house," she said. "Too much chance of being intercepted. I'll walk out and meet you by the road."

Colin massaged his jaw, releasing a faint groan. He was a libertine with prodigious experience. She was a naïve bluestocking still tasting her first kiss. This was an exceedingly bad idea. No matter how much he wanted to leave Spindle Cove, no matter how much she claimed to want this journey . . .

It could not happen. Because now he wanted *her*.

"Colin?"

He shook himself. "Yes?"

She met his gaze. The vulnerability shining in her eyes plucked at his conscience.

"Please," she said. "You *will* be there, won't you? You won't play me another cruel trick and leave me the laughingstock, standing all by myself while the coach passes by?" She swallowed hard. "Should I be worried about you?"

Yes, pet. That's just it. You should be worried indeed.

Chapter Six

He wasn't coming.

Minerva stared off in the direction of the castle. Then she checked her timepiece for the fourth time in as many seconds. Two . . . no, *three* minutes past six.

He wasn't coming.

She should never have dreamed otherwise. She ought to have known he'd let her down.

The ground shivered beneath her. A rumble of hoofbeats reached her ears. Here it came, the coach. And it would pass her by. Leave her standing on the side of the road—an awkward fool of a girl, all dressed up with nowhere to go.

Hopeless.

She stared down the road, just waiting for the black shadow of the coach to crest the distant hill. So strange. The hoofbeats grew louder and louder, but no carriage appeared. By this point, she could actually feel the earth's low rumble in her shinbones. Still no coach. She whirled, feeling confused and frantic.

And there he was. Lord Payne.

Colin.

Charging toward her on horseback, dashing through the

early-morning mist. The wind rippling through his wavy hair. The sight was just like something from a fairy tale. Oh, he wasn't riding a white stallion, but rather a serviceable, sturdy bay gelding. And he was dressed not in shining armor or regal attire, but in a simple, well-tailored blue topcoat and buckskin riding breeches.

No matter. He still took her breath away. As he slid from his horse, he was magnificent. Resplendent. Without a doubt, the most beautiful man she'd ever seen.

And then he spoke.

"This is a mistake."

She blinked at him. "A mistake?"

"Yes. I should have said as much yesterday, but better late than never. This journey would be a mistake, of catastrophic proportions. It can't happen."

"But . . ." Looking around, she realized he had nothing with him. No valises. No bags of any kind. Her heart sank. "Yesterday, in the cave. Colin, you promised."

"I said I'd be here at six. I didn't promise I'd leave with you."

Minerva reeled in her half boots. Deflated and numb, she dropped to sit on the edge of her largest trunk.

He surveyed her baggage. "Good God. How did you bring three trunks all the way up here by yourself?"

"I made three trips," she said weakly. Three cold, hard slogs through the mist. For nothing.

"Three trunks," he repeated. "What could possibly be in them all?"

"Why do you care? You've just said you won't go."

He crouched in front of her, sinking to her eye level. "Listen, Michaela. This is for your own good. Did anyone notice we'd gone missing yesterday? Did anyone see us kiss the other night?"

She shook her head. "No."

No one seemed to suspect a thing. Which ought to have made her feel better, but was somehow the most humiliating part yet.

"Then you're safe, so far. And there's too much at risk for you in this undertaking. Not just your reputation, but your safety. Your happiness. And it all might come to naught." He tipped her chin.

She stared into his eyes. They were red-rimmed and weary. Little lines creased the space between his eyebrows. He hadn't shaved. From a distance, he'd appeared handsome and dashing, but up close . . . "Goodness. You look horrible."

He rubbed his face. "Yes, well. I had a hard night."

"No sleep?"

"Actually, I did try to sleep. That's the problem. I ought to know by now, that never ends well."

Here it came again, that wave of sympathy rolling through her chest. She wanted to touch his hair, but settled for plucking a little burr from his coat sleeve.

"All the more reason you should want to come with me." She tried to make it sound like the only obvious and logical solution, though she knew it really wasn't. "Before the fortnight's out, you could have enough money to return to London and live as you please."

He shook his head. "I don't know how to say this kindly, so I'll just put it bluntly. Forget about me. Never mind your sister. To the devil with the five hundred guineas. Think of yourself. You're betting your reputation, your family harmony—your entire future—on a queer-shaped hole in the ground. I'm a gambler, pet. I know a bad wager when I see one."

"So you don't believe in me."

"No, that's not it. I just don't believe in dragons."

"Is that all? You think I'm fanciful?" She stood and began pulling at the fastened straps of her trunk. "This creature was not a dragon. Not a mythical beast of any kind, but a real, living animal. And I've based my conclusions on years of scientific study."

After a few minutes' fumbling, she finally got the trunk open. "Here," she said, lifting out stacks of journals and setting them atop the other trunk. "All my personal writings and findings. Months of notes, sketches, measurements." She held up a thick leather-bound diary. "This entire journal is filled with my comparisons from the available fossil record. Verifying that no similar creature has been recorded to date. And if all that fails to convince them . . ."

She pushed aside a layer of fabric padding. "Here. I've brought this."

Colin stared at the object in the trunk. "Why, it's the footprint."

She nodded. "I made a casting, from plaster of Paris."

He stared at it some more. In the cave, in the dark, the "print" had looked like a random, three-pronged depression in the ground. The work of time and chance, not some primeval creature.

But now in the sunlight, cast in plaster relief—he could see it clear. The edges were defined and smooth. Just as with a human footprint, the toe prints were individual and separate from the sole. It really looked like a foot. An *enormous* reptilian foot. The print of a creature that could send a man running and screaming for his life.

Colin had to admit, it was rather impressive.

But not nearly as impressive as Minerva herself.

At last, here was a glimmer of that confident, clever woman who'd visited his quarters. The woman he'd been waiting to see again.

The brisk morning air lent her skin a pretty flush, and the misty sunlight revealed it to lovely effect. She'd coiled all that dark, heavy hair and tightly pinned it for the journey—

save a few fetching tendrils that spiraled lazily from her temple to her cheek. Doeskin gloves hugged her fingers like a second skin. Her traveling gown was velvet. Exquisitely tailored and dyed in a lush, saturated hue that danced the line between red and violet. Depending on how the sunlight caught the velvet's thick nap, that gown was either the blaring color of alarm—or the hue of wild, screaming pleasure.

Either way, Colin knew he ought to lower his gaze, back away slowly, and be done with this.

"I will win the prize," she said. "If you still don't believe me, I'll prove it to you."

"Really, you don't need to—"

"It's not only me who believes it. I know you think I'm mad, but he's not." She rummaged through the trunk's interior side pocket and withdrew an envelope. "Here, read it."

He unfolded the letter, holding it carefully by its edges. The message was penned in a crisp, masculine hand.

"'My dear friend and colleague,'" he read aloud. "'I have read with great interest your latest reports from Sussex.'" He skimmed the letter. "So on and so forth. Something about rocks. More about lizards."

"Just skip to the end." She jabbed a finger at the last paragraph. "Here."

"'These findings of yours are exciting indeed,'" Colin read. "'I wish you would reconsider your plans and make the journey to Edinburgh for the symposium. Surely the prize would be yours, without contest. And though it be paltry inducement compared to a purse of five hundred guineas, I would add that I'm most eager to further our acquaintance. I find myself growing most impatient to meet, face-to-face, the colleague whose scholarship I have long admired and whose friendship I have . . .'" His voiced trailed off. He cleared his throat and resumed reading. "'Whose friendship I have come to hold so very dear. Please . . .'"

Colin paused. *So very dear?* In correspondence between a gentleman and an unattached young lady, that was practically a declaration of love.

" 'Please make the journey. Yours in admiration, Sir Alisdair Kent,' " he finished.

He'd be damned. The awkward bluestocking had an admirer. Perhaps even a sweetheart. How quaint. How precious. How unspeakably irritating.

"There," she said. "I'm certain to win the prize. Do you see?"

"Oh, I see. I see your little plan now." He took a few aimless paces, chuckling to himself. "I can't believe this. I'm being used."

"Used? What can you mean? That's absurd."

He made a dismissive noise. "Please. Here I was so concerned that if I consented to this trip, I'd be using you ill." He held up the letter. "But this is all about Sir Alisdair Kent. You were going to pretend to elope with me, on the hopes of seeing him. You're the one using *me*."

She snatched the letter from his grip. "I'm not using you. You would come out richer for this, while I would be utterly ruined. I'm offering you the entire prize. Five hundred guineas."

"A fine price for my tender heart." He pressed a hand over the offended organ. "You meant to ruthlessly toy with my affections. Suggesting we travel together for weeks. An unmarried man and an unmarried woman, trapped in close quarters for all those days." He cocked an eyebrow. "All those *nights*. You'll be casting glances at me over those coy little spectacles, driving me wild with all your polysyllabic words. Sharing my bed. Kissing me like a brazen temptress."

Her lashes worked furiously as she refolded her precious letter. "That's quite enough."

No, it wasn't enough. Not nearly. Colin knew she didn't respect him. But now that he was seized with lust for her, she ought to at least reciprocate with a grudging-yet-helpless infatuation. So much would only be polite. But no, she'd been pining all along for another man. When they'd kissed, had she been practicing for this geologist toad?

She said, "There's no need to mock me. There's no call to be cruel. Sir Alisdair Kent is a colleague, nothing more."

"He holds you dear, that letter says. Not just dear. 'So *very* dear.' "

"He doesn't even—" She made a fist and drew a slow breath. When she spoke again, she'd tempered her voice. "He is a brilliant geologist. And any admiration he feels for me is strictly based on my work. He believes the creature that left this footprint will be recorded as a new species. I'll even get to name it."

"Name it?" Colin eyed the plaster cast. "Why go to Scotland for that? We can name it right here. I suggest 'Frank.' "

"Not name it *that* way. I'll be the one to give the species a scientific name. Besides, this lizard was female."

He cocked his head and stared at the print. "It's a footprint. How on earth do you know?"

"I just know. I feel it." With her fingertips, she reverently traced the three-toed shape. "The creature who left this mark—she was definitely not a 'Frank.' "

"Francine, then."

She exhaled forcefully. "I know this is all a joke to you. But it won't be to my colleagues." She replaced the rolls of fabric around the plaster, packing it tight. "Whatever this creature was, she was real. She lived and breathed, and she left this mark. And now, untold eons later . . . she just might change the way we understand the world."

She shut and locked the trunk, propping one foot atop the

baggage to tighten the leather straps. Her trim, stockinged ankle was revealed to his view. So pale and sweetly curved. He didn't know which he found more appealing—the erotic glimpse of her ankle, or the determined set of her brow.

"Come. Give it here." Colin reached to help with the buckles.

At his urging, she ceased wrestling with the straps and surrendered the task to him. In the transfer, the back of his hand brushed her calf. A jolt of desire rocked him in his boots. *Lord.* This was precisely why he couldn't agree to this wild scheme.

He finished fastening the buckles and stood tall, clapping dust from his gloved hands. "He's probably ancient, you know. Or warty."

"Who?"

"This Sir Alisdair fellow."

Her cheeks blushed crimson.

"I'm just saying, he's likely older than Francine. And less attractive."

"I don't care! I don't care if he's ancient and warty and leprous and hunchbacked. He would still be learned, intelligent. Respected and respectful. He would still be a better man than you. You know it, and you're envious. You're being cruel to me to soothe your pride." She looked him up and down with a contemptuous glare. "And you're going to catch flies in your mouth, if you don't shut it."

For once, Colin found himself without words. The best he could do was take her advice and hoist his dropped jaw.

An air of determination settled on her. The curves of her face became decisive angles. "That's it. I'm going to Edinburgh, with or without you."

"What? You mean to travel almost five hundred miles alone? No. I can't let you do that. I . . . I forbid you."

It was Colin's first attempt at forbidding anyone to do anything, and it worked about as well as he'd expected it to. Which was to say, not at all.

She sniffed. "Stay here and marry Diana if you must, but I won't be a party to it. I can't simply stand by and watch."

"God, is that all that's worrying you?" He put his hands on her shoulders to make sure she was paying attention. "I won't marry Diana. I never had any plan to marry Diana. I've been trying to tell you as much for days."

She stared at him. "Truly?"

"Truly."

The distant rumble of hoofbeats and carriage wheels shook the ground. As they stared at each other, it gathered strength.

"That'll be the coach," she said.

Colin glanced down the road. Yes, here it came. The moment of decision.

"Come now," he said. "Let me help you take your things back to the rooming house."

She shook her head. "No."

"Min—"

"No. I can't go back. I just can't. I left a note, saying we've eloped. By now, they're probably awake and reading it. I can't be the girl who cried 'elopement.' The pathetic thing who gathered all her hopes and packed three trunks, and went out to stand at the road at dawn only to slink back home defeated and hopeless. My mother would . . ." She drew a deep breath, stood tall, and lifted her chin. "I just can't be that girl anymore. I won't."

As he watched her, Colin was visited by the strangest feeling, unfurling warm and buttery inside him. It was a sense of privilege and mute wonder, as though he'd witnessed one of those small, everyday miracles of spring. Like a licked-clean foal taking its first steps on wobbly legs. Or a new butterfly pushing scrunched, damp wings from a chrysalis.

Before his eyes, she'd transformed into a new creature. Still a bit awkward and uncertain, but undaunted. And well on her way to being beautiful.

Colin scratched his neck. He wished there were someone nearby he could turn to and say, *Would you look at that?*

"You truly want this," he said. "It means that much to you."

"Yes." Her eyes were clear and unblinking.

"If we embark on this journey, there's no going back."

"I know."

"And you comprehend all the implications. Everything you'll put at risk. Hell, everything you'll outright sacrifice, the moment you leave with me?"

She nodded. "I'm exchanging my acceptance in fashionable society for standing within the Royal Geological Society. I understand this perfectly, and I think it a rather good trade. You told me to think of myself, Colin. Well, I'm doing just that."

Turning from him, she popped up on her toes and waved her arms, signaling the coachman. "Stop! Stop, please!"

He stood by and watched her desperate gesticulations, absurdly enchanted by them. *Good for you, pet. Good for you.*

As the carriage rolled to a halt, she reached for her smallest trunk. She looked to him, smiling. "Last chance. Are you coming or aren't you?"

Chapter Seven

The road to London was dusty, rutted, bumpy, and miserable.

And Minerva rejoiced in every passing mile.

That was to say, she rejoiced quietly, and without moving so much as a muscle. She hadn't any space to move at all.

Inside the coach, they were packed four to a seat. Two more passengers shared space with the driver. Minerva was almost afraid to count how many people rode atop the carriage. From her view through the carriage window, their legs hung down like stalactites. Beyond them, she caught the occasional glimpse of Colin, riding on horseback alongside the coach. She envied him the fresh air and freedom of movement.

But all in all, she was thrilled. The agonized decisions and frantic preparations were behind her, and now she could simply bask in the exhilaration of having done it. After spending all of her girlhood fervently wishing she could run away from home—she'd actually done it. And this wasn't a childish dash into the forest with a hastily packed picnic basket and petulant note reading simply, "Adieu." This journey had serious, professional significance. It was practically a business trip.

This morning, she'd taken her life into her own hands.

But she was glad she wasn't making the journey alone.

When they stopped to rest or change horses, Colin excelled at playing the attentive, would-be bridegroom. He stayed by her side and looked out for her in small ways, such as procuring their refreshments or keeping a watchful eye on her trunks. He made a point of touching her often. Subtly laying a hand to her elbow, handing her into the coach.

She knew the touches weren't for her pleasure or his, but for the benefit of those around them. Those small physical cues made a point. Every time he touched her, he said without words, *This woman is under my protection.*

And every time he sent that message, she felt a little thrill.

Minerva was especially grateful for the protection when they arrived in London late that afternoon and reached the coaching inn. She was so road weary, she could scarcely stand. Colin dealt with the innkeeper, registering the two of them under a fictitious name without so much as a blink. He made certain all her trunks came upstairs, ordered a simple dinner, and even sent an errand boy to procure his traveling necessities—a few clean shirts, a razor, and so forth—rather than do his own shopping and leave Minerva alone.

In fact, he made her feel so safe and comfortable, they were halfway through their meal of roast beef and boiled carrots when Minerva felt suddenly struck—smacked in the face—by reality. She was in a small bedchamber, with a single bed. Alone with a man who was not her relation, nor her husband.

She put down her fork. She chased her last bite of food with a healthy swallow of wine. She took a slow look around at the room.

This was it. This was ruination in the making. Roast beef and boiled carrots and ugly, peeling wallpaper.

"You're very quiet," she said. "You haven't even teased me all day."

He looked up from his plate. "That's because I'm waiting for you, Morgana."

She set her teeth. Really, she couldn't even be bothered to correct him anymore. "Waiting for me to do what?"

"Come to your senses." He gestured about the room. "Call this all off. Demand I take you straight back home."

"Oh. Well, that's not going to happen."

"You're not having any second thoughts?"

She shook her head. "None."

He poured them both more wine. "It doesn't make you at all anxious, to share this room with me tonight and know what it will mean for you tomorrow?"

"No," she lied.

Even though he'd been nothing but solicitous and protective since they'd left Spindle Cove, she couldn't help but feel anxious in his presence. He was so handsome, so blatant, so . . . so very *male*. His personality seemed to take up the entire room.

And heavens, she'd agreed to share a bed with him. If his idea of "sharing a bed" entailed more than simply lying next to each other, she didn't know what she would do. Fear and curiosity battled within her, as she remembered his skillful, arousing kisses in the cave.

"If I can't dissuade you . . ." he said.

She closed her eyes. "You can't."

He exhaled expansively. "Then in the morning, I'll see about finding space in a coach headed north. We should try to sleep as early as possible."

She gulped.

While he finished eating, Minerva decided to seek a familiar refuge. Excusing herself from the small dining table, she went to her trunks and opened the smallest—the one that held all her books. She pulled out her journal. If she'd be presenting at the symposium in a week or so, she needed to organize all her most recent findings and add them to the paper.

Taking a pencil and clenching it between her teeth, she shut the trunk and brought the journal back to the table. She moved her empty dishes of food aside and adjusted her spectacles, settling in to work.

She flipped open the journal to the last filled page. What she saw there horrified her.

Her heart squeezed. "Oh no. Oh *no*."

Across the table, Colin looked up from his food.

She fanned through the pages in dismay. "Oh no. Oh God. I couldn't possibly be so stupid."

"Don't limit yourself. You can be anything you wish." To her annoyed glance, he replied, "What? You complained that I hadn't been teasing you."

She stacked her arms on the table and rested her head on them. Slowly raising and lowering her brow, *thunking* her forehead against her wrist. "So. So. Stupid."

"Come now. Surely it's not that bad." He put aside his cutlery and wiped his mouth on a napkin. Then he slid his chair around the table, so that he sat beside her. "What can possibly have you so upset?" He reached for the journal.

She lifted her head. "No, don't!"

Too late. He already held it in his hands. He flipped through the pages, skimming the text.

"Please don't read it. It's all lies, all foolishness. It's a false journal, you see. I stayed up all night writing it. I meant to leave it behind, to give my mother and sisters the impression that we'd been falling in l—" She bit off the foolish words. "That we'd been carrying on for some time now. So they'd believe in our elopement. But obviously, I made a mistake. I brought the false journal with me and left the real one at the Queen's Ruby."

He lingered on one particular page, chuckling to himself. Minerva's face burned. She wanted to disappear.

"Please. I beg you, don't read it." Desperate, she made a wild grab for the journal.

He held it back, rising from his chair. "Oh, this is brilliant. Utterly brilliant. You sing my praises so convincingly." He cleared his throat and read aloud in an affected tone. "'My mother always says, Lord Payne is all that her future son-in-law should be. Wealthy, titled, handsome, charming. I confess . . .'"

"Give it here."

She chased him, but he backed away, scrambling over the bed and continuing from the other side.

"'I confess,'" he continued in that tone of declamation, "'I was slower than most to admit it, but even I am not immune to Payne's masculine appeal. It's so difficult to recall the defects in his character, when confronted so closely by his . . .'" He lowered the journal and drawled, "'By his physical perfection.'"

"You are a horrid, horrid man."

"You say that *now*. Let's see how your tune changes when you're closely confronted by my physical perfection." He strolled back around the bed, toward her.

Now Minerva was the object of pursuit.

She walked in reverse until her back collided with the wall. Like a child with nowhere to hide, she closed her eyes. "Stop reading. Please."

He flipped through the book as he ambled toward her. "Good God. There are whole *pages* of description. The roguish wave of my hair. My chiseled profile. I have eyes like . . . like *diamonds*?"

"Not real diamonds. Bristol diamonds."

"What are Bristol diamonds?"

"They're a kind of rock formation. On the outside, they

look like ordinary pebbles. Round, brownish gray. But when you crack them open, inside they're filled with crystals in a hundred different shades."

Why did she bother? The man wasn't even listening.

"'No one around us could guess our connection,'" he read on. "'To the observer, it would seem he only speaks to me to tease. But there is a deeper sentiment beneath his teasing, I know it. A man might engage in flirtation with disinterest, or even disdain. But he never teases without affection.'" He speared her with a look. "Those are *my* words. That is blatant plagiarism."

"I'm so sorry. Falsehood doesn't come so easily to me as it does to you." She threw up her hands. "What does it matter? The words were a lie when you spoke them, and they were a lie when I wrote them. Don't you understand? It's a false journal, all of it."

"Not this part." He pointed a single finger in the center of a page. "'We have kissed. He has bade me call him by his Christian name, Colin.'"

He fixed her with an inscrutable look. Her heart pounded in her chest, and she found herself swaying toward him. For a dizzying moment, she thought he might kiss her again.

She *hoped* he would kiss her again.

But he didn't. And she was sure she heard someone, somewhere laughing.

"Yes, it's true," she said. "You've bade me call you by your Christian name. And yet, you can't even recall mine." She wrenched the book from his hand. "I think you've more than made up for lost time now. In fact, I'm certain you've exceeded your teasing quota for the day."

"I can't borrow against tomorrow's?"

"No." She snapped the journal shut and tucked it firmly back in the trunk.

"Come along. Don't be upset. You said yourself, it was purposely ridiculous."

"I know. That's not what has me so upset." *Not entirely.* "It's the fact that I left behind the other diary. The real one, with all my latest measurements and observations."

"I thought you had reams of findings."

"I do. But my presentation will be weaker for not having those."

He paused. "How much weaker?"

"Oh, don't worry." She forced a smile and patted the plaster cast in the trunk. "Your five hundred guineas are assured. So long as we still have this."

"Well," he said. "Thank heaven for Francine."

Colin sighed heavily and pushed a hand through his hair. What the hell was he doing? When she'd made her little ultimatum by the road, she'd left him no choice but to accompany her. Simple decency demanded it. But he'd spent the entire day expecting her to come to her senses. To call off the whole mad journey and demand he return her to Spindle Cove, straightaway. Thus far, however, her determination had not wavered. And some strange force wouldn't let him leave her side.

Colin didn't know what the hell that force was. He was here in a coaching inn with her, so he couldn't very well call it honor or duty. Protectiveness, perhaps? Pity? Sheer curiosity? He knew one thing. It damn well wasn't five hundred guineas.

From her trunk, she unpacked a stout roll of something white.

"What do you have there?" he asked.

"Bed linens. I'm not sleeping atop *that*." She indicated the dingy straw-tick bed.

As he watched, she unfurled the roll atop the sagging mattress, stretching and leaning in her efforts to spread the crisp, white linen to all four corners of the bed. Colin noted the edges of the sheet were neatly hemmed, and embroidered with a delicate, stylized pattern that he couldn't quite make out.

She reached for a second roll. The coverlet, he assumed. This one featured the same repeating border. In the center, the fabric was emblazoned with an odd, roundish design the size of a dog-cart wheel. While she smoothed the creases, he cocked his head and stared at it. The careful, embroidered stitches delineated a coil of some sort. It looked rather like a halved snail shell, but the interior was divided into dozens of intricate chambers.

"Is that a nautilus?" he asked.

"Close, but no. It's an ammonite."

"An ammonite? What's an ammonite? Sounds like an Old Testament people overdue for smiting."

"Ammonites are not a biblical people," she replied in a tone of strained forbearance. "But they have been smited."

"Smote."

With a snap of linen, she shot him a look. "Smote?"

"Grammatically speaking, I think the word you want is 'smote.' "

"*Scientifically* speaking, the word I want is 'extinct.' Ammonites are extinct. They're only known to us in fossils."

"And bedsheets, apparently."

"You know . . ." She huffed aside a lock of hair dangling in her face. "You could be helping."

"But I'm so enjoying watching," he said, just to devil her. Nonetheless, he picked up the edge of the top sheet and fingered the stitching as he pulled it straight. "So you made this?"

"Yes." Though judging by her tone, it hadn't been a labor of love. "My mother always insisted, from the time I was twelve years old, that I spend an hour every evening on embroidery. She had all three of us forever stitching things for our trousseaux."

Trousseaux. The word hit him queerly. "You brought your trousseau?"

"Of course I brought my trousseau. To create the illusion of an elopement, obviously. And it made the most logical place to store Francine. All these rolls of soft fabric made for good padding."

Some emotion jabbed his side, then scampered off before he could name it. Guilt, most likely. These were sheets meant to grace her marriage bed, and she was spreading them over a stained straw-tick mattress in a seedy coaching inn.

"Anyhow," she went on, "so long as my mother forced me to embroider, I insisted on choosing a pattern that interested me. I've never understood why girls are always made to stitch insipid flowers and ribbons."

"Well, just to hazard a guess . . ." Colin straightened his edge. "Perhaps that's because sleeping on a bed of flowers and ribbons sounds delightful and romantic. Whereas sharing one's bed with a primeval sea snail sounds disgusting."

Her jaw firmed. "You're welcome to sleep on the floor."

"Did I say disgusting? I meant enchanting. I've always wanted to go to bed with a primeval sea snail."

She wasn't impressed. "I worked hard on this. The calculations were intricate. I counted hundreds of stitches to get every last chamber right." She ran a fingertip over the ridges of thread, spiraling out from the center. "It's not just a haphazard pattern, you realize. Nature adheres to mathematical principles. Each chamber of the ammonite's shell expands on the last, according to a precise, unchanging exponent."

"Yes, yes. I understand. It's a logarithm."

Her head whipped up. She adjusted her spectacles and stared at him.

"You know," he said, "this design begins to appeal to me after all. Sea slugs aren't the least bit arousing, but logarithms . . . I've always thought that word sounded splendidly naughty." He let it roll off his tongue with ribald inflection. "Logarithm." He gave an exaggerated shiver. "Ooh. Yes and thank you and may I have some more."

"Lots of mathematical terms sound that way. I think it's because they were all coined by men. 'Hypotenuse' is downright lewd."

" 'Quadrilateral' brings rather carnal images to mind."

She was silent for a long time. Then one of her dark eyebrows arched. "Not so many as 'rhombus.' "

Good Lord. That word *was* wicked. Her pronunciation of it did rather wicked things to him. He had to admire the way she didn't shrink from a challenge, but came back with a new and surprising retort. One day, she'd make some fortunate man a very creative lover.

He chuckled, shaking off the sudden grip of lust. "We have the oddest conversations."

"I find this conversation more than odd. It's positively shocking."

"Why? Because I understand the principle of a logarithm? I know you're used to speaking to me in small, simple words, but I did have the finest education England can offer a young aristocrat. Attended both Eton and Oxford."

"Yes, but . . . somehow, I never pictured you earning high marks in maths." She reached both hands behind her back, undoing the closures at the back of her gown. As if she'd forgotten he was even there, or felt no compunction about disrobing in front of him.

Colin felt like carving a hashmark in the bedpost. Surely this marked a new level of achievement in his amatory career. Never before had he charmed the frock off a woman with talk of mathematics. Never before would he have thought to try.

Loosening his own cravat, he said, "As a matter of fact, I did not earn high marks in maths. I could have done. But I made certain not to."

"Why?"

"Are you joking? Because no one likes boys who excel in maths. Priggish little bores, always hunched over their slates. They all have four eyes and no friends."

He winced, realizing instantly what he'd said. But it was already too late.

She froze, arms bent in the act of undoing her gown. All amusement fled her expression. She sniffed and stared at the corner.

Damn it, he was always hurting her.

"Min, I didn't mean . . ."

"Turn around," she said, waving him off. "It's late, and I'm fatigued. Spare me the apologies and turn around while I undress. I'll tell you when my four priggish eyes are safely beneath the disgusting sea snail."

He did as she asked, turning away. While he worked his cuffs loose, he tried to close his ears to the rustle of fabric. It didn't work. He couldn't stop his imagination from running wild, painting image after image of her stepping free of her gown, freeing the laces of her stays. He heard a rush of breath, and a thrill raced down his spine as he recognized it as that deep, arousing sigh a woman gave when her breasts were unbound at the end of the day.

Blood rushed to his groin, and he strangled a sigh of his own. He was a man, he told himself. There was an unclothed woman in the room. His physical reaction couldn't be helped. It was simple biology. Birds felt it. Bees felt it. Even primeval sea snails felt it.

He heard soft splashes from the washstand, as she dragged a wet cloth over her every lush, naked curve. Really, she was just torturing him now. He probably deserved it.

At long last, he heard the bed creak. "You may turn now."

He turned, fully assuming he'd find her huddled under the covers, facing the wall. Instead, she lay on her side, looking directly at him.

"I'm going to disrobe," he said. "Didn't you want to turn away?"

"I don't think so, no." She propped her head on her hand. "I've never seen a man naked. Not a real one, not up close. Call it indulging my scientific curiosity." Her gaze sharpened. "Or call it an apology, if you prefer."

Oh, she was a clever one indeed. So, he was to pay for all his teasing and unthinking insults with naked humiliation. Even Colin had to admit, the penalty was just.

"I'd be more than happy to let you survey my physical perfection in its entirety. But only if I get to see you, too." To her shocked silence, he replied, "It's only fair. Tit for tat."

"How is that fair? You've seen countless tits."

Damn, the way she said that word. So plainly, without any hint of missishness. Just when he'd regained control of himself, she had him instantly, throbbingly aroused.

"I don't know why you'd need a peep at mine," she went on. "And since you've proudly waved your . . . *tat* . . . before half the women in England, I find it odd that you'd claim modesty now."

"It's true," he said evenly, "that I've been blessed to view a great many bosoms in my life. But every pair is different, and I haven't seen *yours*."

She shrank in the bed linens, curling into that embroidered shell. "They're nothing out of the ordinary, I'm sure."

"I'll be the judge of that."

Her chin lifted. "Very well. Here is my best offer. Half of my nakedness, for all of yours."

He pretended to think on it. "It's a bargain."

Sitting up in bed, she unbuttoned the front of her chemise.

Then she drew the sleeves down each shoulder, carefully shielding her breasts with her folded legs. Her forearms were toasted by the sun, but her shoulders were pale, swannish curves of loveliness.

Once she'd bared herself to the waist, she hunched behind that wall of knees and issued a challenge. "You first."

He pulled his shirt over his head and cast it aside. Then he undid his buttons and dropped his breeches without ceremony.

Well, not entirely without ceremony. There was a certain amount of fanfare. His rapidly growing erection all but trumpeted for attention, jutting out from its nest of dark hair. Waving in an embarrassing, adolescent way.

"Now you," he said.

True to her word, she lowered her knees and revealed her bare torso.

They took each other in.

She was right, he told himself. Her breasts were nothing out of the ordinary. To begin with, there were two of them. The usual number. They were round and just on the plump side of average, capped with prominent nipples. The room was too dark to discern those puckered nubs' precise shade, but he wasn't choosy. Pink, berry, tawny, brown . . . they all tasted the same in the dark.

No, her breasts, while attractive, were not empirically more or less enticing than most bosoms he'd seen. But what quite stole his breath away was the entirety of her. The picture she made, sitting there half-nude in a rumpled nest of fresh white sheets. Her dark hair tumbling about her shoulders, and those spectacles perched—fetchingly askew—at the tip of her nose. Those lush, plum-colored lips oh-so-slightly parted.

She looked like a memory, interrupted. A torrid dream. Or a glimpse of the future, perhaps.

Stop. Don't think such things.

"Surely it's not always like that?" she asked, leaning forward and peering intently.

"Like what?"

"So . . . big. And active."

His straining cock gave another eager leap. Like a poorly trained hound.

"Did you do that on purpose?" she asked, sounding amazed.

Oh, the devious things Colin suddenly longed to do on purpose. *With* purpose. *For* the explicit purpose of steaming those spectacles and making her mewl with unfettered delight.

"I'm not going to seduce you," he said.

After a moment's delay, she gave her head a brisk little shake. Her gaze wandered back up to his face. With a single fingertip, she pushed her spectacles up on her nose. "Excuse me, what?"

"I'm not going to seduce you," he repeated. "Not tonight, or at all. I just thought I should say that."

She stared at him.

"I mean what I said, that first night at the castle. About not ruining innocent girls. You see, I have rules."

"You have *rules*. For the women you seduce?"

"No, no. For myself."

"So there's an . . . an etiquette to raking. Some seducer's code of honor. Is this what you're telling me?"

"In a way. You see, your average fellow who merely sets out to bed the girls he fancies . . . well, he wouldn't need rules, perhaps. But when a man ventures forth with the quite serious goal of never spending a single night alone . . . a set of guidelines just evolves. Believe it or not, I do have some principles."

"And these rules are . . . ?"

"They start with basic good manners, of course. Saying please and thank you, and adhering to the dictum, Ladies first. I'm not particular about locations, but I do have some prohibitions on ropes and scarves."

Her jaw dropped. "Ropes and—"

"I have no qualms about tying, but I won't be tied. Beyond that . . ." He ticked off the limits on his fingers. "No virgins. No prostitutes. No women in dire financial straits. No sisters of former lovers. No mothers of former lov—"

"*Mothers?*" she squawked.

He shrugged. There was a rather amusing story behind that one.

He said, "Listen, it's not important that you hear *all* the rules. The point is that I have some. As I've already explained, seducing you would break them. So it's not going to happen. And I thought it best to broach the topic now, while I'm standing here naked. Because if I brought it up at any other time, you might take offense and assume I'm just not attracted to you." He indicated his full, turgid, ridiculously optimistic erection. "As you can plainly observe, that's not the case."

She went silent for several moments. Observing.

"You were right," she told his cock. "We do have the oddest conversations."

He rubbed his face with both hands and released a slow, deep breath. "It's not too late to save your reputation, you know. I could take you to Bram and Susanna's town house right now, and you could roll up those sheets and save them. You know, for a man who might be able to fully appreciate . . . the work you put into them. The significance. They're part of your trousseau. They should be special."

If they stayed alone in this room—an unmarried gentlewoman and a known rake—it made no difference what they actually did on these embroidered sheets tonight. Even if the linens remained unsullied by their sweat or his seed or her virgin's blood, they were ruined. When she returned from this adventure unmarried, *she* would be ruined. Unmarriageable, in good society.

She rolled onto her back and looked up at the ceiling. "It's done now, isn't it?"

He pushed aside the surge of guilt, reminding himself this entire trip was her idea, and she knew full well the consequences. She'd literally made her bed, and now she was lying in it. Colin was going to share it with her. That was the bargain.

"I always sleep atop the bedclothes," he said, sitting down on the mattress edge. "So as long as you stay under them . . ."

"There'll be something between us."

Something. Yes. Something with the thickness of a birch leaf.

As he stared up at the ceiling, the memory of her breasts seemed to hang up there in the dark. Like two round, peachy moons mounted from the rafters, tempting him to touch. To taste. Colin knew better than to stretch a hand toward the mirage, but his gullible cock strained and arced, ever hopeful.

He shut his eyes and tried to turn his mind to the least arousing things possible. Spiders with hairy legs. Those bumpy, long-necked gourds that made him think of poxy genitalia. Mashed peas. The dust-and-beeswax smell of impossibly old people.

Then an entirely different image bloomed in his mind. One that made him laugh out loud.

"What's the matter?" She sounded sleepy. He envied her that.

"Nothing," he said. "I'm just picturing your mother's reaction right now."

Chapter Eight

Where *is* that Minerva?" Laying aside her deck of cards, Mrs. Highwood snapped her fingers at one of the Bull and Blossom's serving girls. "You, there. What is your name again?"

"I'm Pauline, ma'am."

"Pauline, then. Do dash over to the rooming house and tell my wayward daughter I wish her to join us here at once. At once! Tell her to put aside that scribbling. She's already missed tea, *and* dinner. She will take her lesson with Miss Taylor, and then she will serve as our fourth at whist. She will be an obedient daughter, or I will no longer claim her. I will wash my hands of her entirely."

With a curtsy, Pauline turned to do as she was bid.

Seated beside Charlotte at the pianoforte, Kate Taylor smiled to herself. Of all the hollow threats. She doubted Minerva would feel a single snowflake's chill of sorrow, should Mrs. Highwood resign her relentless campaign of feminine improvements and give her middle daughter up entirely.

Kate felt a great deal of sympathy for the harangued Misses Highwood—at times, more sympathy than envy, which was saying something. Kate had no family at all, save the circle of female friendship here in Spindle Cove. No home, save for the Queen's Ruby. She was an orphan, raised on the kindness of anonymous benefactors and educated at Margate School for Girls.

For all the nights she'd spent weeping into her pillow in that drafty, austere attic dormitory, pleading and bargaining with God for a mother of her own . . . Occasionally, Mrs. Highwood's behavior made Kate thankful for unanswered prayers. Not all mothers were blessings, apparently.

"Begin again at the coda, Charlotte," Kate told her young pupil. "Mind the rhythm here." She tapped the sheet music with a slender pointer. "Your fingering's all wrong when you hit that run of sixteenths, and it's slowing you down."

Reaching over Charlotte's wrist to demonstrate, she said, "Begin with your index finger, see? And then cross under with your thumb."

"Like this?" Charlotte imitated the technique.

"Yes. Two times slowly, for practice. Then try it up to speed."

As Charlotte repeated the passage, Kate heard a series of subtle cracks from the direction of the bar.

They came from Corporal Thorne. He sat with his rugged profile to them, his only companion a pint of ale on the bar. Whether the repetitive scales, the shuffling of cards, or Mrs. Highwood's shrill pronouncements were to blame, Thorne was clearly unhappy to be sharing the establishment with anyone.

As Charlotte started on her second repetition of the same passage, Kate watched the grim, enormous boulder of a man grimace at his ale. Then he brought his hands together on the counter and began to crack the knuckles of his left hand. One by one. Deliberately. In an ominous, vaguely threatening manner that suggested he might crack something—or someone—if the plodding musical exercise continued.

"Make that *three* times, Charlotte," Kate said, straightening her spine.

Thorne was an intimidating presence, to be sure—but he would not put an early end to their lesson. Repetition was essential to music practice, and the ladies had every right to be here in the Bull and Blossom. It was both their tea shop and the gentlemen's tavern.

Just as Charlotte hit her stride with the coda, playing fluently at tempo, the doorbell jangled and Pauline returned from her errand.

"Well, girl?" Mrs. Highwood asked. "Where is she?"

"Miss Minerva wasn't there, Mrs. Highwood."

"What? Not there? Of course she's there. Where else would she be?"

"I'm sure I couldn't say, ma'am. When I told Miss Diana you were looking for her, she—"

At that moment, Diana burst through the door.

The waxed playing cards slithered to the table as Mrs. Highwood looked up mid-shuffle. "Take care, dear. You'll give yourself an attack."

"She's gone," Diana said, swallowing hard and drawing a slow, deep breath. She held up a piece of paper. "Minerva's gone."

Charlotte stopped playing. "What do you mean, she's gone?"

"She left a note. It must have fallen off the desk. I didn't find it until just now." Diana smoothed the paper and held it out, preparing to read.

As if they were in church rather than the tea shop, the ladies rose from their chairs in unison, preparing to hear the reading. At the bar, even Corporal Thorne perked subtly.

"'Dear Diana,'" the flaxen-haired beauty read from the note, "'I am sorry this will come as such a surprise. You, Charlotte, and Mama are not to worry in the least. I am safe, traveling north with Lord Payne. We have eloped to Scotland to be married. We are . . .'" Diana lowered the paper and looked to her mother. " 'We are desperately in love.' "

The silence was profound.

Charlotte was first to break it. "No. No. There must be some mistake. Minerva and Lord Payne, eloped? In *love*? It's not possible."

"How can they have been gone since morning?" Kate asked. "Did no one notice?"

Diana shrugged. "Minerva's always out exploring the cove and cliffs. It's not unusual for her to disappear before breakfast, only to appear again just as dark's settling in."

Kate gathered her courage and addressed the elephant in the room. "Corporal Thorne?"

He looked up.

"When was the last time you saw Lord Payne?"

The big man frowned at the bar and swore. "Yesternight."

"Then it must be true," Diana said. "They've eloped."

A new concern pinched at Kate's heart. She crossed to Diana and touched her arm. "Are you terribly disappointed?"

Diana looked puzzled. "In what way?"

Kate tilted her head toward the still-stunned Mrs. High-wood. "I know your mother had such hopes for *you* and Lord Payne."

"Yes, but I never shared them," she whispered. "He's charming and handsome enough, but my feelings for him never went beyond friendship. I often thought it would come as a relief, actually, if he were to marry another. But I never dreamed that Minerva . . ."

"Minerva detests the man," interjected Charlotte. "She's told me so, many a time." She snatched the letter from Diana's hand. "I cannot believe she'd elope with him. I would easier believe she'd been kidnapped by pirates."

Kate lifted one shoulder in a shrug. "Sometimes apparent dislike can mask an underlying attraction."

"But for months now, they've done nothing but bicker," said Charlotte. "And half the time, Lord Payne can't even recall her name."

"He did ask her to dance the other night," Diana pointed out.

"That's true, they did dance," Kate said. "But rather disastrously. Still, who could have guessed this?"

"No one. Because it's not right."

Corporal Thorne shoved back from the bar and rose to his feet, nearly bashing his head on the exposed, black-painted rafters. In heavy strides, he crossed to join their group. "Payne's up to something, I warrant. I'll go after them. If I ride out now, I can reach London by morning." He looked to Diana. "If they're anywhere on the Great North Road, Lord Rycliff and I will find them and bring your sister home."

"No!"

Everyone swiveled to face the source of this objection: Mrs. Highwood. The woman remained frozen in place, palms pressed flat to the table, staring straight ahead. Kate wasn't sure the matron had blinked once since Diana read the letter.

"No one is going after them," the older woman said. "I've known from the first, Lord Payne would be my son-in-law. My friends always tell me, my intuition is unparalleled." She pressed a hand to her bosom. "Of course, I thought it would be Diana who'd catch his eye, lovely as she is. But it seems I discounted Minerva's cleverness." Blue eyes gleamed. "I can't imagine what the cunning girl did to snare him."

"Surely Minerva's the one who's been snared," Charlotte argued. "I tell you, she never would have run off with Lord Payne. She might have been kidnapped!"

"I doubt she's been kidnapped, Charlotte," Diana said. "But Mama, you must admit that this turn of events is highly unexpected."

"Unbelievable, more like." Thorne crossed his arms. "He's up to no good."

"Perhaps he's in love," Kate argued. "Like the letter says."

Thorne shook his head. "Impossible."

"Impossible?" Kate was highly annoyed on Minerva's behalf. "Why is it impossible that a man should fall in love with an unlikely girl? Perhaps Minerva's not the prettiest girl in the room. But maybe Lord Payne saw something of beauty in her curious mind, or her independent spirit. Is it truly so unfathomable, that an imperfect girl might be perfectly loved?"

The Highwoods looked away in awkward silence, and Kate knew she'd said too much. This was about Minerva, not her. Their situations weren't the same. Minerva might not be the prettiest girl in the room, but she was still a gentlewoman of good family and modest fortune.

Kate was alone and poor, atop being cursed with physical imperfection. No dashing lords had proposed to elope with her, nor even asked her to dance. But foolish as it might be, she held fast to the hope of love. She'd been holding on to that hope all her life, after all. She could scarcely uncurl her grip now.

"Minerva is my friend," she said simply. "And I'm thrilled for her."

"If she's your friend, you should be concerned." Thorne's glare was intense. "She needs rescuing."

Kate hiked her chin and gave him her profile. Her imperfect, port-wine-stained profile. "Shouldn't that be her mother's decision?"

Mrs. Highwood grabbed her elbow. "Yes, Miss Taylor has the right of it! We should be celebrating. Imagine—my awkward, prickly Minerva, eloped with a viscount. Some might call it unexpected, unbelievable. But unless someone convinces me otherwise . . ." A smile spread across the woman's face, making her look ten years younger. "I call it a *miracle*."

Chapter Nine

Minerva woke in the night.

Tangled with him.

She knew a moment of pure, paralyzing terror, until she recalled exactly where and when she was . . . and with whom. Once she'd remembered that she was in a London coaching inn, and the heavy leg so casually thrown over both of hers belonged to none other than Lord Payne . . .

Then the true fear set in.

He sighed in his sleep, nestling closer. His arm cinched tight about her waist.

Oh, God. His arm was about her *waist*.

And that wasn't the worst of it. He was all over her, and she was all . . . *under* him. His scent and warmth covered her like a blanket. His chin rested heavy on her shoulder, and his nose jutted against the soft place beneath her ear. Yes, the embroidered sheet still formed a soft, pliant barrier between their bodies. But aside from that, they were so closely inter-twined, they might have been one creature.

She stared up at the ceiling. Her pulse pounded in her throat. The desire to move was unbearable, and yet she didn't dare stir.

For untold minutes, she lay still. Just breathing. Staring into the darkness. Listening to the frantic beat of her heart and feeling the soft heat of his breath against her neck.

And then, suddenly, his whole body turned to stone. His grip around her waist tightened to a painful degree, making it difficult to breathe. The leg thrown over hers went rigid as iron. His warm breath ceased washing against her neck.

He began to tremble. So violently, he shook them both.

Minerva's heart rate doubled in both speed and intensity.

What should she do? Wake him? Speak to him? Remain still and simply hope this . . . episode . . . passed?

This dreadful sense of helplessness wasn't new. She felt the same whenever Diana was stricken with an asthma attack. Minerva could never do much to ease her sister's suffering during a breathing crisis, except to stay at her side and keep her calm. To let her know she wasn't alone.

Perhaps that would help him. To know he wasn't alone.

"Colin?"

He drew a harsh, rattling breath. His muscles were coiled as tightly as springs.

One of her arms lay trapped at her side, pinned by the weight of his body. But she had the use of her other hand. She raised trembling fingers and laid a cautious touch to his forearm. With the fire banked, the room had long gone cold. But his skin was damp with sweat.

"Colin." She traced her fingers up and down his forearm in long, calming strokes. She wished she could caress other parts of him—his scalp, his back, his face. But unless he loosened his tight hold on her body, this was as much of him as she could reach.

Her attentions didn't seem to be helping. He shook violently now, and his breathing was erratic. His heartbeat hammered against her shoulder.

This was so much worse than in the cave. There, he'd been

mildly agitated. Now he seemed to be struggling for his very life.

A sound rasped from his throat. A raw, anguished, almost inhuman moan.

"No," he muttered. Then more forcefully, "*No*. Won't let you. Get back. Get back, you bloody bitch."

She winced. She'd never heard him speak in such a savage tone.

Oh God. Oh, Colin. What are you facing in there?

Desperate to do something—anything—to pull him out of that dark, terror-stricken place, she resorted to a trick he'd taught her on the dance floor. She slid her fingers to the vulnerable underside of his arm and pinched him, hard.

He jerked and startled, sucking in a deep, gasping breath. Like a drowning man who'd just surfaced.

"Colin, it's me. It's Minerva. I'm here." She twisted in his slackened embrace and rolled to face him. She stroked calming touches over his brow. "You're not alone. It's all right. Just take deep breaths. I'm here."

He didn't open his eyes, but the tension in his body ebbed. His breathing slowed to a normal rate. Her overtaxed pulse gratefully took the excuse to slow, too.

"I'm here," she repeated. "You're not alone."

"Min." His voice was like a rasp rolled in cotton-wool. Rough and soft all at once. His fingers caught a lock of her hair, and he twisted it between his fingertips. "Did I frighten you?'

"A little."

He muttered a curse and rolled her close to his chest. "Sorry, pet. All's well now." His chest rose and fell with a deep breath. "All's well."

Remarkable. After that episode he'd just experienced, he was the one soothing *her*. And doing a very good job of it, too. His fingers grazed her temple in deft, calming strokes.

The relief of knowing the crisis had passed . . . it left her sapped and boneless. Weak.

"Do you need anything?" she mumbled, pressing her brow to his chest. "Brandy, tea? Would it . . . would it help to talk?"

He didn't answer, and she worried she'd offended his pride.

He pressed a kiss to her crown. "Just sleep."

So she did as he told her. She curled into his strength and let his slow, steady heartbeat lull her back to sleep.

When Minerva woke next, it was daylight.

And she was alone.

She sat bolt upright in bed. Weak sunlight filtered in through the room's single, grimy window. In the daylight, the room looked even shabbier than it had the night before.

After donning her spectacles, Minerva looked around. All of her things were still there. But she saw no sign of Colin. Not his boots, not his coat, not his gloves, not his cravat hanging over the chair back.

Her stomach lurched.

He couldn't have *gone*.

She scampered from bed and began searching the table, the chest of drawers. Surely, he would have left a note, at least. When she found none, she hurried to wash and dress as quickly as possible. Rationally, she knew he was probably just downstairs, but she'd feel much better when she laid eyes on the man himself.

Fortunately, the moment Minerva descended to the breakfast room, Colin rose from his chair to welcome her. "Ah. There you are."

He'd bathed and shaved. She could see that his hair was still damp behind the ears. The worst of yesterday's travel dust had been brushed from his coat, and it made a respectable dark-blue contrast with the snowy white of his fresh shirt and cravat. Someone had blacked and polished his boots to a healthy shine.

He looked well. Truly *well*. Not just handsome, but vigorous and strong. After feeling him groan and tremble beside her last night, this came as profound relief. She'd been so worried for him.

"Colin, I . . ." Strangely overwhelmed, she put a hand to his lapel.

"I do hope you slept well. We've been waiting on you."

Her head jerked in surprise. "We?"

"Yes, dear sister," he said loudly, taking her hand in his. "Allow me to introduce the Fontleys."

Dear *sister*? She gawped at him.

"This is Mr. Fontley and Mrs. Fontley."

He turned her, with all the finesse of a clockwork gear turning a porcelain dancer in a music box. Minerva found herself curtseying to a kindly-looking couple. Silver frosted the gentleman's thinning hair, and his wife smiled from beneath a tidy lace cap.

"The Fontleys have offered you space in their carriage. They're traveling north as well."

"Oh. I'm so pleased to make your acquaintance," Minerva said, with genuine feeling.

With a hand placed to the small of her back, Colin swiveled her to face the other side of the breakfast table. "And here are their children. Mr. Gilbert Fontley and Miss Leticia."

"How do you do?" Gilbert, a young man just on the cusp of adulthood, rose from his seat and made a gallant bow.

"Please call me Lettie," the bright-eyed girl said, offering Minerva her hand. "Everyone does."

Lettie possessed the same sandy hair and flushed complexion as the rest of her family. She looked just a few years younger than Charlotte. Twelve, perhaps thirteen.

Gilbert brought a chair for her, and Minerva sat.

Mrs. Fontley smiled. "We're so pleased to have you join-ing us, Miss Sand. It's our honor to escort you to your rela-tions in York."

Miss Sand? Relations in York? She shot Colin a look full of questions.

The teasing rogue didn't answer.

Mrs. Fontley stirred her tea. "I think it's so beneficial for Gilbert and Lettie to make the acquaintance of young people like yourselves. Doing such good in the world. Gilbert has his eye on the Church, you see. He'll be at Cambridge this autumn."

Gilbert spoke up. "Miss Sand, your brother has been tell-ing us about your missionary efforts in Ceylon."

"Oh, has he?" With an air of utter incredulity, Minerva looked to the "brother" in question. "Pray tell. What tales of our good deeds have you been relating, *Colin*?"

She laid heavy emphasis on his name. His real Christian name. After all, if he were truly her brother, she ought to call him by it.

Now, let's see if he could remember hers. And use it, con-sistently.

She propped her chin on her hand and stared at him, smiling.

He smiled back. "I've just been telling all about our time in Ceylon, dear . . . M."

M. So this was how intended to solve his memory prob-lem. Not by actually remembering her name, but by reduc-ing her to an initial. Magnificent.

"Miss Sand, he's been telling us all about your years of missionary work, ministering to the poor and unfortunate. Feeding the hungry, teaching little children to read and write."

Lettie's eyes went wide. "Did you really spend your schoolgirl years curing lepers?"

Minerva set her teeth. She couldn't believe this. Of all the false identities to assume. Missionaries curing lepers in Ceylon? "Not actually, no."

"What my dear sister means"—Colin slid his arm around the back of Minerva's chair—"is that it wasn't all hard work, all the time. We were children, after all. Our dear parents, may God rest their souls, permitted us ample time to explore."

"Explore?" Gilbert perked.

"Oh, yes. Ceylon's a beautiful place. All those lush jungles and mountains. We'd leave our family hut early in the morning, me and M, with just a bit of bread in our pockets. Then we'd spend our whole day out adventuring. Swinging from vines. Devouring mangoes straight from the trees. Riding elephants."

Minerva looked around at the Fontley family. She couldn't believe that anyone would believe this ridiculous story. Elephants and mangoes? But they all stared rapt at Colin, a mix of wonder and worship in their matching blue eyes.

Well, at least this was some balm to the sting she'd incurred that night in the turret. She wasn't his only dupe. Clearly, he employed this talent for willful, wild exaggeration regularly. And with consistent success.

"You'd wander the jungle all day long?" Lettie asked. "Weren't you afraid of being eaten by tigers? Or getting lost?"

"Oh, never. I might have worried, if I were alone. But there were always the two of us, you see. And we had a little system. A game we played whenever we went out adventuring. If we lost sight of each other in the dense jungle undergrowth, I'd just call out, 'Tallyho!' and M would call back . . ."

Colin turned to her, eyebrows raised, as though waiting for her to put the final link on this epic chain of balderdash.

"You're cracked," she said.

He slapped the table. "Exactly! I'd call out, 'Tallyho!', and she'd call back, 'You're cracked!,' blithe as anything. And that's how we'd keep from being separated."

Each and every member of the Fontley family laughed.

"What a clever game," the beaming patriarch said.

"Nothing will ever separate us, will it, M?" Colin reached for her hand and squeezed it, gazing fondly into her eyes. "I think I'll never feel such kinship with another soul as I do with my dear sister."

Across the table, Mrs. Fontley sighed. "Such good young people."

As the footmen secured her trunks atop the Fontley carriage some time later, Minerva took the first possible opportunity to draw Colin aside.

"What are you doing?" she hissed in his ear.

"I'm making them feel comfortable," he murmured in reply. "They'd never allow you to travel with them if we told the truth."

"Perhaps. But must you make the stories so absurdly exaggerated? Curing lepers and riding elephants in Ceylon? How do you even come up with such things?"

He shrugged. "It's called improvisation."

"These are decent people. It's wicked to tell them such horrid lies."

"We're traveling under false pretenses. On the premise of a false engagement. Using false names. And this was all your idea. This is hardly the time for moral scruples, pet."

"But—"

He raised a hand. "If my entertaining the Fontleys with a few exaggerated tales counts as wicked, I suggest you learn to embrace wickedness. For at least the remainder of the week. Their offer of transport is a true boon. It will save a great deal of money and perhaps preserve your reputation, as well. You have a chaperone."

She knew it was true. "That's all very well. But now I'm the one who must ride in a carriage with them for days, living out your absurd fictions."

"Exactly. So why not have fun with it?"

"Fun?"

He took her by the shoulders and waited for her to meet his gaze. Minerva did so, with no slight reluctance. It was impossible to think clearly when she looked into those brilliant hazel eyes.

"Live in the moment, M. This is your chance to crawl out of that shell. There's an interesting, confident girl in there somewhere. She comes out for a peek every now and then. Try *being* her, for just a few days. You won't progress very far on this journey otherwise."

Minerva bit her lip. She wanted to think there *was* an interesting, confident girl inside her, and that, at last, someone saw that girl clearly. But for all she knew, he was working the same trick he'd played on the Fontleys. Puffing her up with false praises. Telling her just what she wanted to hear.

Lying to her. Again.

"It's only a few harmless exaggerations." He walked her slowly toward the carriage. "Think of it like running down a slope. If you attempt to slow down and choose your steps, you're bound to trip up and stumble. But if you simply let yourself run with the story, everything will come out fine."

"Are you ready, Miss Sand?" Mr. Fontley said. "Mrs. Fontley and the children are already inside."

Minerva nodded.

Colin handed her into the carriage. Once she'd taken a seat beside Lettie and arranged her skirts, her "brother" closed the coach door and popped his head through the open window.

"I'll be riding nearby, M. Never fear. If you have any need of me whatsoever, you know what to do." He flashed a smile and called out, "Tallyho!"

In unison, Lettie and Gilbert called back, "You're cracked!"

With a little groan, Minerva buried her face in her hands.

"It's always been like this between me and M," Colin said. As they walked through a little wooded area, he pushed aside branches so she could pass. "Ever since we were in our cradles."

"Truly?" Lettie asked. "Even as babies?"

Minerva rolled her eyes. How did he have the energy to keep manufacturing this poppycock? She was exhausted. By the time they'd stopped for luncheon and a change of horses, she'd been running down his figurative slope all morning, churning out one vague falsehood after another to satisfy the Fontleys' boundless curiosity. She'd hoped to find some brief escape by declaring her intent to walk and stretch her legs.

But of course, Colin *would* decide to accompany her. And Lettie and Gilbert *would* jump to follow.

"Oh yes," Colin continued, leading them all on the path. "My sister and I have always had this deep, unspoken connection. We have whole conversations without exchanging a word."

He looked to her then. She held his gaze.

He was right. They could have a whole conversation without exchanging a word. And the conversation they had right now went like this:

Colin, shut it.

I don't think I will, M.

Then I'll make you.

Really? How?

I'm not certain, but it will be slow and painful. And I won't leave any evidence.

"She saved my life once," he told the young Fontleys.

"Who?" Lettie asked. "Miss Em?"

"Yes indeed. She delivered me, single-handedly, from death's clutches. It's a grand story."

Striding through the ankle-high grasses, Minerva choked on a laugh. *Oh, I'm sure it is.*

"Do tell us. I'm certain the tale does Miss Sand great credit." Gilbert looked to Minerva with admiration in his eyes. And quite possibly a glimmer of infatuation.

Oh dear. Of all the times for a young man to finally take a fancy to her.

"Well, it all started deep in the jungle," Colin said. "While we were out exploring one day, I was bitten by a rare, highly venomous beetle."

Lettie's eyes sparked. "And Miss Em cut open the wound and sucked out the venom!"

"No, no. She couldn't do that. The poison was too fast acting."

"So she dragged you back home, to get help?"

"I'm afraid not." Colin shook his head. "I was too heavy for her."

"So I left him dying and went home for dinner," Minerva said cheerfully. "The end."

Gilbert laughed. "Of course you didn't. You ran for help, didn't you?"

"She did," Colin said.

They'd reached the stream's edge. Colin propped one foot on a fallen log.

"And I'll wager," said Lettie, flouncing down next to his boot, "that she dashed like mad all the way home, and then made it back just in time. Bringing along some native doctor to cure you with his mystic chanting and powders."

Smiling at the girl's imagination, Colin shook his head. "No. Actually, by the time she returned with help, it was too late. She couldn't heal me. I had died."

Everyone went silent.

"But . . ." Lettie frowned. "But that can't be. Here you are."

"What happened?" Gilbert asked.

Yes, what happened? Minerva almost added herself. Even she was breathless to learn what came next, when he'd lay dying in the jungle after a rare Ceylonese beetle bite.

Nothing happened, you ninny. It's all a lie.

Colin cleared his throat. "Well, I can't tell you precisely what happened. Because I slumped unconscious on the jungle floor, and I don't remember anything after that. I'd fallen into a deep coma, it seems. The signs of life were so faint, my own family believed I was dead. They prayed over me, prepared my body and put it in a wooden coffin. And the next thing I knew, I woke up underground. In the dark. Buried alive."

"Cor," Lettie cried, clinging to his boot. "Whatever did you do?"

"I cried. I wailed. I clawed at the planks sealing me in until my fingernails were torn to bloody nubs. I despaired and trembled. I screamed until my throat was raw." His voice had taken on a strange quality. He looked up, searching Minerva's gaze. "And somehow, she heard me. Didn't you, M? You heard me, calling through the darkness. I was alone and frightened. But in the dark of night, you heard the anguished cries of my heart."

Minerva swallowed back the lump rising in her throat. She didn't like this story anymore. She wasn't sure what Colin was playing at. Obviously this description of his boyhood self, trapped and screaming in the dark, was meant for her. It would seem he hadn't forgotten last night's episode. He remembered it. All of it. And now he wished to . . . what, precisely? Thank her for her help? Mock her for her concern?

He asked, "Do you want to tell the next bit, M?"

She shook her head. "No. I don't."

He turned to the children. "She came running out to the burial site, began digging through the dirt with her bare hands. When I heard those noises . . . well, I thought at first I'd truly died, and the hounds of hell were scratching at my coffin."

Lettie squeaked and bit her knuckle.

"To this day, I have no fondness for dogs," he said.

"Oh, how sad."

In her memory, Minerva heard the echo of his savage cries. *Get back, you bloody bitch.*

"I tried to call out, but couldn't. The air was growing more and more close, and I could scarcely take a breath. As the sounds drew nearer, I managed to suck just a gasp of air into my lungs. Enough to call out one word." He paused dramatically, then whispered, "Tallyho?"

The children held their breath.

"And you can guess what sweet magic I heard in return."

"You're cracked," they replied in hushed unison.

"Exactly," Colin said. "She'd saved me from the very clutches of death. My dear, daring sister."

Their eyes met, and Minerva had to look away. She didn't know what to feel, but she felt . . . something. And she felt it deeply.

Gilbert turned to her. "How brave you were, Miss Sand."

She fluttered a hand. "Not really."

"She's too modest. Always was." Rising from the fallen log, Colin playfully chucked her under the chin before leading the way back to the road. "Just wait until you hear about M and the cobra."

Chapter Ten

nd that"—Colin tapped his fork against his now-
empty dinner plate—"is the story of the cobra." He
sat back in his chair, feeling satisfied.

All the Fontleys turned their gaze from him and looked to
Minerva, awed.

Minerva glared at him. "I am not a snake charmer."

"Of course not. Snake charmers need a flute." He turned
to the Fontleys. "I tell you, she had the creature entranced
with her sweet voice alone. It wouldn't leave her side after
that day. The scaly thing slithered in her footsteps, all over
Ceylon. We made a pet of it. Named it Sir Alisdair."

Under the table, something sharp jabbed him in the thigh.
He covered his yelp of pain with a cough.

Colin knew he'd pay for this later. But he couldn't resist
provoking her. Never had been able to resist it, ever since
they'd first met. Today, of all days, he wanted to draw her
out, push her beyond those boundaries she'd erected.

He wanted to be surprised.

And more than that—he wanted to keep the attention on
her. Because if he gave her the chance to direct conversa-

tion, he knew she'd steer it in an unpleasant direction. One that involved last night. He didn't want to discuss last night. In his own, circumspect way, he'd told her all she needed to know. As much as he'd ever told anyone.

"Miss Sand," Gilbert Fontley said, "how can we convince you to sing?"

Shock flared in her eyes. "You can't."

"Mr. Fontley is quite the lover of music," their mother said, patting her husband's arm. "As am I. Miss Sand, we would be so pleased to hear you. Do oblige us, dear. There's a pianoforte, just there."

"But . . ." She swallowed hard and said weakly, "I couldn't possibly."

Colin watched her as she surveyed the inn's crowded dining room. In a village as small as this one, the inn's dining room also served as the village public house. There were probably above thirty souls in the room, equally divided between travelers passing the night and local men enjoying a pint with the fellows. A good crowd.

Young Miss Lettie joined the campaign. "Oh please, Miss Em. Do sing for us."

"Come on, M," Colin said jovially. "Just one or two songs."

Minerva's jaw tightened. "But *brother*, you know I gave up singing. After that horrific incident with the . . . millipede and the coconut and the . . . the stolen rubies." Before he could press for details, she jumped to add, "Which we have sworn a pact on our parents' graves to never, ever discuss."

He smiled. Now she was catching the spirit. "That's true. But it's my birthday. And you always make an exception on my birthday."

"You know very well it's not—"

"It's your birthday, Sand?" Mr. Fontley exclaimed over her. "Well, why didn't you say so? We should drink to your health." The older gentleman called the serving girl and ordered sherry for the table.

As glasses were passed around, Minerva said pointedly, "But brother, you never drink spirits."

"I do on my birthday." He raised the glass in salute, then drank.

He heard her growl.

"Won't you sing, Miss Em?" Lettie pleaded again. "I so long for a bit of music. And it is Mr. Sand's birthday."

Soon all the Fontleys joined in the encouragement.

She turned to him and said simply, "*Colin.*" Her wide, dark eyes held a frantic plea for reprieve. *Don't make me do this.*

He felt a twinge of conscience, but he wouldn't intervene. He'd come to recognize that look in her eyes. Her eyes always caught that wild, desperate spark just before she did something extraordinary.

"Fine," she said. "I'll sing."

She lifted the sherry glass in front of her, drained it in a single swallow, and set it down with a decisive *clink*. Then she flattened both hands on the tabletop and pushed to her feet.

In slow, determined strides, she walked to the pianoforte. She removed her spectacles and held them folded in her hand. She pressed her finger down on a single piano key and, closing her eyes, hummed the pitch.

And then she opened her mouth and sang.

Well. She sang very, very well.

Surprise.

The crowded room went so quiet, so quickly, Colin could practically hear the jaws dropping. The song she'd chosen was an old, familiar ballad. No fancy scales or operatic trills. Just a simple, straightforward melody that suited her clear, lyrical voice. It wasn't a song fit for a musicale, or even one of the Spindle Cove ladies' salons. But it was perfect for a small country inn. The sort of tune that didn't gavotte, didn't mince around. That didn't bother dazzling the ear or engaging the mind, but went straight for the guts.

And the heart.

Good Lord. It was a bloody fool thing to think—let alone *say*—but her song arrowed straight for his heart.

No way around it. Colin was charmed. As charmed as a Ceylonese cobra.

More than that, he was proud.

When the ballad's lovers met their inevitably tragic end, and the crowd broke into enthusiastic applause, Colin clapped along with the rest. "That's my girl," he murmured.

Though she wasn't, really. He had no right to claim her. To think that all this time—every day that he'd resided in Spindle Cove—this had been inside her. This glorious, soul-stirring song. The courage to unleash it before a crowd of strangers. The sweetness to calm him in the night, when he clawed his way back from hell.

How had he never seen any of this? How had he never known?

The Fontleys—and everyone else—shouted for another song. Minerva shook her head, demurring.

"Just one more," Colin called to her, cupping his hands around his mouth. "Sing my favorite."

She gave him a look of strained patience, but she relented.

Another key struck. Another quietly hummed pitch.

Another moment of sheer revelation.

She'd warmed to it now. The singing, the attention. Her voice gained strength and confidence. She sang with her eyes wide open, and she sang directly to him. Well, he'd asked for that, hadn't he? And it was the best not-an-actual-birthday gift Colin had ever received. Those sultry, ripe lips held him in thrall. Every time she drew a quick breath between phrases, her breasts fairly jumped for his attention.

If her first song had touched his heart . . . well, this one stroked him a ways lower.

It occurred to Colin that he should probably take pains not to be caught slavering over his own "sister." But a glance around the place told him he wasn't the only male in the room so affected.

Gilbert Fontley, in particular, was very bad off.

Without taking his eyes from Minerva, the young man leaned toward Colin. "Mr. Sand, do you think it's possible to fall in love in the space of a single day?"

He smiled. "I wouldn't know. I only fall in love at night. Never lasts beyond breakfast, though."

Gilbert sent him a confused look. "B-but . . . But I thought you—"

"We all have our demons, Gilbert." He clapped the young man on the shoulder and leaned close. "A word of advice. Cleave to the bosom of the Church."

Minerva finished her ballad, and this time he could tell no amount of calling or applause would persuade her to sing again. Even as everyone in the room leaped to their feet, shouting encouragement, she replaced her spectacles and began to make her way back to the table.

Colin pushed back his chair, meaning to welcome her back with some words of sincere praise. But as she started across the room, a large, unshaven man holding a tankard lumbered into her path. He engaged her in some sort of conversation. Colin couldn't make out their words over the din, but he didn't need words to understand what was happening.

That disgusting lout wanted his girl.

And Minerva wanted nothing to do with the disgusting

lout. The brute put a grimy paw on her arm, and she stumbled in her effort to pull away. Her spectacles went just slightly askew. That small detail—that tiny evidence of her disquiet—was enough to make Colin see twenty shades of red.

He punched to his feet, craving blood.

"Sir, unhand me." Minerva tugged against the revolting brute's grip. His breath reeked of ale and garlic. His body reeked of . . . other things, better left unnamed.

"Jes' another song, love." He held her elbow with one hand and pawed at her waist with the other. "Come sit on my lap, give me a private performance."

His hand brushed her bottom.

Minerva recoiled. She felt dirty. Other women might know how to deflect this kind of unwanted attention, but she didn't. This never happened to her.

Then she caught sight of Colin, cutting a path to her through the crowded room. His stride was almost easy, unconcerned. But as he drew close, she could view the tense set of his jaw and the cold fury in his eyes.

He nudged the drunken lout with his arm. "Excuse me," he said, "but is that your hand on my sister?"

The burly man straightened and adopted an affected, aristocratic tone. "I rather think it might be, guv."

"Well, then." Colin clapped him on the shoulder. "This is my hand on you."

He drove a full-force punch straight into the lout's gut. Then followed it with a smashing blow to the face.

Minerva's hands flew to her own mouth, covering her startled cry.

The man didn't even reel or blink. He simply went down. Hard. Taking an entire table and the accompanying glassware with him. The sounds of breaking glass and splintering wood crashed through the room, drawing everyone's attention.

Colin stood over the brute, shaking out his hand and breathing hard. The look on his face was one of barely restrained fury.

"Don't touch her," he said, his voice like cold steel. "*Ever.*"

He put a hand to Minerva's elbow and, with a nod in the Fontleys' direction, ushered her from the room. As they left, the dining room erupted into chaos. She flinched at the sounds of chairs scraping across floors, and angry voices lifting.

She distinctly heard Mr. Fontley shout, "How dare you molest that young lady."

And then Gilbert's reedy tenor. "You'll burn in hell for that. She's a woman of God."

They both paused on the bottom riser of the stairs. And broke into simultaneous laughter.

"We'd better get upstairs," she said.

"Are you well?" he asked, stopping her in the upstairs corridor. His gaze scanned her from head to toe. "He didn't harm you in any way?"

"No. No, thank you." She swallowed. "And you?"

He unlatched the door. "Best birthday ever."

They tumbled through the entry of their suite, laughing. As Minerva went to light the lamp, Colin slung his weight into a chair.

"You," she said, "are unbelievable."

"Come now." He grinned up at her. "Admit it. That was fun."

She felt the corner of her mouth tip, despite her. "I . . . I *never* do that."

"You never do what? Sing ballads in a public house? Inspire tavern brawls?"

"Any of it. I never do any of it. I never even do this." She reached for his hand, turning it over in the light. "Oh, you're bleeding."

"It's nothing. Just a scratch."

Perhaps, but Minerva hurried to fetch the washbasin and soap. She needed something to do. Otherwise, this restless, coursing energy she felt would spill out in other ways. Dangerous ways.

Even as she gathered the materials, her hands trembled. The man was a devil. Mayhem personified. She never knew what wild tale he'd spin or what ill-considered action he'd take next. Over the course of their journey, he could put everything at risk—her reputation, her safety, her scientific standing.

Perhaps even her heart.

But she had to admit . . . he did make things fun.

Returning to the table with a clean handkerchief, she examined his wound more closely. He was right, it was just a scratch along his knuckles. But he'd incurred the injury defending *her*. Minerva wanted to kiss this brave, wounded hand. She settled for dabbing it with a moist cloth.

She touched his signet ring. "I wager that man will be wearing your family crest on his cheek for weeks."

He laughed a little. "Good. He deserved far worse."

"I couldn't believe how easily you laid him flat," she said. "And he was so big. Where did you learn to fight like that?"

"Boxing club." He stretched his fingers and winced a bit. "All the London bucks are mad for boxing. Gentleman Jackson's and so forth. The better question is . . ." His voice darkened. "Where did you learn to sing like that?"

"Like what?" She kept her head bowed, examining his wound.

"Like . . . *that*. I've been living in Spindle Cove more than half a year now, and I've attended countless numbers of those wretched salons, not to mention all the informal soirees at the rooming house. Church on Sundays. I've heard Diana sing many times. I've heard Charlotte sing many times. For God's sake, I've even heard your mother sing. But never you."

She shrugged, tearing off a strip of linen for a bandage. "I'm hardly an accomplished songstress. All I know are the ballads I learned as a girl. Once I grew old enough, I shirked my music lessons whenever possible. I hated the bother of practicing."

"I won't believe singing's a bother to you. And I won't believe you never practice either, as easily as the words came to you downstairs."

Minerva felt herself blush. She did practice, when no one was about. Singing to herself when out on her rambles. But since singing to oneself looked about as odd as reading while walking, it wasn't something she'd admit to him. "I leave the singing to Diana."

"Ah. You don't want to outshine her."

She laughed. "As if I could ever outshine Diana."

"Diana *is* rather shiny, I suppose. Golden hair, luminous skin. Sunny disposition. All things radiant. Perhaps you couldn't outshine her." He cocked his head and regarded her from a new angle. "But Min? You could out*sing* her."

"We're sisters. Not competitors."

He made a dismissive noise. "All women are competitors, and sisters most of all. Ladies are perpetually jockeying for position, sizing themselves up against their peers. I can't tell you how often I'm enjoined to comment on which lady is the prettiest, the wittiest, the most accomplished, the lightest on her feet. And who solicits these opinions? Always women, never men. Men could not care less. About those comparisons, at least."

She eyed him warily. "What comparisons do men discuss?"

"I'll answer that some other time. When I'm not bleeding and at a disadvantage."

Minerva wrapped the bandage tight. "We're not talking of callow young ladies in society. We're speaking of Diana. I love my sister."

"Enough to hide your one talent, just so she won't suffer by comparison?"

"My *one* talent?" She cinched the bandage, and he grimaced with pain. "It's hardly my one talent, or even my best talent."

"Ah. Now I see how it is." He nursed his bandaged hand. "You're every bit as competitive as the rest of them. Only you're vying for a different title. That of least attractive, least congenial. The least *marriageable*."

She blinked at him. He'd doubtless meant the words to tease her, but something in them rang rather true.

"Perhaps I am." She folded the surplus linen and replaced it in her trunk. "I'm committed to my studies, and I'm not sure I ever want to be married at all. Not to the sort of man my mother would wish, anyhow. So yes, I've always been content to let Diana be the prettiest, the most elegant, the kindest. The best singer. She's welcome to have all the suitors."

His eyebrows lifted. "Except me."

"You're a special case."

"I'll take that as a compliment."

"You really shouldn't."

And he really shouldn't look at her that way. So intensely. Searchingly.

"Why didn't you marry long ago?" she blurted out. "If you don't want to sleep alone, marriage would seem the logical solution. You'd have a wife beside you every night."

He chuckled. "Do you know how many husbands and wives actually sleep in the same bed after the honeymoon?"

"Some marriages are affectionless arrangements, I'm

sure. But more than a few are love matches. I can't imagine you'd have trouble getting women to fall in love with you."

"But if I married, I should have to *keep* a woman in love with me. Not just any woman, but one particular woman. For years. And what's more, I should have to stay in love with her. If by chance I met the woman I wanted to try this with—and I haven't yet, after years of sampling widely—how could I ever be certain of achieving that? You're the scientist. You tell me. How can love be proved?"

Minerva shrugged. "I suppose it must be tested."

"Well, there you have it. I always fail tests."

She gave him a pitying look. "Yes, of course. We both know that's why you never earned high marks in maths. It had nothing to do with a lack of effort. You simply couldn't pass the tests."

He didn't answer. Just leaned back in his chair, propped his hands behind his head, and regarded her with an inscrutable expression. Whether his was a gaze of annoyance, admiration, appreciation, or anger, she could not have guessed.

With a sigh, she rose from the table. "We might as well sleep."

The suite had two connecting bedchambers–to keep up appearances for the Fontleys. But they both knew they'd only use this one. She crossed the room and began unbuttoning her spencer. She felt his eyes on her as she shook the garment from her shoulders, pulled her arms free, and set it aside. Didn't he have manners enough to look away? Her body warmed under his appraisal, growing light and hot as a cinder swirling through the smoky air.

She turned away from him and reached to loosen the hooks down the back of her gown.

"Allow me," he said, suddenly behind her.

She froze for a moment, seized by the instinct to shrug

away. But this dress had stubborn fastenings. She would appreciate a little help.

"Just the hooks," she said.

"Of course."

Brushing some loose strands of hair aside, he began at the base of her neck. He loosed the hooks slowly, one by one. She crossed her arms over her chest, holding the gown in place as her neckline began to gape.

"How did you know?" His voice was a gentle murmur, sliding over her neck.

"Know what?"

"'Barbara Allen.' How did you know it's my favorite ballad?" The husky intimacy in his voice undid her.

"Isn't it everyone's favorite?"

His soft laugh in response was warm, authentic. "Did we just find something in common?"

"We have all kinds of things in common," she said, feeling the familiar stupidity descend. Here it came, the inane babble. "We're both humans. We both speak English. We both understand what a logarithm is. We both have brown hair, two eyes . . ."

"We both have skin." His fingertips grazed her exposed shoulder, and sensation rippled down her arm. "We both have hands. And lips."

Her eyes squeezed shut. She held her breath for a long moment, before realizing she'd braced herself for a kiss that wasn't coming. She cursed him, cursed herself. She needed to put all thoughts of his kiss out of her mind. It was just— she couldn't stop picturing the way he'd stared at her while she was singing downstairs. The way he'd moved toward her, scything his way through the crowd.

The way he'd laid that man flat, and bled for her.

She cleared her throat and stepped forward, still facing

the wall. "Thank you for your assistance. Will you turn, please?"

"I've turned." The floorboards gave a weary creak of confirmation.

Minerva swiveled her head, stealing a glance in the mirror to make sure. She almost wished she would find him stealing glances at her, too. But evidently he'd seen enough last night. He remained with his back to her as she drew her gown down over her hips and stepped out.

Once she'd stripped down to her shift, she dove under the bed linens and turned her face to the wall. "It's safe now."

"Safe." He made a wry, disbelieving noise. "For whom?"

She tried to feign sleep as he moved about the room, removing his boots, casting watch and cufflinks aside. Stirring the fire. Making all sorts of unapologetic, manly sounds. Men never hesitated to declare their presence. They were permitted to live aloud, in reverberating thuds and clunks, while ladies were always schooled to abide in hushed whispers.

The bed creaked loudly as he dropped his weight next to her. His arm brushed against her back. Just that slight contact set her whole body humming. As he settled into the bed, she was so aware—so clearly, perfectly aware—of every part of him. Every part of her. Everywhere their bodies touched, and everywhere they didn't.

"Will you be able to sleep?" she asked, after a few minutes.

"Eventually."

"Did you want to talk?" she asked the wall. She felt like a coward, unable to turn and face him.

"I'd rather listen to you. Why don't you tell me a bedtime story? One you read as a child."

"I didn't read any stories as a child."

"I don't believe that. You always have your nose in a book."

"But it's true," she said quietly. "When I was a girl, it took them ages to realize my farsightedness. Everyone thought

I was just mischievous at best or dull witted, at worst. My mother chided me for frowning, for daydreaming. Diana would always be reading tales from her storybooks, but no matter how she tried to teach me, I couldn't make sense of the letters. We had a nursemaid who sang ballads as she went about her work. I used to follow her everywhere and listen, memorizing as many as I could. They were my stories." She closed her eyes. "Eventually, a governess realized I needed spectacles. When I first put them on my face, I can't even tell you . . . it was like a miracle."

"Finally seeing properly?"

"Knowing I wasn't hopeless." A knot formed in her throat. "I'd believed there was something incurably wrong with me, you see. But suddenly, I could see the world clear. And not only the parts in the distance, but the bits within my own reach. I could focus on a page. I could explore the things around me, discover whole worlds beneath my fingertips. I could be good at something, for once."

She didn't know if he could understand, but this was why the symposium was so important to her. Why Francine meant *everything*. This was why, a few mornings ago, she'd opened up the trunk that held her trousseau and swapped out those bridal fantasies for new, scientific goals. Minerva had never been the daughter her mother would have wished. She was different from her sisters, and she was reconciled to the fact. She could live with being a hopeless excuse for a fashionable, elegant lady . . . so long as someone, somewhere, respected and admired her just for being *her*. Minerva Highwood, geologist and bookworm and . . . and after tonight, sometime troubadour.

"Once I learned to read," she said, "they couldn't tear me away from books—still can't. But I'd already outgrown the fairy tales."

"Well," he said, sounding drowsy. "That was a fine bedtime story. Downtrodden girl. Kindly nursemaid. Happy ending. The fairy tales are pretty much all like that."

"Really? I was under the impression most of them feature a handsome, charming prince."

The silence was prolonged. And miserable.

"Well, yours does have a knight," he finally said. "Sir Alisdair the Colleague."

"I suppose." Hoping her voice didn't betray any disappointment, she curled her fingers in the bed linens, drawing them close.

His weight shifted beside her. "You know, I've been wondering something. If that diary that so rhapsodically extolled my charms was the false one . . . what on earth did the real one say?"

Chapter Eleven

Kate Taylor cringed into her water goblet. This just didn't seem right.

Across the dining table in the Queen's Ruby, Charlotte flipped through a small leather-bound book. "This and that . . . something more about rocks . . ."

"Keep looking," Mrs. Highwood said. "It's Minerva's only diary. She must have mentioned him somewhere."

Mrs. Nichols, the rooming house's aging proprietress, directed the servants to serve dessert. As an apron-clad serving girl placed dishes of syllabub before each plate, Kate exchanged glances with Diana. She knew they had to be sharing the same mix of curiosity and mortification.

Naturally the elopement had been the talk of Spindle Cove, and Kate was as eager as anyone to learn the particulars of Minerva's unlikely romance. But reading her diary aloud at the dinner table? It did seem rather tasteless.

"Really, Mama," Diana put in. "Is it necessary to read Minerva's journal? Aloud? Shouldn't she be allowed some privacy?"

Mrs. Highwood considered. "Ordinarily, I would never snoop. Would I, Mrs. Nichols?"

Mrs. Nichols shook her head. "Never, Mrs. Highwood."

"But in this case, the circumstances justify some investigation. Don't they, Mrs. Nichols?"

"Of course, Mrs. Highwood."

"That Corporal Thorne keeps insisting he should chase after them, or at the least, alert Lord Rycliff. He seems to be under the mistaken assumption that Lord Payne is up to some sort of devilry. But I would never believe that of him. Would you, Mrs. Nichols?"

"Absolutely not, Mrs. Highwood. He's an excellent young man. Always praises my pies."

"Oh, here. Here's something about a grand discovery," Charlotte announced, opening the journal wide to a middle page.

Everyone at the table perked.

Charlotte scanned a bit further. "Never mind. It's about lizards."

"Lizards!" With a groan, Mrs. Highwood pushed away her serving of syllabub. "I don't know how in the world she managed to snag him."

"She didn't snag him, Mama. I keep telling you, she's been *snagged*." Charlotte flipped another page. "If she liked him, wouldn't she have confessed it to her own diary? I know I'd fill whole books with poetry if a man so handsome as Lord Payne took a fancy to me."

Kate accepted a slender glass of cordial from a serving tray. "Perhaps Minerva just isn't given to poetry."

"But she ought to say something favorable, at least. See, look. She only just mentions him here, halfway through. And clever as she's supposed to be, she can't even spell his name. P-A-I-N, she has it."

Kate smiled down at her lap. Somehow, she doubted Minerva had written it that way by mistake.

"Never mind about the spelling, child," Mrs. Highwood urged. "Just read it. What does she say?"

Charlotte sipped her lemonade in preparation. "'As today was Thursday, we were made to suffer Lord Payne's presence at dinner. I don't know whether to attribute my acute indigestion to his presence, Mother's fawning, or Mrs. Nichols's eel pie. It was a most disagreeable evening, all around.'"

"Is that dated last summer?" Diana asked.

Charlotte shook her head. "Last week."

Kate knew this would be the moment to defend poor Mrs. Nichols's eel pie. But really, the stuff was indefensible. By mutual, silent agreement, everyone took a spoonful of syllabub instead.

Then a sip of cordial.

Then syllabub again.

"Well, there must be more." Mrs. Highwood waved her spoon at Charlotte. "Read on, dear."

"I am reading on." Charlotte flipped through the remainder of the diary pages. "There isn't much else to read. It's all rocks and shells and lizard prints. The only man she mentions regularly is some scientist. Sir Alisdair Kent. She seems to admire him a great deal. When she spares a word for Lord Payne, it's never kind." She snapped the journal closed. "I told you she doesn't love him, Mama. She's been taken against her will. You must allow Corporal Thorne to find them."

Mrs. Highwood reached across the table. "Give it here, child."

She took the journal from Charlotte, flipped it open to the last written page, held it at arm's length, and peered at it. Her frown of concentration quickly melted to an expression of delight.

"Aha. Here we are. An entry dated just three nights past.

'Distressing news at All Things. It's rumored that Payne will propose to D. The vile, deceitful man. After all he promised me last summer. I cannot allow it.' And then, a few days later is her last entry. The day after the dancing, my dears." Mrs. Highwood arched a brow. "'Payne now convinced. Plan sealed with kiss. We leave on the morrow.'"

She flung the book to the table, rattling the crystal. "There you have it, Diana. Your sister is a scheming, cunning temptress. She stole Lord Payne from right under your nose, and she's been plotting it since last summer. From the very first. Imagine."

"He was never mine to steal." Diana blushed. "I'm sure it's not how it sounds."

"Perhaps not," Kate said, trying to wrap her mind around the idea of Minerva Highwood as a shameless seductress—and failing utterly. "But I think we can safely conclude that wherever Minerva went with Lord Payne, she went of her own accord. She certainly wasn't abducted."

"Devious thing." Mrs. Highwood spooned a large bite of syllabub into her mouth. "When did this happen? She never showed any interest in men. I wouldn't have dreamed Minerva knew a kiss from a carbuncle. And now . . ."

"Oh," Charlotte breathed, suddenly freezing in place and staring rapt at her spoon. "Now. Just imagine where she must be *now*."

Kate choked on a laugh.

Diana squeezed her eyes shut. "Charlotte, please. Let's not."

Chapter Twelve

For the second time in as many nights, Minerva woke to tortured groans.

This time, they weren't Colin's.

When she jolted awake, she found him sleeping peacefully at her side. Through the wall, however, horrid noises reached her ears. Violent thumping and desperate cries.

"Colin. *Colin!*" She shook his arm. "Wake up. Someone's being murdered."

"What? Who?" He sat bolt upright in bed, and his head bashed against the sloping rafter. "Besides me, you mean?"

She laid a touch to his arm and gave a meaningful tilt of her head. "*Listen.*"

He closed his eyes.

The sickening sounds of violence continued. She heard a woman's shriek.

"Well?" she prodded, growing frantic. "Shouldn't you dress, and quickly? Ring for the innkeeper, at least? We must do *something*."

He sighed and rubbed his face. "That is not murder you're hearing. No one's dying. Except in the French way."

"What? What can you mean, 'the French way'?"

"Copulation," he said, flopping back on the bed and flinging his wrist over his eyes. "They're not fighting, whoever they are. They're having a grand time indeed." Under his breath, he added, "Curse them."

"Is it always so loud?" she asked.

"Only when it's good."

"Good?" Minerva frowned, listening. Nothing about that sounded good. The poor woman was even crying out to God.

"How is it you're so curious and educated, and yet so naïve? You do understand copulation, don't you?"

"Of course I do. The science of it, anyhow." A shriek pierced through the wall. She clutched his arm. "Colin, are you *sure* . . . ?"

"*Yes.*" He covered his face with a pillow and groaned into it. "And here I thought bedding down alone would be the keener torture."

The rhythmic banging grew louder, faster. A low, masculine bellow joined the woman's shrieks.

And then it stopped.

"There," Colin said, propping the pillow back under his head. "They're finished. Now it's over, and we can get some sleep."

Several minutes passed.

"You're not sleeping," he said.

"Neither are you."

"Can't. Deuce it. My body's too suggestible." He rolled to face her, and his fingertips caught the edge of her sleeve. "Perhaps yours is the same? Are you aroused?"

She didn't know what to make of her body's warm flush. Nor the way his thumb caressed her arm.

She said, "I mainly feel confused."

He laughed softly. "I won't believe you're *that* innocent." His hand swept down the side of her body. "You do understand there's pleasure in the act?"

"I've gathered as much, yes. But if that's the case, why doesn't it sound more pleasant?"

"Because the act of love is not civilized. It's nature at its purest, most basic form. Primal and wild. You ought to understand a little, if you've ever . . ." She could all but hear his eyebrows shooting up. "Wait. Don't tell me you haven't. You, the woman of science, who can recite the logarithm that defines the precise shape of an ammonite's shell. Don't tell me you don't understand the workings of your own body."

"I'm not telling you anything." Her breath grew shaky.

"Surely it can't be," he said, his hand stealing over her thigh, "that this intrepid explorer of underwater caverns hasn't explored her own little cove?"

Through the bedsheet, he touched her. *There.* Between the legs. White sensation arced through the darkness. A tiny gasp escaped her, but she quickly sealed her lips.

"Did you say something?"

She shook her head. Her heart drummed in her chest.

"Hm. I think you do understand pleasure." His touch moved in a devious circle. "But only the hushed, secret kind. You've always been surrounded, haven't you? By sisters, servants. Did you stroke yourself this way? Clamping that jaw tight, turning your head to the pillow to be very, very quiet?"

His fingertips made gentle sweeps, feathering over her intimate places in strokes so light they might have been excused as incidental, unintentional. But she knew better, and her body did, too. Her nipples drew to tight puckers, and dampness gathered between her thighs.

The forbidden, unexpected nature of his touch was almost more arousing than the physical contact.

A man was touching her, *there.*

Colin was touching her, there.

This couldn't be happening. She could not be *allowing* this to happen.

But it was happening, and she was allowing it, and— sweet heaven, it was marvelous. Through the layers of her shift and the bed linens, he drew a single fingertip up her inner thigh, and her breath caught.

"Colin—"

"No, no. If I'm wrong, don't tell me. I'm enjoying this idea far too much. The little scientist, conducting quiet surveys beneath her night rail. Or in the bath, perhaps. Curious fingers wandering, exploring. Chasing that pleasure 'round and 'round as it builds . . . and builds." His voice was dark, decadent. "Until the crisis shudders through you in perfect, devastating silence."

He gently cupped her mons and groaned a little. "By God, Min. A man's erotic imagination is powerful indeed. But I think that is the single most arousing image I've ever entertained."

"But . . . but you're wrong. Mostly."

He paused. "Mostly?"

Good heavens, what had possessed her to add that word? This entire discussion was too mortifying to be believed. Had she conducted her own explorations? Yes. Had those furtive moments ever amounted to a shadow of the exhilaration she felt right now, with him? God, no.

She'd never felt anything like this. Evidently, she was both a naughty girl and a poor scientist. A failure, all around.

"I think we need another lesson, Min."

His words sent a thrill racing through her. "You do?"

"Yes." He stroked his hand up to her belly. "Yes, you need to understand this. The wildness of it. How good it can be, when it's raw and lusty and loud." He flipped his hand, tracing the backs of his fingers just under the curve of her breast. "You need to know what you deserve from a man. Or you'll end up in some passionless marriage. Tethered to an ancient, dusty geologist whose ideas might inspire your admiration, but whose touch will never, ever make you writhe and moan and scream."

His touch slowed, then drew to a halt on her breastbone.

"Do you trust me?" he asked.

"With what?"

"With your body. With your pleasure."

He said it so baldly. She didn't know how to respond. She'd already trusted him with her safety and her possessions. She might even trust him with her virtue. But she knew she could never trust this man with her heart. And didn't that organ come part and parcel with her body?

But she wanted, *needed* his touch so badly. Her lips and tongue were clumsy with desire. She couldn't make herself say no.

"Close your eyes," he said. "Close your eyes, and think of him."

She closed her eyes. "Think of whom?"

"Of him, whoever he is. Sir Alisdair Kent. Or the fairy-tale prince. You must dream of someone. All young ladies do."

She supposed they did. All girls had a dream suitor, and Minerva was no different.

But most of them never had this chance, to lie next to him in the flesh. This was happening to her. Because—though she tried not to indulge in fanciful dreams—when she did give in and imagine herself feeling safe and adored in the arms of a handsome, charming, unattainable man . . .

That man looked a great deal like Colin.

She hated admitting it, even to herself. And the idea that *he* might suspect . . . that was too miserable to contemplate.

She felt the bed shifting. And then she felt his weight settle *atop* her. An entire man's worth of heat and muscle stretched over her body, with only a linen bedsheet to separate them.

She tensed. Everywhere.

"Hush," he murmured, gently but insistently spreading her

legs to accommodate the breadth of his hips. "It's all right. I won't hurt you. I won't lift this sheet. You're safe beneath it. Just keep your eyes closed and your lips parted. And learn how this should feel."

Learn how this should feel. Shouldn't this feel tender and romantic?

Shouldn't lovemaking feel like love?

But this wasn't love. It was a diversion, a lesson. Just another elaborate pretense.

Her body's reaction, however, was real. Her limbs were restless beneath his. She was breathing so hard, she grew dizzy and faint.

He cupped her breast through the linen, circling his touch around its widest circumference before spiraling inward, toward the rapidly hardening peak.

"A good lover," he murmured, planting hot kisses just beneath her ear, "will take time for you. He will always put your pleasure before his own. He will make you free to experience, free to touch. Free to ask for whatever it is your body craves."

His touch grazed her nipple. Just lightly, like the pass of a feather. The sensation was startling, exquisite.

"Did you like that?" he asked. "Do you want more?"

Yes. Yes, and yes, please.

"Then you must tell me so. Not in words, if you don't wish. When you're caught up in lovemaking, words can—and should—fail you. But a man does perform best with encouragement. So if you wish for more, you must tell me so. With a gasp, or a sigh, or a little moan of pleasure. Let's try again, shall we?"

Once again, his fingertip teased over her taut, aching nipple. Gone, almost before she could register the sensation.

And then nothing.

She bit her lip. She knew he was waiting on her response. Horrid, teasing man. He would drive her to the brink of trembling, molten pleasure, and then abandon her there. Unless she begged for more.

Minerva lay still and silent for what seemed an age, doing battle with herself. Struggling between the desire to take just a little more, and the fear of surrendering far too much.

Raw need and curiosity carried the day.

Her lips parted, and she released her breath as a slow, almost musical sigh.

He answered with a deep, resonant groan. "Yes. That's the way. Sigh for me again."

He pressed his thumb to her nipple and rolled it, teasing around and around the puckered nub. She sighed again, with more feeling this time, and he rewarded her with a light pinch. She arched into his touch, and her head rolled to the side.

"Do you like it?" He tweaked her nipple. "Answer."

A low moan eased from her throat. He was right. Giving voice to the pleasure made it that much sweeter, sharper. Real.

"Yes. God, yes. This is how to drive a man wild, pet." His hand shaped and molded her breast as he trailed kisses over her elongated throat, sipping and licking at her skin. "Once I've made you sigh, all I can think is how to make you moan. Then whimper. Then cry out in helpless ecstasy."

He shifted over her, redistributing his weight. He was so hard all over, pressing against her soft flesh. His muscled chest flattened her breasts. His knee wedged her thighs apart. And then that hard, eagerly thrusting organ she'd brazenly observed and admired last night . . . he pressed it against her sex.

Pleasure rocketed through her. Intense. Consuming. Like nothing she'd ever known.

She moaned, deep and lustily. Because she wanted more. More of his hardness, his heat. More of this enticing friction rubbing her through that cool, smooth linen.

He gave her just what she craved. He set a rhythm, slow and steady, rocking against her as he kissed her throat and nuzzled her linen-sheathed breasts.

"Yes?" he prompted, sucking her earlobe into his mouth.

"Yes."

"More?"

"*More*."

"Tell me with your hands now. Hold fast to me. Move with me."

She clung to him, shameless, sliding her hands around his shoulders. Her arousal only climbed as she felt the flex and strain of his muscles beneath her palms. He was laboring so hard, and for her. All for her. She loved feeling the strength in his body as he moved over her, rubbed against her. Again and again and again.

Soon, he had her moaning with every delicious stroke. The louder she called to him, the more resounding his response. The mattress joined the erotic symphony, creaking in time with his strong, rhythmic thrusts. He quickened his tempo, and the bedpost added thumping percussion as it knocked against the wall.

"Yes, Min. This is how it should be." Raw need edged his voice. "Never settle for less. Be fearless. Wild and loud and lovely. God, you're so lovely."

It was dark, and she knew he could scarcely see her. But it didn't matter. She felt lovely. Beneath her touch, his fevered skin slid hot and beautiful. Together, they'd made this stunning, gorgeous pleasure.

She chased the sensation, tilting her hips and riding his thrusts as they came faster, stronger.

Then something changed. Suddenly, the pleasure was chasing *her*. Hunting her down with ruthless intensity. She couldn't hide from it, couldn't escape.

Her eyes flew open, wide and unfocused in the shadowy dark. "Colin."

"Yes." He stroked on, relentless. "Yes, call my name. Louder."

"Colin, I—" Her voice caught on a fearful gasp. "I can't . . ."

"Don't fight it. All's as it should be. It's perfect." As he surged on and on, his brow dropped to her shoulder. "You're perfect."

Here it came, the pleasure. Swirling, taunting. Pulling at her from the inside. Dragging her into some dark, strange place. She grasped him tighter, pressing her nails into the flesh of his shoulder.

Don't let me go.

He kissed her cheek, her lips. "Come for me, darling. Come for yourself."

At last, she surrendered to it. She heard herself cry out as the bliss finally caught her, lifted her. Pulled her to fragments. Wrung her limp. Left her gasping for breath and changed inside.

And still he moved on, pumping his hips at a tortured, frantic pace. He framed her face in his hands, then drove his fingers back to twist in her hair. The delicious pull sent pleasure rushing through her again.

He held her still and tight, grinding his hardness against her. "Sorry," he groaned. "Too good. Can't stop."

With a growl, he shuddered and jerked in her embrace. Then slumped heavy atop her, panting into the curve of her neck.

Her fingers relaxed their grip on his shoulders. Her hands trembled. She didn't know how to touch him. A bead of sweat trickled along her collarbone. She wasn't sure if it was hers or his.

What did this all mean? It wasn't really copulation, much less lovemaking. But it was real in some way. She didn't know how to think of him now. Much less how to look at him, speak to him in the morning. How did she think of herself, after she'd moaned and sighed his name? Was she ruined? Was she a wanton?

He rolled to the side, one hand still tangled in her hair. His chest rose and fell with a heavy sigh. "Good Lord, woman."

Woman. She was a woman.

"You are forever catching me by surprise. I begin as your tutor, teaching the lesson. And then somehow . . . minutes later, I'm spilling like a schoolboy." He gave a husky, intimate chuckle.

And what seemed like seconds after that, he was snoring.

Chapter Thirteen

"Jesus." Wincing at the too-bright morning, Colin speared a hand through his hair. "I can't believe this happened. I never do this. Never."

Minerva rolled over sleepily, rubbing her eyes. "What is it?"

"Get dressed, and quickly. We've overslept."

Thus began a mad, mutual dash to wash and dress and pack up all their things. The haste was convenient, in some ways. It postponed any discussion of last night.

It did not, however, erase his memories. Her every sound, every motion aroused him. The way she tugged her hairbrush through that love-tangled jumble of dark curls. The way her breasts jounced as she hopped on one foot, struggling to jam the other into her half-boot. When she reached out and clutched his shoulder to balance, Colin thought he might unman himself yet again. He hadn't been exaggerating last night. She made him randy as a youth, and twice as stupid.

Damn it, man. What were you thinking? You have rules about this.

Yes, he conceded. But he hadn't broken those rules. He'd merely stretched them.

Stretched them. Stroked them. Humped them. Made them moan and sob.

He shook himself. Bloody hell. And here he had another long, dusty day of riding horseback facing him. Excellent. At least he wouldn't need to schedule additional time for guilt and regret.

Hopefully the grooms downstairs had already selected a horse and readied it with his tack and saddle. As travel went, renting a posting horse every twenty miles wasn't ideal. It wasn't doing his arse any favors, either. But to keep up with a coach's pace, Colin really had no alternative.

She drew aside the curtains and peeked out the window. "Oh, I see the Fontleys. They're getting in the carriage already. Surely they wouldn't leave without us."

"Surely not." He joined her at the window. The Fontleys were, indeed, almost ready to depart. "They can't do that to you. Today's *your* birthday."

"Don't start." She cast him a chastening look through askew spectacles. Then self-consciousness flickered across her face, as if she'd felt some echo of the night before. She blushed, swallowed, and looked away.

He had the sudden, inexplicable urge to kiss her. But that would almost certainly be a bad idea, and anyway—there wasn't time. They hurried down the stairs with a thunder of footfalls, struggling with the trunks as they came.

"Here we are," Colin called, hurrying ahead of Minerva. "We're coming! Tallyho!"

One of the Fontleys' footmen stood perched on the back of the coach. Colin heaved the smallest trunk up to him, for storage. Then the second.

"Don't forget this one," Minerva called, dragging the third trunk behind her. The one that held Francine.

As Colin turned to help her with it, he heard the crack of a driver's whip. Before he even understood what was happening, the coach had rolled into motion.

The Fontleys were driving away. Without them.

"Wait!" Minerva called. "Come back!"

Mrs. Fontley's head poked out the window. "And subject my children to such reprehensible characters? I will not." As the coach trundled away at a clip, they heard her shouting, "You are not good people!"

Minerva turned to him, stunned and breathless. "What can she mean? Surely it wasn't the fact that you punched that man last night."

"Couldn't be. I can't think what we did to change their opinion, unless . . ." His stomach rolled.

"Unless what?"

"Unless they somehow heard us. Last night."

She paled. "Oh, sweet heaven." Her lip folded under her teeth. "But how could they have . . . ?"

"They couldn't have."

"No, they couldn't have, unless they were right next door. Unless . . ." Her gaze met his, wide and horrified. "Unless *they* were the ones *we* heard."

Colin blew out a slow breath. He turned his head and stared after the coach. "Well. Good for them. Well done, Mr. Fontley."

Minerva didn't share his amusement.

"Oh God." She sat down on her one remaining trunk and dropped her head in her hands. "They must think us scheming charlatans. They know every word we said was false. Ceylon, the lepers, the stupid beetle bite. They know we're liars."

He ducked his head and scratched the back of his neck. "Let's *hope* that's what they concluded."

She looked up at him. "What else would they think? That

we weren't lying? That we really are brother and—" He watched the look of abject revulsion creep across her face. "No. *No.*"

"Don't worry," he said hastily. "I'm sure they concluded the first."

"Ugh." She shuddered violently. "I think I'll be sick."

"There's no need for that, pet. *We* know the truth."

"Do we?"

He felt the barb in her remark. Neither of them knew exactly what they were to each other, after last night.

But that conversation would need to wait. For the first time, Colin noticed how many people around the area were watching them. The look in their eyes wasn't friendly. As he turned casually to face the inn, the door slammed. He heard a latch scrape shut.

Renting a fresh horse was apparently out of the question. And he didn't suppose any of these villagers would be offering them a ride.

"I should have known it was a bad idea," she whimpered. "I should have known I'd pay for it somehow. Whenever you touch me, I end up humiliated."

He cleared his throat and drew near to Minerva. "We'd best leave this place. As soon as possible. Whatever the Fontleys concluded about us, it seems they shared those conclusions with everyone here."

"But where will we go? How will get there?" She gestured after the long-gone carriage. Despair weakened her voice. "They took all my clothes, all my things."

He crouched before her. "You still have your purse?"

She nodded.

"And you still have Francine. You're sitting on her."

She nodded again. "My scientific findings are in this one, too."

"Then those are the most important things. Everything

else is replaceable. We'll just walk to the next town up the road, and from there we'll start anew. All right?"

She sniffed. "All right."

He helped her to her feet, then stared at her trunk, considering how best to carry the thing. On his shoulder?

She clutched one handle with her gloved hand and lifted. "I'll take this side, and you take the other. It will be faster this way."

His sense of chivalry rebelled, but she was right. Carrying the thing between them was really the best way.

"Now, then," he said, as they walked down the road that led out of town, carrying a giant lizard's footprint. "Let's have a smile. We'll be back underway in no time."

It took hours.

The next town couldn't be far, Minerva had reasoned. A few miles at most. But Francine hampered their progress. They kept stopping to rest, to change sides, to readjust the weight. And though Minerva kept telling herself the low shadow of cottages and a church would surely appear over the next rise, or just around the next bend in the road . . .

They walked for hours. Nothing.

Coaches and carriages passed them regularly. But either they were full to capacity or they'd been warned in the previous town to avoid a pair of charlatans walking north. Even if one of the coaches had slowed, it wouldn't have helped. Colin wouldn't ride in one. No, they had to walk for miles, hoping to find some village where she could find space in a carriage and he could rent a fresh horse. Who knew how far that would be?

The sun was high overhead, and she was growing faint. They'd never even eaten breakfast. Fatigue and hunger conspired within her, whispering to each other in irritable voices. Thirst thickened her tongue.

She drew to an abrupt halt by the side of the road. "That's it. I won't go any farther."

He put down his side of the trunk. "Very well. We'll rest."

"No. I don't want a rest, I want a coach. Perhaps one will stop for me, if I'm alone. I'll stay here. You can keep walking."

He shook his head. "Out of the question. I know you don't have a high opinion of my character. But if you think I'd abandon an unprotected gentlewoman by the roadside, you're mad. Do you know what kinds of brigands loiter along these coaching routes?"

"Yes, I believe I do know." She stared at him pointedly.

"So I'm a brigand now."

"You landed us in this predicament."

He stepped back. "You think this is all my fault?"

"Of course it's all your fault! I didn't ask you to tell the Fontleys all those wicked lies. I didn't ask to be made a party to your incorrigible behavior. I didn't ask you to teach me any . . . lessons."

"Oh, of course not. You merely showed up at my door in the middle of the night and begged me to take you to Scotland." He jabbed a thumb in his chest. "You kissed *me* outside the Bull and Blossom. You dragged *me* into a bloody cave. I didn't ask for any of that."

"You're ruining this journey," she all but shouted. "You ruin everything."

"Well, I beg your pardon, but I believe you signed on to be ruined!"

Her hands clenched in fists. She tried to calm herself. "We made a simple agreement. You take me to Edinburgh. I give you five hundred guineas. I don't recall any negotiations about lying or singing or . . . or moaning."

"No, I threw those in the bargain for free. You're welcome." The infuriating man walked in a slow circle, swinging his arms. "We'll rest a few minutes. And then we'll continue walking. The next village can't be far now."

"I will not be moved from this spot."

He came to a halt behind her. His hands gripped her shoulders. "You will be," he muttered, "even if I have to forcibly move you."

"You wouldn't dare."

"Oh, yes I would." His hands massaged her neck and shoulders muscles—not tenderly, but in the way a manager might loosen a boxer for a fight. It felt maddeningly wonderful.

Crouching, he swiveled her so that she faced the road ahead. "Yes," he whispered in her ear. "I will push you, pull you, rattle you as I see fit. Because you've a sparkling wit lurking beneath that dull exterior. Because you can sing, but you don't. Because you've a fiery passion inside you, and it needs release. Because you *can* keep walking. You just need someone to push you over that next horizon."

Surely it was the effect of hunger and fatigue, not his rough, intimate voice. But she trembled, just a little.

"Those are rather ironic words," she said, turning her head to face him. "From a man who won't even ride in a coach."

His hands tensed.

"Ho, there!"

On the road beside them, a carriage rolled to a halt. A young woman with a gaily beribboned bonnet called to them from inside.

"My goodness, what misfortune has befallen you? Do you need assistance? Can we offer you some help?" She opened the door. "It's just my sister and our companion with me, you see. Plenty of space."

Minerva rose from her trunk and looked to Colin. "Well? Must I push *you*?"

"No," he said grimly. "I'll ride. Just until the next town."

Minerva assessed the young woman in the carriage. She looked about the same age as Diana, and her bonnet and carriage marked her as a lady of some wealth. Judging by the fact that she was stopping to offer rides to strangers, she must be either exceptionally kind or rather stupid.

More likely, she was simply the sort of privileged, high-spirited girl who couldn't imagine anything bad happening to her—because nothing truly bad ever had.

"You're so kind to stop for us," Minerva said, dropping a curtsy. "I'm Miss Sand, and this is . . . my brother. We've had quite the misadventure this morning, I'm afraid. If you could only take us to the next town, we'd be so grateful."

"So we're still brother and sister?" he murmured, lifting her trunk.

"Yes," she whispered back. "But keep it simple. No more missionaries. Or cobras. And most importantly, no more . . . *you know*."

His eyes were hard as he looked her up and down. "Believe me. You needn't worry on that score."

Minerva absorbed the swift, ruthless stab to her pride.

"Just slide your trunk here, in the compartment," the young lady directed. "There's no more room up top, I'm afraid. Cordelia *will* bring a half dozen hatboxes on every journey."

After Minerva climbed into the carriage and took a place on the rear-facing seat, Colin lifted the trunk inside and slid it back as far as possible. Finally, taking one last deep breath as though he were preparing to submerge himself in the sea, he entered and settled his significant bulk beside her. His legs were nearly folded double.

"Carry on, John Coachman!" the young lady called.

As the carriage jolted into motion, Minerva felt Colin's muscles go rigid as iron. She knew that familiar pang of sympathy for him—but truly, he had no one to blame for this situation but himself. And it would only be a short ride.

He'd survive.

"I'm Miss Emmeline Gateshead." The beribboned young woman stuck out her hand, and Minerva shook it. "This is my sister, Miss Cordelia Gateshead, and our companion, Mrs. Pickerill."

Minerva made her polite greetings to all three. She might as well have saved her breath. All three young women were instantly riveted to Colin. No surprise. The man drew female attention like a sponge draws water.

"And what takes the two of you north?" Miss Gateshead asked. "I didn't quite catch your names."

"Oh." Minerva was suddenly panicked. "Well. We . . ."

"Don't tell us! We'll guess," Cordelia said, smiling. "It will help to pass the time." She tipped her smile in Colin's direction. "Are you an officer, back from the war?"

"No, miss. I'm no hero."

Minerva would have said the same, a few minutes ago. But now she wasn't so sure. From the moment they'd entered the coach, she'd been aware of the tension in Colin's body. Now, her spectacles had begun to fog over from his shallow breaths. But no one else in the carriage suspected his struggles. He was enduring the torture quietly, manfully.

Perhaps even heroically.

"Pity, for you'd look so fine in uniform." Emmeline's remark prompted a chastening harrumph from her companion. "Did you come from Town?"

"We came through it," Minerva answered. "But home is rather further south. On the coast."

Cordelia gasped. "I know. He's a pirate!" The younger lady collapsed into giggles.

Emmeline turned her head and regarded Colin askance. A coquettish lilt stole into her voice. "Well, I would believe it of him. He does have that roguish air."

Miss Gateshead, you have no idea.

"Perhaps a spy." This, from Mrs. Pickerill.

Minerva's annoyance neared its boiling point. She couldn't take any more of this silliness from the women, and Colin's quiet misery had her truly concerned. Now he seemed to have stopped breathing entirely.

"Why don't you just tell them the truth, brother?" Perhaps it would help him to talk. He did love spinning outlandish tales. And if he were speaking, he'd simply *have* to start breathing.

He cleared his throat. "Oh, I don't like to say."

Mrs. Pickerill looked suspicious. "It's simple enough, isn't it? Names, destination."

"Yes, of course," Minerva jumped to agree, casually sliding her arm through Colin's. "But it's not a matter of how we are," she improvised. "It's who we *might* be that complicates matters."

"And who might you be?" Miss Cordelia Gateshead inched forward on her seat.

"Do tell them, brother," Minerva urged. "It's so very diverting. And I think what we need right now is a little diversion."

She gave his arm a surreptitious squeeze. *I'm here. You're not alone.*

He nodded. "Well, you see . . . the truth of the matter is . . ." He put his hand over Minerva's. "We might be royalty."

Every lady in the coach gasped, Minerva included. Well, she'd asked for this. At least there'd be no cobras or lepers this time.

"Royalty?" Miss Gateshead sat tall. "How astonishing."

"That was our reaction, when the solicitors found us." Colin began to sound himself again. His incorrigible, devilish self. "But it's recently come to light that our father was possibly descended from the line of Prince Ampersand, ruling monarch of Crustacea."

"Crustacea," Cordelia echoed. "I've never even heard of it."

"Neither had we!" he exclaimed. "We had to dig out the atlas from our father's library and dust it off when we received the letter last month. A very small principality, apparently. High up in the mountains, along the border of Spain and Italy. The entire economy is based on the export of calendula and goat cheese."

Minerva bit back a laugh. Any imbecile with an atlas knew Spain didn't border Italy. And good luck growing calendula on a mountaintop.

"What did the letter say?" Cordelia asked.

"You see, some months ago, tragedy struck the tiny alpine paradise. The entire Crustacean royal family was wiped out by a particularly virulent strain of violet fever."

"I've never heard of violet fever."

"Neither had we," Colin said. "We had to break out father's old medical tomes next. Didn't we, M?" He patted her hand. "It's very rare. But almost always deadly." He clucked his tongue. "A true tragedy. It wiped out the prince, the queen mother, all the royal children. Unless they want to hand over the realm to this vile, sniveling, warty usurper called . . ." He looked to Minerva. "Sir Alisdair, was it?"

She snorted.

"They had to find someone in the royal line. They searched far and wide, and then they found us. So we're off to the ancestral family home, you see. To retrieve our birth records and the family Bible and such. By this time next month, you could be looking at the prince and princess of Crustacea."

Emmeline sighed. "It's like a fairy tale."

Yes, Minerva thought. Just like a fairy tale. Absolute rot, from beginning to end.

"Oh, it's no fairy tale," Colin said. "Don't envy us our sudden elevation. If we are royalty, our lives will cease to be our own. We'll have duties, won't we? We'll have to leave England—our beloved homes and friends—behind. And then there's abandoning the hope of love." His expression went somber. "A prince can never expect to find love."

In unison, the sisters pressed their hands to their hearts.

"He can't?" Cordelia asked.

"No, he can't." With an air of thoughtful sincerity, he leaned forward. "You see, if I remained just poor, simple Mr. Colin Sand of Sussex, I could take a fancy to a pretty girl I met while traveling. Ask permission to court her. Take the time to become better acquainted. Share with her all my dreams and fancies and secrets, and learn hers. Bring her sweets and bouquets." He cast a wistful glance out the coach window. "Like any man, I've enjoyed my youth, sown my wild oats. But deep down, I always wanted that tender romance with the right girl. Someday."

Good Lord. He spun these tales so convincingly, even Minerva had to remind herself it was all fabrication. She'd once made the mistake of believing those lies. *It's you, Minerva. It's always been you.* She could still hear the mocking laughter ringing off the turret walls.

This time, at least, she could have been the one to laugh. The young Misses Gateshead were so far gone, they'd all but tripped over the horizon.

Such charm was a talent, she had to give him that. Twenty minutes in the same carriage, and he had two well-bred gentlewomen utterly enamored with a reluctant prince who'd turn down the riches of the world for a chance at true love. Their hearts, souls, smiles, and virtues could be his for a single, smoldering gaze. They'd probably queue up to take turns.

Minerva suddenly realized that he'd never unleashed his

full seductive potential in Spindle Cove—at least, not with Diana. A strange surge of gratitude took her by surprise.

"If I'm a prince," he said, smiling in that disarming, bashful way—the way that revealed his single dimple as though it were a secret vulnerability only the love of a good woman could cure—"I of course will do my duty. I will do my best. But sometimes, I think it might be a relief to find it's all just a grand mistake."

The coach lurched to a sudden halt.

"Oh," exclaimed Emmeline, falling forward. "What's that?"

Minerva looked out the window for the first time in several minutes. This stretch of road passed through a wooded area. Perhaps they'd come to a turnpike, or the road was muddy ahead.

Without warning, the door of the coach opened, just a crack.

In the opening, the barrel of a pistol gleamed.

"Stand and deliver."

Chapter Fourteen

Colin very nearly laughed. Not out of amusement, but irony. It was really, truly absurd that part of him welcomed this turn of events. That he'd rather face a highwayman at gunpoint than ride one minute longer in this hellish, suffocating coach. Even spinning outlandish claptrap and enjoying the company of three ladies couldn't distract him from the too-close walls and the too-warm air. When the carriage had lurched to its unexpected stop, Colin had gone a bit wild inside.

He'd wanted out.

At the sight of the pistol, he'd almost begged, *Yes, shoot me. End this misery.*

Until that pistol turned in Minerva's direction, and clarity descended. Now Colin wasn't panicked.

He was pissing angry.

He cleared his throat, drawing the bastard's attention. "If you must point that thing at someone, point it at me."

The highwayman obliged him and threw a canvas pouch through the open door. "Pass the sack. Coin, jewels, watches, rings. All of it goes inside." An ominous click sounded as he cocked the pistol. "And quickly."

The Misses Gateshead cowered together with their companion.

Colin retrieved the canvas pouch from the floor. As he teased the drawstring open, he spoke to the ladies in his calmest, most reassuring tone. "It'll have to be done, I'm afraid. We'll do as he asks, and then we'll continue on. Everything will be well."

Damn it all. Colin knew handing over the valuables was the only safe and responsible choice. Except for a knife buried deep in his boot, he was unarmed and at a distinct disadvantage. Presumably, the robber had associates holding the carriage driver and footmen at gunpoint, too. Any heroics Colin might attempt would doubtless end in someone's injury or death. With four ladies in the carriage, he couldn't take the risk. Still, he hated giving in. He cursed his own thoughtlessness. Why hadn't he brought a pistol on this journey?

The answer was simple. Because he hadn't expected to actually *leave* on this journey. He'd tried to cancel the whole thing, that first morning by the road.

He should have tried harder.

With shaking fingers, the trio of ladies removed their lockets, bracelets, rings, and hair combs. He shook the few coins he carried from his own pocket.

"What about her?" The robber thrust his pistol in Minerva's direction.

"She's not wearing jewels," Colin said, angling himself between the pistol and her body.

"What about that reticule?"

Colin held out the canvas bag. "The reticule, Min."

"But . . ." Her dark eyes were wild with apprehension. "But it has all my—"

All her money. All *their* money. Yes, Colin knew. And from the look in her eyes, he knew she would likely do something very stupid to save it, if he didn't take command of this scene.

"Give it here," he said firmly. "Now."

Her face blanched to the color of parchment as she un-looped the reticule from her wrist and dropped it in the canvas bag.

"There." Colin pushed the heavy bag at the highwayman. "Take it and begone. Before I change my mind and crush your miserable, reeking face with my boot."

"Not so fast." The robber flashed his pistol in the direction of Colin's signet ring. "Your ring."

"Won't come off." Colin demonstrated, tugging at the gold band. "If you want it, you'll have to take the finger."

The ladies gasped at this suggestion, drawing the high-wayman's notice. From beneath his wide-brimmed hat, sharp eyes scanned the compartment.

His pistol pointed in Francine's direction. "What's in the trunk?"

"Nothing," Minerva jumped to answer. "Nothing at all."

Bollocks. *Wrong answer, pet.* That trunk's contents were of no value to anyone, save Minerva herself. And a few dusty scientists, perhaps. But with her hasty denial, she'd just given the impression that the trunk was filled with gold doubloons. Now the robber would not rest without taking it, and Minerva would not surrender.

He leaned toward her. "Min, it's not worth your life."

"It *is* my life. Without it, I've done this all for nothing."

"Give me that," the highwayman ordered, holding the pistol steady with one hand and reaching for the trunk's handle with the other.

"No," Minerva cried, holding it back. "Please."

Colin's heart careened in his chest. Good Lord, the girl would get herself killed.

"Leave the trunk," Colin said. He turned to the highwayman. "Leave the trunk, and you can have me."

The robber's lip curled. "You're not my sort. But perhaps I'll take the trunk *and* the girl. I like 'em spirited."

It took everything Colin had not to slam his fist into the man's throat, that instant. Pistol or no pistol, he could pulverize the blackguard. He felt sure of it.

But there were others, he reminded himself. Outside the coach. An untold number of men, most certainly armed. He couldn't risk them firing on the ladies.

Colin steeled his jaw. "What's the girl worth to you? A few minutes' fun? I'm worth a fortune in ransom." He flashed his signet ring and brought out his most aristocratic accent. "Thousands. Let the ladies pass unmolested, and I'll come with you. No struggle."

He watched greed and suspicion wrestling in the robber's eyes. The man wanted to believe Colin, but he wasn't sure he could.

And then, from the opposite seat, Miss Cordelia Gateshead gave Colin the best, most timely gift he could ever hope to receive.

The girl clasped her hands together and sighed, "Oh, your royal highness. You mustn't."

Well. That sealed the bargain nicely.

As Colin made ready to leave the carriage, he pinned Minerva with a stern glare. "Listen to me," he whispered fast and fierce. "You go to the next town. You find a safe inn. You send word to my cousin, and then you bloody well stay there until he arrives. Do you hear?"

Her eyes shimmered with fear. "But, Colin—"

"No arguments, damn it. Just do as I say. I need to know you're safe."

She nodded. Her bottom lip trembled, and he couldn't

resist soothing it with a brief, if rather unbrotherly, parting kiss.

"God be with you, Prince Ampersand," said Emmeline Gateshead, weeping into her handkerchief. "And with the people of Crustacea."

As Colin alighted from the coach, he assessed the scene. As he'd suspected, the highwayman had associates. Two that he could see, both armed. A stocky man held the horses by their leads and had a pistol trained on the driver. The third, youthful and lean, stood several paces to the rear, keeping a musket shouldered and cocked.

The first highwayman nudged Colin with a pistol to the back. "Look what I have here, boys! It's a prince."

"That don't look like a prince. He's got too many teeth."

"Whoever he is, let's get him away from the road." The stocky man released the horses' leads and nodded to the driver.

The Gatesheads' coach jolted into motion, and Colin rejoiced to see it carrying all four—five, if he counted Francine—innocent females well away. He took his first deep breath since entering that godforsaken conveyance some miles back. So long as Minerva was unharmed, he could endure whatever came next.

If she'd been hurt in any way, he could not have lived with himself.

Still prodding him along with the pistol, the highwayman pushed him toward the woods.

"My cousin is the Earl of Rycliff," Colin said, as they crunched over ferns and wove through stands of coppiced hazel. "He's trustee of my fortune. Send him a letter sealed with this"—he wiggled his signet ring—"and he'll arrange for whatever ransom you demand."

Possibly. Or, his cousin might send them a letter back saying, "Go ahead, do me a favor and send the scoundrel to the devil." Depended on Bram's mood that day. It didn't really matter, as Colin had no intent to remain in the brigands' custody that long. These were petty thieves, not kidnappers by trade. They'd surely slip up and give him a chance to escape. Perhaps before the morning was out.

Or perhaps not.

Once they'd made their way well into the woods, his captor spun him about. He struck Colin across the face with the pistol. The blow sent his head whipping sideways and his brain reeling off to some sparkling, painful place.

All three of the men closed around him.

"A prince, eh?" The stocky one made a fist. "Don't be expecting the royal treatment from us."

Colin straightened. Thanks to years of boxing at the club, he knew how to weather a few blows. He also knew he couldn't put his fists against three armed men. But he would not cringe or beg. "I'm actually not a prince. I'm a viscount. If that helps."

It didn't help. But it did earn him another blow, this one to the gut.

And so, as it happened, by the time the morning was out, Colin had *not* found an opportunity for escape.

Rather, he'd found himself beaten, bloodied, and tied to a chestnut tree.

Staring down the barrel of a gun.

Chapter Fifteen

Jt was a fine day for target practice. Mild, sunny. Not overly breezy.

Kate Taylor cocked her pistol and stared down the distant bull's-eye.

Weekly shooting lessons were the legacy of Miss Susanna Finch, a gentleman gunsmith's daughter and Spindle Cove's first patroness. She believed every young lady should know how to defend herself.

Susanna had married Lord Rycliff last year and was presently staying with him in London. So Kate had taken responsibility for the ladies' schedule in her absence.

On Mondays, they had country walks. Tuesday's sea bathing was on hiatus until summer, of course, but on Wednesdays, they turned their hands to gardening. And on Thursdays . . .

Bang.

Thursday was their day to shoot. Here at Summerfield, the Finch estate. Sir Lewis Finch always made the young ladies welcome, offering his finest weaponry and refreshments for their enjoyment. The old man obviously missed his daughter greatly, and took some comfort in hosting her friends. And for her part, Kate couldn't get enough of being in a family home. Even if it wasn't her own. She loved soaking up the sense of shared history, old portraits, fond memories.

Charlotte Highwood tugged at her sleeve. "Miss Taylor, look. Is that the militia?"

Kate turned her gaze, staring over the open meadow. Indeed, the members of the local militia were dressed in full uniform and marching in formation. Straight for them, it would seem.

Strange.

"I didn't think they had drill today," Diana said.

"Neither did I." And even if they did, why would they be marching here, toward Sir Lewis Finch's estate?

"It's like a sham battle." Charlotte perked with excitement. "Ladies versus gentlemen. Can we fall into a formation of our own? Fix bayonets and charge?"

Diana tugged her sister's hair. "Goose."

As the column of red-coated men approached, Kate recognized Corporal Thorne leading them. He wasn't difficult to make out. He stood several inches taller than most of the men. His shoulders were near twice as broad.

And his demeanor was a thousand times more unpleasant.

"Ladies," Kate called, keeping her voice even. "Weapons down, please. It seems the men have something they wish to discuss."

With a barked command, Thorne brought the men to a halt. Another harsh order, and they'd fallen into a single line, facing the ladies.

He approached Kate. She grew uneasy, her spine withering in that massive shadow that completely blocked the sun. She hated his effect on her. So the man didn't like her. What of it? He didn't like anyone, and why should she care? Why should she allow him to make her feel so small, so powerless?

"Corporal Thorne," she said, nodding in lieu of a curtsy. "To what do we owe this . . . interruption?"

"I mean to conduct an inquiry. Of your ladies and my men. I want to know if anyone has reason to believe that Miss Minerva Highwood and Lord Payne were . . ."

"In love?" she finished.

"Involved. In any way."

Kate shrugged. "I should think the fact of their elopement might serve as ample evidence of their involvement, Corporal Thorne."

He shook his head. "It's not right. There's something not right about it."

"Mrs. Highwood has said—"

"I know that, Miss Taylor. I'm not stupid."

"I didn't say you were."

"I know what Mrs. Highwood has said," he said, "and I've decided I don't care. In Lord Payne's absence, I'm in charge of the militia. And that means, I'm responsible for the safety of this place and every man, woman, and child in it. Including Miss Minerva. If her health, happiness, or virtue is endangered in any way, it's my responsibility to see her back home. Safe."

"And what if she's not endangered, but merely eloped, happily?"

"That's what I'm here to find out."

He took a few backward steps and called out. "I'm going to walk down this line of my men, and then going to walk up the line of ladies. And I'm going to ask each of you the same question. Prior to their disappearance, did you have any reason to believe Lord Payne and Miss Minerva Highwood were . . ."

"In love," Kate supplied for him, once again. "You seem to have a problem with that word, Corporal. Or is it a problem with the concept?"

He betrayed no response.

"I don't understand that man," she muttered to Diana. "Either he has rocks in his head or a stone for a heart."

Diana smiled. "I doubt it. If either were true, Minerva would have been taken with *him*, and not Lord Payne. She does so love rocks and stones."

Corporal Thorne stood before Mr. Fosbury, the Bull and Blossom's proprietor. "Fosbury."

"Yes, sir."

"Before they disappeared, did you have any reason to believe Lord Payne and Miss Minerva held one another in affection?"

Mr. Fosbury chuckled. "The two of them? No, sir. That came as a true surprise."

Thorne moved down the line, to the blacksmith. "Dawes. Same question."

The big man tipped a gaze in the ladies' direction. "No, Corporal. From everything I saw, I would have marked him as fancying Miss Diana. And lieutenant or no, I think he's a right bastard for leading her on. If you do go after him, I'd ask to join the pursuit."

"Well, that's . . . kind of him, I suppose," Kate murmured to her friend. "If unnecessary."

Diana didn't answer.

Corporal Thorne continued down the line, interrogating each of his men in turn. The vicar, a few farmhands. After the eighth or so staunch denial, Thorne slid Kate a brief, smug glance. A look that said, *I told you so.*

She merely raised her eyebrows in reply.

"Hastings," he barked, moving on to the next man. A fisherman, by trade. "Before they run off together, did you have any reason to believe Lord Payne and Miss Minerva Highwood were involved?"

Hastings squared his shoulders. "I did, sir."

Thorne pulled up short. He'd already started moving on to the next militiaman. But in the wake of Hastings's reply, the hulking officer turned. He turned only his head, not his body. The motion struck Kate as menacing and unnatural.

He said, "What was that, Hastings?"

Even Hastings looked unnerved. "I . . . I said I did, sir. Have reason to believe the two of them was carrying on."

"Why? What? How?" He fired the questions like howitzers.

Kate laughed nervously. "One question at a time, Corporal. Allow the poor man some opportunity to answer."

Oh, and the look he gave her then. It was pure dark, demanding threat. Well, Kate threw it right back. She was not one of his soldiers to be disciplined. Even without fortune or family, she was a gentlewoman. He had no power over her.

She thrust her hand behind her back, lest he see it trembling.

Hastings found his voice. "I saw them together in the cove. Just a few days ago, as I was headed out with my nets in the early morning. Miss Minerva was in her bathing costume, and Lord Payne was stripping down to his breeches."

"A swim?" Diana said. "In April?"

"I don't know what they done afterwards. I just know what I saw." Hastings shrugged. "And when I come back in, a few hours later, they were just leaving."

"I know it's not my turn yet," Rufus Bright called from the end of the line, "but I saw them together too."

"When?" Kate and Thorne spoke in unison, much to their shared dismay.

"The other night, when I was standing watch at the castle. Sometime after . . ." Rufus shot a glance at the women and tugged his collar. "Sometime after midnight, I saw Miss Minerva leaving Lord Payne's quarters. Alone."

Charlotte shrieked, then clapped both hands over her mouth. Diana tried to soothe her sister.

"Why didn't you say something that night?" Thorne demanded. "You let her walk home alone, unprotected?"

"Well, you have to admit it weren't the first time he's entertained a lady visitor after dark."

Oh dear Lord.

Kate strode forward. "Corporal Thorne, isn't this enough? You wanted evidence. I believe Hastings and Rufus have given you ample proof. Now can we conclude this public inquisition, before we unearth more details that prove unnecessarily embarrassing to the Highwood family?"

The big man released a slow breath. "You really think Payne will marry her."

"I do," she answered.

"Well, you're right on that score. He *will* marry her. I'll see to that. The only question is whether he's doing it willingly now, or whether he'll marry her when he comes back"—the big man cracked his neck—"at the point of my pistol."

Chapter Sixteen

God preserve him from incompetence.

As he sat on the forest floor, arms wrenched behind his back and tied around the trunk of a chestnut tree, Colin felt a pang of wistful nostalgia for the Spindle Cove militia. They might have been a sorry group of volunteers at the outset, barely able to march in time—but this band of fool highwaymen made them look like a crack infantry unit by comparison.

First the thieves had argued for a good half hour over whether to believe he was a prince, a viscount, or a charlatan. Then they'd argued for a similar length of time over what to do with him. Colin, of course, had plenty of suggestions—each of which earned him another cuff across the face.

So far, these criminals had proven skilled at only one thing: Tying knots.

Finally, they'd decided to report back to their leader—some boss of their thieving gang, apparently. And so they'd tied Colin to the chestnut tree and left their youngest, most anxious-looking member to watch over him. The young man sat about ten feet distant, keeping a pistol trained on Colin's chest.

It wasn't the boy with the gun that troubled Colin, it was

the ropes lashing him to this tree. He hated feeling confined, couldn't abide being bound to anything.

Stay calm. You'll be released. Eventually.

He was simply too valuable to kill. But the longer he remained tied here, the captive of the robbers' indecision, the longer it would take word to reach Bram. And the longer Minerva would be on her own, alone and penniless.

The thought of her huddled frightened and hungry in a strange village . . . it made him shake with impotent anger. He raged and strained against the chafing ropes.

Enough with patience. There was no waiting this out. He had to escape.

"Why you?" Colin asked his captor, trying to sound calm.

"What's that?"

"Why'd they leave you in charge of a valuable hostage? You look barely old enough to shave."

"I'm nineteen this summer." The robber scratched his jaw. "Reckon Grubb and Carmichael wanted to be the ones to tell the boss. They're probably fighting over it right now, who gets to tell the tale."

"Ah." Colin tilted his head. Behind the tree, he struggled and pulled against the ropes binding his wrist. No slack. Damn it, if only he could reach the knife in his boot . . .

"So," he said, "this . . . Grubb and Carmichael, was it . . . wanted the glory for themselves?"

"That's how I see it."

"I'm sure you're right." He nodded. "Very astute. But you know, you probably shouldn't have told me their names."

The younger man's eyes went wide. He cursed unimaginatively.

"Don't worry. I'm sure Grubb and Carmichael won't kill you."

He waved the pistol at Colin. "Don't . . . don't . . . don't you say those names again."

"Well, it's not like I can just forget them, is it?"

The young man pushed to his feet. "You'll forget them if I shoot you."

"But then you'd be in a very bad situation. Once Grubb, Carmichael, *and* this boss of yours come back and find you've killed their valuable hostage?" Colin whistled low. "You'd not be long for this world then."

The robber's hands started to tremble. "I didn't agree to this. I was just supposed to be lookout, while they done the robbing."

"No," Colin said smoothly. "Of course you wouldn't agree to this. Kidnapping a peer of the realm? That's not like you."

"It's not, is it? I only wanted a few bob to take my sweetheart to the fair."

"Buy her a trinket, slide a hand under her skirts . . ."

"Exactly."

Colin paused. "I'll tell you what. These boots I'm wearing? They'll fetch a tidy sum in any city. If you untie me, you can have them. Run off, make your money, take your sweetheart to the fair. When the law comes looking for Grubb and Carmichael—and mark my words, they will hang—you'll be long gone. Forgotten. I don't even know your name."

The youth eyed him warily, slowly approaching. "I have a better idea. Mayhap I'll just take your boots. And then I'll leave you here."

A sliver of fear pierced Colin in some vital artery. His composure bled from the wound in gasping spurts. Just the image of being left alone, tied to a tree . . . with night coming, eventually . . .

He could have begged the man to shoot him dead.

Instead, he closed his eyes.

Stay calm. This was what you wanted. What you knew he'd do.

Still holding the gun with one hand, the youth began tugging at Colin's left boot with the other.

"You'll never get it off that way," Colin said, forcing a nonchalant tone despite the sweat trickling down his back. "You may as well set aside the gun. There's nothing I can do, trussed like this."

After a few more moments of struggling, the robber swore and did as Colin suggested, setting the pistol to the side and wrestling the boot with both hands. At last, it slid free with a *whooshing* sound.

Casting the first boot aside, he started to work on the other.

"Slowly, now," Colin joked. "Have a care for my aging joints."

In actuality, he cared nothing for his joints. He was wagering everything on the hope of that small folding knife secreted in his right boot. If the thing slid free where he could see it . . . and if his captor didn't notice it . . . and if he could somehow manage to get the knife into his hands . . . in a matter of minutes, he could cut himself free.

But if any one of those things went wrong, he'd remain tied here. For only the Devil knew how long. Until night, most likely. Until the dark descended, thick with ominous rustling. Until thirst and hunger became animate demons, tasked with his ceaseless torment.

Until the wild dogs came.

Jesus. Please, God, no.

His heartbeat thundered in his chest.

As the youth lifted his leg and tugged on the boot, Colin flexed his leg muscle, pulling the boy close. He had to keep that knife within reach when it fell. If the thing went flying when the boot came off . . .

"Easy," he said through gritted teeth. He could feel the boot starting to give way.

Crack. A faint snap in the undergrowth drew his attention.

His captor didn't notice the sound. He was too absorbed in his struggles with the boot. But Colin slid his gaze to the side, and what he saw there stalled his pounding heart.

Minerva.

Minerva Highwood, in her governess-blue traveling gown, slowly emerging from the undergrowth. Creeping toward them with all the stealth of a cat, intent on grabbing the discarded pistol. She put a finger to her pursed lips, gesturing for Colin's silence.

Colin made his eyes wide. *No*, he mouthed. *No. Go back.*

She crept closer still. Her foot snapped a branch.

This time, the robber noticed. His head whipped up, swiveling toward Minerva.

With a vicious growl, Colin gathered his strength and kicked him in the face. Scissoring his legs, Colin caught the man by the throat. He had him stunned and caught off guard. But he wouldn't be able to hold him long.

"Get the pistol," he managed.

As Minerva dove to retrieve the weapon, Colin tightened his legs about the highwayman's neck.

"I know what you're thinking," he said, his voice strained with effort. "You're thinking that she's just an innocent miss with spectacles. That she can't possibly know how to fire that weapon. But you're wrong. She's had training." He raised his voice. "Min, show him. Shoot that birch tree over there."

"I'm not firing at a tree! I'd waste my shot, and I haven't more powder. Then what help would I be? Really, Colin."

"See?" Colin said to the suffocating man. "She knows what she's doing." He released the robber with one final half-strength kick to the jaw. "No sudden moves."

Minerva focused her gaze and held the pistol steady. "Do I shoot him?"

"No. No, there's a knife in my right boot. Fetch it, kindly."

Keeping the pistol trained on the robber at all times, she moved sideways until she could reach the boot. She found the knife with one hand and fumbled it open, wielding it like a dagger.

"All right," she said, glaring down at the highwayman. "So where do I stab him?"

Stab him? Colin stared up at her, amazed. Her hair was hanging half loose, curling around her shoulders. Her eyes sparked with feral intensity. Her plump lips curled in a little snarl.

He'd seen this wild, savage look on her face before. In Spindle Cove, he'd known her to fell a grown man with her rock-filled reticule, and once she'd even challenged Colin to a duel. She wore that look of righteous fury when she thought her sister was in danger, or one of her friends. Even Francine.

But this was the first time she'd worn that look defending *him.*

Amazing. She wasn't supposed to be here. But here she was, for him. Willing to shoot or stab a man in his defense. And she was goddamned beautiful.

"You don't stab him, pet," he said gently. "You use the knife to cut me loose."

"Oh. Oh yes." A drunken laugh bubbled from her throat. "I suppose that makes more sense."

Working one-handed, she couldn't free him as quickly as he might like. But a few minutes' sawing and hacking at the ropes, and she had him freed.

Colin took the pistol from her the first instant he could, and promptly bashed it across the robber's face, knocking him cold. He plucked the powder horn and spare lead shot from the man's insensible form.

He turned to Minerva. "Hurry. We must be gone before he wakes."

"Oh, Colin. They hit you." She took a handkerchief from her pocket and dabbed at the bloodied corner of his mouth, wincing as she did.

"It's nothing."

"What about our money?" she asked, looking around.

"Gone with the other robbers."

"Oh. At least I still have a sovereign. It's sewn in the lining of my stays."

"Well," he muttered, cramming his left foot back into its boot. "Aren't you resourceful."

"You sound upset." She balled the handkerchief in her hand.

"I am upset." He pushed to his feet and began walking in the direction from which she'd come. They needed to be gone, as soon as possible. "I can't believe you're even here. Minerva, I gave you specific instructions to ride on to the next town. Where you'd be safe."

"I know. But I made Miss Gateshead let me out, a quarter mile down the road. I . . ." She grabbed for his wrist. "I couldn't just leave you."

He turned and stared at her.

God, he didn't know how to feel. Relieved to be free? Infuriated with her for flouting his commands? Overwhelmed with gratitude to see her whole and safe, and to have her here with him? The emotions seething within him were some mixture of all these.

He knew one thing. He didn't dare touch her right now. Whether he ended up shaking her senseless, clutching her mindlessly to him and sobbing into her skirts, or tupping her on the forest floor until his bollocks ran dry . . .

She'd get hurt, one way or another. And that would make this whole damned ordeal for naught.

"Wait." As they left the small clearing, she called him

aside. "My trunk's over here. I hid it under some branches."

"You brought Francine?"

So that's why she'd made such a delayed appearance.

"Well, I couldn't leave her behind." She knelt on the forest floor and began clearing branches from atop her hidden trunk. "Not after what you'd done to save her."

"After what I'd done to . . . to save *Francine*?" He crouched beside her, helping in the excavation. "You are an intelligent girl, Min. But sometimes you can be remarkably stupid. I wouldn't give two fingernail shavings to save this miserable piece of plaster. Much less risk my life."

"But the five hundred guineas."

"Believe me, you couldn't pay me five *thousand* guineas to sit roped to a tree like that. I would never have left with those highwaymen if you hadn't forced me to do it."

"Forced you?" Her tone jumped an octave. "I didn't force you. I could have throttled you myself when you volunteered. I was so frightened."

"Well, it was either volunteer or watch you be murdered. You'd have risked everything to save this wretched lizard, if I hadn't intervened. And you'd have ended up dead. Or worse."

"So you did it for me?"

"Minerva." He started to reach for her, then thought better of it. He gestured impatiently instead. "You left me no choice."

"I'm sorry." She touched a hand to her hair. "I'm sorry to have put you in that position. It's just . . . my life's work is in this trunk. It's my one chance at gaining recognition from my peers, my one chance at success. I've already risked so much for it. When that highwayman tried to take it, I didn't think, I just . . . reacted." Sniffing, she looked up at him. "Can you understand?"

"Oh, certainly. I understand. What's in this trunk is your life's work, and I'm just the useless fellow traveling with you this week. Of course, Francine's safety comes first."

"No." She shook her head so hard, her spectacles went crooked. "That's not fair. You're twisting my words. Colin, listen. In that frantic moment in the carriage, yes—I might have risked my own life to save this trunk. But you must believe me when I tell you this. I did not mean to risk yours. That's why I came back."

He nodded slowly. Hard to argue further, when she put it that way.

Truly, what could he say? Admit that he'd been harboring some absurd male fantasy of her running through the woods to save him, hair flowing loose behind her, breasts heaving with every pace . . . aided by helpful songbirds chirping directions . . . simply because she'd known in her heart that he needed her help? Because the moment the Gatesheads' carriage had rolled away, she'd realized that science meant nothing—absolutely nothing—to her without him, and now she would fall at his feet and beg to be his sultry-lipped love slave forevermore?

No. Of course not. She'd come back because it was expedient to her goals, and the decent thing to do. She was both driven and loyal, as ever. Nothing between them had changed.

Damn it.

He rose to his feet and took one of the trunk handles in his hand. "We need to be moving. The young one I clobbered won't give chase. He'll be too busy running for his own life. But once his associates realize I'm missing . . .

"Oh dear." She lifted her side of the trunk. "They might be after us."

Chapter Seventeen

They walked on and on through those woods, carrying Francine between them. By the position of the afternoon sun at their backs, Minerva knew they were traveling north. They hadn't crossed any large bodies of water, so she assumed they were still on British soil. Beyond that, she could not have said. She wasn't sure Colin knew, either.

Goodness, had it really been just that morning when she'd plunked herself on the side of the road and declared she could not walk another step? Colin had insisted she had the strength in her, and it annoyed her to admit he'd been right. She'd walked miles and miles farther now, with nothing to eat since last night's dinner.

Putting one boot before the other required all her powers of concentration. Hunger dogged her every step, gnawing at her from the inside.

"I'll be damned." Colin stopped in his tracks. "And here I thought I hated the country."

Minerva looked up. They'd entered a clearing. A wide, green meadow in the middle of the forest. The entire space was carpeted with bluebells. Thousands upon thousands of sweetly curving green stalks, their tips heavy with sprays of blue-violet blossoms. The sunlight shone from above and slanted through the trees, catching the blooms at different angles. The whole scene sparkled.

It was magical.

Colin said, "Even I, jaded as I am, have to admit that's bloody lovely."

Minerva was so famished, all she could think to reply was, "Do you suppose they're edible?"

He laughed. She smiled. And just like that, their mood lightened. The highwaymen were behind them. They were healthy and whole, and they still had Francine. Her stomach might be empty, but a sense of hope swelled within her breast.

Perhaps all was not lost.

As they strode through the meadow, she had the eerie sensation of walking atop waves. Except this was a sea of petals, not saltwater. Her toe caught on a fallen branch, and she stumbled a bit.

"Are you all right?" Colin asked.

She nodded. "I was just distracted. Wondering how much loam is in this soil."

"What?"

He set down his side of the trunk. Minerva did the same.

"You know," she said. "Loam. A mix of clay and sand. In order for the soil to support this many bluebells, it would—"

"You're standing in the middle of *this*"—he spread his arms wide to indicate Nature's splendor—"and you're thinking about loam in the soil? You spend far too much time staring at the ground."

Rounding the trunk, Colin plucked her off her feet. With gentle strength, he tumbled her into the bluebells. She lay flat on her back, breathless and dizzy from the sudden inversion. From the sudden nearness of him.

He lay down next to her. "There. Have a rest. Look up at the sky for a change."

Minerva stared up from the uneven ground. Her heart-beat drummed in her ears, and a crushed green scent engulfed her senses. The grasses and bluebells towered over her, swaying in the gentle breeze and dripping loveliness. Above everything, the sky hovered brilliant and blue. Nearly cloudless, save for a few wispy, changing puffs of white that were apparently too proud to mimic rabbits or dragons or sailing ships.

"What am I supposed to be seeing?" she asked.

"I don't know. What do people see when they gaze at the sky? Inspiration? Beauty?" She heard him sigh. "Truth be told, this view always intimidated me. The sky's so vast. I can't help but feel it has expectations of me. Ones I'm already failing." He was silent for a long moment. "It reminds me of your eyes."

She dug her elbow into his side. "My eyes are brown. And my back's growing damp. This is definitely very loam-rich soil. I just needed to look at the sky to realize it."

With a chuckle, he rolled over and pinned her with one leg. "Do you know, you are the most surprising woman."

Her breath caught. "You have a way of surprising me, too. Not always pleasantly."

"If surprises were always pleasant, there wouldn't be much surprise in them."

"I suppose that's true."

He brushed a few wisps of hair from her face, then removed her spectacles and laid them atop the trunk.

Minerva's pulse pounded as he slowly lowered his head and kissed . . . the tip of her nose.

She blinked up at him, trying hard to focus and read his expression. Was it teasing or affectionate? She couldn't tell. "Why did you do that?"

"Because you weren't expecting it. Which kind of surprise was it? Pleasant or otherwise?"

"I'm not sure."

"Then I'll try again."

He bent his head and kissed her temple. Then her chin, her jaw, the place between her eyebrows.

His tongue flicked over her ear.

Slid down her neck.

Dipped into the warm, sensitive valley between her breasts. She gasped. "Colin."

He clutched a fistful of her skirt and brought her pelvis flush with his.

"Min," he groaned against her neck. "I know it's mad, but I need this right now. Right here, in the midst of all this beauty. I need to feel you hot and alive beneath me."

As he leaned in to kiss her mouth, she put a hand to his chest. "I don't think this is a good idea."

His hand swept over her body. "Last night wasn't good?"

Shadowy memories of that frantic, wicked, grinding pleasure assailed her. She grew damp between the legs, and it had nothing to do with the loamy soil.

"It was very good. But it was confusing."

"This doesn't have to be complicated." He cupped her breast and thumbed her nipple to a stiff, aching peak. "It's physical. Instinctual. Releasing tension in a mutually pleasurable way."

He seeded kisses along her neck, and tendrils of desire unfurled from each one. Still . . .

"I'm not . . ." She gasped at another greedy kiss. "I'm not sure I'm comfortable being the instrument of your release."

"You make it sound so one-sided. I promise, you'll enjoy it, too."

She didn't doubt that. His hand found its way under her neckline, and he slipped his fingers beneath the fabric to curl around her breast. With practiced skill, he eased the soft globe up and free.

"God," he breathed, circling her bared nipple with his fingertip. "You're so soft. So warm and soft and sweet."

He took her nipple in his mouth. He moaned, drawing lightly on the tip with delicious suction, then swirling his tongue around the peak.

Minerva reeled with the exquisite sensations. The way he was touching her, kissing her, licking and suckling her . . . it felt so good. The pleasure was so sharp, it made her ache deep inside. It was impossible to feel this and not crave more.

But Colin wasn't the only one with principles. He wasn't the only one who could make rules. She just couldn't take any more "lessons" or pretending. She only wanted this if it was *real*.

His leg snaked between hers. "You have so much fire in you, Min. A natural talent for passion."

A talent for passion? *Her*?

"Even if that were true," she said, "look where indulging it has landed me." Thrown off one carriage, robbed on the next. Lost in the woods. Hungry, almost penniless.

"It's landed you *here*. In the most beautiful afternoon to ever grace the English countryside. Sprawled on a lush carpet of bluebells, staring up at a heartbreakingly blue sky."

"With you."

"With me."

They were silent for a time. Then she sensed his demeanor make a sudden shift. The muscles of his chest tensed beneath her touch. His tone changed.

"I see," he said, withdrawing his fingers from her bosom. "So that's the problem. Not the setting, not the notion of pleasure. It's me. You think you're here with the wrong man."

"Colin—"

He rolled away from her. "You'd rather be sharing all this with someone else. Someone like Sir Alisdair Kent. Talking of loam and soil composition, and denying the part of yourself that screamed my name last night."

Blushing, she tucked her breast back into her bodice and fumbled for her spectacles. "There's no need to be cruel."

"I'm not being cruel." He pushed to his feet, brushing off his dirt- and grass-streaked breeches. "I just feel sorry for you, is all. I've been trying to break you out of that shell, teach you how to enjoy life. But now I can see you don't want it. You're going to die curled up in that hard, brittle cage you've constructed. I hope Sir Alisdair doesn't mind cramped quarters."

"So now I should apologize? For wanting something more than carnal 'lessons' on your charity? After all, that's the best an awkward bluestocking like me could hope for. Is that it?" Minerva struggled to her feet. "At least Sir Alisdair would remember my name."

"Perhaps." He closed the distance between them, standing so near his chest grazed her breasts. "But could he kiss you so hard, you forget it?"

For a hot, confusing moment, his breath mingled with hers.

But before she could think of any possible retort, he retreated. He picked up the trunk and shouldered it.

"Come along," he said irritably. "By this time, we must be nearly there."

"Nearly there? Nearly where?"

Minerva lagged behind him, trying to understand his irrational anger. And here common wisdom would argue that women were the sex with changeable moods.

They walked on for perhaps a quarter hour more, and then they emerged from the woods at the edge of a crest.

In the distance, down the slope, sat an immense stone manor house, bordered by gardens and outbuildings.

"Good heavens," she breathed. "What is that place?"

"Winterset Grange," he answered. "I knew we had to be

close. A good friend of mine resides there. We need a place to stay the night. To lie low, in case those highwaymen are still sniffing about."

"And we're going to just appear on your friend's doorstep? Uninvited, out of nowhere?" She waved a hand between them. "Looking as we do?"

"Oh, no one will blink. Guests are always coming and going from Winterset Grange. Whenever the duke's in residence, it's one never-ending bacchanal."

Minerva stared at him. "The *duke*? We're going to be guests of a duke?"

"He's not a *royal* duke," he said, as if this should be some comfort. "Hal's an amiable fellow, you'll see. He's patron of a popular gambling circle called the Shilling Club. I'm a member. He'd never begrudge my lack of an invitation, so long as I show up with money to lose at his card table."

"But you *haven't* any money to lose at his card table. We have precisely one sovereign to our names."

"Details, details."

They started down the grassy slope. The vast, sprawling manor house seemed to inflate as they approached. As if some mischievous boy were behind the thing, huffing air into it like a scraped pig's bladder. It was just grotesquely large, its windows deep-set and hooded, like leering eyes.

She didn't like this. Not one bit.

As they neared the drive, Colin pulled her into the gardens, behind a windbreak of cypress trees. After dipping a handkerchief into a trickling fountain, he swabbed his face and neck clean, then retied his cravat. He brushed the dust from the front of his coat and gave a brisk, jaunty toss of his head that instantly tamed his hair.

So wretchedly unfair. Thirty seconds' *toilette*, and he looked better than she could have managed with hot tongs, curling papers, and the assistance of two French lady's maids.

"Am I presentable?" he asked.

"You're every bit as unjustly handsome as always."

He cocked his head and peered at her. "Now, what can we do about you?"

She snorted. What indeed. "Likely nothing, my lord," she said acidly.

"Well, you can't go in looking like that—all pinned and laced and buttoned up. Not if you're meant to pass as my mistress."

"Your . . ." She lowered her voice, as though the cypresses had ears. "Your *mistress*?"

"How else am I to explain your presence? I've been friends with the Duke of Halford for years. I can't tell him you're my sister. He knows very well I have none." His hands went to the buttons of her traveling spencer. Beginning at the one nearest her throat, he slipped them loose, one by one. "First, we need to do away with this." When he had the two sides divided, he pushed the garment from her shoulders and shook loose the sleeves. All the while, Minerva stood there numbly, not even knowing how to protest.

He folded her jacket and tossed it aside. "This won't do either," he grumbled, eyeing her shot-silk traveling gown. "You should have worn the red today."

Minerva bristled. "What's wrong with this gown?" She *liked* this gown. It was one of her best. The peacock blue suited her coloring, or so she'd been told.

"It's too modest by far," he said. "You look like a governess, not a mistress."

Modest? She stared down at the silk. The bodice fit close across her bosom, and the empire waist cinched her tight around the ribs, flaring to a full, draped skirt. It was a form-fitting, curve-emphasizing silhouette—one that had felt positively daring, in the seamstress's fitting. The sleeves, especially. They puffed a bit at the shoulder, then gathered with a ribbon garter just at the top of the arm. From there, they hugged her arms tight, all the way down to the wrist.

He reached for one of those ribbon bows, worrying the lace between his fingertips before skimming a light touch all the way down to her cuff. A heady sensation slid through her, coasting on the sheen of silk.

See? These sleeves were cunning, *sensual* sheaths of fabric. Nothing modest about them at all.

"Perhaps this will help." He closed his fingers about the cuff and gave it a ruthless yank.

"No, don't!"

And just like that, the cunning sleeve was gone. His sharp tug made a rent in the seam below her ribbon ties, and he frayed the rest of it loose with devious fingers. Within moments, he had the entire sleeve destroyed and he'd set to work on the other.

In the end, he left her with abbreviated puffs of fabric covering her shoulders. Two little apostrophes of silk, where full parentheses had been.

After standing back a moment to look at her, he untied one of the ribbon bows and left its ends dangling.

"Why would you do that?"

His eyebrow arched. "It makes a suggestion."

"The suggestion being that I'm *loose*?"

"Your words, not mine." He framed her waist in his hands, and spun her around—so that she faced away. His hands went to the row of hooks down the back of her dress. Beginning at the base of her neck, he undid them one by one.

"Now this is too much," she protested, trying to wriggle away. "I won't be made to look slatternly."

He held her tight. His breath fell hot and rough on her neck. "You'll be made to look the way I wish you to look. That's the point of a mistress, after all. No doubt Sir Alisdair Kent likes his women looking prim and demure, but you chose me as your travel partner. I have a reputation to maintain."

He unhooked her dress to the midpoint of her back, just between her shoulder blades. Then he worked the widened neckline over the slopes of her shoulders, shimmying it down to a most indecent latitude. The edge of her chemise was exposed, making a lacy ruff of white to frame her exposed cleavage.

After whirling her back to face him, he surveyed his handiwork. Minerva flushed with shame. He'd taken her perfectly respectable traveling gown and turned it into an off-the-shoulder ensemble befitting a pirate wench.

And he wasn't through with her yet. He lifted his hands to her hair and began plucking the pins from her failing chignon. If she weren't faint with hunger and terrified of being stranded penniless in the Midlands, she would not have stood for such treatment.

This went beyond teasing. Could he . . . could he possibly be *envious*?

"Really, Colin. I'm sorry if you resent my regard for Sir Alisdair. But humiliating me this way is hardly going to earn you my good opinion."

"Perhaps not." He pulled the last of the pins free and shook her hair loose about her face. "But I'm convinced it will add greatly to my personal satisfaction. And it will save us both a great many prying questions."

He removed the spectacles from her face and folded them, tucking them inside his breast pocket.

"I need those." She reached for them.

He caught her wrist. "No, you don't. From the moment we walk through those doors, you're not leaving my side, do you hear? Believe me, you don't want any of Halford's guests thinking I mean to share you."

Share her? What sort of den of iniquity were they entering?

"For my part," he said, "I'll behave as if I'm your slavish, besotted, jealous protector."

She bit back an unladylike laugh. "Now *that* will be the role of a lifetime."

"And you . . ." He tipped her chin with a single fingertip. "You had better play your part to perfection, my pet."

"*My* part? I don't know how to be a mistress." Certainly not among dukes. She became an absolute pudding around powerful men.

"Oh, don't sell yourself short. I think you'll do very well indeed. You see, a mistress is a sharp, savage little creature. When it suits her, she can make a man feel as though he's irresistible, desirable, endlessly fascinating. The only man in the world." He leaned closer, lowered his voice to a dark whisper. He was too near for comfort or clarity, just a blur of male ferocity. "She moans as if she means it. And when she's got what she wanted, she'll make it bitingly clear that the man means nothing—absolutely *nothing*—to her at all. I think you were born to that role. Don't you?"

"No, I don't," she said, her voice wavering. "How dare you suggest that I'm some sort of . . . Last night was all your idea."

"I know it."

"And I can hardly be the first woman to pass an enjoyable night in your arms and want little to do with you the following day."

"Of course not. You're merely the most recent in a long, distinguished line. And don't harbor any illusions you'll be the last."

"Then why are you so angry? Why am I singled out for such cruel retribution? What wound can I have possibly caused you, save a miniscule twinge to your pride?"

He stared at her for a long moment. "I don't know."

Then he reached up with both hands and pinched her cheeks. Hard.

"Ow!" Reeling, she clapped her hands over them. "What was that for?"

"You need a blush on those cheeks if you're to play my trollop, and we haven't any rouge." One of his arms shot around her, gathering her close. He traced her bottom lip with his thumb. "And these lips are looking entirely too pursed and pale."

Bending his head, he caught her mouth in a harsh, bruising kiss. His tongue thrust between her lips, making a thorough, claiming sweep of her mouth. Then he caught her bottom lip and gave it a teasing, puppyish tug with his teeth. He left her mouth swollen, stinging with pleasure and pain.

She dug an elbow into his side, using all the strength in her arm to lever some distance between them. He released her, and she stumbled a few steps back.

She touched her fingertips to her mouth, checking for blood. "Are you satisfied now?"

He released a long, frustrated breath. With some distance between them, she could better make out his expression. It was one of lean, wary hunger.

"Not even close, Min." He bent to pick up the trunk. "Not even close."

Chapter Eighteen

I f Winterset Grange looked austere and forbidding from
the outside, its interior resembled something out of Ancient Rome at its peak of debauchery and excess.

Being without her spectacles was both a hindrance and a
blessing. Everywhere Minerva turned, she saw blurred de-
pictions of flesh. Paintings of lascivious nudes covered the
soaring walls, stacked bosom-to-backside three tiers high.
Decadent sculptures winked out from alcoves. Some ambitious decorator had splashed gold leaf over everything.

The sculpture nearest Minerva appeared to be Pan, ca-
vorting and twisting atop a Corinthian column. If she
squinted, she could make out the fine silver and rosy veins
of the stone. Italian, most definitely.

"Such lovely marble, to be so misused." She ran her fingers over the cool, smooth stone. Then withdrew her hand
immediately when she realized the cylindrical protuberance
she'd grasped was not a horn, nor a pipe.

Casting about for a safe place to rest her gaze, she looked
to the wallpaper. A traditional, pleasant gold-and-white toile
pattern of couples dancing. Or *were* they?

She squinted and peered closer, forcing the pattern into focus.

No, the couples weren't dancing.

"Payne! It is you." A man sauntered across the hall to them, dressed in a lazily tied banyan. He seemed young—near to Colin's age, she'd imagine—and he brought with him an air of cultivated dissipation and the vague scent of opium smoke. He was flanked by two women even more scantily clad than he—one smooth and fair, the other titian-haired. Minerva couldn't make out the women's expressions, but their sensuality was a palpable force. She felt their gaze on her, cool and prickling.

This mousy girl can't be one of us, she imagined them thinking.

I'm not, she wanted to shout. She had this brief, vivid vision of giving Colin, his debauched friend, and these two loose women a good dressing down, smashing priapic Pan to the floor, whirling on her heel, and—

But she had no money. Nowhere to go, and no means of getting there. She didn't even have her spectacles.

So Minerva lifted her chin and cocked her hip. She shuffled closer to Colin and moved to prop her arm on his shoulder. Of course, with her vision so hampered, she misjudged and propped her arm on air. She stumbled and fell into him instead, splaying one arm over his chest and trying for all the world to look as though she'd meant to do that.

She didn't think anyone was fooled.

One woman began giggling. The other laughed out loud.

Minerva wanted to sink through the floor.

"Ladies," the man she presumed to be the Duke of Halford said, "you remember my good friend Payne."

"But of course," one of them cooed. "We're old friends, aren't we?"

Now Minerva wanted to sink through the floor and die

there. She understood Colin was angry, but how could he do this to her?

Colin inclined his head. "Always a pleasure, Hal. Sorry to arrive unannounced. Hope you don't mind the imposition."

"Never an imposition! But gods, you did appear from nowhere. I didn't even hear your carriage in the drive." The man relinquished his hold on one of the ladies and gave Colin a genial punch on the arm. "The butler told me you'd arrived, and I didn't believe him. Last I heard, that cousin of yours had you on a short leash."

"I've slipped it, apparently."

"Good for you. Your timing couldn't be better. Prinny's expected to pop round later this week. Girls, go find that puckered housekeeper of mine and tell her to ready Payne's usual suite."

"Yes, your grace."

Halford sent the ladies on their way with a resounding smack to the backside. Then Minerva felt the duke's gaze slide to her. Her skin crawled.

"Now," he said, "let's see to your baggage. Aren't you going to introduce her, Payne? Don't believe I've seen this one before."

"No, you haven't." Colin trailed a reassuring touch down her back. "Melissande is new."

Melissande? She briefly closed her eyes to avoid rolling them.

"Not your usual sort, is she?" the duke asked.

"I've always enjoyed variety. She may look innocent, but in the bedchamber she's very surprising."

"Is she, now?" The duke spoke to her. "Well, then Melissande. Surely my friend will have told you, we're all friends at Winterset Grange. Aren't you going to show your host a bit of appreciation? Perhaps you could start with a kiss."

Her stomach lurched.

Colin's arm tightened around her waist, lashing her to him and forbidding her to move. He said easily, "You'll have to excuse her. She doesn't speak a word of English."

"Not a word?" The duke chuckled. "*Parlez-vous francais*?"

"No French, either. She hails from some tiny Alpine principality. Can't even recall the name of it. They have their own dialect."

"Hm." The duke considered. "Fortunately, pleasure is a universal language." He swept a finger over Minerva's bared shoulder.

She glared at him, seething. Duke or no duke, ruse or no ruse, symposium or no symposium—Minerva refused to abide such treatment. Even if she lacked a proper lady's beauty, accomplishments, and social graces, she was a gentlewoman and a free-thinking individual. She had her dignity.

When Halford's presumptuous touch trailed downward, teasing toward her décolletage, she bristled—and smacked his hand away.

Then she bared her teeth and gave a little growl. Violence was a universal language, too.

"Watch yourself, Halford." Colin tensed. No good humor in his voice now, only threat. "This one's not to be trifled with. A friend of my cousin's in the War Office asked me to keep on eye on her. There are rumors, suspicions. The Crown's intelligence suggests she's either a princess in exile or a cold-blooded assassin."

The duke gave a bark of laugher. "Judging by that bruise on your jaw, my wager's on the latter. But speaking of wagers, come along. Everyone's in the card room."

The duke turned on his heel—his bare heel, for he seemed to be wearing nothing beneath the banyan—and padded down a long corridor.

Colin and Minerva lagged several steps behind.

"Now I'm a cold-blooded assassin?" she hissed. "Where do you come up with these things?"

He shushed her, purposely slowing his paces so that they'd drop even farther behind. "It's called improvisation, remember? I had to offer some explanation for your behavior."

Ahead of them, the duke called out to a friend as he turned a corner.

Once Halford was out of sight, Minerva stopped dead in the corridor, wrenching out of Colin's embrace. She didn't understand how he could do this to her—be so protective and self-sacrificing one moment, and then so patronizing the next.

"I do not deserve this," she whispered. "Just because I made the mistake of accepting your . . . *attentions* . . . last night, that does not make me a whore. How dare you lump me in with those debased women?"

"Believe me, those women would not call themselves debased. And what makes you think they're whores? Perhaps they're ladies, every bit as pedigreed and well-bred as you, who understand what you don't. How to enjoy themselves. How to have a good time."

"What?" She jabbed a finger in her own chest. "I understand how to enjoy myself. I understand how to have a good time."

He cocked his head and drawled, "Oh, of course you do."

"How dare you." Now she jabbed the same finger in his chest. "How dare you bring me to this place and subject me to that leering, grabby duke."

He grasped her wrist and lowered his voice. "How dare I, indeed."

She didn't have to see his expression to know he was angry. The fury radiated from him.

"How dare I risk my life to save yours, when you all

but threw yourself to the highwayman. How dare I bring you to a comfortable house, where we can find food and a night's shelter after a day of rambling woods and fields. How dare I."

His hands slid up her shoulders and stopped halfway between her head and neck. As though he were trying to decide whether to kiss her or throttle her.

She would put up a fight, either way.

"We're going to go into that card room now. We will eat, drink, and play their game. As soon as we're able, we'll slip upstairs and have a good night's sleep. I swear to you, you'll leave this house tomorrow morning with both your virtue and that disapproving personality intact—tucked safe inside your little shell—so long as you do two things." He gave her head a little shake. "Stay close to me and play your part."

"The part of a cold-blooded assassin? I could get inspired for that."

"The part of my lover." His fingers slid up and through her hair, dragging exquisite sensation over her scalp. "Search deep inside this clever mind, and try to see if you can't dredge up the imagination to pretend. To convince those around us that you find something in me to admire. That against all odds, you actually prefer my company to a clod of dirt."

The ragged hurt in his voice took her by surprise. So here was the reason for his changing moods and erratic behavior. Somehow, in attempting to guard her own fragile emotions, she'd managed to make *him* feel lower than dirt.

"Colin . . ." She stroked his lapel. "I can convince them I like you. That won't require imagination."

This thumb traced her jaw, and his voice went husky. "Won't it?"

"But no one will believe we're lovers. You heard those

women laugh. You said it yourself, back in Spindle Cove. No one will believe you want *me*."

With a groan, he slid his hands down her back. Cupping her backside in two hands, he lifted her and pressed her into the nearest alcove. The possession in his manner thrilled her, and so did the press of his hard, muscled body against hers.

He pressed a kiss to her ear. "What if I said I was an idiot that night?"

"Then I would agree."

"What if I told you everything's changed?" He kissed her neck. "That in the past four-and-twenty hours I've wanted to murder three different men just for daring to touch you— one of them a duke. That I am desperate with longing, consumed with wanting you. As I've wanted no other woman in all my debauched, misspent life."

His tongue traced her pulse, and her breath caught. "Then I would doubt you," she breathed.

Why?"

"Because . . ." *Because I doubt myself.* "Because I know how easily you lie."

He clutched her bottom, bringing her pelvis flush with his. His hardness ground against her, sending pleasure rushing through her veins.

"Feel that?" he growled.

She nodded. Good Lord, how could she not?

"I've been hard for you for days, Minerva. Since before we even left Spindle Cove. If you believe nothing else, believe this." He rocked against her. "This doesn't lie."

Colin was done pretending.

He ushered Minerva into the card room. After he'd greeted the half dozen familiar faces assembled about the green felt tabletop and introduced his feisty foreign mistress-or-murderess Melissande, he took his own chair.

And taking Minerva by the hips, he put her on his lap. Nestled her sweet little backside on his left thigh, draped one arm about her shoulders, and let his hand dangle directly over her breast. With lazy motions, he traced the delicate border where her altered neckline chafed against her exposed décolletage.

"Stay close," he whispered, nuzzling her ear. While he was in the neighborhood, he took the chance to catch her tiny earlobe with his teeth.

In sum, he made the two of them very, very cozy. Not to create appearances for Halford's sake. Not to prove a point to her, or to anyone.

Simply because he wanted her. And he was done pretending otherwise.

"Well, Payne." The duke reached for the deck of cards. "The game is brag."

Colin surveyed the coins and gambling tokens scattered on the table. "Stake me a sovereign's worth, will you? I'm not carrying much coin on me."

"But of course." The duke slid him two stacks of shillings, each ten pieces tall.

Minerva tensed in his lap.

"Hush," he murmured against her hair. "Trust me." She should understand this was necessary. A few hours at the card table earned their board and keep.

She made a doubtful noise in her throat. But she kept still.

"Be a good host, Hal, and have one of these liveried jackanapes fetch my lady food and wine? She could do with some nourishment."

"So could you, from the looks of you."

"Yes, well." Colin grinned. "We've quite exhausted each other over the past few days."

The gamblers around the table laughed heartily. The duke merely waved for servants to bring refreshments and began to deal the cards. Halford was always all business, in the card room.

Colin turned his attention to the cards. Minerva turned hers to the food.

She took care of him, in small ways. While he concentrated on the hand he was dealt, she had his glass filled with claret. Now she prepared for him a slice of roast pork, sandwiched between two halves of a buttered roll. In the process, she dabbed a bit of butter on her thumb. She put her thumb to her mouth and sucked it clean. Colin knew she didn't intend the motion to be coy or provocative. Which made it arousing as hell.

He'd noted this about her, ever since that first night in the turret. There was an earthy, natural sensuality in her, but it only emerged when she felt confident. Or when she'd had a little wine. He wondered what it would take to coax *this* Minerva out into the world, permanently. She would need a steady supply of assurance, he supposed. Perhaps her participation in the Royal Geological Society could give her that, to some degree. But the right man could do far more. The right man could plant seeds of confidence, deep inside her, and nurture them to healthy, robust vines that reached and stretched, offering sweet, bountiful fruit.

The only fruit *she* cared for at the moment was the plate of grapes and apricots before them. Filling her famished belly was clearly her primary goal, and she went about it with energy—devouring wedges of cheese and slices of ham. When a passing servant offered her a tray of bite-sized tarts, she abandoned her wineglass with an eager gasp and reached for a tart with either hand.

She popped one in her mouth and offered the other to him.

Rather than take it with his fingers, he grasped her wrist to hold it steady. Then he devoured the morsel of pastry directly from her fingers, letting his tongue swirl over her fingertips. She sighed, and the little sound was more honey-sweet and sinfully delicious than a jam tart could ever hope to be.

Halford cleared his throat. "It's your bet, Payne."

Colin shook himself and sent a shilling wobbling toward the center of the table. "Yes, of course."

He played, they ate. When they'd both consumed their fill, Colin waved for servants to remove the plates and trays.

Minerva made herself comfortable in his lap. Her fingers curled into the fringe of hair at his nape, toying idly. She stroked up and down the tendons of his neck, soothing away the tension coiled there. Little brushes of kindness he didn't deserve.

He pressed his lips to her ear and whispered, "You do know I'm sorry? For earlier."

She gave a slight nod.

With a breathy groan, he slid his arm to her waist and gathered her close. She laid her head on his chest.

He kissed her crown. "Sleep, if you wish."

She released a full-body sigh and melted in his embrace. This easy intimacy between them . . . it made sense, he supposed, given their adventures over the past few days and nights. But still, it came as a surprise.

He'd been physically intimate with many women, and he'd felt emotionally close to others. But thus far, he'd assiduously worked to keep the two social spheres separate. There were women Colin counted as friends, and then there were women he bedded. Anytime he'd allowed the two groups to overlap, it meant trouble.

Minerva Highwood had meant nothing but trouble to him, since the very first.

But by God, he'd returned the favor. As she curled into his chest, she felt so small and fragile against him. In the past four-and-twenty hours, she'd walked untold miles across the

English countryside, surrendered all her money at gunpoint, pulled a knife on a highwayman, and entered a house that oozed such Bacchanalian excess as to send a gently-bred virgin screaming. And all this, just one day on the heels of her first proper orgasm.

Never once had she dissolved into helpless tears. Or begged him to just please take her home. Not one woman in a hundred would handle herself so well in similar circumstances.

He made a vow to himself, then and there. If he did nothing else right in his life, he would do this: deliver Minerva Highwood to Edinburgh for her scientific presentation. On time, in one piece. And with her virtue intact.

Some way, somehow, he would make *these* good intentions come out right.

He gently stroked her hair and back with his left hand as he gathered his cards with the right. "Sleep," he murmured again.

As she shifted in his lap, her thigh rubbed against him. His body's reaction was immediate, instinctual. Blood rushed to his groin, hardening his cock and loosening his tenuous hold on those cherished principles. He wanted her physically, and he couldn't pretend otherwise.

But he must endeavor to hide this other, more visceral reaction—the overwhelming, tenderness rising in his chest.

The simple, unthinkable fact that he *cared*.

Chapter Nineteen

Once again, Minerva woke in his arms. She was growing accustomed to waking like this—embraced by his heat, his strength, his clove-spiced scent. She didn't hurry to rouse herself, but hovered in that half-dream world for just a minute longer. Sighing into his waistcoat and hugging his neck tight.

She trusted this man. He was a known liar and shameless rake, but she trusted him. Enough to fall asleep in his arms amid all this debauchery.

She blinked at the card table, trying to bring the confusion of cards and coins into focus. How much time had passed? It felt very late. Most of the players seemed to have already retired for the night. Only Colin and Halford remained.

She stared hard at the heap of shilling pieces in front of them. Had he increased their funds enough to continue their journey? Those coins had numbered twenty at the outset of the game.

Now she counted . . .

Four.

Her heart stopped. Oh, God. How could he? She'd *trusted* him, and he was losing everything.

Then she shifted her gaze to the cards in Colin's hand. What she saw gave her reason to breathe again. His cards looked promising. She couldn't make them out exactly—not without her spectacles. But she could see they were all red and they were all face cards. Simple logic told her, that had to add up to something good. A pair of knaves, at the least.

She looked to the center of the table, heaped with coins. More than enough money to replace what the highwayman had taken. Perhaps this was all part of Colin's plan.

"A poxy pair of nines, that's all." The duke threw down his cards. "I'm sure you can do better, Payne."

Yes! He could. She curled her fingers around the edge of his waistcoat pocket, faint with excitement.

Colin held his silence for a time. "Sorry to prove you wrong, Hal," he said, "but you have me beat." He laid his cards facedown on the table before him.

With a greedy laugh, the Duke of Halford gathered his winnings.

Minerva's hand slipped from Colin's pocket. She was stunned. Aghast. Four shillings. They were down to four shillings now. She had to get him away from this card table before he lost everything they had.

But how? She couldn't even speak to him, thanks to his wild tales. These people all believed her to be Melissande, a refugee princess from some tiny Alpine principality. Or, alternatively, an assassin who just might garrote them all in their sleep. And in her spare time, Colin's mistress.

His worldly, sensual mistress.

Minerva bit her lip. Perhaps there was a way to lure him from this betting table without words.

Adjusting her weight in his lap, she stretched up one hand to stroke his hair. The heavy brown locks sifted between her fingers, stroking like feathers over her palm. With her other hand, she teased loose his cravat knot until the entire length of fabric slid from his neck in a slow, sensual glide. She thought she heard him moan, a little.

She nuzzled into his neck. The scent of brandy clung to his skin, dark and intoxicating. Without her spectacles, at this close range, he was little more than an unshaven blur. But he was an achingly handsome blur, nonetheless. Craning her neck, she kissed his cheek.

His breath caught, and she almost lost her nerve to continue. But she'd started this, and now there was no retreating.

Tilting her head, she pressed a kiss to the underside of his jaw.

Across the table, the duke gave a dry laugh.

Minerva's heart stalled. She froze, lips pressed to Colin's unshaven throat. What had she been thinking? A brazen seductress? *Her*? Of course Halford wouldn't believe it. No one in his right mind would believe it.

"Payne," the duke said, "perhaps you'd care to sit out this round? It would seem the fetching Melissande needs putting to bed."

Colin's Adam's apple bobbed in his throat. "She can wait."

"Perhaps," the duke replied, with a knowing chuckle. "But can you? I've never seen a man's knuckles quite that shade of pale."

Exhilaration swarmed through her body. Halford *did* believe it. Colin *was* affected. She *was* a seductress. But she still hadn't succeeded in her goal—pulling Colin away from the card table.

Minerva redoubled her efforts. She wove her fingers tight into his hair. She licked his neck, dragging her tongue from his pulse to his earlobe. With the tip of her tongue, she traced his ear's every whorl and ridge.

"Upstairs," she whispered. "Take me upstairs. Now."

Colin's hand fisted in the back of her dress, stealing her breath with a swift yank. But the sharp, secret rebuke only inflamed Minerva's rebellious nature. Whose idea had it been for her to play this role? He had no right to complain. Besides, a part of her was enjoying this. Judging by the hard, heated ridge pulsing against her thigh, a part of him was enjoying it, too.

This doesn't lie.

She kissed his collarbone, dropping her fingers to his shirt closures. Slipping loose one, then two, and snaking her fingers inside to caress his smooth, muscled chest.

The duke observed, "You're getting rather low in your stack, Payne. Since you're so uninterested in enjoying Melissande yourself, perhaps you'd care to make a friendly wager. I'd lay a great deal of money against such obvious and abundant . . . charms."

Minerva had to work, very hard, not to betray her understanding with a sour look. Or a violent heave of her stomach.

Colin tensed as well. "Tread with caution, Halford."

"Why? It's not as though she can understand a word we say." The duke shuffled and dealt the cards. "One hand, one winner. You put your girl on the table, and I'll toss in one of mine. Whoever wins can enjoy double the amusement tonight."

Every muscle in Colin's body went instantly hard as stone. One of his hands balled in a fist. The other went to the pistol tucked at his hip.

Minerva's blood turned icy in her veins. These protective impulses were all well and good, but the last thing she needed was for Colin to start trouble with the duke. They'd be cast out from Winterset Grange—running through the night this time, with nothing but the clothes on their backs.

A matter of minutes stood between them and disaster. But she could tell from his stormy expression, Colin wasn't thinking more than ten seconds into the future.

Lifting Minerva off his lap, he pushed to his feet. He leveled a finger at the duke. "Don't you *ever*—"

Smack.

Minerva slapped him, square across the face.

Colin blinked at her, clearly stunned.

She lifted her shoulders. He'd left her no choice. She had to stop the men's argument somehow. And Colin couldn't start a fight with the duke if she started a fight with Colin first. So . . .

Smack. She used her left hand this time, whipping his head the other direction.

Then she stood back, seething as dramatically as she imagined a dark-haired Alpine princess-assassin with hot blood could possibly seethe. Adopting a nonspecific accent—something halfway between Italian and French—she narrowed her eyes and said, "Yoooo. Bass. *Tard*."

His brow wrinkled. "What?"

Oh, for God's sake.

"Yoo!" She shoved at his chest with both hands. "Bass. *Tard*."

Rising from his chair, Halford laughed. "I believe she's calling you a bastard, friend. You're in for it now. Seems the wench understands a bit of English after all. Whoops."

At last, Colin caught on. "B-b-but Melissande, I can explain."

She circled him, snarling. "Bass. Tard. Bass. Tard."

When he spoke again, she could tell he was struggling not to laugh. "Calm down, pet. And whatever you do . . . please, I beg you, don't go into one of your fits of wild temper and uncontrollable passion."

Incorrigible rogue. She had no doubt he meant that as a dare.

Well, then. She would accept it.

Minerva reached for a glass of claret on the table. She downed most of it in a single gulp, then dashed the remainder straight in Colin's face. Wine splashed them both. Ruby-red rivulets streaked down his stunned expression.

With a little growl, she threw herself at him, catching him by the shoulders and wrapping her legs over his hips. She licked the wine from his face, running her tongue over his cheeks, his chin . . . even his eyebrows. And then she ended her madwoman mistress performance with a slow, deep, savage kiss on the lips that had him moaning into her mouth and clutching her backside in both hands.

"Upstairs," she growled against his lips. "Now."

At last, he carried her from the room. And kissed her until they were halfway down the corridor. There he stopped, apparently unable to hold back the laughter one moment more. He pressed her to the wall and wheezed helplessly into her neck, shaking with laughter.

Well, she was glad someone found this amusing.

Still laughing, he set her on her feet and tugged her up a flight of stairs and down a side corridor. He flung open the door of a suite, obviously familiar to him. In decor, it suffered the same excess of gold leaf and dearth of good taste as the rest of Winterset Grange.

"Oh, Min. That was excellent."

"That"—she banged the door shut—"was humiliating."

"Well, it was a first-rate mistress performance." He shrugged out of his coat, set aside the pistol, and began unbuttoning his waistcoat. "What the devil was that, with the . . . the licking, and the wine? And how on earth did you think to—"

"It's called improvisation! Running down the slope and all." She thrust her hands through her wild, unbound hair, making a frantic survey of the room until she found Francine's trunk, tucked neatly beneath a scroll-legged side table. "I had to get you away from the card table before you lost all our money and ruined everything. We already owe him sixteen shillings from my sovereign. Aren't debts of honor supposed to be paid immediately?"

She crossed to him and boldly reached inside his waistcoat. As her fingers brushed against his chest, she heard his breath catch.

"I need these," she explained, suddenly timid. She withdrew her spectacles from his inside pocket and fit them on her face. It felt good to put the room in focus.

She only wished the lenses could help her make Colin out. Just what had he been doing downstairs? *Trying* to end their journey here? Perhaps he'd had enough of her and Francine and had decided he'd rather sponge off the duke's generosity at Winterset Grange until his birthday.

"It's the Shilling Club," he said. "We play with shillings, but they stand for a hundred pounds each."

"A hundred pounds? *Each*?" She felt faint. She pressed a hand to her brow. "But how will we—"

"We won't." He removed the waistcoat and set it aside. "I always lose, I never pay. They know I'll be good for it in the end."

"But why lose at all? I could make out your cards on that last hand. They were better than the duke's. You *let* him win."

He tugged loose his cravat and slung it over the back of a chair. "Yes, well . . . everyone loves a gracious loser. That's why I'm always welcome at any card table, any evening, here or in London. I have no shortage of friends."

"*Friends*." She spat the word. "What makes people like that your friends? The fact that they'll allow you to sit at their table and lose heaps of money? That hardly fits any definition of friendship I know."

He didn't answer. Merely sat on the edge of the bed to remove his boots.

"They don't respect you, Colin. How could they? They don't know you at all. Not the real you."

"And what makes *you* an expert on the real me?"

"I suppose I'm not. I'm not even certain *you* know who you are. You just become whomever the situation requires."

He kicked his boots aside and passed wordlessly into a connecting room. Presumably a dressing or bathing area. She heard the sounds of water splashing into a basin.

She raised her voice. "I mean, I am beginning to notice a pattern. All your guises are variations on the same theme. The charming, fun-loving rogue with the not-so-deeply hidden pain. Obviously, it works for you nicely. But doesn't it grow tiresome?"

"Tiresome indeed." He strolled back into the room with his hair damp and his shirt untucked and cuffed to the elbows. "Min, please. I'm a little drunk and extremely fatigued. Can we hold the rest of this character dissection for the morning?"

She released a sigh. "I suppose."

"Then get in bed. I'm exhausted."

With a bit of contortion, she managed to undo the hooks at the back of her gown. She drew the tattered, wine-stained silk down over her hips and cast it aside on the chaise longue. The thought that she had nothing else to wear tomorrow was lowering indeed. At least in the morning, she could ring for a proper bath. For now, she did her best with the washbasin and soap.

After rebuttoning her shift, she lay down on the bed next to him, staring up at the ceiling.

A few minutes passed.

"You're not sleeping," she said.

"Neither are you."

She bit her lip. Something lay heavy on her mind, and she didn't have anyone else to tell. "He doesn't know me, either."

His reply was groggy. "Who doesn't?"

"Sir Alisdair Kent." At the mention of his name, she felt

the sudden tensing from Colin's side of the bed. "I mean, he knows of my scientific findings, and he admires my intellect. But he doesn't know the real me. I've conducted all my Society business through written correspondence, and I've always signed myself M. R. Highwood. So Sir Alisdair . . . well, he thinks I'm a man."

Several moments passed.

"He's in for a great surprise."

She giggled up at the ceiling. "Indeed he is." Whether it would be a pleasant or unpleasant surprise, she was afraid to guess.

"But that's odd, " he said. "There was genuine affection in that letter."

"Mere friendly interest, I'm sure."

"I'm not so convinced. Perhaps he's in love with you."

Her heart gave a queer flutter. Not at the idea, but at the sound of that word from his lips: *love*.

"How could that be?" She rolled onto her side, bending her elbow and propping her head with her hand. "Didn't you hear what I just said? Sir Alisdair thinks I'm a man."

"Oh, I heard you." Devilish eyes slid to meet hers. "Perhaps he thinks you're a man, and he's in love with you. Poor fellow has some heartbreak ahead of him, if so."

She frowned, unsure of his implications.

He chuckled low. "Don't listen to me, pet. My bollocks are aching, and my pride is smarting. I'm foxed, and I'm feeling very wicked tonight. If you know what's best for you, you'll ignore me and go to sleep."

"Why are your bollocks aching?" She sat up. "Were you injured somehow? Was it the highwayman?"

With a groan, he threw his wrist over his eyes. "My dear girl, you might be a brilliant geologist, but your grasp of biology is dim indeed."

She dropped her gaze to the front of his breeches. They were impressively tented.

"Go to sleep, M."

"No, I don't think I will. Not yet." With sudden determination, she plucked at the buttons of his falls. She had one side completely unfastened before he managed to struggle up on his elbows.

"What are you doing?"

"Indulging my curiosity." She snaked her hand under the fabric, and he flinched. A heady surge of power rushed through her. The wine she'd drunk downstairs was doing its work, melting away her inhibitions. She wanted to know and see and touch it—this most honest, *real* part of him.

This doesn't lie.

She said, "I did as you asked and played your mistress downstairs, and I've earned this much. I want to see and touch it properly. I never had the chance, before."

"Mother of—"

"Do be calm. What was it you told me? Think of it as an . . . an excavation." Smiling, she curled her fingers around his hard, hot length. "It's in the name of science."

It's in the name of science.

Hah. That was a first-rate line, that was. Ranked right up there with, "You could save my life tonight," and "Darling, teach me what it means to love." Colin made a mental note to remember that one for the future.

Then her hand closed around his swollen cock, and his mental slate blanked.

"Good Lord," he heard himself mutter. This was dangerous. He was half drunk and scarcely in control of himself as it was.

Rules, he reminded himself. He had rules.

But curiously, none of them covered virginal caressing in the name of *science*. Leave it to Minerva Highwood to transform bedsport into a completely new endeavor.

She held him gently for a moment, rubbing her thumb up and down the underside of his cock. The slight, delicious friction did more to tease than satisfy. Then she released her grip and began tugging down his breeches and smallclothes, wrestling them over his hips.

"They're in the way," she explained, when he sent her a scandalized look.

He let his head fall back on the pillow, resigned. He had no idea how to arrest this scientific exploration, and truthfully—no desire to do so anyway. He helped her by lifting his hips and kicking out of his breeches, once she had the fabric bunched around his knees.

"Oh, why stop there," he muttered, gathering his shirt in both hands and drawing it over his head before flopping back onto the mattress. "There. Now you have your life model. Explore at will."

And she did. She explored his body—every inch of it—at a leisurely pace that made him fair crazed with desire. He began to regret offering himself as a subject of experimentation. When she dragged a light touch down the center of his chest, a damned snail could have raced her fingertip.

Too exhausted and intoxicated to do otherwise, Colin simply lay there and endured. Suffered her slow, sweet exploration of his arms, chest, abdomen—God, his *nipples*. He emitted a sound that he feared was not quite manly when she grazed his nipples. All the while, his ignored cock leaped and strained for her attention, arcing up to his navel in what he assumed must be quite livid shades of plum and dusky red.

"If you mean to torture me," he gritted out, "you're doing an excellent job of it."

"Am I?" She skipped her fingers over his collarbone. She was deliberately teasing him now, the minx.

With a curse, he grabbed her hand and dragged her touch where they both wanted it. The relief was immediate, intense. And nowhere near enough.

"Goodness." She spoke the word in an awed, highly gratifying tone that made him wonder why he didn't debauch virgins more often. "It's so very . . . stiff."

"You make it that way." Unable to resist, he curled his hand over hers and silently urged her to grip tighter, showing her how to stroke. She obliged him for a few tantalizing pulls.

"What do you call it?" she asked. "I know there are different names."

"Names? Like Peter, Belvedere, Sir Charles Grandison?" His breath was shaky. "It's just my cock, pet."

She stroked down to the root and grasped the base tight. "Your cock."

Oh, holy God. She drove him wild when she talked that way.

"I quite like your cock. Smooth as talc on the outside." She slid her hand up again. "But like granite beneath."

He laughed. A strained, *ha, ha, ha, I may die of this* laugh. "Well. We both know how you love rocks."

"I do love rocks, as a matter of fact." A coquettish smile crept into her voice. "I find them utterly fascinating. I'm forever taking them in hand. Exploring their every ridge and contour." She skimmed a petal-soft fingertip over the head of his cock, tracing the flared ridge of the crown and the dewy slit at the tip. Then her touch teased down his length, all the way to the root. "Some of them have very interesting veins."

"I don't suppose you ever—in the name of science, of course—put these utterly fascinating objects in your mouth?"

She froze. "What?"

He slapped a hand over his eyes. This—*this*—was why he had the rules about virgins. The lewd request had just flowed out of him, in a lascivious drawl.

"I'm drunk, Min." He waved his hand in dismissal. "Forget I said anything."

"How could I forget you said *that*?" Her hand gripped his cock tight, as if she could wring an answer from its tip. "What a suggestion. Do women really . . ." She swallowed, audibly. "*Really?*"

"Would you like to hear a very bald, very earthy, completely scientific truth?" He struggled up on his elbow, reaching one hand toward her face. He cupped her cheek in his hand, traced her parted lips with his thumb. "You," he whispered hoarsely, "have the most goddamned erotic mouth I've ever seen. These sweet, plump lips drive me wild. It's impossible to look at you and not . . . not *wonder*, how it would be."

Her eyes went wide. "You've *wondered*."

He nodded. "Oh yes."

"Y-you've actually spent time—"

"Hours, probably, if you added it up."

"Thinking about—"

"This." He slid his thumb between her startled lips, pressing it deep into her hot, wet mouth. "Yes."

They stared at each other, unmoving. Then, after a prolonged, excruciating hesitation, she closed her lips around his thumb. Her tongue curled beneath it, gently tickling. Stroking. A bolt of sensation shot straight to his cock. He groaned with helpless pleasure.

"God, *yes*. That's the way." He slid his thumb out half an inch, then pushed it in again, deeper. Her cheeks hollowed as she lightly suckled. "You are unspeakably clever, Min. And so . . . so damned lovely."

She moaned a little as he withdrew his thumb from her

mouth. Her lips cinched him so tightly, he heard a small popping sound when it finally slipped free.

"Holy God," he muttered, collapsing to the mattress. "You'll kill me."

She regarded his cock, holding it steady in her grip and giving it a bold, assessing look. Just the thought of watching his length disappear into her mouth . . . it was almost enough to bring him off, right then.

But then his damned conscience caught up with him. "Min, you needn't . . . hell, you really shouldn't."

"Why not? You want it, don't you?"

"With every corpuscle in my body, believe me. But I can't ask it. And you shouldn't offer. It would . . . it would make things awkward in the morning."

She convulsed with laughter. "We can't have that. Because we've been getting along so smoothly as it is."

With a toss of her head, she flipped that mane of long, dark wavy hair over her shoulder, and then her head—that enticing mouth—began a slow yet steady descent. She was true scientific adventuress, this girl.

Rules.

He had to have some rule against this. And even if he didn't have a standing rule—any code of conduct that allowed him to slide his cock into a virgin's mouth but not her cunny? Well, that code probably needed some rethinking.

But then her sweet kiss was upon him. And then he was *in* the hot, slick heaven of her mouth. No more thinking would happen tonight.

"Oh," he moaned, as her warmth enveloped him. "Oh, Minerva."

Her lips slid downward, slipping over the swollen crown of his erection and partway down the shaft. Then she suckled lightly, her tongue caressing him in sweet waves. His hips arched off the bed, and he cursed.

She pulled away, leaving his cock glistening, aching, and quite possibly hard enough to crush stone. Colin struggled to master his disappointment. She'd performed her experiment, and now she was satisfied. He would not, could not ask for more.

But rather than abandon him entirely, she began to press little kisses up and down his length. He closed his eyes, reveling in the coy whispers of sensation. It was the sweetest torture he'd ever known.

When she took him in her mouth again, he slid deeper this time. Near halfway inside. Her slow, slippery retreat drove him wild with need. He writhed on the bedclothes, grappling for restraint.

No restraint to be found.

Rutting bass-tard that he was, he reached for her and did what he'd been longing to do for ages. He tangled his hand in all that dark, silky hair and made a tight fist. And then he guided her, teaching her how to please him. Dragging her lush, hot mouth up and down his length, in a deep, steady rhythm.

He was a cad. He was a monster. He was going to burn in the fires of hell.

It would be worth it.

"Yes," he told her, wincing at the exquisite pleasure. "Min, that's so good. You're so good."

He relaxed his grip on her hair, and she backed off him again, sitting straight.

"You don't—" He gulped for air. "You don't have to continue." As if that made him some kind of generous saint.

She only smiled. First, she removed her spectacles, folded them, and set them aside. Then she readjusted her position, hiking her shift to her knees and straddling his sprawled leg as she bent to once again take him in her mouth.

He groaned. She was such a quick study. This was serious

now. Shameless, he watched those plump, ripe lips sliding up down his cock. The tight, wet friction was only part of the pleasure. The rest came from the sweet triumph of being stroked by *her*, pleased by *her*. Most of all, just being *inside* her, in some way. He'd been wanting this so damn badly. Those nights of lying *next* to her, wanting to be inside her. To be part of her.

To feel joined, and not alone.

He stroked a fond caress down her body and reached for the hem of her shift, drawing it up. He slid a hand beneath the frail linen, sliding a touch up the bare expanse of her thigh. She moaned, spreading her legs a little. He took the encouragement, stroking higher still. Until he cupped her sex in his hand, dewy and flushed, guarded by enticing curls.

Yes. God, yes.

He slid a finger between her slippery folds, rubbing up and down her sex. She whimpered and ground her hips, seeking his touch. He slipped his middle finger inside her tight sheath, moving in slow, shallow thrusts that she began to mimic with her mouth. When he moved faster, so did she. When he pressed his finger deeper, she sank down, taking him almost to the root.

The pleasure was so acute, so intense. He couldn't take much more of this.

He cupped his hand, so that the heel of his palm would rub against her pearl. Moaning with pleasure, she pressed into his touch. She rolled her hips at a brisk, frantic pace, and for the first time, her own rhythm faltered.

"*Min*," he gritted out.

She lifted her head, glassy-eyed and flushed with arousal. His left hand remained blissfully lodged between her thighs. He put his right hand over hers where she gripped the base of his erection.

"Like this." He dragged her hand up and down. "Yes."

They worked each other in a firm, steady rhythm, staring into one another's eyes as the pleasure mounted. Until her eyelids flickered closed, and little frown lines appeared between her eyebrows.

"Colin," she gasped.

"Yes, love. That's it." His own head rolled back on the pillow, as he stroked them both faster. "That's it. That's—"

She cried out. Her intimate muscles clenched and pulsed around the buried girth of his finger. And then his own climax erupted, sending pure bliss quaking through his body and white light flashing behind his eyelids.

In the aftermath, he kept his eyes closed. He slid his finger from her sex and drew her shift back down her thighs. His chest rose and fell with his heavy breaths. He tried to coax her down to lie beside him, but she stayed where she was— straddling his leg, hand curled around his flagging erection.

Now that curiosity had been satisfied and her own need slaked, he expected her to recoil from him. Surely she'd realize how callously he'd just used her, and what liberties he'd taken with her body and her trust. He fully expected her to hate and loathe him with a renewed—nay, unprecedented passion.

When he finally summoned the fortitude to lift his head and gauge her reaction, he found her replacing her spectacles. Her expression did not hint at hatred or loathing, but rather . . .

Scientific interest. Of course.

"Oh, Colin." She dabbed a fingertip to his sticky abdomen, then rubbed her fingers together, as though testing the quality of his seed. "That was *fascinating*."

Chapter Twenty

He'd been right. Things were a bit awkward in the morning.

Leaving Colin to his sleep, Minerva crept out of bed as stealthily as possible and rang for the maid. She met the servant at the door to the suite, using ridiculous pantomime to ask for a hot bath drawn in the adjoining room.

She felt a pinch of anxiety as the servants brought up the heated water and tub, cringing to imagine how this all looked. A young, unmarried woman sharing a room with a naked, sleeping lord? But the maids acted bored and businesslike, not shocked. Minerva soon realized that for servants at Winterset Grange, this was hardly a scandal. It was merely . . . Friday.

Lord, it was *Friday*. The number of days before the symposium was dwindling, and here they'd barely made it one third of the way to Edinburgh.

Despite the urgency that calculation implied, she took her time in the bath. The maids had brought her scented oils and soaps, rose petals for the bathwater and cool cucumber slices to soothe her eyes. Minerva accepted assistance in washing her hair. Then she dismissed the servants and lingered in the tub until the water went cool, feeling the soreness and tension ebb from her muscles.

As she toweled dry, she rued the fact she had nothing to wear but the same beleaguered shift and ruined silk gown from yesterday. Perhaps there were spare clothes to be found somewhere in this house, but she didn't know that she could stomach wearing some mistress's castoffs. But then her eye fell on her trunk. The trunk that held Francine's footprint, Minerva's scholarly notes, and . . .

Her trousseau.

Wrapped in the towel, she padded across the room and undid the buckles on the trunk. Carefully laying aside all her journals and papers, she removed the rolls of white cloth padding the plaster cast. For the most part, these bulky cylinders of white were embroidered bed sheets and tablecloths and pillowcases. But there were other items, of a more personal nature.

Lacy chemises. Gauzy fichus. Bosom-lifting corsets. Silk stockings and ribbon garters.

She'd forgotten these things, tucked inside her trunk for years now. It had seemed she'd never have a use for such sensual, indulgent attire. She'd all but given up on the idea of marriage.

After this journey—heavens, after last *night*—marriage seemed less likely than ever. But that didn't mean she couldn't use these things, or that she must deny this side of herself. The items in this trunk were elegant and sensual, and they were *hers*. Whether or not she had a husband to display them for.

She unfurled a pristine white chemise, low-cut in both the front and back and worked with lace at the neckline. Setting aside the sprig of dried lavender tucked inside for freshness, she drew the sheer fabric over her body and stood before the mirror.

Twisting to view herself from different angles, she ran her hands down her torso, pulling the sheer fabric tight. Until the wine-colored buds of her nipples showed through, and the dark triangle between her legs as well. She skimmed her hands down her body again, enjoying the soft heat of her flesh beneath the cool fabric. The gentle curves of her breasts, belly, and hips. As she watched her own hands stroking over her skin, her pulse quickened.

This body *wanted*.

This body *was* wanted, by him.

In the bedchamber, Colin stirred and mumbled in his sleep. Minerva jumped, then pressed her hands to her mouth to keep from laughing aloud.

She donned a pair of sheer silk stockings and tied them with pink ribbons. She called the maid back in to lace her into a French *divorce* corset that lifted and separated her breasts to quite flattering effect. With reluctance, she put on the blue silk again. But the effect was much better with her pristine, lacy chemise peeking out at the top. And she found an embroidered white overskirt in her trunk, rather like a pinafore. It covered most of the wine stains.

Her hair was still damp, so rather than pin it all up, she merely gathered a few locks from the front and secured them with tortoiseshell combs. The rest of her hair hung loose and heavy about her shoulders.

"Good morning."

She turned to see Colin tangled in the sheets, propped up on one elbow and rubbing his unshaven face with the other hand.

"Good morning," she said, resisting the urge to make a girlish twirl and beg for his approval.

He blinked and focused his gaze. A smile crooked his lips. "Well, Min. Don't you look pretty."

Giddy joy fizzed through her. It was a simple compliment,

but a perfect one. She would have doubted him, if he'd called her "lovely" or "beautiful" or "stunning." But "pretty"? That, she could almost believe.

"Really?" she asked. She wouldn't mind hearing it again.

"You're the picture of a fetching country lass." His gaze raked over her body and lingered on her enhanced, lace-framed cleavage. "You make me want to find a hayloft."

She blushed, just as she supposed any fetching country lass would.

He yawned. "How long have you been out of bed?"

"An hour. Perhaps more."

"And I didn't wake?" His brow wrinkled. "Remarkable."

The maid brought a breakfast tray. While Colin rose from bed and went about his own toilette, Minerva feasted on coddled eggs, buttered rolls, and chocolate.

"Did you save me any?" he asked, strolling back into the room some quarter-hour later.

She looked up, saw him, and let her spoon clatter to the table. "Now, that's just unfair."

Fifteen minutes. Twenty, at most. And in that time, he'd bathed, shaved, and dressed in a spotless pair of new breeches and a crisp, laundered shirt.

Perhaps she looked 'pretty,' or 'fetching.' But he looked magnificent.

He adjusted his cuff. "I always keep a few items of clothing here. No coat though, unhappily. I'm stuck with the same one I've been wearing."

It was petty of her, to take that as some consolation. But she did.

"Now." He sat down across from her and plucked a thick slice of toast. "About last night."

She flinched. "Must we discuss last night?"

He buttered his toast in slow, even strokes. "I think we must. Some apologies are probably in order."

"Oh." Nodding, she swallowed hard. "I'm sorry for taking advantage of you."

He choked on his bite of toast.

"No, really," she went on. "You were exhausted and more than a little drunk, and I was unspeakably shameless."

He shook his head and made noises of disagreement. He washed his toast down with a quick sip of tea.

"Minerva." He reached across the table to touch her cheek. "You were . . . a revelation. Believe me, you have absolutely no reason to apologize. The shamelessness was all mine." His eyes grew troubled. "I don't think we should continue this journey, pet. I told myself I'd see you to Scotland unharmed. But if we continue sharing a bed, I'm at serious risk of harming you. Irrevocably."

"How do you mean?"

One eyebrow lifted. "I think you know what I mean."

She did know. He meant that he wanted her, more than he'd wanted any woman in his debauched, misspent life—and he wasn't certain he could honor his promise not to seduce her.

Her pulse pounded. With exhilaration, with fear. "But we can't go back now. We can't just give up."

"It's not too late," he said. "We could be back in London tonight. I'd take you to Bram and Susanna's house, and we can tell everyone you've been their guest all this time. There may be some talk, but if my cousin throws his name behind you—you won't be ruined."

She stared at the tablecloth. The thought of simply turning around and returning to Spindle Cove, without ever reaching Edinburgh . . . she'd been prepared to go back ruined and disgraced. But she didn't know that she could live with going back *defeated*.

And how could she return to her old life, and just pretend none of this ever happened? Impossible.

"Min . . ."

"We can do this, Colin. We can reach Edinburgh in time. And I can keep you in your place, if that's what you're worried about. I'll go back to being shrewish and unattractive. I—I'll stash a cudgel under my pillow."

He laughed.

"Anyway, I'm satisfied now. You know, in terms of my curiosity. After last night, I'm sure I've seen all there is to see."

His voice darkened in a thrilling way. "Believe me. You haven't seen a fraction of what I could show you."

Oh, don't. Don't tell me that.

"Colin, please." She squeezed her eyes shut, then opened them. "Think of the money. Think of the five hundred guineas."

He shook his head. "It's not the money, pet."

"Then think of Francine."

"Francine?"

"Think of what she represents. What if long ago, before the first man ever drew breath, there were creatures like her everywhere? Giant lizards, roaming the earth. Even flying through the air."

"Er . . ." She could tell he was struggling not to laugh.

"I know you find it amusing, but I'm being serious. Discoveries like her footprint, they're changing history—or at least, our understanding of it. And there are a good many people who don't like that. Geologists might seem boring, but we're really renegades." She smiled. "I know you've been with a great many women, but Francine just might be the most scandalous, heretical female to ever share your bedchamber."

He did laugh then, good-naturedly.

Impulsively, she grabbed his hand. "Colin, please don't take this from me. This is my dream, and I've already risked so much. I'd rather fail than forfeit."

He drew a deep breath.

She held hers.

"Halford never rises before noon," he said. "We should slip out as soon as possible, to avoid questions."

The relief seeped through her, warm and sweet.

"Oh, thank you." She reached for his hand and squeezed it. "But we have so little money. Where will we go?"

He bit into his toast and chewed. With a shrug, he eventually answered, "North."

It was truly amazing, she thought, how far a man could travel on charm alone. By midmorning, Colin had wheedled them a chain of rides with tradesmen and farmers, working them toward a place where they could rejoin the Great North Road.

After pausing to chat with a local gentleman farmer, he strode back to Minerva where she waited by a rail fence.

He squinted at her through the bright morning sunlight. "He says he can offer us a ride to Grantham this afternoon, in exchange for a few hours' work this morning. He has his farmhands thatching a cottage roof. If we help, we can have space in his wagon afterwards."

"A ride all the way to Grantham? That would be wonderful. But . . ."

"But what?"

She tilted her head. "I take it he doesn't realize you're a viscount."

"A viscount? Wearing this?" Smiling, he indicated his dusty, bedraggled topcoat. The fabric retained just a memory of its original deep blue. His boots hadn't been blacked in days. "Not a chance. He assumes us to be common travelers, of course."

"But . . ." How to put this in a way that wouldn't offend his pride? "Colin, have you ever thatched a roof before?"

"Of course not," he said gamely, helping her lift Francine's trunk over the stile. "This is my grand opportunity."

She took a deep breath. "If you say so."

They crossed a hopfield, lined with neat rows of poles and ambitious green tendrils just starting to climb them. Minerva could see the cottage in the distance. Several men were scaling ladders and carting up bundles of fresh, golden longstraw to layer on the roof. They looked like ants swarming over a dish heaped with yellow custard.

"Here." Colin removed his cravat and wound it around the pistol before shoving both into his coat pocket. Then he removed the coat altogether and handed it to her. "Look after this."

With that, he joined the men at their labor. Minerva found herself quickly drafted into the women's portion, sorting and bundling the straw as it was forked from the wagon. She supposed if she could be a convincing missionary or assassin, she ought to be able to do this. After all, she was used to working long hours with her rock hammer.

An hour later, her back was aching and her exposed forearms had acquired a thousand tiny abrasions. Her head felt swollen with the thick, sweet scent of the straw. She wasn't particularly good at the work, and she could sense that she was coasting by on the other women's forbearance. But she wouldn't give up.

She stood tall for a minute to stretch her back. Shading her eyes with one hand, she scanned for Colin among the men. There he was, near the top of the roof, fearlessly straddling two rafters. Without a moment's hesitation or a hint of imbalance, he walked across ten feet of narrow, sloping beam to accept a fresh bundle of straw. Of course, he'd taken to this easily—the same way he took to everything.

She watched him for a few minutes. Placing the straw in a thick layer, then pinning it down with twists of split hazel. He lifted a flat-head tool that looked something between a currycomb and a mallet. With swift, strong arcs of his arm, he pounded the thatch into place. He paused to wipe his brow and toss a comment to his fellow laborers. From the way they all laughed, she supposed it must have been a good joke.

Minerva found herself caught between admiration and envy. She seemed doomed to move through life feeling the perpetual outsider, whereas Colin could fit in anywhere. But for the first time, she saw his charm in a different light. Not as lubricant, of either a social or sexual variety, but simply as an expression of his true self.

He caught sight of her and lifted a hand in greeting. "Tally-ho!"

She couldn't help but smile and shake her head, whispering, "You're cracked."

Cracked indeed.

Cracked open, more like. Come out of his shell.

How funny. He was forever chiding Minerva, telling her to emerge from her protective cage. But didn't everyone have a shell? Hard, external armor protecting the soft, vulnerable creature beneath?

Perhaps, she thought, people were more like ammonites than one would suppose. Perhaps they too built shells on a consistent, unchanging factor—some quality or circumstance established in their youth. Each chamber in the shell just an enlargement of the previous. Growing year after year, until they spiraled around and locked themselves in place.

Colin's shell had been formed by tragedy. His parents' death had defined the shape of that first protective chamber. He'd owned it, grown to fill the shape of it, enlarged it with room after mournful, troubled room. But what if the person inside those many hollow, echoing chambers wasn't a tragedy at all? Just a man who genuinely enjoyed life and loved people, but happened to have two dead parents and a stubborn case of insomnia?

And who was *she*, beneath all her layers? A bookish, awkward girl who couldn't be bothered to care for anything but fossils and rocks? Or a bold, adventurous woman who'd risked everything—not on the hopes of achieving professional acclaim, but on the slim chance of love. Of finding that one person who could understand her, appreciate her, and let her understand and appreciate him.

She couldn't lie. In Spindle Cove, she'd entertained vain fancies that Sir Alisdair Kent might be that man. But now, looking back, she had to own another difficult truth. Whenever she'd imagined herself with Sir Alisdair—gazing deep into eyes that reflected acceptance, desire, affection, and trust—those eyes had looked a great deal like Bristol diamonds. And they were anchored by a strong jaw and single, reluctant dimple.

She was so confused. In the immediate future, she wanted—*needed*—to share Francine's footprint with the scientific community. Beyond that, Minerva didn't know what she wanted anymore. And even if she could discern what future she wanted . . .

How would she bear it if that future didn't want her?

When the thatching was finished, the laborers gathered at long, planked tables for a simple midday meal. Minerva helped the other women pass baskets of fresh bread, sausages, and hard cheese. Ale flowed freely from a cask.

The general mood turned from one of work to one of anticipation. The men washed and put on their coats, and the girls removed aprons and tied ribbons in each other's hair. The wagon that had so recently been heaped with straw for thatching was swept and hitched to a strong, sturdy team.

"Our chariot awaits." Colin extended a hand to Minerva. "After you."

He helped her into the wagon, and then loaded the trunk. She pushed it to the far end of the wagon bed, and they sat in a row—all three of them. Minerva folded her legs beneath her. Colin stretched his out. Francine kept her foot in the box.

"You don't mind the wagon?" she asked him.

He shook as head. "Not so long as it's open."

All the other farm workers crowded in, and just before the rear gate was latched, a half dozen pink, squirming piglets were added to the mix. One of them found its way to Minerva's lap, rooting adorably in the white folds of her overskirt, where the keen little creature knew she'd saved some cheese from their luncheon.

"Are we *all* traveling to Grantham?" Minerva wondered aloud, feeding the piglet a morsel of cheese.

The young woman seated across the wagon stared at her, as though she were a simpleton. "It's fair day, isn't it?"

Ah. Fair day. This would explain the air of excitement. And the piglets.

As the wagon started off down the road, the girls in the wagon shifted and coalesced, forming a loose knot. They whispered to each other, shooting furtive glances at Colin and Minerva.

Minerva could tell they were speculating on their relationship. Wondering whether or not this handsome stranger was available. After a bit more whispering and nudging, they seemed to nominate a bold-looking brunette to find out.

"So, Mr. Sand," she said, smiling. "What takes you and your lady friend to the Grantham fair?"

Minerva held her breath, foolishly hoping to be claimed as something other than his sister. Something more than a mistress.

"Business," Colin said easily. "We're circus folk."

Circus folk?

"Circus folk?" several of the girls echoed.

"Yes, of course." He lazily riffled a hand through his hair. "I walk the tightrope, and my lady here . . ." He stretched his arm around Minerva, drawing her close. "She's a first-rate sword swallower."

Oh my God.

Minerva clapped a hand over her mouth and made helpless snuffling sounds into her palm. "Caught a bit of straw dust," she explained a few moments later, wiping the tears of laughter from her eyes.

She slid a look at Colin. The man was unbelievably shameless. Incorrigibly handsome. And—oh, heavens. She was a feather's brush away from falling hopelessly in love with him.

"A sword swallower," the brunette echoed, casting a skeptical glance at Minerva.

"Oh yes. She has a rare talent. You must believe me when I say, I've spent several years in the circus world, and I've never seen her like. You should have seen her performance just last night. Sheer brilliance, I tell you. She has this way of—"

Minerva elbowed him, hard.

"What?" He caught her by the chin, turning her face to his. His eyes danced with amusement. "Really, pet. You are entirely too modest."

She took a long, dizzying tumble through his warm, affectionate gaze. And then he kissed her. Not quite on the mouth, not quite on the cheek. Just at the corner of her smile.

The wagon hit a rut in the lane, jolting them apart. Minerva laid her head on his shoulder and sighed with happiness.

Across the wagon, the rest of the women sighed with disappointment.

Yes, girls. Go weep in your aprons. He's taken. For today, at least.

Minerva laced her hand with Colin's and gave it a squeeze of thanks. Along with all the blissful pleasure he'd so masterfully coaxed from her body, he'd now introduced her to an entirely new sensation.

So this was how it felt to be envied.

"Well," said the brunette, "you never do know who you'll meet along the Great North Road, do you? Just yesterday, my brother said one of his friends passed time with a long-lost prince."

Everyone in the wagon laughed, except Minerva. Colin's arm tightened around her shoulders.

"No, really," the girl went on. "He was a prince, traveling in common clothes."

Beside her, another young woman shook her head. "Your brother's spinning tales again, Becky. Imagine, a long-lost prince in disguise, traveling this stretch of road. What's he doing? Coming to the fair?" She giggled. "I'd never give that tale any credit."

"I don't know." Minerva smiled to herself, nestling closer to Colin. "I could believe it."

"Well." The brunette arched an eyebrow. "If this prince does exist—he'd better hope he doesn't meet with my brother's friends. They've a score to settle with His Majesty."

Chapter Twenty-one

There was no leaving Grantham tonight. Not for love, money, giant lizards, or whatever fool motive was now driving Colin on this quest.

Every wagon, coach, and pony cart in the county must have been rolling into town for the fair. None of them were leaving.

He fought his way through the jostling throng of horses and carts, back to where he'd left Minerva. As a cartload of crated chickens rolled out of his way, he caught sight of her through the flurry of white feathers.

He stopped dead in his tracks, transfixed. Admiring.

She sat atop her precious trunk of course, chin propped in her hand. She'd allowed her spectacles to slide down toward the tip of her nose, so she could peer over them—as she always did when regarding something more than a dozen paces distant. Her long dark hair tumbled about her shoulders in fetching waves, and the late afternoon sun gave it warm, reddish highlights. With her teeth, she worried that plump, sweet bottom lip, and her toes tapped in time to some distant music.

She was lovely. Just the picture of a wide-eyed country lass, taking in the fair.

"Nothing," he said, approaching her. "Perhaps we'd have better luck later this evening." He cast a look over his shoulder, toward the bustling green. "For the meantime, we might as well see the fair."

"But we haven't any money." She pushed her spectacles back up on her nose and held up a thin gold coin between her fingertips. "This one sovereign must stretch all the way to Edinburgh."

He took it from her and slipped it in his breast pocket. "It costs nothing to look. And we'll need to eat something, sometime. But we'll be frugal."

"A frugal brother and sister?" she asked, peering up at him. "A frugal gentleman and his mistress? Or frugal circus folk?"

"Frugal sweethearts." He extended a hand to her. "Just for today. All right?"

"All right." Smiling, she put her hand in his, and he pulled her to her feet.

Ah, the sweet, unveiled affection in her eyes . . . it warmed his heart, and then wrung it fierce. A better man wouldn't play this 'sweethearts' game with her when he knew very well it couldn't lead to more.

But he wasn't a better man. He was Colin Sandhurst, reckless, incorrigible rogue—and damn it, he couldn't resist. He wanted to amuse her, spoil her, feed her sweets and delicacies. Steal a kiss or two, when she wasn't expecting it. He wanted to be a besotted young buck squiring his girl around the fair.

In other words, he wanted to live honestly. Just for the day.

He hefted Francine's trunk and balanced it on his right shoulder, offering Minerva his left arm. Together they moved through the crowds and past the church. They walked down the rows of prize livestock brought for show, giving the pigs and stoats ridiculous names, then debating which deserved the ribbon and why.

"Hamlet must get the ribbon," Minerva argued. "His eyes are the brightest, and his haunches the most fat. He also keeps himself quite clean for a pig."

"But Hamlet is a prince. I thought you bestowed your greatest favor on knights." He pointed. "Perhaps you'd prefer Sir Francis Bacon over there."

"The filthy one wallowing and grunting in the mud?"

"I understand grunting is a mark of porcine intelligence."

"Please." She gave him a look. "Even I have standards."

"Good to hear." He added under his breath, "I think."

They wandered down rows of booths displaying as exotic an array of wares as one could hope to find in the English Midlands—everything from oranges to ormolu clocks, French bonnets to scented bootblack. Colin wished he could buy her one of everything, but settled for spending sixpence on a length of blue ribbon to match her gown.

"In case you're wanting to tie back your hair," he said.

"Did you want me to tie back my hair?"

"Not at all. I quite like it down."

She shook her head. "You're nonsensical."

He made a show of bristling in mock offense. "You just don't know how to take a gift."

"A gift?" She laughed and nudged his side. "You bought it with *my* money. But thank you." She kissed his cheek.

"That's better."

For a shilling and scattered pence, Colin purchased their supper—a small pitcher of fresh milk and two meat pies. They found a clear place on the green and sat facing each other on the trunk. Minerva spread out her handkerchief as a makeshift tablecloth.

"I'm so hungry," she said, staring at the food.

He handed her one of the pies. "Then have at it."

She bit into the crescent-shaped pastry, slowly sinking her

teeth through the layers of flaky crust. Her eyelashes fluttered, and she gave a moan of pleasure.

"Oh, Colin. That's marvelous." She swept her tongue over those ripe, sultry, pouting lips.

He stared at her, suddenly helpless to move or speak. Raw, animal lust gripped him, and gripped him hard.

He *had* to feel those lips on him again. Had. To. This wasn't a mild expression of preference. This was an imperative. His body was insistent. To continue his existence on this earth, he now needed the following: food, water, shelter, clothing, and Minerva Highwood's lips.

Sending him a coy glance through her dark eyelashes, she took a sip of milk. Then she licked her lips again.

Correction. He needed food, water, shelter, clothing, Minerva Highwood's lips, *and* . . . Minerva Highwood's tongue.

Memories of the night before flashed through his mind. He didn't even try to force them back. No, he let them surface, taking time to engrave each carnal, erotic moment on his memory. Each blissful moment must be recorded, so he could mentally relive that scene in months and years to come. Out of not just desire, but *need*.

Those lips. That tongue.

"Aren't you going to eat?" she asked.

"No. Er . . . yes." He shook himself. "Eventually."

Colin bit into his own pie. It was good and savory, still warm from the oven. He enjoyed it. But not nearly as much as he enjoyed viewing her enjoyment.

Remarkable. He'd wooed lovers with jewels and Venetian lace, taken them to view operas from the most lavish box in the theater, fed them oysters and sugared berries from silver trays. But he'd never known the sort of pure, honest pleasure he felt right here, right now. Devouring meat pies with Minerva Highwood in the middle of a country fair.

Licking her thumb clean, she tilted her head to regard the sky. "It'll be twilight soon. Should we try our luck finding transport?"

"Probably."

They picked up Francine and carried her between them, ambling toward the carriage mews and stables. As they went, they passed a row of booths and carnival games.

A small girl yanked at Colin's coat front. She was waifish but bright-eyed, dressed in a patched yellow dress.

"Won't you and the lady have your fortune told, sir?" The girl indicated a tent a few paces away. "My mum tells fortunes for a sixpence. She can see the future, clear as looking through a glass windowpane. She'll tell you everything you want to know about your life, love, and children. Even the day of your own death!" She all but chirped this last.

Colin smiled, setting down the trunk. "Well, that's a tempting offer."

"Colin, we can't," Minerva whispered in his ear. "We've only eighteen shillings to our names. We can't be wasting any of it on fortune-tellers."

He knew she was right, but something in the girl's gap-toothed smile tugged at him.

"What's your name, pet?" he asked the girl.

"Elspeth, sir."

"Well, Elspeth." He leaned down close. "I'm afraid we can't buy a fortune from your mother. I'm a rather fragile soul, you see. I'm not sure I could bear up under the revelation of my future loves and children, much less the date of my own death. So why don't I tell your fortune instead?"

"My fortune?" She narrowed her eyes with precocious cynicism. With her tongue, she worked a loose front tooth back and forth. "How are you going to tell my fortune?"

"Oh, easy as anything." Colin drew a penny from his pocket and placed it in the girl's hand. "I see a sweet in your future."

Elspeth smiled and closed her hand around the penny. "All right then."

As she scampered off, he cupped a hand around his mouth and called after her, "A sweet, remember. Don't go making me a charlatan. Be sure not to spend it on anything else."

He turned to find Minerva staring up at him.

"It is true," she asked, "what you told her just now?"

"What did I tell her just now?"

"That you fear the future."

His chin ducked, as if he were instinctively dodging a blow. His brain rang, as though he'd failed to evade it. "I didn't say that."

"You said something quite like it."

Had he? Perhaps he had.

"It's not that I *fear* the future. I just find it's best not to form expectations. Expectations lead to disappointments. If you expect nothing, you're always surprised."

"But you're never really satisfied. You never experience the joy of working toward a goal and achieving it."

He sighed heavily. Must she always be so damned perceptive?

Doesn't it grow tiresome? she'd asked him last night, referring to his live-for-the-day, Devil-may-care, insert-blithe-motto-here lifestyle.

Yes, it did rather grow tiresome. Colin envied men like his cousin, who had their sense of duty and purpose whittled so sharp, it could balance on a rapier's edge. Men like Bram woke up each morning knowing exactly what they meant to accomplish, and why, and how. Hell, Colin envied the men he'd worked with this morning, thatching a cottage roof.

And he envied Minerva her scholarly dedication and discoveries. More than she could ever suppose.

"If you're asking me, don't I want to do something useful with my life . . . ? Of course I do. But I'm a viscount, pet.

There's a responsibility inherent in that. Or there will be, once I finally gain control of my accounts. Mostly, my task is to stay alive and not cock things up. I can't risk my life purchasing an officer's commission, or sign on with a pirate crew for larks."

"Aren't lords supposed to manage their lands?"

"Who says I don't?" He threw her a look. "Believe it or not, I go through pots of ink every month, ensuring that my estate is well managed. And I do my part to keep it in excellent condition by staying far away, myself." He shrugged. "I know some gentlemen develop intellectual interests or political pursuits to occupy their time. But what can I say? I'm not a specialist. I'm passably good at a thousand things, but I don't particularly excel at any of them."

"Jack of all trades," she said thoughtfully.

"Well, something like that. If I could engage in trade, which I can't."

They were silent for a few moments.

"You do have talents, Colin."

He gave her a lascivious wink. "Oh, I know I do."

"That's not what I meant."

"Let's see. I'm good at lying, drinking, pleasuring women, and inciting tavern brawls." Pulling up short, he stopped before a booth with a toss game. "And this. I'm good at things like this."

He picked up one of the round wooden balls, tossing it into the air and catching it in his hand. Testing its weight as he rolled it from palm to fingertips and back.

"How do I play?" he asked the woman behind the table.

"Three pence for a try, sir. You throw the ball in the baskets." She waved to a large basket right up front. Behind it, a series of similar baskets were lined up—in gradually diminishing sizes. "A pitch in the first basket earns you an apple. Next basket, an orange. Then peaches, cherries, grapes." She swept to the end of the row and pointed out a tiny woven basket, probably smaller than the ball itself. "Hit the last, you've won yourself a pineapple, direct from the Sandwich Islands."

Right. Colin smirked. The stumpy, shriveled pineapple on display looked to have come from a fruitier's glasshouse, via several weeks' travel around the English countryside.

Easy enough to see how the game worked. In essence, players traded three pence for an apple. If they had a bit of skill, they took away an orange, as well.

Clearly, no one ever won the pineapple.

He laid three pennies on the table. "I'll have a go."

The apple came easily, as it was supposed to do. He handed the shiny round fruit to Minerva, who'd taken a seat on the trunk. "Go ahead," he urged. "Life's uncertain. Eat it now."

By the time he'd won her the orange and a trio of fine, ripe peaches, Colin had amassed a small crowd of children. As he sized up his toss for the cherries, he slid a glance to the side and instantly gathered where they'd come from. Little Elspeth had joined Minerva on the trunk. Peach juice dribbled down her chin as she bit into the fruit from one side, carefully avoiding her loose tooth. Apparently, the penny sweet hadn't been enough for her. She'd come back for more, and she'd brought all her friends.

When he'd tossed and won, Colin passed the net of cherries to Minerva for distribution. "One apiece," he called to the gathered boys and girls. "No spitting the stones."

From the cheer that rose up, one would think he'd passed around gold coins.

Minerva was pressed and jostled from all sides, but she flashed him a wide smile as she opened the net. "Don't you want one?"

He shook his head. Her smile—genuine, adoring—was the best reward he could imagine.

"Grapes next!" called one boy. "Cor, I've never even tasted a grape. Not in all my life."

The stout woman behind the table crossed her arms. "Greedy little beggars. Go on with you. He won't win the grapes."

"We'll see." Colin rolled the wooden ball in his hand, assessing. The basket he needed to hit was some ten paces back, and approximately the size of a saucer. If he lobbed it too directly, the ball would glance off the basket's edge. His best shot was a high arc, to send the ball sailing up and then directly down.

He lofted the ball high in the air. The children held their breath.

And a few moments later, Colin was handing round clusters of red grapes. They were seedy and a bit shriveled. Half on their way to becoming raisins, in some cases. But a boy who'd never tasted a grape before wouldn't know to complain. The children popped them into their mouths and made a contest of outdoing one another's sounds of delight.

"The pineapple!" they all called next, jumping up and down. "Win us the pineapple!"

Colin's mouth tugged sideways. The pineapple basket looked about the size of a teacup. He wasn't sure it was even possible to fit the wooden ball inside it, let alone do so from a distance. "Don't get your hopes raised, children."

"Oh, but I've dreamed of pineapples."

"My mum's a housemaid. She's tasted 'em. Says they're like ambrosia."

"You can do it, sir!" Elspeth cried.

Colin tossed the wooden ball to the plucky girl. "Rub it for luck, pet."

Smiling, she did so and handed it back.

He gave Minerva a wink and a shrug. "Here goes nothing."

Then he eyed the basket, sized up his shot . . . and threw the ball.

Chapter Twenty-two

As the wooden ball sailed through the air, all the hopeful children clutched their hands together and held their breath. Minerva held her breath along with them. And she didn't even care for pineapples.

Go in, she willed. *Go in*.

It didn't go in.

When the ball bounced off the basket's rim and thudded to the ground, she couldn't resist joining the collective groan of disappointment.

Colin shrugged and pushed a hand through his air. "Sorry, lads and lasses. Did my best." He was good-natured in defeat. A gracious loser, as always. But she could tell he was disappointed, too. Not over his bruised pride, but on account of the children. He wanted to give them a treat to remember, and who could blame him?

Thrusting caution and frugality aside, Minerva pushed her way to the table and addressed the booth's mistress. "How much for the pineapple? Will you take three shillings?"

The woman's eyes flared with greed, but her mouth was firm. "It's not for sale."

"I'll have a go, then." A well-dressed young gentleman

stepped to the fore. He looked to be the local version of a dandy—probably the son of some country squire, unleashed on the fair with a generous allowance of pocket money and an inflated sense of self-importance. He was flanked by a couple of friends, both of whom looked eager to be amused.

"Sorry, gents." The stout woman crossed her arms. "This booth is closed."

"Pity," said the suave-looking young gentleman, casting a superior glance at Colin. "I'd rather looked forward to showing this fellow up."

His friends laughed. Meanwhile, the children gathered around Colin, as if they'd claimed him for their own and must come to his defense. It was terribly sweet.

"Well," said Colin amiably, "you're still welcome to have a go. If it's a contest of marksmanship you're after, one can be arranged. With targets and pistols, perhaps?"

Excitement whispered through the assembled children. Apparently, the promise of a shooting match was an effective balm to their disappointed pineapple hopes.

The young man looked Colin up and down, smirking. "I warn you, I'm the best shot in the county. But if you insist, I should be glad to trounce you."

"Then you should be glad to take my money, too. Let's place a wager on it."

"Absolutely. Name your bet."

Colin rummaged through his pockets, and Minerva grew alarmed. He might well be an excellent shot, but surely he wouldn't risk *all* their money.

"Five pounds," Colin said.

Five pounds?

"Five pounds?" the young gentleman echoed.

Minerva couldn't help herself. She went to his side, whispering, "Five pounds? Are you mad? Where do you mean to come up with five pounds?"

"Here." From his innermost pocket, Colin drew a small, folded square of paper. "Just found it in my coat pocket. Must have been there for months. I'd forgotten it."

She unfolded the paper and adjusted her spectacles. It was indeed a bank note for five pounds.

Five pounds. All this time she'd been fretting over how to stretch their shillings and pence, and he'd been carrying five pounds in his pocket. The impossible knave.

"You can't risk this," she whispered. "It's—"

"It's a wager." The dandy pulled out a coin purse and shook loose five sovereign pieces. He dumped them into Minerva's hand. "Five pounds."

Oh dear. She didn't have a good feeling about this.

They made a veritable parade, the whole group of them trooping to the edge of the fairgrounds, where a shooting contest could safely be staged. Dusk was gathering by the time a straw-stuffed target had been mounted, and a sizable crowd had amassed to watch—not just the children, but adults, too.

"One shot each," the overconfident dandy said, tilting his head toward the bull's-eye lodged in the center of a freshly plowed field. "Closest to center wins."

"Sounds fair," Colin said. "You first."

The younger man made a show of cleaning and loading his expensive, polished double-barreled pistol. It was a Finch pistol, Minerva noted with some amusement. Her friend Susanna would have a good laugh at that.

With pomp and an undue air of gravity, the self-styled dandy leveled his pistol and made his shot. A dark circle appeared on the target, several inches left of center.

The younger man accepted the smattering of applause with a bow. Minerva rolled her eyes. The ladies of Spindle Cove could shoot better than that.

Surely Colin could, as well.

For once, Colin didn't attempt any showmanship. He merely shook off his coat and swept a hand through his wavy hair. And those two small gestures were enough to make him the desire of every woman, the envy of every man, and the idol of every child in attendance. Good heavens, he was beautiful.

She was so dazzled by his good looks, Minerva nearly forgot to work herself into a state of sheer anxiety. Before she knew it, he'd stepped up, leveled the pistol, and made his shot. As the smoke cleared, she whipped off her spectacles to stare at the target.

Dead center, of course.

The children went wild with whoops and hollers. A few of the older boys tried, unsuccessfully, to lift Colin on their shoulders for a victory salute.

And Minerva curled her fingers over the small fortune in her hands. Ten pounds. Ten pounds changed *everything*. Now they were truly back on schedule. They would make it to Edinburgh. Francine would have her day.

When Colin untangled himself from the jubilant children and turned to her, grinning . . . oh, she could have kissed him. Right in front of all these people.

But the defeated dandy wanted words with him first.

"You're a cheat." The young man stared Colin down. "I don't know what kind of swindler you are, but my father's the magistrate in these parts. I think he'll need to have a talk with you. And that five-pound note will need to come along, as evidence. Surely you've stolen it."

Stepping back casually, Colin slid his arms into his coat sleeves. "I don't want any trouble."

The man's friend stepped forward, brandishing a fist. "Well, you've found some."

Minerva knew that in a fistfight Colin could take one or

both of these young men easily. But if the dandy were truly a magistrate's son, a brawl would be a very bad idea.

And must they always flee a scene in the mayhem of violence and rioting? Could they walk away just this once, with ten pounds in their pocket and some levity in their step? Just this once?

"Listen," Colin said, clapping each man on the shoulder. "Perhaps you're right, and it wasn't very sporting of me. But surely we can settle this without involving magistrates. How about this—just to prove I'm a decent fellow, I'll give you a chance to win it all back. Double or nothing."

The dandy sneered at him. "If you think I'm going to—"

"No, no," Colin replied, speaking in a smooth, conciliatory tone. "Not you and me. We'll have our seconds shoot it out. Your man here"—Colin tapped the friend on the shoulder—"against my girl." He looked to Minerva.

Oh, no. Colin, don't do this to me.

"Against your girl?" The dandy chuckled.

"She'll even remove her spectacles." Colin raised open hands in a gesture of surrender. "I told you, I don't want trouble. You can lead me away in shackles and throw me in the stocks, but you won't get any richer. There's five pounds in it for you this way."

The dandy pulled straight and smiled. "All right, then. As you say."

"Double or nothing." Colin called Elspeth to his side, picked her up by the waist and set her atop the fence. "Little Elspeth here will hold the purse." He took the ten pounds from Minerva and put it in the girl's hands.

The young gentleman raided his coin purse and borrowed a few pounds from his friends. Finally, he'd cobbled together his portion and gave it to smiling Elspeth, who knotted it all in a handkerchief.

He handed his pistol to his eager companion, who quickly proved to be a middling marksman as well. He hit the target, but well wide of the center.

It was Minerva's turn. Her nerves did a frantic jig in her stomach.

"Give us a moment," Colin said to the gentlemen, smiling. "Let me show her how the thing works."

The men had a good laugh amongst themselves as Colin drew her forward, to the shooter's mark.

"Colin, what were you thinking?" she whispered, trembling. "What am I to do?"

"You're going to shoot, of course. And you're going to hit the target, dead center." With confident fingers, he removed her spectacles, folded them, and tucked them into his coat pocket.

He put the reloaded pistol in her hand. Then, approaching her from the back, he wrapped his arms around hers and raised the gun, as though teaching her how to shoot.

"After you make your shot," he murmured in her ear, "you grab the purse from Elspeth. I'll get Francine. And we'll run, as hard as we can, down that lane." He pointed the pistol to the side, indicating the direction. "Don't stop for anything. Don't even pause to look back. I'll catch up to you, promise."

She leaned back, savoring the comfort of his strength and warmth. "But . . . but what if I miss?"

"You won't miss." He pressed a kiss to her earlobe, then stepped back, releasing her arms. "Go on, then. Make me proud."

Minerva leveled the pistol at the target, giving her eyes time to focus. Her hands trembled. She tried to remember all the tips Susanna and Miss Taylor had given her. Like all the Spindle Cove ladies, she'd learned to shoot—but her marksmanship had never been especially consistent. Mama had made no secret that she found Minerva's participation in the activity laughable.

A mostly blind girl, armed with a pistol? Mama would say. *My dear, the gentlemen already keep their distance. There's no need to frighten them off with guns.*

Minerva took a deep breath and tried to banish the sounds of laughter.

"Francine," she whispered, "this is for you."

And just she began to squeeze the trigger, a voice called out about the crowd's hushed silence—freezing her finger in place and turning the blood in her veins to ice.

"That's him, right over there!"

No. It couldn't be.

"Go get him, boys!" the voice shouted. "There he is! It's Prince Ampersand of Crustacea!"

Stunned, Minerva lowered the gun and looked to Colin.

"*Shoot*," he said, eyes wide and fierce. "Now."

"Right."

With a sudden, stone-cold certainty, Minerva raised her arms, took aim, and fired the pistol. Without pausing to see how her shot had landed, she grabbed the money from Elspeth and ran. The children's wild cheer of triumph told everything she needed to know. What she'd already known, in her bones.

She'd hit dead center. Just as Colin had said.

Grinning to herself, she ducked her head, pumped her arms and legs, and raced down the lane.

Her breath and heartbeat pounded so loud, she could barely hear her own boots slapping the dirt. But soon she became conscious of another set of footfalls behind her. She didn't dare slow or turn to ascertain whether they belonged to Colin. She just kept running like the Devil was on her heels.

And it occurred to her, as she made that mad dash down the lane—clutching a blazing hot pistol in one hand and a fistful of money in the other—that this surely must mark some turning point in her life. Really, there was no going back from *this*.

Today, all her mother's judgments had been proved false. She wasn't plain, but pretty. She wasn't distracted and awkward, but confident and a crack shot.

Most of all, Minerva was not hopeless. She had twenty pounds. She had an important scientific discovery.

And she had Colin, the most handsome, charming devil in England, coming fast on her heels. Save for the ransom-minded highwaymen and angry magistrate's son chasing after them . . .

Life had never been so good.

"This way," he called, overtaking her as they neared the town's borders. He had Francine lifted in his arms, leading the way as he turned down an alleyway. They clattered down the narrow, shadowy corridor, then found an arched passage that led through the churchyard wall and out into the countryside.

Carrying Francine between them now, they ran into the sunset. Only when they'd covered two meadows, vaulted a stile, and crested a hill did they pause for breath and dare to look back.

They saw no one.

"How did you get away?" she asked.

"Elspeth and her army. They provided a diversion. But we're not safe yet." Panting, he nodded toward a nearby hut. "Over there."

It wasn't a dwelling proper. Just a cramped shelter for shepherds to sleep in while their flock grazed these fields. Tonight, it was empty. Likely all the sheep had been penned somewhere so the shepherds could enjoy the fair.

Colin had to stoop to fit through the small doorway. Inside, they found just a small cookstove, a lamp, various crooks and other shepherding implements . . . and a narrow cot.

Still breathing hard from exertion, Minerva found a flint and lit the lamp. "Do you want to know something?" As the yellow light warmed the space, she turned her gaze to Colin. "Today is my birthday."

He laughed. "Really?"

"No. Not really." She giggled helplessly. "But if it were, it would have been the best one ever. Colin, you were unbelievable."

"You were amazing." He took her by the waist. His chest rose and fell with a resonant sigh. "You *are* amazing."

His words of praise gave her gooseflesh. But as he pulled her close, a strange round obstacle squished between them.

His brow wrinkled in confusion.

"Oh," she said, laughing. Pulling back a bit, she fished the obstacle out of her overskirt pocket and held it up for his view. "I saved you a peach."

He looked at the peach. Then he looked at her.

"*Minerva.*"

Awareness tingled over every inch of her skin. The hunger in his eyes, the smoldering heat between their bodies . . . this wasn't a lesson, or an experiment to satisfy scientific curiosity. It wasn't pretense of any sort.

This was *real*.

He bent his head by slow degrees, teasing out the moment. Making her reach for him, stretch for him, ache for him. Until finally, his hand slid to cradle her neck and he took her mouth in a deep, passionate kiss.

She let the peach slip from her fingers and tumble to the straw-covered ground, the better to fill her hands with him. They kissed and grappled, tangling tongues and weaving their fingers into each other's hair. It seemed they couldn't get close enough, couldn't kiss deeply enough, couldn't press enough skin to skin.

Her nipples came to tight points. She felt the hard ridge of his erection, jutting against her belly. And her mind slowly caught up to what their bodies already knew. There was only one way to satisfy this need. Only one means of achieving the closeness she craved.

"Minerva." He slid his tongue from her throat to her ear. "I want to make love to you."

Just at the words . . . that bold, unequivocal statement of intent . . . fire raced through her veins. Hot, powerful, consuming.

There were a dozen reasons why she might refuse him. But they were all someone else's reasons. Her mother's, her peers', society's. She'd already left all those expectations behind. If Minerva consulted herself, there was no question. Her body craved the feel of his skin against hers. Her ever-curious intellect was eager to experience physical passion, with him. And her heart . . .

Oh, her heart was already his for the breaking.

His hands went to the knotted overskirt ties. With deft motions, he untied them and slid the garment free. Then he started on the row of hooks down her back.

His voice grew rough with need. "I promised you I wouldn't do this. Hell, I promised myself I wouldn't do this. But I can't help it, Min. I want you so badly."

She kissed his throat and pressed her body to his, hoping to show him what she couldn't quite find words to say. That she wanted him, too. Needed his touch. As he worked the closures of her gown loose, she tangled her fingers in his wavy hair.

"Colin," she sighed.

His hands went to her shoulders. His gaze searched hers. "If you don't want this, tell me so." He swallowed hard. "Say the word, and I'll stop."

In answer, she merely drew the sleeves of her gown down her arms and pushed the blue silk to her feet. He took one of her hands to steady her as she stepped free of the gown.

Standing back a pace, he made a wistful noise in his throat. "Just look at you. So lovely."

She warmed with pleasure as he surveyed the items she'd drawn from her trousseau that morning. Her lacy white chemise, bosom-flattering corset, and silk stockings. If she'd been saving them for anything other than this moment with him, she couldn't remember it. This mad, triumphant day at the fair; this snug, humble place to spend the night. The unveiled desire in his eyes as he regarded her.

This felt like all she'd ever wanted.

She opened her trunk and found those embroidered sheets she'd stitched and saved for some unlikely wedding night. Together, they spread them on the narrow cot.

Even if she went to her grave a spinster, she would still have known more passion in this one night than some women experienced in a lifetime. She vowed to savor every touch. Remember every caress. Keep her eyes open for each and every moment. Even now, as he kissed the soft place beneath her ear.

He took her by the waist and spun her around. With her back to him, she trembled as he worked the laces of her corset loose. At last, the restrictive garment fell away from her body, and she drew a deep, intoxicating breath.

With a soft groan, he gathered her close. The solid muscles of his chest supported her weight as he lifted and cupped her breasts through her chemise. Her breath quickened as he stroked and caressed the soft globes, thumbing her nipples to taut, eager peaks.

She turned in his embrace, wanting her turn to touch. Sliding her hands under his lapels and toward his shoulders, she cleaved the coat from his body. He shook the heavy garment down his arms and tossed it aside. She gathered the loose fabric of his shirt and yanked it free of his waistband, sliding her hands beneath to explore the smooth, muscled contours of his torso.

He lifted his arms overhead—as much as he could, with the low ceiling—and she drew the shirt up and over his shoulders. Once his shirt was removed, he directed her to do likewise. Minerva stretched her arms tall as he gathered the thin, gauzy fabric of her chemise and drew it up her body. Slowly, reverently. Until he pulled the shift over her head and arms. With a flick of one hand, he tossed it aside. Then his hands made a slow, languid sweep back in reverse— skimming down her stretched arms, over her breasts, her waist, her hips. Awakening every part of her with his touch. His palms were a little roughened from his thatching work that morning, but the delicious friction only increased her excitement.

It let her know this was real.

She stood before him bare, save for her stockings and garters. He ran one hand over her backside and down her thigh. She thought he would untie her garter, but instead he smoothed his hand over the delicate silk. Lifting her leg, he wrapped her thigh over his hip, drawing her close. Her breasts met his bared chest, and as they kissed she couldn't help but rub them against his solid heat, easing their dull ache. He moaned into her mouth.

He worked a hand between them, gently cupping and stroking her sex. A muscle in her inner thigh quivered, and she felt herself growing damp.

He pressed two fingers inside her, pushing deep. Until the heel of his hand rested firm against her mound. Her body's reaction was immediate, intense. As he rocked his hand back and forth, she moved with him, riding his motions and moaning in time to his gentle thrusts.

So close. She was already so close.

He withdrew his fingers, and she whimpered at the sudden loss.

As he lifted her and lay her down on the bed, his voice shook with need. "Damn it, I know I should be selfless. I should give you pleasure first. But I want to be in you. I want to be so deep inside you when you come."

To that, she could muster no protest.

She watched him as he sat on the trunk and wrestled out of his boots and breeches. As his erection sprang free of his unbuttoned falls, she reached for the enticing, dusky curve. He made her free to explore, spreading his thighs wide so she could stroke his full length and cup the vulnerable sac beneath. He sighed deeply as she caressed him. She dabbed at the bead of moisture welling from his tip, spreading it with circling motions of her thumb.

He grabbed her wrist, staying her hand. With a hoarse chuckle, he said, "I can't take much more of that."

"Then come to me." The words made her feel bold and seductive. She stretched sinuously on the cot, making her whole body an invitation writ in pale pink calligraphy.

He wasted no time accepting. He moved between her legs, spreading her thighs wide. The full length of his shaft teased up and down her sex, making her mindless with pleasure. By the time he positioned the broad, smooth head of his cock at her opening, she ached to be filled.

"You're so wet," he groaned, pushing forward. "So wet and so tight."

At the slow, startling invasion, she couldn't suppress a sharp cry of pain. Her eyes flew wide, and she gasped for breath.

It was done. He was *in* her. They were making love.

It felt . . . wonderful and terrible, all at once. The flood of sensations and emotions overwhelmed her. Her breasts molded to the firm weight of his chest. Her heart swelled with a poignant tenderness.

But mostly—between her legs, it hurt like the devil.

Colin knows what he's doing, she told herself. Surely it would start to feel marvelous soon.

Any moment now.

He slid out a little, then pushed back in. Plunging deeper this time, and stretching her wider. She knew from her own explorations, he was thickest at the root. The further he advanced, the more the pain increased. She wavered on the brink of begging him to stop altogether.

"Can you . . ." She panted for breath. "Just wait. A moment."

With a curse, he pressed his brow to her shoulder. "I hate that I've hurt you. I hate that I've done this to you at all." He lifted his head. "God, Min. I'm so sorry. I'll make it up to you, I swear. I don't know how, but . . . I'll make it right."

"Just make it good." She gave him a brave smile. "You do know how to do that?"

His mouth tipped in a lopsided, arrogant grin. "That much I hope I can manage."

He didn't press any deeper. Instead, he gave her the pause she'd requested and refocused his attention on matters close to hand. Balancing his weight on one elbow, he framed her breast in his cupped fingers and sucked her nipple into his mouth. He mouthed her lazily, swirling his tongue around and over the sensitive peak. With every flick of his nimble tongue, a shiver of bliss spread through her body.

As he transferred his attentions to the other breast, the pain where they were joined began to ease. Her intimate muscles relaxed around his girth, and the swollen bud at the crest of her sex ached for attention. Instinctively, she arched and rolled her hips, seeking friction. She found it—but the motion also pulled him deeper, brought them closer.

She gasped, surprised by the sudden pleasure. He moaned around her nipple.

All pain was forgotten as she tried to duplicate the sensation, writhing against him again. Then again, and again. Taking him deeper in tantalizing increments. With each motion, his pelvis rubbed hers just where she needed it, taking her arousal to new heights.

"Yes," he said, shifting his weight and driving forward. "That's it, love." He slid one hand beneath her bottom, lifting her up and against him as he thrust deeper still. "It's better now, is it?"

"Yes," she whispered.

He thrust harder. "Yes?"

"*Yes.*" She clutched his shoulders. "Oh, Colin. It's so good."

Burying his face in her neck, he muttered something that sounded like, *Thank God.* He set a rhythm, strong and steady, probing just a bit deeper with every stroke. She felt him reaching places she hadn't dreamed existed. And still, she craved more. When his full length was at last buried inside her, he rested a moment, holding their bodies close and joined.

His eyes shone with emotion. "I've been wanting this, Min. For longer than you could know."

She touched his cheek. "So have I."

He kissed her sweetly as he began to thrust again. Deep and steady. Real and true. She arched into his motions, growing desperate for more. At his silent urging, she wrapped her legs over his, and he slid deeper still. Now he stroked against some dark, sweet, *essential* place inside her, wrenching a joyful sob from her throat with each teasing thrust. She clutched at his back, digging her fingernails into his flesh. Her teeth scraped his shoulder.

Don't stop. Please, don't ever stop.

She rode the wave of pleasure higher and higher, until it broke. He held her tight, stroking on and on as she spiraled and tumbled through bliss.

He raised up on his arms, working her from a new, deeper angle. His pace accelerated, and the force of his thrusts increased. She loved feeling the need strung tight in his muscles. Loved knowing how much he wanted her, seeing the pained expression of desire on his face. Loved taking him just as deep and as hard and as fast as he wanted to go. As though if they collided hard enough, they might be meshed into one person.

They *could* be meshed into one person, if he didn't take care.

"Colin," she panted. "We must be careful."

"I know. I know. You just feel . . ." He groaned on a deep, hard thrust. "So sweet. So right. So good. So . . . very . . . very . . . *very* . . ."

With a deep, guttural cry, he pulled free of her body. He slumped forward, shuddering in her arms. His seed spilled over her belly like a confession of some kind. A warm, vital secret.

She stroked his back as his breathing eased. He was so quiet. This was Colin in her arms, and he was *never* quiet. As he lay there, heavy and silent atop her chest, she began to worry. Had she . . . *performed* . . . well? Perhaps she hadn't done enough, or maybe she'd done too much. Perhaps he would have wished her to be louder or bolder or . . . just different, somehow.

She was on the verge of apologizing and begging him to give her a second chance, when he rolled to the side.

"Oh, Min. That was unbelievable. I never dreamed how good it could be with . . ." He smoothed her hair back from her face. "With you."

Tears of relief and happiness pricked at the corners of her eyes.

He flopped onto his back and propped his head on one arm. "You know, I probably shouldn't say this. But you could ask me for anything right now—anything at all—and it would be yours."

"Truly?" She giggled. "Whatever would I wish for? Gold, silver, pearls, rubies . . . ?"

"Done. And done and done and done."

"The moon."

"Yours. I'll go snag it for you, just as soon as I've caught my breath. A few stars as well, if you'd like."

She nestled close to him. "Don't bother. I can't imagine anything that would make this moment better."

But that was a lie. There was one thing she wished she dared ask of him. If she could have anything she desired, she would ask only this.

Love me.

Love me, and let me love you.

The words burned on her tongue, but Minerva couldn't give them voice. What a hopeless coward she was. She could pound on his door at midnight and demand to be respected as an individual. She could travel across the country in hopes of being appreciated for her scholarly achievements. But she still lacked the courage to ask for the one thing she wanted most.

To be loved, just for herself.

Chapter Twenty-three

S omewhere, a dog howled in the night.

Colin sat up with a start, shaking and drenched in sweat. He flung open the door of the shepherd's hut and drew greedy gulps of the fresh, cool night air. As his pounding heartbeat slowed, he leaned his brow on his wrist and swore violently.

Light, soothing caresses trailed up and down his back. Her touch didn't ask questions or make demands. It simply let him know he wasn't alone.

"Can I help?" she eventually asked.

He shook his head. "It's nothing out of the usual. Just took me by surprise. The last few nights, I haven't woken at all. I'd almost begun to think . . ."

"That I was your cure?" He heard a wry smile in her voice. "I think I hoped so, too. But I suppose it was a foolish notion."

"Not foolish." He exhaled, running his hands through his hair and gathering his wits. "It's just this place, I think."

"It's too small and dark. We can take our blankets and lie under the stars. Or we can just give up sleeping altogether and walk toward the road."

"No, no. It's ages before dawn yet. I can go back to sleep,

but I think . . ." He fumbled for his discarded neck cloth and wiped the sweat from his brow and neck. "I think perhaps I'd like to talk."

The words came as a surprise to them both. They didn't pretend that he had the weather or coaching routes or any other topic on his mind. She knew instantly what he meant.

"Of course." She sat up. "Shall I light the lamp?"

"No. Don't bother." With the door open, some moonlight shone through the opening. He could discern the silvered outline of her profile, and the concerned glint in her dark eyes. That was enough.

He drew her down beside him, nuzzling in her thick, jasmine-scented hair. He was unsure how to begin. He'd never spoken of that night with anyone, not in detail. But years of keeping his silence hadn't seemed to help matters. Perhaps it was time to try talking instead. He had to do something, if he was ever going to put this behind him. To seize control of his days *and* his nights, and weave them into some semblance of a normal, boring life.

He wanted that kind of life. He wanted Minerva to be part of it.

"It will be unpleasant to hear," he warned her. "Are you certain you won't mind?"

She snuggled against his chest. "You *lived* through it, Colin. I can find the strength to listen."

"Perhaps we should wait for daylight."

"If you want to wait, we can wait. But I'm ready now if you are."

He took a deep, slow breath and then plowed straight in. "I've no idea what caused it. The accident, I mean. We were coming home from a visit with some neighbors. It wasn't a long trip. We had no footmen with us, only a driver. I'd fallen asleep on the rear-facing seat. My parents sat together, across from me. I remember listening to them talk and laugh about something. My mother was teasing my father for his overindulgence, I think. I drifted off to the sound of their voices. And then I woke sometime later. To screams."

She slipped her arms about his torso. "You must have been so confused."

"Completely. I had no idea what was happening. It was dark, and we'd careened off the road. I'd fallen from the seat. Somehow, I learned that the carriage had overturned and I'd landed atop the door. I'd cut my head on the latch."

"Here." She felt for the scar on his temple.

He nodded. "Other than that, I seemed to be unharmed. But I was terrified. The darkness was so complete. Like wearing a blindfold. And the smell of blood . . ." His gut clenched, and he paused to master his composure. "It was so thick. Smothering. I called for my mother, and she answered. Her voice was weak and strange. But she just kept telling me over and over that all would be well. That I must be brave. That surely someone would come to help us soon. I wanted to believe her, but I knew she was unable to move."

"Where was the driver?"

"Severely injured. He'd been thrown from the driver's box some distance back, but we couldn't know it at the time. We only heard the horses in agony. Theirs were the cries that woke me."

"And your father?"

"Dead."

"You knew that already?"

"No, but my mother did. The way they'd landed . . ." He drew a shaky breath. "This is the unpleasant part, pet."

"Go on." She stroked his shoulder. "I'm listening."

"There was a spike of some sort. To this day, I'm not certain whether it was part of the carriage or something in the ditch. A bit of fence, perhaps a branch . . . but they were impaled on it. The both of them. It went all the way through my father's chest and then into my mother's side."

She shuddered in his embrace. "Oh. Oh, Colin."

"It gets worse, I'm afraid. As long my mother kept talking, I knew she was alive. And even when she couldn't speak anymore, her breathing was so raspy and loud. But when even that stopped . . . I went utterly mad. I panicked. I wanted out. I screamed and beat on the carriage walls until I think I went unconscious. And then—" He choked back his emotion. He'd come this far. He had to get it all out now. "And then the wild dogs found us. Drawn by the noise and the scent of blood. They finished the horses. I passed the first half of the night screaming to get out, and second half praying they wouldn't get in."

"Oh God." He felt her tears, hot and wet against his skin.

"I'm sorry," he said quickly, holding her tight. "I'm sorry." He knew well what a disturbing picture it made. Which was precisely why he'd never shared it. Not with anyone. He hated that such a gruesome tableau would be seared on her imagination. "I shouldn't have told you."

"Of course you should." Sniffing, she lifted her head. "You did absolutely right. To think, you've been keeping that to yourself all these years? I'm the one who should be sorry." She worked her arms around his neck and hugged him tight. "Colin, I'm sorry. They're pathetic words, and they're not enough. But I'm so, so sorry. I wish with all my heart you hadn't suffered so. But I'm glad you told me everything."

He buried his face in her hair. For a moment, he feared he would weep. And then he realized, if he did weep—even noisily, messily, uncontrollably—she wouldn't shrink from him. She probably expected him to shed some tears. These soft, sweetly fragrant arms would hold him as long as he needed to be held.

So he decided to let the tears come.

And then they didn't. Odd.

For whom should he cry? For his parents? He'd grieved their loss, yes. And he missed them still. But mourning only lasted so long. It was the horror of that night that had lingered. The fear. And the shame.

The deep, buried, unvoiced shame.

"For years," he said quietly, "I thought it was my fault. That if I hadn't fallen asleep, it wouldn't have happened."

She gasped. "But that's nonsensical."

"I know."

"Of course it wasn't your fault."

"I know."

"You were a child. There was nothing more you could have done."

"I know. And as a grown man, I understand that, rationally. But . . ." But he'd never managed to rid himself of the notion. It was as though he needed someone else to confirm his innocence. Someone very intelligent and logical. Someone he could trust to always give him the unvarnished truth.

Someone like Minerva.

"It wasn't my fault," he said.

"No," she answered. "It wasn't."

Sweet, darling Min. From the first, this was what he'd loved most about her. Her certainty.

She pressed a kiss to his jaw. He took a deep, slow breath. Remarkable, how much lighter he felt. As though without her arms anchoring him, he might simply float away.

"Do you know something?" he asked drowsily. "I've always thought my parents' death was like something from a ballad. They loved each other so very much. Even as a boy, I could see it. It seems almost fitting that they met such a poetic end. Always together, united even in death. As tragedies go, you must admit—it's a rather romantic one."

She was quiet for a long time, but he knew she wasn't sleeping. Her fingers teased through his hair.

He'd almost drifted off when he heard her reply.

"If you write the verse, I'll sing it."

Minerva didn't sleep any more that night. Her heart and mind were too full. And somehow, she knew he'd sleep more soundly if she kept the vigil for him.

As the first rays of dawn seeped into the hut, she stretched her left arm. First overhead, drawing blood to her numbed, stiff fingers. Then habit and necessity drew her arm to the side, where she groped for her spectacles.

With an incoherent murmur, Colin turned in his sleep. He threw a leaden arm over her torso, and his fingers fumbled for her breast.

Oh, heavens. Her heart froze for a moment, refusing to beat. Then it underwent a rapid, prickling thaw. It hurt, the way snow-numbed fingertips stung, when thrust in a basin of warm water. Breathing suddenly required conscious thought.

She reached for her spectacles every morning, first thing. Because she could make no sense of the day without them.

Colin reached for *her*.

She couldn't "heal" him. No woman could. Events that far in the past just couldn't be undone. But perhaps he didn't need a cure, but . . . a lens. Someone who accepted him for the imperfect person he was, and then helped him to see the world clear. Like spectacles did for her.

An hour from now, the idea would seem absurd. But these first misty rays of morning forgave all kinds of foolishness. So just for a moment, she let herself dream. She let herself imagine how it would be to wake like this every day, feeling essential to him. The last thing he touched at night, and first thing he reached for every morning—out of familiarity and a desire to feel whole.

By the time he stirred with wakefulness, pressing kisses to her cheek, she wanted it so keenly, so desperately, some raw, throbbing part of her heart was already mourning the disappointment.

She turned away from him, onto her side—not wanting to explain how she'd managed to make herself so overwrought even before breakfast. He nestled behind her, cradling her body with his own. The pose emphasized all the contrasts of their physiques. The hard contours of his chest pressed along her back. The coarser hair of his legs rubbed against her smooth thighs.

Beneath the linens, his hands roamed her curves with hot, possessive intent. Cinching an arm about her waist, he drew her close. His arousal pulsed against her lower back.

"Min," he breathed, nuzzling the curve of her neck. "I need you again. Can you take me?"

She nodded her assent. But before she could turn to face him, he'd cupped and lifted her leg, shifting position behind her. His hardness wedged between her thighs.

She tensed, uncertain.

"It's all right." He kissed her neck as his fingers slid down her belly, working their way to her cleft. "Let me show you."

He caressed her intimate flesh with skill and patience. Until she was not only ready, but desperate for him.

"Love me," she begged. Because she could speak the words right now, without risking too much.

He took his erection in hand, tilted her hips to just the right angle, and eased inside.

She was tender from the night before. But he was gentle, holding her curled in his arms and loving her in slow, deliberate strokes. The sweet warmth between them grew and spread. She relaxed her body, undulating with his thrusts so that they moved as one.

He palmed her breast and pinched her nipple. Then his touch drifted down her body.

Yes. Lower. Touch me there.

He knew what she craved. He caught her pearl with his fingertips and worked her in tight, feverish circles until she shuddered and cried out with the exquisite pleasure. As her climax receded, he withdrew, finishing with a few hard, desperate thrusts between her thighs. As he came, she savored his low growl.

"Good morning." She felt his smile against her nape.

"Is it?"

His tone changed. "Don't you think so? Are you wishing we hadn't—"

"No." Screwing up her courage, she twisted to face him. "I have no regrets. None. But I want assure you, just in case it needs saying . . . I don't have any expectations."

Only hopes. Wistful, foolish hopes.

He blinked. "You don't have any expectations."

Surely he must understand what she meant. "What we shared was wonderful. But I don't want you to worry that I'm expecting something more."

"Well," he said dryly. "How very generous of you."

"Aren't you relieved?" She didn't understand the annoyance in his voice.

He rolled onto his back, rubbing the bridge of his nose. "Minerva, I can't decide which of us you're insulting more. After last night, you *should* have expectations."

"Expectations of what?" She swallowed hard.

"Of *me*."

"I thought you were the one who argued against having any expectations at all. Isn't that your grand life philosophy? You said expectations lead to disappointments. That if you expect nothing, you're always surprised."

He gave a bark of laughter. "In that case . . ."

He turned to her. His hazel eyes sparked with intensity.

"Surprise." He kissed the tip of her nose. "You're marrying me."

Chapter Twenty-four

Well, Colin thought. He'd certainly managed to surprise her.

Whether the surprise fell into the "pleasant" or "unpleasant" category, he wasn't sure. The latter, he suspected.

She didn't move a muscle. But behind her spectacles, her eyelashes worked like twin ebony fans. "Marry? *You*?"

He tried not to take offense. "I must say, Minerva. That's not exactly the breathless, overjoyed acceptance a man might wish to hear."

"That wasn't exactly the ardent, heartfelt proposal that might warrant one. In fact, I'm not sure it counts as a proposal at all."

"Fair enough, I suppose." He lightened his tone. "You have a temporary reprieve. Right now, out of bed with you. We have to make haste if we're going to reach York tonight."

"Wait, wait." As he sat up, she grabbed his arm. "I'm so confused. Is this like one of those silly duels gentlemen arrange for show? You fire off a haphazard proposal at dawn, it sails straight over my head, and somehow honor is satisfied?"

"No, it's not like that at all. I'm serious. I mean to marry you."

"But I thought you'd sworn off marriage."

He shrugged. "I seem to recall you saying something similar."

"Exactly. Colin, I do appreciate the gesture." She bit her lip. "I think. But I won't marry you simply because you're feeling a sudden twinge of conscience. We both knew from the outset I'd be ruined."

"In appearance, yes. But this is actuality."

"In actuality, I don't feel ruined at all." She gave him a sheepish half smile. "Only a bit tender in places. Did last night feel like some grave mistake to you?"

He touched her cheek. "God, no. The furthest thing from it."

He let his gaze wander her sweet, lovely face. After the night they'd shared, something in his soul finally felt put right.

"Then what's this truly about? What on earth can you be thinking?"

She struggled to sit up. The bedsheets slipped to her hips, revealing her bare torso.

Colin's breath left his body. Damn if she didn't look just exactly the way she had that first night. Her spectacles slipped to the end of her nose, her unbound hair tumbling about her shoulders, her bared breasts tempting him with their touchable perfection.

A low groan rattled loose from his chest.

"I'm thinking," he said, "that last night was inevitable, and I should have known as much the day we left Spindle Cove. I'm thinking that what I *ought* to do, as a gentleman, is call an immediate halt to this journey and make swift arrangements for a proper wedding." He stayed her objection with a touch to her lips. "I'm thinking what I'd *like* to do is push you back on that bed, bar the door, and spend the next week learning your body from the inside out. But mostly, Min . . ."

He pushed her spectacles back up her nose, so that she could focus on his face.

"I'm thinking that I made you two promises. To get you to your symposium, and to do so without seducing you. I've broken one of those. But I damn well mean to make good on the other." He rose from the bed and offered her a hand. "So I'm thinking this conversation will have to wait. We have no time to waste."

With a bewildered shake of her head, she took his hand. "All right."

Taking a leather bucket from the shepherd's hut, Colin fetched water from a nearby stream. While Minerva performed her ablutions inside the dwelling, he doused himself in the frigid water—shirt and all.

His shirt needed washing, and he needed a bracing, icy bath to punish his lustful loins into submission. He'd taken her virtue last night. Then he'd taken her again this morning. He'd broken all his own rules, forsaken what few remaining principles he held. No matter what objections she raised or how many of his own stupid words she threw back at him, his conscience insisted there was only one course of action.

He must marry her.

But he *had* to get her to that symposium first.

She didn't want to marry him simply because he'd ruined her, and Colin didn't want that either. No, he wanted her to marry him because he'd helped her triumph. He would prove to her—to himself—that he could be good for her.

As he submerged himself in the cold water, an insidious, shadowy doubt swirled through his thoughts.

The road to Edinburgh is paved with good intentions.

He forced the doubt away, rising to the surface and pushing the water from his face. This time was different. Today, everything was different. For God's sake, he hated the country—and yet, here he was in the middle of a pasture, making his way to a shepherd's hut, absurdly wishing he could lease it as a summer home.

When he returned to the hut, soaked and shivering, Minerva gave him a baleful look through her spectacles. "You'll catch cold."

He shrugged, wringing out his shirttails. "The sun will dry it soon enough. First order of business when we reach York"—he yanked his breeches up and fastened them under his dripping shirt—"is fresh clothes."

"Are you sure it's even possible to make the symposium?" She counted the days on her fingers. "Only three more nights between now and then."

"We will make it. We'll reach York tonight. From there, with our replenished funds, it's a new journey. We'll take just a few hours to eat and shop and hire a post-chaise, and then we'll be off."

"But you'll be miserable. Post-chaises are so small and cramped. Not to mention expensive. We won't have enough funds to rent you horses past York."

"They're the fastest way. If we travel straight through, we'll make Edinburgh just in time."

"Travel straight through? We won't stop for nights?" Her eyes filled with concern.

He shook his head. "There won't be time."

"But Colin—"

"And we haven't time to debate it, either." He picked up one side of Francine's trunk. "Let's be on our way."

Money made everything easier. They found a proper breakfast, a ride to the next coaching town, and from there, Colin rented a horse to ride alongside her coach. His last horse of the journey.

They reached York in late afternoon. He sought out the

largest and best of the coaching inns. Holding Minerva close at his side, he approached the innkeeper.

"What can I do for you, sir?" the distracted innkeeper asked.

"We'll need a good dinner. A few hours' use of a room, just to rest and change. And then I'll need to inquire about hiring a post-chaise to take us north."

"How far north are you traveling?" the innkeeper asked.

"Edinburgh. We mean to travel straight through."

"Is that so?" The man eyed them with suspicion, his rheumy eyes ranging over their bedraggled attire.

"I'll pay in advance," Colin offered.

"Oh, indeed. That you most certainly will." The innkeeper cocked one eyebrow and rubbed the top of his head. He named a figure, and Colin counted out the money.

He leaned forward and addressed the man in low tones. "Listen, perhaps you can help me with something else. My lady here's been parted from her baggage. Before we continue, I need to find her a new gown. Something pretty."

The innkeeper eyed Minerva. "My missus can find her something, I warrant."

"The finest quality this will buy." To the amount he'd paid for the post-chaise, Colin added several sovereigns.

Minerva gasped. "Colin, don't. We can't afford it."

"It's not negotiable. You must have it."

"But . . ."

The innkeeper laughed. "Come now, miss. Surely he don't have to draw you a picture. Elopement or no, a man wants his bride dressed proper."

"But . . ." Minerva called after him as he shuffled off, disappearing through a doorway. "Sir, we're not eloping."

"Of course you aren't," he called back. "None of you young lovers are."

She turned to Colin.

He shrugged. "There's no use arguing. Do you think he'll believe we're headed for a geology symposium?"

"It's strange," she said, as they sat down at a table to order their dinner. "We have had uncommonly good luck today. Reasonably fine weather, except for that short rain. No loss of money or belongings. No fisticuffs. No highwaymen. I keep looking over my shoulder, expecting to see those kidnappers chasing after Prince Ampersand."

"Oh, don't worry about them. We will have left those highwaymen far behind. Believe me, that group wasn't sufficiently organized or industrious to follow us beyond their own county." He rubbed his jaw. "But I have to admit, I wouldn't be at all shocked to see someone else catch up to us."

"Who?"

"Bram. Or Thorne, or both. When my cousin heard of this, I can't imagine his reaction was favorable. He knew I had no plan of marrying, as of two days before we left. And if Susanna expressed any doubts as to your willingness . . . I wouldn't put it past him to decide you needed rescuing."

The serving girl brought them two glasses of claret. Colin ordered them a hearty meal of beefsteak, fish stew, sauced vegetables, and apple tart. His stomach growled with hunger.

"But I left a note," Minerva said, once the serving girl had gone. "I told my sister we'd eloped."

"Slim evidence, on its own. You forgot to leave behind that false journal."

"That's true. And the real diary was less than complimentary to your character." She cast him a cautious glance over her wineglass. "But that wasn't all I left behind. There was something else."

"Oh, really?" Intrigued, he leaned forward. "What?"

"You, um . . ." Blushing, she took a large gulp of wine. "You might have written me a letter."

Chapter Twenty-five

"Corporal Thorne!"

Samuel Thorne paused in the act of lifting his shovel. He'd know that voice anywhere.

Damn it. Not her. Not now.

"Corporal Thorne, I—" Miss Taylor turned a corner and stopped short when she caught a glimpse of him. "Oh. There you are."

Blast. Weren't gently bred ladies supposed to have some rules of decorum that prevented them from surprising half-dressed men at their labor? How the hell was he supposed to greet her with mud streaking his shirt and sweat matting his hair to his scalp?

Throwing aside the shovel, he hastily wiped his face with a bit of sleeve. He jerked his collar closed.

She didn't even have the good sense to avert her eyes. She just stared at him, wide-eyed and curious. He had half a mind to pull the shirt over his head, cast it aside, and say, *Here. Look your fill. This is what years of thieving, prison labor, and battle do to a man.*

He almost chuckled at the thought. Oh, she'd run screaming then.

She cleared her throat. "I'm sorry to interrupt your . . . digging."

"Why are you here, Miss Taylor? What can I do for you?"

She waved a paper clutched in her hand. "I've come to prove it to you. The truth of the elopement. I have here a love letter, addressed to Minerva Highwood from Lord Payne himself. Miss Charlotte found it in Minerva's stocking drawer."

"Impossible." Thorne would swallow nails before he'd believe Payne to be in love with Miss Minerva Highwood. It still ate at him, that he hadn't chased after the couple that very first night. But what was he to do, when the girl's own mother forbade it?

Now if only Miss Taylor would let the topic rest. He suffered enough torment in her presence already, without this added deviling.

She approached and offered him the letter. "Read it for yourself."

Good God. Now she meant to test his alphabet. Thorne eyed the envelope. A queasy feeling curdled in his gut. He knew his letters reasonably well—better than most men of his station—but he needed time and concentration to sift through a missive of that length. And he'd have an even harder time of it, trying to read with a raging beauty hovering over his shoulder. How was he supposed to put two sounds together in her presence?

He held up his grimy hands in excuse. "You'll have to read it to me."

She shook open the paper. " 'My darling beloved Minerva,' " she read aloud.

And that was the last bit he heard. Oh, she kept reading. And he kept listening. But he wasn't hearing the words anymore—just her clear, bright voice.

So strange. She had music in her voice, even when she

wasn't singing. The melody hummed in his body. Not in a pleasant way. It hurt. The same way it would feel if he drove his shovel full-strength into soil and met unyielding rock instead. The shock of it reverberated all through his bones, his teeth.

His heart.

And now he hadn't a damned idea what the hell she was reading anyway. He would have had better luck staring stupidly at the paper himself.

"Enough." He held up a hand. "Payne did not write that."

"He did. He signed his name."

Thorne cocked his head and stared at the address on the paper's reverse. "That's not Payne's handwriting." That much he could discern without effort.

"What?" She flipped the paper back and forth.

"It's not his hand. I know it's not." Wiping his hands on his breeches, he strode over to the turret Payne had been using as his personal quarters. He unlocked and opened the door, proceeding straight to the small writing desk.

He rifled through a stack of papers until he found one in the right penmanship. Then he handed it to her. "See?"

She held up the two and compared them. "You're right. It is different penmanship."

"I told you so. He didn't write that letter."

"But I don't understand. Who else would write this, then sign it with Lord Payne's name?"

He shrugged. "A cruel joke, perhaps. To build up her hopes. Or maybe she wrote it herself."

"Poor Minerva."

He watched as Miss Taylor's bottom lip folded beneath her teeth. Then he forced himself to look elsewhere.

She said, "But somehow, it seems to have worked out anyway. They did elope together."

He snorted, resisting the urge to tell her everything he'd

learned from Mrs. Ginny Watson the other day. When confronted, the young widow had told him all about Miss Minerva's midnight visit to Rycliff Castle. Thorne knew the truth now, beyond all doubt.

Payne and Miss Highwood had not eloped.

They would, however, end up married. He would ensure that much. If Payne dared to come back from this jaunt a bachelor, he would not remain so long. He'd walk Miss Minerva down the aisle of St. Ursula's if Thorne had to prod him at knifepoint. Protecting the women of this village was his duty, and he took it seriously.

Which was exactly why he kept his mouth shut now.

Miss Taylor didn't need to know the particulars of all Mrs. Watson had told him. If it pleased this girl to believe in true love and tales that ended happily for all concerned, Thorne would carry all manner of unpleasant truths to his grave. After all, this secret was hardly the first. Just one of many he'd vowed to keep, for her happiness's sake.

She sifted through the papers.

He crossed his arms. "What, are you snooping now?"

"No," she protested. "Well, maybe. Goodness, he writes a great many letters to his stewards."

"Listen, I have a well to dig, and—"

"Wait." She plucked a paper from the stack. "What's this?" She read aloud. " 'Millicent . . . Madeira . . . Michaela . . . Marilyn . . .' And this *is* written in his hand."

"So? It's a list of names."

"Yes. A list of women's names, all of them beginning with M." A flush rose on her throat. "The letter means nothing, but this . . . this is proof. Don't you see?"

"No, I don't. Not at all."

"Lord Payne always acted as though he couldn't remember Minerva's name. Calling her Melissa and Miranda and every other 'M' name under the sun. But he must have done it on purpose, don't you see? Just to tease her. He even went to the trouble of writing out this list."

"That proves him even more of an blackguard, to my mind."

She clucked her tongue impatiently. "Corporal Thorne. You really don't understand a thing about romance."

Thorne shrugged. She was right. He understood desire. He understood wanting. He understood loyalty and bone-deep devotion that stretched back to a time before this woman's earliest memories.

But he didn't know a damn thing about romance.

She ought to thank God for it.

There she went, right now—flashing him a fearless smile. No one smiled like that at Thorne. But she'd always been this way. Cheerful, in the face of everything. Singing like a little angel, even when she stood at the very gates of hell.

"Don't you know?" she said. "Apparent dislike often masks a hidden attraction."

He felt his face go hot. "Not in this case."

"Oh, yes. This list doesn't prove Lord Payne's a black-guard." She tapped the paper against Thorne's chest. "It proves he was *smitten*."

Chapter Twenty-six

"I demand to know what was in this letter." Wearing a devilish grin, Colin chased her up the coaching inn staircase.

Minerva cringed. She never should have mentioned it. "Can we move past this, please? You plagued me all through dinner. I've told you, I don't recall."

"And I told *you*, I don't believe you."

"It doesn't matter whether or not you believe me."

She opened the door to their chambers. While they'd been eating downstairs, a manservant had been dispatched to fetch a few gentlemen's necessities for Colin. And the finest secondhand gown three pounds could purchase had been laid out by the maid. A surprisingly lovely muslin frock— ivory, block-printed with tiny pink sprigs.

A banked fire smoldered in the hearth. And the bed, heaped with pillows and quilts . . . oh, how Minerva's road-weary body yearned to sink into that bed and stay there for *days*.

"I'm going to change before our post-chaise is ready." She ducked behind a dressing screen in hopes of hiding from this conversation.

"Then I'll have a shave." She heard him cross to the washstand. "But I'm going to keep on deviling you, until you confess everything. Did I compose pages of description? Compare your eyes to Brighton diamonds?"

"They're *Bristol* diamonds. And no, you did not."

"Aha. So you do remember the contents."

She huffed out a breath. "Very well. Yes. I do remember. I remember that letter word for word."

Water splashed in the basin, and she heard the scratch of his shaving brush against his stubbled jaw. The familiar scent of his shaving soap filled the air. It smelled of cloves.

"I'm listening," he prompted.

Behind the screen, she picked at a ragged fingernail. "You wrote that you'd been studying me, when I wasn't aware of it. Stealing glances when I was lost in thought, or when my head was bent over a book. Admiring the way my dark, wild hair always manages to escapes its pins, tumbling down my neck. Noting the warm glow of my skin, where the sun has kissed it. You wrote that you're consumed by a savage, visceral passion for an enchantress with raven's-wing hair and sultry lips. That you see in me a rare, wild beauty that's been overlooked by other men. Sound familiar?"

"Oh, you didn't." He muttered a curse and tapped his razor on the washbasin. "You couldn't have remembered *everything* I said that night."

"Certainly I could. And what better words to fill a forged letter from you? They were all yours, after all." She sniffed. "You wrote that I was the true reason you'd remained in Spindle Cove all those months. And the letter ended with the sweetest words. 'It's simply you, Minerva. It's always been you.'"

He was quiet for a long time. For as long as it took her to undo fourteen hooks at the back of her abused blue silk gown and pick loose the knots of her corset laces and unbut-

ton all the tiny closures of her shift. For as long as it took for
him to finish shaving and cross the room in slow, measured
footfalls.

She heard a creak as he flung himself on the bed. "God, I
was such an ass."

She didn't offer any argument to the contrary.

"And do you know the most ironic thing about it, Min?"

"What's that?"

"I always liked you."

Minerva paused in the act of tying her garter. She allowed
herself one moment of absurd, heart-pinching hope before
making a loud sound of disbelief. "Please."

"No, really," he insisted. "All right, perhaps I didn't always
like you."

See? She yanked her petticoat laces tight.

He went on, "But you have to admit, there was something
between us from the first."

"Something like antagonism, you mean?" She stepped
into the new gown and bounced on her toes, tugging the
fabric over her petticoats and stays. The fit was rather tight.
"The hostility of two barn cats fighting in a sack?"

"Something like that." He chuckled. "No, it's just . . ." His
voice went thoughtful. "I always felt that you could see me,
somehow. In a way no one else did. That with those fetching
little spectacles, you could peer straight through me. And
you made no secret of the fact that you despised what you
saw, which marked you as far cleverer than most. I couldn't
rid myself of this fascination with you. Your sharp gaze,
your enticing mouth, your complete invulnerability to all
my charms. If I treated you poorly—and I know I did, to my
shame—it was because I always felt rather hopeless around
you."

Her spine snapped straight. She couldn't believe what she
was hearing.

She poked her head around the dressing screen and stared at him. He lay on the bed, freshly shaven and washed, legs crossed at the ankles and arms propped behind his head. His posture said, *Yes, ladies, I truly am this handsome. And I don't even have to try.*

"You," she said. "Felt hopeless around *me*? Oh, Colin. That is too much."

"It's the truth." His gaze was sincerity itself.

Minerva took refuge behind the screen. She was surprised her pounding heartbeat hadn't knocked it over.

"I never despised you," she said. "Just so you know."

It was his turn to make a sound of utter disbelief.

"Very well, I may have despised you a little. But only because . . ." She sighed, unable to deny it any longer. "Only because I was so wretchedly infatuated with you. I didn't want to be, but I couldn't help it. All you had to do was glance my direction, and my heart would go all fluttery. Every time I tried to say something witty in your presence, it came out shrewish or dull. I've always considered myself an intelligent person, but I vow, Colin—no one has ever made me feel so stupid."

"Well. That's . . . oddly gratifying."

She laughed a little at the memories, and at herself. "And all the while, everyone in Spindle Cove would talk about what a perfect match you made for Diana. I heard it at the tea shop, at the All Things, around the fire of an evening . . . Just underscoring again and again, no one would ever pair you with a girl like me. And that much I could have lived with, but the prospect of being your sister-in-law?" She swiped at a welling tear with her wrist. "I love my sister. I've always tried not to envy Diana her sweetness or elegance or beauty. But I would have envied her *you*, and the thought made me ill. So if we're vying for the crown of Most Hopeless, I do think I had it won."

After a long silence, he clapped his hands together. "I hope you're ready to trade that crown for a five-hundred-guinea prize. I see our post-chaise out the window. It's nearly ready."

She emerged from behind the dressing screen. "How do I look?" She turned and fretted in the mirror. "Will the gown do?"

He came to stand behind her, settling his strong hands on her shoulders and waiting until she went still. "The gown will do. You, on the other hand . . ."

She . . . ? Wouldn't?

Out of self-preservation, she tried to twist away from their reflection. His hands tightened on her shoulders, forbidding her to move. She watched him carefully, cautiously in the mirror as his gaze wandered her form.

She couldn't take the suspense. "For God's sake, Colin. What's wrong?"

"You're beautiful, Min," he said, in a tone of wonderment. As if his own words took him by surprise. "Lord above. You're stunning."

She huffed a protest. "I'm not. You know I'm not."

"What makes you so sure?"

"No one's ever called me so before. I'm twenty-one years old. If I were beautiful, surely someone would have noticed by now."

He seemed to think on this for a moment, dropping one hand to straighten the trim on her sleeve. "It *is* hard to imagine anyone overlooking beauty on this magnitude. Perhaps you weren't beautiful until very recently."

A nervous laugh rose in her throat. "I'm sure I haven't undergone any dramatic transformation." She searched her own reflection, just to make sure. The same wide brown eyes stared back at her, encircled by brass wire rims. They anchored the same rounded face and funny, heart-shaped mouth. Her skin had freckled and tanned over recent days, but other that that . . . "I'm the same as I ever was."

"Well, I'm not," he said simply, still drinking in her reflection. "I'm altered. Destroyed. Utterly laid waste."

"Don't. Don't tease me." *I can't bear to be hurt like that again.*

"I'm not teasing you. I'm complimenting you."

"That's just it. I don't want compliments. I'm not fanciful that way."

"Not fanciful?" He laughed. "Min, you have the wildest imagination of anyone I know. You can look at a queer-shaped hole in the ground and see a vast, primeval landscape overrun with giant lizards. But it's too much to believe you're beautiful?"

She didn't know what to say.

He mused, "Maybe 'beautiful' isn't the proper word. It's too common, and the way you look is . . . rare. You deserve a rare compliment. One sincerely meant, and crafted just for you. So there will be no doubt."

"Really, you needn't—"

"Hush. I'm going to compliment you. Honestly. No raven's-wing nonsense. You needn't say a word in return, but I will insist you stand there and take it."

She watched him in the mirror as his brows drew into a frown of concentration.

"Once," he said, "years ago, I heard this fellow speak at the Adventurers Club. He talked about his journeys into the Amazonian jungles."

Minerva didn't like where this excursion was headed. She had the dreadful feeling he was going to compare her to some strange carnivorous plant. One that lured its prey with garish red flowers and the scent of decaying meat.

"He was an entomologist, this fellow."

Oh God. Worse! *Insects.* He was going to compare her to

some giant hairy-legged jungle insect. One that spat venom, or ate small rodents.

Calm down, she told herself. It might be a butterfly. Butterflies were pretty. Even beautiful, depending on the variety. She heard they came big as dinner plates, in the Amazon.

"Anyhow, this fellow had spent all this time with the natives, in the thick of the jungles, hunting down hard-shelled beetles."

"Beetles?" The word came out as a whimper.

"Can't remember, to be honest. I slept through much of his talk, but what I recall is this: this native people he lived with, deep in the jungle—their language had dozens of words for rain. Because it was so common to them, you see. Where they lived, it rained almost constantly. Several times a day. So they had words for light rain, and heavy rain, and pounding rain. Something like eighteen different terms for storms, and a whole classification system for mist."

"Why are you telling me this?"

His touch skimmed idly down her arm. "Because I'm standing here, wanting to give you a fitting compliment, but my paltry vocabulary fails me. I think what I need is a scientific excursion. I need to venture deep into some jungle where beauty takes the place of rain. Where loveliness itself falls from the sky at regular intervals. Dots every surface, saturates the ground, hangs like vapor in the air. Because the way you look, right now . . ." His gaze caught hers in the reflection. "They'd have a word for it there."

Entranced by his touch and his warm, melting tone, she watched her own eyes go glassy in the mirror. She leaned back a fraction, resting against his chest. His heartbeat pounded against her spine, echoing through her chest like some distant drum.

"There'd be so many words for beauty there," he went on, bringing his lips close to her ear and dropping his voice to a murmur. "Words for everyday showers of prettiness, and the kind of misty loveliness that disappears whenever you try to grasp it. Beauty that's heralded by impressive thunder, but turns out to be all flash. And beyond all these, there'd be this word . . . a word that even the most grizzled, wizened elders might have uttered twice in their lifetimes, and in hushed, fearful tones at that. A word for a sudden, cataclysmic torrent of beauty with the power to change landscapes. Make plains out of valleys and alter the course of rivers and leave people clinging to trees, alive and resentful, shaking their fists at the heavens."

A hint of sensual frustration roughened his voice. "And I will curse the gods along with them, Min. Some wild monsoon raged through me as I looked at you just now. It's left me rearranged inside, and I don't have a map."

They stared into the mirror. At each other, at themselves.

"I've fallen in love with you," she said, with quiet resignation. "If I appear changed somehow, I can only imagine that's why."

She watched him carefully for his reaction. His face became a mask, frozen in time. Eternally handsome and emotionless.

And then, finally . . . a hint of a roguish grin cracked at the corner of his mouth. "Oh, Min—"

"Stop." She stood tall, putting distance between them. She just knew he was going to make some jesting remark to dispel the tension. *Oh, Min, don't fret. You'll get over it soon.* Or, *Oh, Min, think of poor Sir Alisdair.*

"Don't you do that." She turned away from the mirror, toward him. "Don't you dare make a joke. It took a great deal of courage to say what I did. And you don't have to speak a word in return, but I will insist you be man enough to take it. I won't have you making light of my feelings, or making light of yourself—as if you're not worthy of them.

Because you are worthy, Colin. You're a generous, good-hearted person, and you deserve to be loved. Deeply, truly, well, and often."

He looked utterly bewildered. Well, what did he expect, after the power he'd given her? He couldn't compare a woman to a torrentially beautiful monsoon, and then look surprised that he'd gotten wet.

"You reckless man." She laid a touch to his cheek. "You really should be more careful with those compliments."

"So it seems."

She sighed and straightened his tattered lapels. "I know you have this idea that we'll marry in Scotland. To satisfy honor, I suppose. While you've given me this momentary burst of courage, I'll tell you this. I will not marry you to satisfy honor."

"You won't?"

"No." Difficult as it was, she forced herself to meet his gaze. "I will only marry you if you love me, and if you can allow me to love you." A bittersweet smile curved her lips. "That first night in the turret, you gave me a taste of how it would feel to have your love. It was the most thrilling sensation I've ever known. For a moment, I felt as though anything—absolutely *anything*—could be possible. When it turned out to be false . . . it crushed me, Colin. More than I care to admit. I would rather die a spinster—poor, ruined, scorned, and alone—than suffer that heartbreak daily."

Regret creased his eyes at the corners. "That's just it, pet. I start with good intentions, but . . . the people around me get hurt."

So there it was. Her emotion-swelled heart was beating on borrowed time.

Seeking consolation from the man who'd soon break it seemed stupid indeed, but she did so anyway. She let her forehead lean against his shoulder. He put his hands on her arms, rubbing lightly up and down. His chin rested square and heavy on her head.

"I will get you and Francine to Edinburgh in one piece." He pressed a firm kiss to the top of her head. "If I can promise you nothing else, I promise you that."

Chapter Twenty-seven

For the love of tits.

Colin considered himself a patriot and a devoted servant of the Crown. But by God, right now he hated England. This damnable country, plagued with endless rain and cursed with muddy, rutted, barely passable roads.

Their first day out from York had gone well. Smooth transitions when they changed horses. He passed a few brief stints inside the coach, but spent most of the journey riding next to the postilion. The roads and weather had stayed fair. His hopes had run high.

Then, today, the rain had started. And it had kept on. And on.

At one coaching stop, they had waited an hour before a fresh team was available. The road conditions were so poor in stretches, their pace slowed to a crawl.

And all along, a clock ticked down inside Colin's mind. Every hour of slow, inching progress set them further and further behind schedule. The delay was making him wild inside.

He *had* to get Minerva to her symposium on time. He'd *promised*. If he couldn't see this journey through, how could he ask her to trust him with the rest of her life? Good intentions and pretty compliments weren't enough. He had to prove this to her, and to himself.

All was not lost yet. They still had enough time to reach Edinburgh, but their cushion was dwindling. There was no more room for error. When they'd taken luncheon a few hours ago, Colin had told himself—from here on out, everything needed to go right.

Some fifteen miles after that, they were stuck.

The crisis had started at the last coaching inn. There were no horses to be hired, and—due to the rains and mud—no horses expected to come available. Colin had used all his powers of persuasion and a significant sum of money to convince the postilion to forge ahead with the same team—promising him if he turned onto a side road, Colin knew of a place some miles distant where strong, fresh horses could be had.

And that would have worked brilliantly, if they hadn't lurched into a rut halfway there, burying two of the wheels spoke-deep in mud.

Colin tried to lighten the weight. It didn't help.

He went round the back of the coach and pushed with all his might as the postilion whipped the horses. It didn't help.

Now soaked with rain and covered in mud, he struggled to hold despair at bay. This could be accomplished. It wasn't too late. They might have been able to pull free with a fresh team, but these poor beasts were simply exhausted. After discussing matters with the postilion, he helped the man unhitch the team and returned to Minerva.

"What's going on?" she asked, opening the door to speak with him. "Is he walking away with the horses?"

"Yes. They're too tired to pull out of this mire, so he's going to switch them for new. I told him of a place nearby. We'll just wait here until he returns."

She eyed him closely. "Wait here?"

He nodded.

"In the rain?"

He tilted his face to the sky. "I think it's clearing a bit."

"In that case." She opened the door and stepped out from the post-chaise, immediately sinking ankle-deep in mud. "I'll wait outside with you."

"No, no," he urged. "Get back in the coach. The rain's not really clearing at all."

Raindrops dotted her spectacles. "So even that was a lie?"

Bloody hell. "I was trying to sound optimistic."

"Why bother?" Staring down the road, she shook her head. "Colin, you have to admit it's—"

"Don't." He knew what words were coming, and those words would have destroyed him. "Don't say it."

"I'm merely stating facts. Even if the postilion returns, we'll still be hours behind schedule. And with this rain—"

"Don't *say* it." He grabbed her by the upper arms, turning her to face him. The rain had plastered little wisps of hair to her cheeks. "It's not over, Min. I made you a promise. I will get you and Francine to Edinburgh in one piece." He slid his hands up and down her arms, chafing them over the fabric. This scrap of cloth the innkeeper had sold them was much too thin for this weather. "Now get back in the coach before you catch your death."

She started to reply, but the distant slap of hooves against mud interrupted her. Colin turned in surprise. A carriage was approaching, drawn by an impressive team of four.

"See?" he said, releasing her. "I told you. Look, here comes our salvation now."

As the coach drew closer, Colin stood to the side of the road, waving his arms. The driver slowed the team.

One glass window swung open, and a face peered out. A kind-faced woman with graying hair and a lace cap. Wonderful. Colin was a wild success with silver-haired ladies.

This particular one narrowed her eyes and said, "*You*."

Damnation. Really, what were the chances?

"Why, Mrs. Fontley," he said, forcing a grin. "How lovely to see you again. And fortunate, too. As you can see, we're in a bit of a muddle."

"You ought to be in prison, you villain."

"I say." Mr. Fontley's face squeezed into the frame. "You have quite a lot of nerve, Sand. If that is your real name."

"It's not, actually. I lied to you in London, and that was wrong. But I'll tell you the truth now. I'm a rather useless insomniac viscount, but"—he gestured at Minerva—"my companion here is a brilliant geologist. There's a symposium, you see. We need to get to Edinburgh by tomorrow, so she can present her findings about giant lizards and possibly alter our understanding of the world's natural history."

Mrs. Fontley squawked in disbelief. "Lizards? First cobras, now lizards."

"No, no. This is nothing like the cobras. I swear on my life, this time I'm telling you the absolute truth."

Mr. Fontley signaled the driver with a knock on the roof. "Onward."

"Please. You can't leave us here." Colin grabbed the door latch.

Through the window, Mrs. Fontley beat at his fingers with a folded parasol. "Get away from our carriage, you vile people."

"Gilbert!" Minerva rapped at the coach's front window. "Gilbert, please. Can't you convince them to help us?"

The youth pressed his fingertips to the glass and gave her a sorrowful look. "I'll pray for you."

The driver whipped the team into motion, and Colin had to pull Minerva away lest she be caught under the wheels. As the coach departed, the footmen tossed down two rectangular objects. They landed in the center of the road with a sick thud, spattering them both with mud.

Minerva's trunks.

Colin stared at them, trying to laugh. He couldn't. None of this was amusing anymore.

Pushing rain off his face, he turned to Minerva and found her watching him.

"Don't bother," he told her. "I know what you're going to say."

"You do?"

He nodded. "You're going to say that this is all my fault. That if I'd never lied to the Fontleys, they would have helped us just now."

She didn't say anything. Just crossed her arms and looked at her boots, encased in mud.

"But then I would say to *you*," he went on, "that if I hadn't lied to the Fontleys, we would have never come this far at all."

She frowned at him. "Do you often have arguments with yourself?"

"And then you'll say, 'But *Colin* . . .'" He raised his voice in a lilting imitation of hers. "'If only we had taken the mail coach, we'd already be in Edinburgh.' And on that score, you would be right."

"Please don't put words in my m—"

He waved her off. "You're shivering. Did you have a cloak in one of those trunks?"

She shook her head. "I'm fine."

"Damn it, don't tell me you're fine." The rain picked up strength, and he had to raise his voice to shout through it. "You're wet, and getting wetter. You're here, and not in Scotland. You're . . ."

You're with me, and not some better man.

"So don't tell me you're fine, Min."

"Very well," she finally shouted back, balling her hands into fists. "I'm not fine. I'm disappointed and heartbroken and m-miserably cold. Are you happy now?"

God damn it. He pushed both hands through his hair and stared down the road. Such a simple thing, a road. Just a strip of dirt running from one place to another. And everyone else in the civilized world, when they wanted to travel from one place to another, would simply get inside a blasted carriage and ride there. Any other man in England could have already delivered her to Edinburgh.

Any other man would be waiting out this downpour with her in a safe, dry place.

He strode to the post-chaise door and held it open. "Get inside."

Minerva gave up arguing and got inside. Colin joined her, shutting the door behind them. It was a tight fit, what with three occupants. Francine had been riding inside the cab ever since the rain began.

Once he'd wrestled out of his wet coat and draped it over her lap, Colin unknotted his neck cloth. He slid the length of fabric free, using the drier bits to swab his face and neck.

She watched him with concern.

"I'm fine," he said. "It won't be long. I gave the postilion explicit directions. He'll return soon, and we'll be on our way. Everything will be fine."

"Then what are you doing with the pistol?"

As she looked on, he retrieved the gun from under the seat and began to load it with ball and powder.

"Simple precaution," he said. "Stuck like this, we're a sitting target for thieves."

She didn't know how to interpret his dark mood. This was more than just the closeness of the carriage. He seemed to be blaming himself for everything, the weather included.

And she was angry with herself for letting him goad her into heaping yet more recriminations. None of this was his fault.

"Colin, this entire journey was my idea. I'm sorry to have put you—"

"We don't need to discuss it." He recapped the powder horn.

She tried to respect his wish for silence, but it wasn't easy.

After a minute, he said lightly, "It's just a shame it's not better weather. His fingers drummed against the window-pane. "All sorts of impressive crags and boulders in this area. You'd be in heaven."

She flicked a glance at the window and the square of gray downpour it held. "So you've journeyed this way before."

"Oh, countless times."

Countless times? That made no sense. She thought he'd avoided the country, ever since . . .

"Oh dear." The chilling realization sank into her bones. She reached for his hand. "Colin. We're not close to your home?"

The silence confirmed what he wouldn't say. Her heart pinched. So this was why he knew where the postilion could find fresh horses. He'd simply sent the man to his own estate.

"Was it very near here?" she asked. "The accident?"

He drew a slow breath that seemed the product of great effort. "Actually, no. It wasn't terribly near."

But neither was it terribly far, she imagined.

Overwhelmed with emotion, she nestled close, lacing her fingers tight with his. He was in a cramped, stuffy carriage with her, with night coming on, stuck on the very same roads that had claimed his parents' lives and destroyed his innocence.

This was as close as Colin Sandhurst could come to walking barefoot down the brimstone avenues of hell, and he was doing it for her.

For her.

She clutched him tighter still. *Thank you*, she wanted to say. *Thank you for believing in me. For braving this for me. If I didn't love you so madly already, I surely would now.*

But she knew tearful professions were hardly what he needed at the moment. This situation called for distraction.

She said, "I'm sure it won't be long. What shall we do with ourselves to pass the time?"

"Why don't you read me your presentation again, and I can pretend to pose thoughtful questions?"

She laughed a little.

His voice warmed. "No, truly. I like listening to it. I can't pretend to understand every word in your presentation, but I don't have to be an expert to know you've something important to say. I don't need to be a geologist to understand that it's well-written and carefully reasoned. And the way you pronounce all those polysyllabic words?" His thigh nudged hers. "Makes me rock hard, every time."

She blushed. Not just at the carnal suggestion, but at his honest appreciation for her scholarship. For all his teasing over the months, she had to give him this: he'd never once suggested she lacked a mind of her own, or insinuated her sex must be an intellectual handicap. How many men of his rank and importance would so readily recognize a young unmarried woman as their academic superior?

She supposed she'd find out when they reached Edinburgh.

If they reached Edinburgh.

"We will make it," he insisted, as though he could read her thoughts. "Go ahead, read through the presentation again."

"It's growing too dark for me to read my notes."

"Oh." Looking drawn and tense, he leaned against the carriage wall. He tugged at his open collar. "Night will be coming on soon, I suppose."

Drat. Minerva winced. Of all the stupid things to say.

He was working mightily to conceal his physical discomfort, but she knew this was misery for him.

"Colin, why don't we just get out and walk?"

"Because it's pouring rain."

"A little wet won't hurt us."

"It would chill you. And it would demolish Francine. In a lighter rain, the trunk might keep her dry. But a downpour like this? You know the rain will pound right through the seams. The plaster would disintegrate."

"So we'll just leave her here in the carriage."

He snorted. "Out of the question. I've done far too much and come much too far with that scaly old girl. She's not getting out of my sight now. I'm fine. I can do this, Min. The postilion will be back soon with fresh horses, and we'll be moving on."

The tone of his voice would brook no argument.

"Well, we must have *some* distraction in the meantime." She perked. "I know. Let's list naughty-sounding mathematical terms." In her most tarty, breathy voice, she whispered, "*Parabola*."

After a pause, his fingers squeezed hers. "Tessellation."

"Binomial."

"Why stop there? Trinomial."

"Now that's just wicked."

"That's nothing. I've been saving this one." He leaned close to whisper in her ear. "*Annulus*."

Laughing, she crawled into his lap. "Oh, Colin. This is why I love you."

His hands went to her waist. "For God's sake. Because my adolescent mind always wandered to ribald places when I should have been attending my studies?"

She shrugged. "Did I need a better reason?"

"I should think so. Yes." His brow met hers, and his voice dropped to a raw whisper. "That's why I'm here, Min. You must know that's why. You need a much better reason to love me, and I'm trying like hell to give you one."

Dear, foolish man. By shifting her weight and pulling at her skirts, she managed to straddle his lap. "Just kiss me."

Framing his face in her hands, she brushed her lips against his. Then he kissed her back, fierce and deep. Their tongues tangled and played.

She guided his hand to her breast. He moaned into her mouth as he cupped and kneaded, smoothing his palm over the fabric-cloaked bud of her nipple. Their kisses became greedy, urgent. He ravaged her mouth with his lips and tongue, and she gave back as good as he gave.

The firm ridge of his arousal announced itself, thrusting against her inner thigh. His free hand found her backside and grabbed tight, grinding her pelvis against his.

"Yes." She sat back to loosen her bodice. "Yes. Make love to me."

"Min, I want . . ." He worked for breath as he pushed up her skirts. "Jesus, I can't be gentle right now. I can't make love to you. I can't."

She whimpered with disappointment, pressing her body to his. She needed him so badly, and she could feel the significant proportions of his need for her. He couldn't say no.

His sweaty brow pressed against her neck. He licked, then nipped the top of her breast. "You deserve sweet, tender love. A man who'll give you anything you desire. But right now, what I want is to take. To take you hard and fast and wild enough to light up the whole damn night."

His fingers delved under her petticoats and found her sex, plunging deep without preliminary.

She gasped. She was so ready for him, his fingers slipped right in.

"Can I . . ." He pushed deeper, grunting. "Will you . . ."

"Yes," she managed. "Yes."

He withdrew his fingers and began fumbling with the buttons of his breeches falls. "Say it. I need to know you understand, that you're fully willing."

She wasn't merely willing. She was *wanting*, desperately.

"Yes," she whispered. "Take me."

Arousal rushed through her. She actually *felt* herself go damp and pink.

"Take me," she said louder, this time owning the words. Owning the wildness that was a part of her, too. "Take me. Now."

He positioned himself and entered her on a hard, almost painful thrust. She cried out with the joy of it. With fierce digs of his hips, he worked deeper still. Her pelvis banged his, and the entire post-chaise jounced and rattled on its springs.

"Oh, God. Minerva. I don't deserve you. You're so good. So hot and so wet and so very, very good to me. Clever, foolish, lovely thing."

Good Lord, did the man never stop talking? Minerva didn't want to converse right now. She just wanted . . . deeper. Harder. More.

She caught his earlobe between her teeth and growled, spreading her legs to draw him closer still. He clutched her hips and pumped wildly, guiding her up and down his length. She rode his thrusts with abandon, bracing one arm against the carriage roof for better leverage. They clung to each other with teeth and nails, making harsh, snarling, animal sounds.

The whole coach bucked and swayed with their frantic rhythm. The square windowpane fogged over with the heat of their passion.

Her eyelids fluttered closed, blocking out what daylight remained. His arousing words became inarticulate grunts. Their rhythm took on a power of its own, became a force unto itself.

In his arms, she was speechless, helpless, heedless, mindless. She knew nothing but sensation. Nothing but him.

When the climax hit her, she gave a helpless, keening cry of joy. Pleasure racked her body. He withdrew from her all too soon, growling curses and blessings and spurting warmth against her thigh.

"Min." His hot, openmouthed kisses covered her face and throat. His voice was raw with emotion. "Min, don't ever leave me."

She laced her arms around his neck. "Colin, I—"

A loud, brittle *snap* interrupted her. Followed by a creak of metal and a shivering, shuddering moan.

And then they were falling. Falling in each other's arms, as the whole post-chaise toppled to the side.

"Oh no."

Chapter Twenty-eight

Together, they slid to the end of the bench, slamming against the wall of the post-chaise. Then the wall became the floor, as the whole business tipped on its side.

The coach hit the mud with a thick *squelch*. They broke apart, and Minerva's shoulder jarred painfully as she bounced against the side panel.

"Min." He scrambled to her side. "Minerva, tell me you're not—"

"I'm fine," she hastened to say. "Unharmed."

Mostly.

She wouldn't tell him so, but her shoulder did ache a bit. Nevertheless, this was hardly a dramatic, deathly carriage accident. The post-chaise hadn't even been in motion. It was really no more than falling off a fence, or out of a tree.

"Just don't die." He clutched her tight. "If you died, I'd beg God to take me, too."

Lord, what a statement. She forced herself to ignore its implications and keep to the task at hand: reassurance.

"Well, I'm not dying. I'm not even injured."

He searched her face. "Are you certain?"

"Yes."

"You're not bleeding anywhere? You can feel all your limbs?"

"Don't you feel my arms around you?"

She stroked up and down his back, until he released a heavy sigh.

"Yes." He moved his weight off her chest, laughing a bit. He passed a hand over his face. "Good God. I didn't realize how unstable these contraptions are without a team hitched to them. I suppose we were too . . ."

"Zealous?" She smiled. "Well, look at it this way. The wheels aren't stuck in the mud any longer."

"This is true. Let me help you up."

They untangled their knot of limbs. Colin rose first, then offered his hand.

As she got her feet under her, Minerva's boots sloshed. Water was seeping in through the coach's damaged side panels, puddling at their feet.

"Oh dear."

Colin had noticed it, too. He tipped the trunk, using his boot to move it away from the growing puddle. Francine was packed so tightly, she'd no doubt survived the fall—but she wouldn't survive a soaking.

"So it wasn't our . . . you know . . . that toppled the chaise. At least, not entirely."

He shook his head. "The road is flooding. That's why the wheels slid free."

The muddy water lapped at her hem. "We should get out of here. Right away."

"I agree." Colin raised his hands and pushed on the door overhead.

It wouldn't open.

With a curse, he caught the door latch and rattled it violently. "Open, damn you," he muttered. "Open."

"It's all right," she said, trying to keep him calm. "We're not trapped. If you break the window, I can crawl through and open it from the outside."

"Right. You always were the clever one. Move aside and cover your head."

When she'd obeyed, he took a handkerchief from his breast pocket and wrapped it tight about his knuckles. Then he grabbed the pistol by the barrel and used it to smash at the windowpane. Two good swings, and he had it cracked.

Small bits of glass rained down on Minerva's bowed head and shoulders. When the shower of glass had ceased and true raindrops made their way inside, it seemed safe to look up. She glimpsed him clearing the few remaining jagged shards from the edges of the window opening.

"Here." He cupped one hand and held it out. "You put your boot in my hand and your hand on my shoulder. I'll lift you up."

She nodded.

As her head and shoulders emerged through the small opening, Minerva braced her hands on either side of the makeshift hatch. She hauled the rest of her body up and through. Rain doused her instantly, plastering her hair to her neck and brow. She swiped it away, impatient.

Once she had her entire body outside the carriage, she knelt on the top—which had recently been the side—and pulled at the door latch with both hands, rattling and cursing the twisted bit of metal.

"Drat. The latch is jammed from this side, too." She peered down at him. "Just come through the window, like I did. It will be a tight squeeze, but you'll fit."

"I'll fit. But Francine won't." He hefted the trunk with both hands, lifting it above the water. It was far too big to fit through the window. "Go on. Take shelter under some trees. I'll keep her dry until the rain lets up."

"You want me to leave you here? *Alone*?"

A flicker of some emotion passed over his features, but he squelched it. "I'll be fine. We'll stay within shouting distance. You know our system, M. Tallyho, and all that."

She shook her head. Impossible man. Not five minutes ago, he'd clutched her in his arms and begged her to never leave him. Pledged to follow her to the grave, if it came to that. He honestly thought she would abandon him now? Leave him trapped in a darkened carriage, alone, on these same roads that had claimed his parents' lives?

He truly *was* cracked.

"I'm not leaving you in there."

"Well, I'm not leaving this trunk."

She rattled at the door latch again. It still refused to budge. "Perhaps I can break it open. Hand me the pistol, will you?"

Reaching up through the broken window, he handed her the weapon. She unwrapped it, slid her palm around the grip . . .

And then leveled it at him.

"Come out of there, Colin."

She spoke with cool, unruffled calm, shielding the gun from the rain with her body. Minerva didn't mean to really threaten his life. She just hoped to shock him out of his stubborn, foolish wish to stay inside that coffin.

Well, he certainly looked surprised.

His incredulous gaze flicked from her face to the pistol in her hand. "Min, have you gone mad?"

"I might ask you the same! It's over, Colin." Her voice broke. "It's over. We're not going to reach Edinburgh, and this isn't worth another moment of your distress."

"To hell with my 'distress.' This is your life's work in this trunk. I'm not leaving it. And we can still make the symposium, Min. As soon as the postilion returns . . ."

Minerva looked up and around. No sign of the postilion

or horses anywhere. Muddy runnels swelled in the road, carrying a tide of leaves and sticks coursing past. And the rain only pounded harder, pinging and thundering against the shell of the coach.

She had to raise her voice to call over the din. "The water's rising, and night is falling. The post-chaise is damaged. Even if the horses arrive, the road will be impassable. It's *over.*"

"Blast it, Min. Don't you give up on this. Don't you give up on me. I made a promise to you, and I will damn well keep it. I will find a way."

"You can't—"

A startled cry stole the rest of her argument. The overturned coach lurched a half foot sideways. The rising rainwater had buoyed the hollow, overturned post-chaise, allowing it to slip over the mud.

Minerva's gut clenched. She had to get him out. His stubborn insistence on remaining in the carriage was now not only foolhardy, but dangerous. If the water kept rising, they could slip right off the road.

She thrust the pistol forward. "Colin, drop the trunk. We both need to leave this coach. No more arguments."

"No." He shook his head. "I won't do it, Min."

"Then you leave me no choice."

She steadied the pistol, cocked the hammer, aimed—
And fired.

"Holy—"

Bang.

When the pistol went off, Colin's first thought was: *My God. She did it. She actually shot me.*

His second thought was: *When the hell were my blood and guts replaced with gritty white powder?*

As the dust settled, Colin slowly realized that she had *not* shot him. She'd sent a bullet whizzing straight through her trunk. And the plume of white powder that exploded through the dim interior was *not* the remnants of his calcified heart.

It was Francine.

Oh God.

God *damn* it. He wished Minerva had shot him in the guts instead. It would have hurt less. And at least his guts might have a chance of mending. Francine, on the other hand . . .

Francine was gone.

"Wh—?" He choked on the plaster dust. "Why would you do that?"

"Because you left me no choice," she cried, flinging the pistol away. "Now come out of there. It's over."

It's over.

Yes, it was over. All of it, over. She'd just shot a bullet through all her hopes and dreams. It didn't matter if the postilion arrived with four fresh horses. It didn't matter if the clouds suddenly parted and a hot-air balloon descended to whisk them to Scotland. Without Francine, it was over.

He swallowed back the bitter lump in his throat. There was nothing left to do but admit defeat.

He'd failed her. He'd managed to fail her, despite all his best efforts. His good intentions landed like mortar shells, and this time Francine had taken the hit.

He hoisted himself out through the broken window. He jumped from the post-chaise first, landing in calf-deep water. "Jump into my arms," he directed.

Minerva obeyed. She clung to his neck, just as though he were the hero in her fairy tale and not the villain ruining everything. "Where will we go?"

Colin stared down the road, peering through the tapering rainfall. Could those shadows be . . . ?

Horses. Yes, they were. A fine team of four from his own

stables. At last, here came the postilion—accompanied by two of Colin's own grooms from Riverchase.

He released his breath and told her, "Home. We go home."

The distance to Riverchase was only a few miles, but the road conditions forced him to take those miles at a painfully slow walk. He held Minerva in front of him on his horse, trying his best to shield her from the cold and wet.

For a while, he thought she'd fallen asleep.

Until she mumbled, "Colin? What is that vast, impressive-looking place in the distance?"

"That's Riverchase. My estate."

"I thought it might be. It's lovely. All that g-granite."

He laughed inwardly. She *would* notice that first. "It's local stone."

"I'd bet it sparkles in broad daylight."

"It's luminous."

He tightened his arm about her, drawing her close. For the first time, he noticed how violently she shivered against his chest.

"Are you well?" he asked.

"Just cold. So c-cold."

Swearing under his breath, Colin nudged the horse into a trot. The rain was dwindling to a mere trickle, but she'd already been soaked through. He had to get her before a fire, and quickly.

At least the Riverchase staff had been warned by the postilion that their master was in the neighborhood. The entire house had been thrown into readiness. When Colin rode up in the drive, the front door opened and a bevy of servants sallied forth.

Colin slid from the horse first, then helped Minerva drop into his arms. Sliding one arm about her back and lashing the other beneath her thighs, he carried her up the fourteen granite stairs and through the main entry.

The old, familiar housekeeper, Mrs. Hammond, hurried to greet him. It must have been almost two years since he'd seen her, but he cut the salutations short.

"Have you laid a fire?" he asked.

"In the drawing room, my lord."

Shifting Minerva's weight in his arms, he strode past the housekeeper and turned directly into the drawing room. He laid Minerva's sodden, shivering form on a plush divan and pushed the entire thing—furniture and woman—forward, until it sat a few feet from the hearth. The fire was young and blazing. Scorching flames leaped and danced.

"This is a lovely room," Minerva said weakly. "I'm so gl-glad to—" Her teeth chattered. "To have this chance to see your home."

"Shush. Don't try to talk. You can have the grand tour later."

"All right."

Her thin, quivering attempt at a smile made him want to howl with anguish. It should not be this way. He slipped the spectacles from her face, wiped them dry, and replaced them on her nose.

Mrs. Hammond stood in the doorway.

"Bring blankets," he ordered. "A clean shift, I don't care whose. Hot tea immediately, and other refreshment as you're able."

"Yes, my lord."

Once the woman disappeared, Colin set about the work of removing Minerva's soaked clothing. She tried to help him, but her fingers were shaking too hard.

"Be still, pet. Allow me."

In the end he gave up on the buttons and hooks and drew the folding knife from his boot, using it to slice her gown at the seams. He peeled the drenched fabric from her body, tossing her garments into a heap by the fire. As he hacked away at the sweet, gauzy muslin, he wanted to weep.

A week ago had he harbored some vague concern that he might ruin this girl? Taint her reputation beyond repair? Or, horrors—steal her virtue?

She should have been so lucky.

Look at her now. Curled up, shivering uncontrollably. Skin pale, lips blue, gown in rags. Dreams left shattered and strewn on a country road, and all her hopes for the future vanished. As he undressed her, he found a horrific bruise swelling on her shoulder.

This went beyond social ruin. This was complete and total devastation he'd wrought upon her.

The deep, eviscerating pain Colin felt at that moment told him two things, both equally tragic.

He loved her, beyond anything.

And she was lost to him, forever.

Chapter Twenty-nine

mazing, what an hour's rest, a warm fire, and a spot of doctored tea could do for a girl's constitution. As she snuggled into her warm nest of blankets, Minerva decided fleecy quilts were her new favorite attire.

And she'd yet to have the promised grand tour, but judging by what little she'd glimpsed thus far, Riverchase was the finest home Minerva had ever dripped inside.

If only Colin would abandon his post by the hearth and come sit next to her, she would feel completely restored. He looked so miserable. She started to rise and go to him. But he stayed her with an outstretched hand and single, harsh word.

"*Don't.*"

His voice and his eyes were so cold. Minerva shrank back into the divan.

He stared into the fire. "I'm sending you back to London. Tomorrow."

"You're . . ." Her breath caught painfully. "You're sending me to London? Not taking me."

Now that Scotland was no longer their destination, she

supposed it made sense that they would turn back. But tomorrow? Separately?

He nodded. "It's safer that way. And more expedient. Naturally, you'll have outriders for your security. Mrs. Hammond, my housekeeper, will travel as your companion."

"What about you?"

"I'll ride ahead to warn Bram, so he'll be expecting you."

"Lord Rycliff? But what will you tell him?"

"The truth." He gestured vaguely. "Some version of it. That we left Spindle Cove with plans to go to Scotland, but it didn't work out. And that I'm asking his and Susanna's help in salvaging your reputation. We'll tell everyone you never traveled past London. That you fell ill that first night, and you've been staying with them the whole week."

The prospect of so much deceit made Minerva's stomach churn. "Susanna is my friend. I don't want her to lie for me."

"Such things are done all the time."

Minerva knew this much was true. More than one of the young ladies she'd met in Spindle Cove had been sent there to weather a scandal or indiscretion. As the village's erstwhile patroness, Susanna kept a great many secrets. And society at large owed her a great many favors of discretion, no doubt.

But it would be one thing to conceal this journey from public notice, and another thing to banish it from their own memories. He spoke as if they would be strangers to each other, from this point forward.

"This is what you truly want?" she asked him. "To just pretend none of this happened?"

"No matter what occurs, you will never lack for anything. Once I gain control of my accounts, I'll quietly settle some money on you. Enough that you'll be able to live as you desire. Set up house in any place you wish. Devote your life to your scholarship. You and your sisters will always have my protection."

"Your *protection*? Am I to be your mistress, then?"

"God, no."

"Oh." She swallowed a sob. "Not even that?"

With a muttered curse, he crossed the room and sat beside her. "Minerva, I would never degrade you that way. After all the pain I've caused you, I wouldn't blame you if you banished me from your sight." He dropped his head to his hands. "Don't make me list all the ways I've failed you."

"Then I'll list everything you've given me. Hot tea and blankets. A day at the fair. An apple, an orange, peaches, cherries. The chance to win twenty pounds in a shooting contest. The courage to sing in a tavern. My first honest compliments. Breathless passion, and enough adventure to last a lifetime. Just think, in this one week alone I've been a missionary, an assassin, a long-lost princess . . . and, we can't forget, a sword swallower."

"Believe me." Looking up, he gave her a half smile. "So long as I live, I will never, *ever* forget that."

Her heart warmed to see that flash of his familiar good nature. This was the Colin she knew and loved.

She shrugged. "After all that adventure, perhaps being a simple geologist would have come as a disappointment."

"Don't. Don't lie to me, Minerva." His hand went to her cheek. "I know how much it meant to you. You can't tell me you're not disappointed."

No, she couldn't. And she couldn't hold back the tears any longer. He held her in his arms while she had a good little cry for poor, pulverized Francine and all those smashed scientific ambitions.

After a few minutes, she wiped her eyes. "I just wanted to leave a footprint. Make my own lasting mark on this earth, the same way Francine left hers. To post a little sign that will survive for generations to come: 'Minerva Highwood was here, and the world is just a little different for her presence.' I just wanted to make an impression."

"Yes, and you should have done." He rose from the divan and strode to the hearth, where he tapped the mantel with his fist. "You would have done. Your only mistake was joining up with me."

"That wasn't a mistake."

"Of course it was. Haven't you noticed, Min? I leave impressions everywhere. Except in my case, they're not footprints. They're more like craters."

With a single finger, he nudged a porcelain shepherdess toward the edge of the mantel and then—

Smash it went on the hearthstone.

"Oh look," he said dryly. "Colin Sandhurst was here." He sent another figurine careening to its doom. "And here." A third *crash*. "Here, as well."

As the melody of destruction trailed off into silence, Minerva took a deep breath and forced herself to be calm. "Colin, do you . . ." She steeled her nerve. "Could you love me?"

He stared at her. "For God's sake, don't ask me that."

"Why not?"

"Because I can't answer you. Because no matter what I say, I'll make a hash of it somehow. I can't even get your plaster lizard footprint to Scotland. How could I ever be trusted with something so precious as your heart?"

Drawing a blanket about her shoulders, she pushed to her feet. She crossed the room and moved to stand at the opposite corner of the hearth.

"Colin, if you could love me . . . nothing else would matter. You're worth so much more than a science prize of five hundred guineas."

"Oh, do you think?" He cast a pointed glance around the magnificently furnished drawing room. "Yes, I'm worth a great deal more."

"That's not what I mean, and you know it."

"But this was never about the money. I know how much it meant to you. You were so driven to attend that symposium. You've risked everything, Min. Security, reputation. Your very life. And I destroyed those dreams."

She touched his wrist and waited until he met her gaze. "You didn't destroy my dreams. You broke me out of my shell. There was bound to be a bit of a mess."

He brushed a light caress against her cheek and whispered, "Min."

She smiled and wiped a lingering tear. "Despite everything, this has been the most exciting, magical week of my life. I'm only sad that it's ending this way."

"I know, I know. It's just wrong, isn't it?" He took up the poker and stirred the fire with agitated motions. "I had this idea, you see. More of a foolish hope, I suppose. That all through this mad, tumultuous journey . . . we'd been writing the story of our future."

She laughed a little. "Do you mean we were actually going to become missionaries in Ceylon? Or join up with a circus?"

"No, no. I don't mean that we'd been *foretelling* our future. I meant, I hoped we'd been writing the *story* of our future. The tale we would tell and retell, over goblets of wine at dinner parties, and on dreary spring days when it's too muddy for lawn bowls. Do you know what I mean? That it would be our story, Min. One we'd remember and laugh over for years to come, even tell some bits to our . . ." His voice trailed off as he replaced the poker in the andiron.

"To our what?" Her heart missed a beat. "To our children?" Had he been dreaming of a life with her?

"Minerva, you're the most clever person I know. You can look at a queer-shaped hole in the ground and see a rich, vibrant ancient world. Look at me now."

Looking him in those fiery Bristol-diamond eyes was never a trial.

"Tell me the truth," he said. "Do you see a pleasant future with me?"

She reached for him, teasing her fingers through his hair. "Honestly?"

"Honestly."

"When I look at you, my thoughts are something like this: God only knows what trials lie down that path." Smiling, she slipped her arms around his neck. "But take heart, Colin. Some women like to be surprised."

He was silent for a long, breathless moment.

"Well, then," he said darkly. He caught her up in one swift motion. "Surprise."

Chapter Thirty

Colin flattened her to the wall, greedily clutching her everywhere he could reach. Pressing fervent kisses to her brow, her cheek, her lips.

He needed this. Needed *her*.

Needed it *now*.

He yanked the buttons of her shift loose. Unfastening some, simply popping others from their threads. Soon the frail linen garment lay discarded at her feet.

"*Minerva*." With a resonant sigh, he pressed the full length of his clothed body to her nakedness. Bracing his hands against the wall, he nudged her thighs apart with his knee. Bending his head, he kissed and licked her neck, all the while grinding his desperate erection against her heat.

A groan welled in his chest. "I need you, Min. Need you so much."

"I'm here," she breathed. Her arms draped over his shoulders. "I'm yours."

I'm yours. A sweet pang of emotion wrenched his heart. Still, he kept his hands braced on the wallpaper—not trusting himself to touch her yet.

He backed up a bit, wanting to see. To admire.

She reached for him. "Colin . . ."

"Wait." His voice shook with desire. "Let me look at you."

She fell back against the wallpaper, displaying herself for his view. He'd never dreamed a woman could be so beautiful.

She looked more luminous against this wall than a Dutch master's painting ever could. Her flawless skin would make a porcelain shepherdess weep bitter, envious tears. And her breasts . . .

He didn't have a decorative parallel for her breasts. But they made *him* hard as the parquet floor. Her breasts were every bit as wildly arousing as the first time he'd glimpsed them in that London inn.

He kissed his way down her elegant throat, pausing to suckle each of those luscious nipples as he sank to his knees. When his knees met the floor, he made himself comfortable there, resting on his haunches. Pressing light kisses to her navel. Nuzzling her thigh. Settling in for a nice long visit.

"God." He nudged her legs apart and sifted through her dark curls. "I've been wanting this forever."

She laughed nervously. "We've been traveling a week."

"It's been forever." He parted her with his fingers, exploring her folds and circling his thumb over her swollen pearl. "You can't know, Min. You can't know how long I've been waiting for you."

He pressed a single, chaste kiss to her sex. Just a prelude, so she wouldn't be too shocked.

Then he slid one arm under her knee, hooking it over his shoulder. With his hands, he bracketed her hips, reaching toward her sex with both thumbs to spread her wide to his view. To his kiss.

She made a strangled noise. "Colin—"

"Shush." He blew the word over her delicate flesh. "You had your chance to explore every bit of me. Now it's my turn."

And explore he did. Most thoroughly. He ran his tongue—just lightly—over every flushed, dewy petal of her sex. Down one side, up the other . . . until he centered on that swollen bud at the crest. Again, teasing lightly. Just lightly. Until her breath went ragged and she arched her hips, digging her heel into his back to pull him close.

Yes. That's it. Hold me close and tight. Claim me. Make me a slave to your pleasure.

But something wicked in him wouldn't give her what she craved. Not yet. He kept up his light, teasing attentions. Until she rocked against his mouth in an urgent rhythm, and needy whimpers eased from her throat.

"Oh, Colin. Oh, God."

So blasphemous, but he loved being classed above the divine in her universe. Even if only for a brief, wanton second.

"Yes, darling?" he murmured, between slow, languid strokes of his tongue.

"I need . . . I need something."

"This?" He dipped his tongue inside her.

She gasped and bucked. "More."

Her grip twisted in his hair. Her heady taste lingered on his tongue. He needed more, too. And he couldn't wait a moment longer.

Lowering her leg to the ground, Colin pushed to his feet and hastily stepped out of his unfastened trousers. He pulled his shirt over his head and cast it aside. Clutching her backside in both hands, he lifted her against the wall. He pinned her with a fierce gaze, determined to read her every emotion.

"Do you want me, Min?"

"Yes."

"Need me?"

"*Yes.*" She writhed against him, wild and slick and hot.

"Love me?" His voice was so hoarse with yearning, the words got lost in his throat. He slid into her, pushing his hard length into her tight body. "Love me," he grunted, driving the words home on a thrust. "Love. Me."

"Yes." She gasped with pleasure, canting her pelvis to take him deep. "Yes."

He pumped her steadily, driving into her at just the angle he knew she craved. "Love me. Don't ever stop. You hear me? It won't be this good with anyone else. Only me, Min. Only me."

"*Colin*." She dug her nails into his shoulders and pulled herself off the wall, confronting him face to face. Her tongue made a quick, hungry swipe at his. "I love you. Stop talking."

Fair enough.

He pressed her back against the wall. No more discussion. Only joining and clasping and thrusting. And kissing, hot and wet and deep. Only this desperate, visceral need to get closer, in every possible way.

Without warning, her body bowed and tensed. She clung to him as the crisis hit, crying out against his ear. Her intimate muscles tightened, sending pulsing waves of friction down his cock.

This time, he didn't hold back. Couldn't, even if he tried. He rode the crest of her pleasure, thrusting frenzied as her climax pulled him straight into his own.

When he came inside her, the sheer blinding joy of it was like nothing he'd ever known. It took him outside himself. Sent him spinning into a strange, dark place. He was lost there, for a moment, stranded in bliss. But soon, her soothing caress led him back.

She would always lead him back from the darkness.

How could she not? She held his heart.

"Minerva." Spent and trembling, he buried his face in her neck. "I need to ask you something."

"You do?"

"Yes. This is a very important question. One I've never

posed to any woman before. I want you to think carefully
about your answer."

She nodded.

"After all this madness is over, and I see you safely back
home . . . do you think you could see fit to . . ." He swallowed
hard and lifted his gaze to hers. "To let me court you?"

Her lips fell apart. "*Court* me. You . . . you want to *court* me?"

"Yes. Very much so. More than anything."

"Colin, you do realize you're currently inside me."

"I'm exquisitely aware of that, yes."

Her fingers sifted through the hair at his temples. "Then
the horse is through the gate, isn't it? Don't you think formal
courting would be an unnecessary bother at this point?"

"Not a bother at all." He kissed the confused twist from
her lips. "And I think it's necessary indeed. You deserve to
be courted, Min. Flowers, picnics, walks in the park, and all
the rest of it. And if I do say it myself, I have a suspicion I'll
be rather brilliant at courting, once I apply myself."

"I'm very sure you will be, but—"

"The season will be in full swing soon." He gently withdrew from her, then set her back on her toes. "I'll convince
your mother to send you to London, so I can lavish attention
on you in front of the entire *ton*."

"How on earth would we manage that, after we've returned unwed from this scandalous journey? Even with your
cousin's help, the gossip will be vicious."

He tsked. "Even if there is some scandal and we're denied
vouchers at fusty old Almacks, what of it? We'll be welcome
any number of other places. Balls, opera, the theater, Vaux-
hall. We'll be the talk of London."

"Yes, I can imagine. They'll all be wondering what that
awkward little bluestocking slipped in your wine to make
you go so addled."

"No. Don't speak that way." He propped a finger under her chin. "I hate it when you speak ill of yourself, Min. I'd visit bodily harm on anyone who dared insult you, but I don't know how to guard you from yourself. So kindly do me a favor, and just . . . don't. All right?"

"All right."

Her bottom lip trembled. He traced it fondly. "Spoiling you will bring me so much pleasure. I'll make you feel like a queen. I'll do everything I can to win you."

"But Colin, don't you realize . . ." Affection warmed her brown eyes. "There's no need to win me. I've told you, I'm yours."

He scooped her into his arms and carried her back to the fire, setting her on the carpet. Her chemise was rumpled and torn, so he retrieved his shirt and helped her into it. He fit it over her head, lifting her dark, lovely hair through the collar and arranging the locks about her face. His shirt looked well on her, the open collar offering a saucy glimpse of her unbound breasts. Her eyes shone, and a pretty blush kissed her cheeks.

God, he loved the look of her well tumbled. His heart and his loins argued he should marry her at once and keep her here, so he could start enjoying this sight every day. Every night.

But for once, he was going to let his brain make the decisions. When he acted on impulse, even his best intentions went bad. A hasty marriage, tempting as it sounded, simply wasn't the right way.

He pulled on his discarded trousers and sat cross-legged with her, before the fire.

"You're so young," he began.

"I'm only five years younger than you. When my mother married, she was seventeen and my father was forty-three."

"You're young," he insisted. "And this week has been tumultuous, to put it mildly. I want to give you some time, back in the normal world, to make sure of your feelings."

"I *am* sure of my feelings."

"You deserve to be courted. You deserve to know you have choices before you go committing your life to anyone—least of all a blighter like me. You deserve a look at Sir Alisdair Kent. He might not be so warty after all."

She touched his face. "I love *you*, Colin. Nothing's going to change that."

"Dear, sweet girl." He gathered her in his arms and held her imprudently tight.

I love you. Nothing's going to change that.

Oh, how he wanted to take that bold, unequivocal statement and grasp it as truth. Carve it in stone, tattoo it on his flesh, spell it out in little mosaic tiles embedded in this very floor. The Gospel According to Minerva, never to be doubted. But he'd learned too much—from her, from life— and he knew well how little she'd seen of the world. His jaded soul craved assurance. At least a few months' worth of it.

Of all people, she ought to understand the value of a scientific test.

"If what you say is true . . ." He pulled back to look her in those dark, beautiful eyes. "Then there's no harm in waiting, is there?" He caressed her cheek, trying to coax a smile. "I'm no stranger to impulsive decisions. They don't turn out well. When I marry you, I want everyone to know—and that includes the two of us—that it's not a rash, impetuous whim. I want to wait until after my birthday, so there'll be no suspicion that gaining control of my fortune had something to do with it, either."

"After your birthday? You're suggesting we live separately, for months?"

He nodded. "I suppose so, yes."

"What about the nights, Colin? How do you plan to get through all those nights?" She swallowed hard. "I don't think I could stand it if . . ."

He hushed her with a kiss. "The wedding vows must wait. But I swear to you here and now, Minerva"—he took her hand and pressed it to his heart—"so long as I live, I won't pass a night in any other woman's arms. I can't pretend waiting for you will be pleasant, but I'll muddle through. It'll be a great deal easier to stand the darkness if you're the warm, lovely beacon of light at the end of it."

She looked disappointed, and he hated himself for that. But of all the things he'd ever done in his life, he needed to take care and do this right. If that meant moving at the pace of a sea snail, so be it.

"Don't worry," he said. "This is ideal, you'll see. We do everything backward. It's just how we are. We began with an elopement. After that, we made love. Next, we'll progress to courting. When we're old and silver-haired, perhaps we'll finally get around to flirtation. We'll make fond eyes at each other over our mugs of gruel. We'll be the envy of couples half our age."

She smiled. "Oh, Colin. If they could see me right *now*, I'd be the envy of every woman in England."

"A few in Scotland, too. You forget, I was raised very near the border."

He made the comment lightly, but its import sent a shiver of excitement through his bones.

Scotland.

The change in Colin was immediate. Minerva watched the expression on his face shift from warm affection to cold determination, in an instant.

She dragged a coy, sensual touch down his chest, hoping to change it back.

It didn't work.

He pushed to his feet, offering her a hand. "Come, now. Quickly."

"What? Why?"

"I'll explain on the way upstairs. We've no time to lose."

Bewildered, she accepted his hand. He helped her up, then gathered all their discarded clothes. "By now your rooms will be prepared. They'll have fetched your trunks from the road. I'll see you to your suite, then send a maid to help you bathe and dress."

"In the middle of the night?"

He glanced out the open window. "Dawn will be coming on soon."

He put a hand to the small of her back and gathered her close, leading her out of the room and to a grand, sweeping staircase. As they rushed up the steps, Minerva tried not to think too hard about the fact that she was tiptoeing barefoot through one of England's grandest, most historic estates in nothing but Colin's lawn shirt. Scandal personified.

But then . . . someday she would be this house's mistress. Perhaps. Assuming the courtship went smoothly.

Lord, she was so confused.

"And while I'm bathing and dressing, where will you be?"

"I'll be doing likewise," he said. "Bathing, dressing. And then seeing to the horses."

"Horses?"

"Yes. We'll need to leave as soon as possible." He stopped. "Which door was it . . . ? Aha. Here's your suite."

He led her into an exquisite sitting room decorated in ivory and sage green. Minerva could barely spare a glance to admire the carved moldings, or to emit a sigh of pleasure, as her travel-weary toes sank into the plush carpet pile.

"Colin, we just arrived here. We've barely slept in days.

Can't we at least rest before we go dashing off again? This is the most beautiful room I've ever seen."

"You look beautiful in it." Leaving her standing in the center of the carpet, he made a circle of the room. First, he pulled back the drapes. A silver glimmer of dawn filtered through the floor-to-ceiling windows. "Your dressing room's here," he said, indicating an open door. "And the bedchamber's through that. I hope you'll have more time to explore it the next time we come through." He passed closed doors, pointing. "Bath. Closet."

She closed her eyes, then opened them again. "Colin. Where on earth do you mean to take me?"

"To Scotland. To the symposium."

"But . . . it's too late. The symposium is today."

"I know. That's why we must hurry. We'll arrive late. It can't be helped."

"How would we even arrive at all? No more coaches, Colin. We can't." She knew how miserable he'd been in the post-chaise last night. She wouldn't put him through that again, ever.

"I have a plan," he said. "You'll see."

"But Francine—"

"Still exists. Plaster cast or no plaster cast. Her footprint exists. She left her mark on the world." He approached and took her hands in his. "And so will you, Min. Perhaps you won't be assured the prize without the evidence in hand. But you'll be there, and you'll make your impression."

She didn't know what to say.

A maid appeared in the bathing-room doorway. She cleared her throat and bobbed in a curtsy. "My lady, your bath is prepared."

Colin dismissed the servant with a nod.

He squeezed Minerva's hands. "We've come this far.

We're not giving up now. This is the story of our future—the one we're going to tell our friends and dinner guests and children and grandchildren—and the story doesn't end with defeat. It ends in triumph. *Your* triumph."

He lifted her hands to his lips. Kissed one, then the other.

She melted inside.

"Just trust me to get you there," he said. "And then make me proud."

"This?" An hour later, Minerva stood on the Riverchase front steps, dressed in her best remaining traveling habit, made of a dark green twill. She hoped she looked optimistic, if she didn't quite feel it. "We're journeying to Edinburgh in *this*?"

She peered into the misty dawn. In the drive sat the highest-sprung, most richly upholstered and gaily-painted phaeton she'd ever seen in her life. The narrow seat, built to accommodate only two persons—one driver, one passenger—must have hovered at least six feet from the ground. The little sporting carriage was hitched to two of the finest, most perfectly matched black warmbloods Minerva could imagine. They looked more like racing stock than coaching beasts.

"That can't be safe," she said.

"It isn't exactly the family model."

"We'll glow in the dark." She winced as the first ray of sunlight hit daffodil-yellow lacquer.

"It's garish and flashy and reckless, yes." Colin tugged on a bit of leather tack, testing its strength. "But it is the fastest conveyance to be had in England. Won it in a game of cards, a few years back."

"You *won* it. But do you know how to *drive* it?"

He shrugged and smiled. "We'll find out."

Minerva approached the phaeton with no small degree of trepidation. But she forced the nerves down, determined to be brave. Colin was putting all his faith in her. She had to make this worth it.

With a groom's assistance, she managed to climb into the seat. The team danced with impatience, and the phaeton swayed on its springs. Minerva's head spun.

Don't look down, she told herself.

Of course, the next instant she looked down. Did such prohibitions ever work?

Hoisting himself into the seat, Colin landed next to her. He pulled down the brim of his hat and gathered the reins. "Seventy-three miles. That's the distance to Edinburgh. If the weather holds, we can cover twelve miles an hour, easily, in this phaeton. Fifteen, if I press. With any luck, we'll arrive by noon. We can do this, Min. We really can."

She nodded. "You do . . ." Threading her arm though his, she swallowed hard. "Colin, you do know how to drive this thing, don't you?"

He smiled. "You keep asking me that."

"You keep refusing to answer."

He turned his gaze to the road and flicked the reins, nudging the team into a walk. "I don't like to *ride* in carriages. *Driving* is a different matter."

Once they'd rounded the turn in the drive, Colin snapped the reins and gave the horses their head, urging them into a canter.

They didn't canter. They *flew*.

"Oh!" The wind took her startled laughter and whipped it across the sprawling grounds of Riverchase.

This must be what a bullet feels like.

Powered by those two majestic, elegant animals, the phaeton rocketed down the straight gravel drive like the angels' divine chariot. The seat was so lightly sprung, Minerva scarcely felt the ruts in the road.

When they reached the end of the drive, Colin slowed the

team and guided them onto the main road with skill and ease. He looked as though he'd been born with reins in hand.

She leaned closer, forced to shout over the roar of wind and hoofbeats. "Teasing man. You *do* know how to drive it."

"Four-in-Hand Club!" he called back, giving her a sly wink. "All the rage in Town."

Laughing, Minerva clapped a hand over her bonnet, was too exhilarated by the rush of wind and speed to complain. Yes, of course. The rascal was a member of every club that would have him. Gentlemen's clubs, boxing club, gambling club, adventurers club. Why not a driving club, too?

That was his life, in London. All those clubs. All those friends. All those glittering, opulent amusements.

All those *women*.

As they raced northward, her mind spun faster than the phaeton wheels.

His suggestion of a public courtship thrilled her, to be sure. Attending balls and operas on the arm of the dashing, handsome Lord Payne? The thought alone made her heart skip beats. And she believed him when he said he cared for her. He wouldn't lie about that.

He's driving breakneck to Scotland for you, she told herself. *Of course he cares.*

Then again . . . just a few days ago he'd devoted an afternoon to thatching a cottage roof. He'd thrown himself into the menial labor with strength and enthusiasm and good humor. But he hadn't pledged to spend the rest of his life doing it. Was his sudden attachment to Minerva just a product of the extreme circumstances?

And if she was doubting his attachment, maybe he doubted her love.

Or maybe he simply doubted *her*. Perhaps he doubted she could make a proper viscountess, and who could blame him? For God's sake, think of that enormous, beautiful

house and estate. Who would ever think Minerva could be
its mistress? She'd already left the drawing room a sham-
bles and dripped rainwater all over the entry carpet. The
servants would hate her.

She couldn't help but worry over a hundred separate
things. Colin must be worried, too. He'd admitted his uncer-
tainty. That's why he wanted to wait.

Waiting was wise, she reasoned. Delaying an engagement
was the sensible, prudent course of action.

So why did it terrify her?

They stopped thrice to change horses and take refreshment, always hurrying back to the road at the first possible
moment. The landscape rolling by was green and lushly
curved. A recumbent goddess, awakening from her winter
sleep.

The wind, by contrast, was a cold, cruel witch.

Minerva huddled under a woven rug for warmth, but the
chill clawed straight through it. When the road straightened
and he could spare some slack on the reins, Colin drew her
close, putting his arm about her shoulders. She nestled into
his side, comforting herself with his familiar warmth and
scent. Watching his gloved hands guide the team with arousing, confident motions.

She slid an arm about his waist, hugging him tight. It
didn't matter what happened today, or tomorrow. This—just
this—was worth everything.

They neared Edinburgh just as the midday sun reached
its zenith.

"Almost there," he said, climbing back into the seat after
stopping to ask directions of a tradesman. "Ready for your
grand moment?"

"I . . ."

*I don't know, I don't know. They don't know I'm a woman.
I've lost all my notes and sketches. They won't believe me*

about Francine without the evidence. And after traveling seventy miles in a single morning, my hair must be a perfect fright.

They're all going to laugh. Oh God. I just know they'll all laugh.

Terror had her insides knotted. But she refused to give her fears a voice. She'd promised Colin she wouldn't speak ill of herself again.

"I think so. If you're with me, I'm ready for anything."

He drew the horses to a halt, right in the middle of the street.

"Are we there?" she asked, looking about.

"Not quite." With a single gloved fingertip, he turned her face to his. "But I didn't think I should do this on the doorstep of the Royal Geological Society."

He bent his head and kissed her. Right there in the street and with such sweet, tender passion, all her worries receded, pushed aside by the swelling emotion in her heart.

"Better?" he asked, gathering the reins.

She nodded, feeling her confidence return. "Thank you. I needed that."

Another few minutes' travel down crowded, cobbled streets, and Colin pulled the team to a stop in front of a stately brick edifice. He tossed the reins and a coin to a waiting boy before rounding the phaeton to help her alight.

"Hurry, now. You're just in time to make a fashionably late entrance."

Arm in arm, they raced up the steps. Minerva was so occupied trying not to trip over her skirts, she didn't notice a doorman—or anyone, for that matter.

Until a deep voice drew them to a halt.

"I beg your pardon. Just where do you think you're going?"

Chapter Thirty-one

inerva winced. She should have known it couldn't be so simple.

"We're here for the geology symposium," Colin told him. "And we're running late, due to a travel mishap. So if you'd kindly step aside . . ."

The bearded man stood firm. He thumped a paper clipped to a writing board. "I'm sorry, sir. But admittance is for Society members only."

"I am a member." Minerva came forward. "I'm a member of the Society. My name's M. R. Highwood. It must be on your list."

"You?" Behind his gray beard, the man flushed an unseemly shade of red. "You would claim to be M. R. Highwood?"

"I would do more than claim it. I am Miss Minerva Rose Highwood. I can't believe the name would be unfamiliar to you. My findings have been published in no fewer than five issues of the *Royal Geological Journal* in the past seventeen months."

"Really, Min?" Colin's hand brushed the small of her

back. "Five times? That's brilliant, darling. I'm so proud."

She blushed a little. At least *someone* appreciated her accomplishment. Someone marvelously handsome and kind and intelligent and, against all odds, purportedly devoted to her.

This pompous oaf standing before her, waving his silly list . . . he couldn't intimidate her. Not anymore.

"Madam, there must be some misunderstanding. The members of this Society are all gentlemen."

"There has definitely been a misunderstanding," she said, smiling patiently now, "but the misunderstanding isn't mine. For the past two years, I've paid my dues and submitted my findings and engaged in written correspondence as a full member of this organization. I have never claimed to be male. If the membership made the mistaken assumption otherwise, I cannot be responsible for it. Now will you kindly allow me entrance? I have a paper to present."

"I don't think so." He pulled up straight and turned to Colin. "We cannot allow this. Unless she has some—"

"Excuse me, why are you talking to him?" Minerva interrupted. "I'm standing right here, and I can speak for myself."

The man sighed heavily. "My dear girl, I—"

"I'm not a girl. Nor am I 'dear' to you, unless—" Good Lord, she hoped this red-faced prig wasn't Sir Alisdair. Sir Alisdair had seemed so much more reasonable than this. "Listen, Mr. . . . ?"

"Barrington."

"Mr. Barrington." She smiled with relief. "I'm here to present my findings at the symposium. I'm an esteemed member of the Society, with an impressive record of scholarship, and I have something of value to contribute to these proceedings. I also happen to be female. I'm a woman who knows a great deal about rocks. I suggest you find the stones to deal with it."

Beside her, Colin choked on a laugh. "Well done, love. Brava."

"Thank you."

Mr. Barrington looked decidedly less amused. "This symposium is restricted to members of the Royal Geological Society and their guests. And as membership is restricted to gentlemen, so this door is barred to you."

"Come now." Colin intervened. She recognized him bringing forth his most commanding, lordly tone. "We can settle this some other way, surely. I happen to be rather fond of joining clubs. Now, what must a man do to become a member of your Society?"

"There's a lengthy application process. A letter of inquiry must be made, including a personal statement of research interests and any relevant publications. References must be provided—three, at the minimum, and no more than—"

"Yes, yes. Here's my application, if you'd be so good as to take dictation. I'm Colin Frederick Sandhurst, Viscount Payne. As for geological interests, I'm told my estate sits atop the largest vein of usable granite in all Northumberland. For references, I name my cousin, Lord General Victor Bramwell, the Earl of Rycliff. Second, my dear friend the Duke of Halford. And thirdly . . ."

Minerva cleared her throat. "Ahem."

"Thirdly, M. R. Highwood," Colin finished.

"Sir, I—"

"Ah." Colin raised a finger. "I believe that's 'my lord' to you."

"My lord, I'm sure the Society is honored by your lordship's interest. However . . ."

"Did I mention that in lieu of the regular dues and as a concession to my expedited application process, I'm willing to pledge an annual sustaining subscription of . . . say, a thousand pounds?"

Mr. Barrington seized.

"Oh, very well. You drive a hard bargain, Barrington. Make it three." He smiled broadly in the face of silence. "Well. Now that that's all settled, I'll be entering the symposium. Miss Highwood will come as my guest."

"But, my lord, unmarried women cannot attend as guests. It's not proper."

"For the love of ammonites, man! That's just stupid. Why on earth would the Society need to protect unmarried women from bone-dry lectures regarding soil composition? Do your members find themselves whipped into some sort of dusty frenzy, from which no delicate lass would be safe?"

Mr. Barrington tugged on his coat. "Sometimes debate does get heated."

Colin turned to her. "Min, can I just hit him?"

"I think that's a bad idea."

"Run him through with something sharp?"

"Probably a worse idea."

"Then there's no getting around it." He sighed.

"I know. You'll just have to go in and give the presentation for me."

"What? No." He shook his head. "No, I can't do that."

"Of course you can. You've heard me read it so many times. I know it contains a great many polysyllabic words, but you'll rise to the challenge."

"Minerva, these are your findings. These are your peers. This should be your moment."

"Yes, but . . ." Tears prickled at the corners of her eyes, and she impatiently blinked them back. "They won't let me in."

"They won't let *unmarried* ladies in. So marry me. Right here and now."

She stared at him, shocked. His Bristol-diamond eyes shone, brilliant and sincere. "Marry? But we . . . we can't possibly—"

He took her hands. "This is Scotland, Minerva. We don't

need a license or a church. We only need witnesses. Barrington here can serve as one, and—"

He turned, just as another man opened the door and joined them on the stoop.

"What's going on here?" the newcomer asked in a deep, solemn voice.

Minerva's eyes swept him from boots to crown. He was tall and handsome and . . . well, tall and handsome some more. He struck quite the fine figure, silhouetted in the door.

He asked, "Barrington, who are these people?"

"Oh, good," Colin said. "This fine-looking fellow can serve as our second witness. We have Mr. Barrington, and we have"—he clapped the newcomer on the shoulder— "Mr. . . . ?"

The man blinked at Colin's presumptuous gesture. "I'm Sir Alisdair Kent."

Minerva clapped a hand over her shocked laughter.

"Right." Colin's hand made two slow, heavy pats on Sir Alisdair's shoulder, as he sized the man up with a sweeping gaze. "Right. You would be." He heaved a sigh and turned to Minerva. "This is probably where I should step aside and let you two get more acquainted—"

No!

"But I won't," he finished.

Her heart flipped. Thank heaven.

He wrapped her gloved hands in both of his and stared deeply into her eyes.

"Minerva, I love you. I'd been waiting to tell you so at a better moment. In some more romantic time and place." He threw a glance at their surroundings. "But here and now will have to do."

"Here is fine," she managed. "Now is good."

He squeezed her hands. "I love you. I love that you're clever and loyal and curious and kind. I love that you're often so fearless and bold and strong—but I also love that you're occasionally not, because then I can be strong for you. I love that I can tell you anything. Anything at all. And I love that you always have something surprising to say. I love that you call things by their right names. That you aren't afraid to call a tit a tit, or a cock a—"

"I beg your pardon," Sir Alisdair interjected, "but what in God's name are you on about?"

Minerva couldn't help but laugh.

"Do you mind?" Colin told the man irritably. "I promised this woman months of tender courtship, and thanks to your Society and its inane, archaic rules, I must cram it all into the space of five minutes. The least you could do is not interrupt."

Sir Alisdair spoke directly to Minerva. "Is this man harassing you, Miss . . ." He paused. "It is *Miss* Highwood?"

"Yes," she said gently. "Yes, it is *Miss* Highwood. I apologize for the confusion. And I'm so sorry if I've caused you any . . . disappointment."

His mouth quirked as he looked her up and down. "Merely surprise, Miss Highwood. Merely surprise."

"Yes, yes. She's a very surprising woman." Colin cleared his throat. "Once again, man. Do you mind?"

Smiling, Minerva pulled Colin a few steps away. "Never mind him. Carry on."

Once they had a bit of privacy, his eyes gentled. "As I was saying, pet. I love that you call things by their right names. That you're bold enough to call a tit a tit, and a cock a cock. But most of all, I love that even after this mad, reckless week with me—even with your heart and reputation and future hanging in the balance—you were brave enough to call love love." His hands framed her face. "Because that's exactly what this is. I love you, Minerva." A look of exultant joy lit his eyes, as though he'd just unearthed the scientific discovery of a lifetime. "We love each other."

A knot rose in her throat. "Yes. We do."

"I want to be with you, for the rest of our lives."

"I want that, too."

"Then here." He released her hands. Catching his glove between his teeth, he tugged it loose and then discarded the thing entirely. His fingers went to the signet ring on his little finger, and he twisted it back and forth. And back and forth. He grimaced. "This may take a moment."

"Colin, really. You don't have to—"

"Almost have it," he said through gritted teeth. His face was red and contorted with effort. "Wait . . . wait . . ."

He turned away and crouched, still tugging at the ring. Minerva began to grow worried for him.

"There." Panting for breath and wearing an expression of triumph, he held up the ring for her inspection. "I haven't removed this ring since I was a boy. It was my father's of course, and it came to me after his death. It started out on my thumb, then made its way down every finger. It's been on that last finger so long, it almost became a part of me. But now I want you to wear it."

"Oh, I couldn't."

"No, you must." He turned her hand palm up and dropped the ring in it. "It's my most cherished possession, Min. You must wear it. That way, I'll always know the two things dearest to me are in the same place. It will be a true help. Most convenient."

She stared at the ring. Then she stared at him, breathless with emotion.

"Didn't—" He cleared his throat. "Didn't you want to marry me?"

"Of course I do," she hastened to assure him. "Of course

I want to marry you. But I thought you wanted to wait, go slowly. Have a proper courtship. It seemed so important to you."

"This"—he gestured at the door and the symposium going on within—"is important to you. Which means it's everything to me."

Stunned, she watched as he sank to one knee.

"I love you, Minerva. Stay with me forever. Let me cherish you always. Give me the lasting joy of calling you my own." He slipped the signet ring on her gloved finger. "But marry me today. So I can share you with the world."

She gazed down at him, her heart swollen with love—and her mind decided that the world would never see a better man.

With a few hasty vows uttered right here on these steps, he offered to make all her dreams come true. And she could make Colin all hers. Forever.

"Well, girl?" Behind them, Mr. Barrington thumped his board. "Do you mean to marry the fellow or not?"

Chapter Thirty-two

"Can I interest you in some lace today, Miss Taylor?" As Kate entered the All Things shop, Sally Bright straightened behind the counter. The fair-haired young woman laid aside the newspaper she'd been reading. "Or a new ribbon, perhaps?"

Kate shook her head, smiling. "Just some ink. I haven't any reason for new lace or ribbons today."

"Are you certain?" Sally plunked a bottle of ink on the counter. "That's not what I hear."

The sly note in the girl's voice made Kate snap to attention.

"What did you hear?"

Sally feigned innocence. "Only that someone made a trip up to Rycliff Castle the other day. Alone."

Kate felt her cheeks heating. Which annoyed her, because she had nothing whatever to feel embarrassed or ashamed about. "Yes, I did walk up to the castle. I needed to speak with Corporal Thorne. We had a . . . a disagreement to settle."

"Ah." Sally's brow arched. "A disagreement to settle. Well, that all sounds very proper."

"It wasn't improper, if that's what you're suggesting."

Kate declined to mention the fact that she'd come upon the man at his labor. Half-dressed, drenched with perspiration. All that bronzed skin stretched over a hard, muscled body . . . his broad-shouldered silhouette was burned into her memory now. As though she'd stared directly at the sun, and the impression lingered on her retinas.

"I'm just teasing you, Miss Taylor. I know there's nothing untoward between you. But mind you be careful. You don't want the wrong idea getting around. Else you're sure to suffer a plague of small mishaps. Salt will find its way into your sugar bowl, pins will be left in your hemmed skirts, and so forth."

Kate frowned. "How do you mean?"

"Envy. Half the women in the village will be wishing you ill."

"They'd envy me? Why?"

"Cor, you truly don't know." Sally straightened the pieces of jewelry in the display case. "From the moment Lord Rycliff's party rode into the village last summer, I know all you ladies of the Queen's Ruby had your eyes on Lord Payne. Dashing, handsome, charming. What gentlewoman wouldn't take a fancy to him? But there's other women in this village, Miss Taylor. Serving girls, sailors' widows, housemaids . . . women who won't bother to dream of a viscount. They've all been jostling to catch Corporal Thorne."

"Truly? But . . ." Kate slapped at a gnat pestering her neck. "But he's so big. And rough. And coarse mannered."

"Exactly." Sally gave her a knowing smile.

Kate wondered at it.

"So far, it's all come to naught. Traps have been laid for him all over this village, but he's evaded every one. Rumor is, he's got himself an 'arrangement' with a widow next town over. Goes to pay her a kindly visit once or twice a month, if you catch my meaning."

Kate did catch Sally's meaning. And it made her suddenly, unaccountably nauseous. Naturally, Corporal Thorne had the right to do whatever he pleased with whomever he pleased. She just didn't like knowing about it.

Much less *picturing* it.

She gave herself a brisk mental shake.

"Well, you can spread the word"—and she knew Sally would—"that the women of Spindle Cove have nothing to envy. There's absolutely nothing between me and Corporal Thorne. Nothing but polite acquaintance on my side, and certainly no affection on his. The man barely tolerates my existence."

Thorne had been only too eager to see Kate leave that day. She recalled the terse impatience in his motions as he'd shown her to the castle gate, once their conversation was concluded. Evidently, digging a well was more entertaining.

Sally shrugged, wiping a dusting cloth over the shelves behind the counter. "You never know, Miss Taylor. No one thought there was anything between Miss Minerva and Lord Payne, either. And look at them."

"That's entirely different."

"How?"

"It . . . just is." Kate was saved by the clip-clop of hoofbeats and a rumble of approaching carriage wheels.

In an acrobatic maneuver, Sally clutched the shelf with one hand and leaned her weight to the other side, craning her neck to peek out the shop's front window. Glimpse achieved, she dropped her dusting cloth.

"Just a moment, Miss Taylor. That's the post. I have to meet it, or they'll be ever so angry. Those mail-coach drivers are surly ones. They don't even like to slow down."

While Sally gathered the post, Kate fished in her reticule for coins to pay for the ink. There weren't all that many coins left. Winter and early spring were lean seasons for a music tutor in a holiday village. She had to exercise constant frugality.

"Do you have change for a half crown?" she asked, as Sally came back through the door.

"Just a moment . . ." The young woman sifted through the small bundle of envelopes and letters. She seized on one missive, separating it from the stack. "Cor. Here it is."

"Here what is?"

"A letter from Miss Minerva."

Kate's heart jumped in her chest. The whole village had been waiting for word from Minerva. She rushed to Sally's side. "That's her penmanship. I'm certain of it."

"Oh!" Sally squealed. "It's sealed with Lord Payne's crest, just look."

Kate ran her fingers over the bumpy red wax seal. "Indeed it is. Oh, this is wonderful news. Mrs. Highwood should have it at once. I'll take it to her at the Queen's Ruby."

Sally clutched the envelope to her chest. "Absolutely not. No one's getting this away from me. I have to be there when she reads it."

"But what of the shop?"

"Miss Taylor, this is the Bright family. There *are* a half dozen of us." Sally dashed to the storeroom door and called through it. "Rufus, mind the counter. I'll pop back in ten!"

Together, they raced across the green and through the door of the Queen's Ruby. They found Charlotte and Mrs. Highwood in the drawing room. The former, working an embroidered pillowcase. The latter, drowsing on the divan.

"Mrs. Highwood!" Sally called.

The matron woke with a snort. Her head swiveled so abruptly, her lace cap went askew. "What? What is it? Who's murdered?"

"No one's been murdered," Kate said, smiling. "But some-one may have been married."

Sally pressed the letter into the older woman's hand. "Go on, Mrs. Highwood. Do read it. We're all desperate to know."

Mrs. Highwood looked at the envelope. Her face blanched. "Oh my saints. My dear, darling girl." With trembling fingers, she broke the seal and unfolded the letter.

Charlotte put aside her embroidery and huddled near.

The older woman thrust the letter at her youngest daughter. "Here, you read it. My eyes are too bad. And my nerves . . ."

Sally clutched Kate's arm, and they all waited in breathless anticipation.

"Aloud, Miss Charlotte," Sally urged. "Do read it aloud."

" 'My dear mother,'" Charlotte began. " 'I know you must be wondering what has become of your wayward daughter. I must admit, the past week has not unfolded quite as I'd planned.'"

"Oh dear," Kate murmured.

"She's ruined," Mrs. Highwood said weakly. "We're all ruined. Someone fetch my fan. And some wine."

Charlotte went on reading. " 'Despite the travails of the road, we—'"

"We!" Sally echoed. "Take heart, Mrs. Highwood. She wrote 'we'!"

" 'We are settled in Northumberland at present.' "

"Northumberland." The color returned to Mrs. Highwood's cheeks. She sat straight on the divan. "His estate is there. He told me so once. Oh, what was the name of it?"

" 'And it's with great pleasure,'" Charlotte continued, " 'that I write to you from . . .'" She lowered the paper and smiled. " 'From the beautiful library at Riverchase.'"

Chapter Thirty-three

Two weeks later

My dear daughter, the Viscountess Payne,

*The bells are ringing in St. Ursula's today! I told the
vicar they must, no matter that you're all the way in
Northumberland. How happy we were to receive your
letter. As my friends always tell me, my intuition is
unparalleled. I always knew that rascal Payne would
be my son one day. But who could have guessed his
viscountess! You have done your mother proud, dear.
Of course, you must take time for your honeymoon,
but do think of returning to Town for the celebrations
of the Glorious Peace. Diana must be next, you know.
She will be well placed to take advantage of your new
connections. I have higher hopes for her prospects
than ever. If you can catch Payne, surely Diana can
snare a duke!*

Yours, etc.
Mama

With an amused smile, Minerva refolded the letter and placed it in her pocket.

She paused in the middle of the path, drawing a lungful of the warm, fragrant late-spring air and loosening her bonnet strings to let the straw bonnet slip down her back. Then with a light step, she continued on the country path that led from the village to Riverchase.

Bluebells waved drunkenly on their slender stalks, begging to be plucked. As she went, she stopped to gather them, along with primrose and a few remaining daffodils. She had quite a posy accumulated by the time she climbed the hill. As she neared the ridge's apex, a smile bloomed across her face. She warmed with joy, just anticipating the sight of the familiar granite facade.

But it wasn't Riverchase she first glimpsed as she crested the hill.

It was Colin, walking down the same path—toward her.

"Hullo," he called, drawing near. "I was just on my way to the village."

"What for?"

"To see you, naturally."

"Oh. Well, I was on my way to see you." She gave him a shy smile, feeling that familiar touch of giddiness.

He gestured at her bouquet of wildflowers. "Collecting flowers today? Not rocks?"

"I like flowers sometimes."

"I'm glad to hear it. Vases of flowers are much easier to send round to the cottage." His gloved fingertip caressed her cheek. "Miss Minerva, may I . . . ?"

"A kiss?"

He nodded.

She offered her cheek to him, leaning in to accept the tender, courtly gesture. But at the last moment, he turned her face to his and kissed her on the lips instead. Oh, he was ever the scoundrel, and she was glad of it. Their kiss was brief, but warm and sweet as the afternoon sun.

After a moment, he straightened. His gaze wandered her form. "You look . . ." He shook his head, smiling a little. "Cataclysmic with beauty today."

She swallowed, taking a moment to recover from his masculine splendor. "You rather devastate me, too."

"I'd like to think my kiss can take all the credit for that lovely blush, but I doubt it's the truth. What has you so self-satisfied?"

"The kiss has a great deal to do with it. But the post came through this morning." She fished a pair of envelopes from her pocket. "I had two rather interesting letters. The first is from my mother. She extends her felicitations on our marriage."

She handed him the letter from Spindle Cove. He unfolded the page and scanned its contents. As he read, the corner of his mouth curled in amusement.

"I'm sorry," Minerva said. "I know she's dreadful."

"She's not. She's a mother who wants the best for her daughters."

"She's mistaken, is what she is. I didn't tell her we'd married. I only said we'd stopped at your estate, and she shouldn't expect me back for a month or more. But she's obviously assumed."

"They've all assumed. I had a letter from Bram just the other day. He wanted to know why I hadn't sent the solicitors written proof of our marriage yet. 'Don't I want my money?' he asked."

Together, they turned to walk toward Riverchase.

"They'll learn the truth eventually," she mused.

"Yes, they will. You said you had two interesting letters. Who sent the other?"

"Sir Alisdair Kent."

She noted a slight hitch in his step. The subtle hint of jealousy thrilled her more than it ought.

"Oh, truly?" he said, in a purposely offhand tone. "And what did the good Sir Alisdair have to say?"

"Not much. Only that the *Royal Geological Journal* has declined to publish my paper about Francine."

"What?" He stopped dead and turned to her. The affectionate sparkle in his eyes became a flash of something irate, verging on murderous. "Oh, Min. That's bollocks. They can't have done that to you."

She shrugged. "Sir Alisdair said he tried to argue on my behalf, but the other journal editors would not be convinced. My evidence was specious, they said; my conclusions were too great of a reach . . ."

"Codswallop." His jaw tightened. "Cowardly bastards. They just won't be outdone by a woman, that's all."

"Perhaps."

He shook his head ruefully. "I'm sorry, Min. We should have gone in to the symposium that day. You could have presented your findings in person. If only they'd all heard you speak, you could have convinced them."

"No, don't be sorry." She reached for his hand and squeezed it. "Don't ever be sorry, Colin. I never will be."

They stood there for a long moment, smiling a little and gazing into each other's eyes. Lately, they could spend hours like this—a palpable happiness and love welling in the space between them.

Minerva couldn't wait to be his wife. But she would never regret refusing to marry him that day in Edinburgh, at the threshold of the Royal Geological Society.

He'd been through so much just to get her to that doorway. Faced his deepest fears, committed feats of daring. Opened his heart to her, and his home as well. He'd given her courage and strength and hours of laughter. Not to mention passion, and all those fervent words of love. In proposing to her, he'd made the bravest leap of faith she could imagine.

In return, Minerva wanted to give him this much, at least. The proper courtship he'd wanted. A chance for their love to take root and grow. When she recited those wedding vows, she wanted him to know they were vows of freely given, lasting devotion, not a hasty grab at scientific glory.

Colin deserved that much.

They'd turned their backs on Mr. Barrington and the Royal Geological Society that day. But Sir Alisdair Kent had the curiosity to follow. He invited them for a meal at the nearby inn, where they spent several hours engaged in scholarly debate with his friends. Sir Alisdair and company listened, questioned, argued, and generally afforded Minerva the respect due an intellectual peer. Colin saw that the wineglasses never went empty and kept his arm draped casually, possessively, over the back of her chair.

No, it wasn't a medallion and a prize of five hundred guineas, but it was a symposium of sorts. And it had been well worth the journey.

Afterward, she and Colin had traveled straight back to Northumberland. Colin installed her in a lovely cottage in the village, with his housekeeper Mrs. Hammond as chaperone. And then he'd gone about living up to all his promises of a tender, attentive courtship. He called on her most mornings, and they went for long, rambling walks in the afternoons. He brought her gifts of sweets and lace, and they kept the errand boys dashing back and forth with notes that needed no signatures. Several times a week, she and Mrs. Hammond dined at Riverchase, and he took Sunday dinner at the cottage.

They also spent time apart. She, writing up her Spindle Cove findings and exploring the new craggy landscape.

Colin, surveying the estate with his land steward and making assessments and plans for the future.

As for plans for *their* future . . . Minerva tried to be patient.

If Colin had taken a hurtling leap of faith when he'd proposed, her gesture of faith had been more of a long, slow skate on thin ice. As much as she'd been enjoying their courtship, she tried not to think about the potential for heartbreak. There was always the chance that he might change his mind.

But in the month or so since returning from Edinburgh, they'd survived their first argument—a dispute over, of all things, a missing pair of gloves. They'd also weathered their second clash. It had begun as a tense disagreement over whether Minerva could safely explore the local crags unaccompanied. (Of course she could, was Minerva's opinion. Colin begged to differ.) The tense disagreement exploded into a grand row that involved loud denouncements of female independence, male arrogance, fur-lined cloaks, rocks of all sorts, and—inexplicably—the color green. But the eventual compromise—a joint excursion to the crags that became a passionate, frantic tryst in the heather—quite took the edge off their anger.

Since then, their courtship had been as sweet and tender as ever—but not entirely chaste.

Minerva put her arm through his, and they resumed walking down the path. "I'm not deterred. I'll find some other way to publish my findings."

"*We'll* find a way. If you can wait five more weeks, I'll celebrate my birthday by printing a copy for every household in England."

She smiled. "A few hundred copies would do, and there's no need to rush. Francine's footprint survived in that cave for millions of years. I can wait a bit longer to make my own mark."

"Would it help if I tell you there's already a deep, permanent, Minerva-sized footprint on my heart?"

"Yes." She kissed his cheek, savoring that hint of cloves from his shaving soap. "Do you have any business this afternoon? I was hoping to spend a few hours poking through the Riverchase library."

He didn't answer for a moment. "If an afternoon in the library is your desire, you shall have it. But I confess, I had something else in mind."

"Truly? What's that?"

"A wedding."

Minerva nearly dropped her posy of flowers. "Whose wedding?"

"Ours."

"But we can't—"

"We can. The vicar's read the banns in the parish church three times now. I sent him a note before I left the house this morning, and I asked the butler to ready the chapel. By the time we return, all should be ready."

Minerva blinked at him. He'd been planning this? "But I thought we agreed to wait until after your birthday."

His arms went around her, wreathing loosely about her waist. "I know, but I can't. I simply can't. I slept well last night. But when I woke this morning, I missed you so intensely. I don't even know how to describe the sensation. I looked at the other pillow, and it just seemed wrong that you weren't there. As though I'd woken up missing my own arm, or half of my heart. I felt incomplete. So I rose, and dressed, and I just started walking toward you—because I couldn't move in any other direction. And then there you were, walking toward me. Flowers in hand."

Emotion glimmered in his eyes, and he touched her cheek. "This isn't a whim. I simply can't stand to spend another day apart. I want you to share my life and my home, and . . ." He cinched her tight, drawing her body in exquisite contact with his. He bent his head, pressing kisses to the soft place beneath her ear. "And I want you to share my bed. As my wife. Tonight."

His kisses made her dizzy with longing. She clung to him tight. "Colin."

"I love you, Min. I love you so much, it terrifies me. Say you'll marry me today."

She pulled back a little. "I . . ." Swallowing hard, she ran a trembling hand down her butter-yellow muslin. "I should at least change my frock."

"Don't you dare." He shook his head, framing her waist in his hands. "You're perfect. Utterly perfect, just as you are."

Emotion swelled in her heart and thickened her throat. She felt like pinching herself, just to make sure she wasn't dreaming. But she never could have dreamed something so wonderful. She was perfect. He was perfect. This moment was perfect. She was afraid to speak, for fear of ruining it somehow.

Don't pause to think. Just run down the slope.

"Yes," she finally blurted out. "Yes. Let's get married."

"Today?"

"This very hour." A giddy grin stretched her cheeks, and she couldn't hold back the pure joy any longer. She launched herself at him, flinging her arms around his neck. "Oh, Colin, I love you so much. I can't possibly tell you. I'll try to show you, but I'll need years."

He chuckled. "We have decades, darling. Decades."

Five minutes' hasty walk saw them to the chapel door. While Colin went to find the vicar and round up a few servants as witnesses, Minerva passed into the small church-yard and came to stand before a slab of flawless granite, polished to a mirror gleam.

She stood there for a long minute, unsure how to begin. Then she took a deep breath and dabbed a tear from her cheek.

"I'm so sorry we'll never meet," she whispered, laying her posy atop the late Lord and Lady Payne's grave. "But thank you. For him. I promise, I'll love him as fiercely as I can. Kindly send down some blessings when you can spare them. We'll probably need them, from time to time."

By the time she left the churchyard and rounded the chapel corner, she caught sight of Colin leading the vicar, butler, and house servants marching in a bemusement-day parade. Holding open the door, he waved them all into the chapel.

"Come along, now," he said, tapping his boot with impatience.

When the rest had all filed in, and only the two of them were left standing at the door, he caught Minerva's gaze. "Ready?"

She nodded, breathless. "If you are."

"I've never been so sure of anything." He reached for her hand and kissed it. "You belong beside me, Min. And I belong beside you. I know it in my heart. I feel it in my soul. I'm certain, in every possible way."

And he'd never been more handsome.

"Certainty becomes you," she said.

Smiling, he laced her arm through his, leading her into the chapel.

And that was how the grand, epic story of their future—the tale they'd tell friends and dinner party guests and grandchildren for decades to come—ended. Just as a proper fairy tale should. With a romantic wedding, a tender kiss . . .

And the promise of happily ever after.

Author's Note

"Francine" was an iguanodon.

Preserved iguanodon footprints can be found in many places along England's southern coast, but Minerva was a few years ahead of her time in identifying Francine's footprint as fossil evidence of what we now call dinosaurs. Sussex geologist Gideon Mantell published his findings on iguanodons in the early 1820s. The discovery of several key fossils is often credited to his wife, Mary Ann.

Perhaps the earliest and most influential paleontologist of all was Mary Anning, who first discovered ichthyosaur fossils on the cliffs of Lyme Regis at the age of twelve. She spent the rest of her life unearthing valuable finds—only to watch them purchased, displayed, and written about by gentlemen of a higher social class.

I made up the Royal Geological Society of Scotland, but the Geological Society of London existed at that time. The Society did not admit women to its membership or its meetings.

In other notes, some readers might wonder why Spindle Cove is celebrating victory in April 1814, more than a year before Napoleon Bonaparte's final defeat at Waterloo. Bonaparte did surrender in France in 1814, and he was exiled to the island of Elba. However, he managed to escape his prison in early 1815, forcing England and her allies to rally for the Hundred Days campaign. So the peace England enjoys in this book is sadly a temporary one—but the characters couldn't know that yet.

Want more Spindle Cove?
Turn the page for a sneak peek at
Tessa Dare's

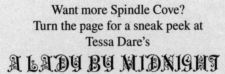

Coming September 2012
From Avon Books

More tea, Miss Taylor?"

"No, thank you." Kate sipped the weak brew in her cup, masking her grimace. The leaves were on their third use, at least. They seemed to have been washed of their last vague memory of being tea.

Fitting, she supposed. Vague memories were the order of the day.

Miss Paringham put aside the teapot. "Where did you say you're residing?"

Kate smiled at the white-haired woman in the chair opposite. "Spindle Cove, Miss Paringham. It's a popular holiday village for gently bred young ladies. I make my living offering music lessons."

"I am glad to know your schooling has provided you with an honest income. That is more than an unfortunate like yourself should have hoped."

"Oh, indeed. I'm very lucky."

Setting aside her "tea," Kate cast a surreptitious glance at the mantel clock. Time was growing short. She despised wasting precious minutes on niceties when there were questions singeing the tip of her tongue. But abruptness wouldn't win her any answers.

A wrapped parcel lay in her lap, and she curled her fingers around the string. "I was so glad to learn you'd settled here in Hastings. Imagine, my old schoolmistress, pensioned just a few hours' ride away. I couldn't resist paying a call to reminisce. I have such fond recollections of my Margate years."

Miss Paringham raised an eyebrow. "Really."

"Oh, yes." She stretched her mind for examples. "I particularly miss the . . . the nourishing soup. And our regular devotionals. It's just so hard to find two solid hours for reading sermons nowadays."

As orphans went, Kate knew she'd been a great deal happier than most. The atmosphere at Margate School for Girls might have been austere, but she hadn't been beaten or starved or unclothed. She'd formed friendships and gained a useful education. Most important of all, she'd been instructed in music and encouraged in its practice.

Truly, she could not complain. Margate had provided for Kate's every need, save one.

Love.

In all her years there, she'd never known real love. Just some pale, thrice-washed dilution of it. Another girl might have grown bitter. But Kate just wasn't formed for misery. Even if her mind could not recall it, her heart remembered a time before Margate. Some distant memory of happiness echoed in its every beat.

She'd been loved once. She just knew it. She couldn't put a name or face to the emotion, but that didn't make it any less real. Once upon a time, she'd belonged—to someone, somewhere.

"Do you remember the day I arrived at Margate, Miss Paringham? I must have been such a little thing."

The old woman's mouth pursed. "Five years at the oldest. We had no way to be certain."

"No. Of course you wouldn't."

No one knew Kate's true birthday, least of all Kate. As schoolmistress, Miss Paringham had decided all wards of the school would share the Lord's birthday, December 25. Supposedly they were to take comfort from this reminder of their heavenly family on the day when all the other girls had gone home to their own flesh-and-blood relations.

However, Kate always suspected there'd been a more

practical motive behind the choice. If their birthdays were on Christmas, there was never any need to celebrate them. No extra gifts were warranted. Wards of the school made do with the same Christmas package every year: an orange, a ribbon, and a neatly folded length of patterned muslin. Miss Paringham did not believe in sweets.

Apparently she still didn't. Kate bit a tiny corner off the dry, tasteless biscuit she'd been offered, and then set it back on the plate.

On the mantel, the clock's ticking seemed to accelerate. Only twenty minutes before the last stagecoach left for Spindle Cove. If Kate missed the stage, she would be stranded in Hastings all night.

She steeled her nerve. No more dithering.

"Who were they?" she asked. "Do you know?"

"Whatever do you mean?"

"My parents."

Miss Paringham sniffed. "You were a ward of the school. You have no parents."

"I do understand that." Kate smiled, trying to inject some levity. "But I wasn't hatched from an egg, was I? I didn't turn up under a cabbage leaf. I had a mother and father once. Perhaps I had them for as many as five years. If only I could remember. All my memories are so vague, so jumbled. I remember feeling safe. I have this impression of blue. A room with blue walls, perhaps, but I can't be certain." She pinched the bridge of her nose and frowned at the knotted carpet fringe. "Maybe I just want to remember so desperately, I'm imagining things."

"Miss Taylor . . ."

"I remember sounds, mostly." She shut her eyes, delving inward. "Sounds with no pictures. Someone saying to me, 'Be brave, my Katie.' Was it my mother? My father? The words are burned into my memory, but I can't put a face to them, no matter how I try. And then there's the music. Endless pianoforte music, and that same little song . . ."

"Miss *Taylor*."

As she repeated Kate's name, the old schoolmistress's voice cracked. Not cracked like brittle china, but cracked like a whip.

In a reflexive motion, Kate snapped tall in her chair.

Sharp eyes regarded her. "Miss Taylor, I advise you to abandon this line of inquiry at once."

"How can I? You must understand. I've lived with these questions all my life, Miss Paringham. I've tried to do as you always advised and be happy for what good fortune life has given me. I have friends. I have a living. I have music. But I still don't have the truth. I want to know where I came from. I know my parents are dead now, but perhaps there is some hope of contacting my relations. There has to be someone, somewhere. The smallest detail might prove useful. A name, a town, a—"

The old woman rapped her cane against the floorboards. "Miss Taylor. Even if I had some information to impart, I would never share it. I would take it to my grave."

Kate sat back in her chair. "But . . . why?"

Miss Paringham didn't answer, but merely pressed her papery lips into a thin slash of disapproval.

"You never liked me," Kate whispered. "I knew it. You always made it clear, in small, unspoken ways, that any kindness you showed me was begrudged."

"Very well. You are correct. I never liked you."

They regarded one another. There, now the truth was out.

Kate struggled not to reveal any sign of disappointment or hurt. But her wrapped bundle of sheet music slipped to the floor—and as it did, a smug little smile curved Miss Paringham's lips.

Beastly, horrid crone.

"May I ask on what basis was I so reviled? I was appropriately grateful for every small thing I was given. I didn't cause mischief. I never complained. I minded my lessons and earned high marks."

"Precisely. You showed no humility. You behaved as though you had as much claim to joy as any other girl at Margate. Always singing. Always smiling."

The idea was so absurd, Kate couldn't help but laugh. "You disliked me because I smiled too much? Should I have been melancholy and brooding?"

"Ashamed!" Miss Paringham barked the word. "A child of shame ought to live ashamed."

Kate was momentarily stunned silent. *A child of shame?* "What can you mean? I always thought I was orphaned. You never said—"

"Wicked thing. Your shame goes without saying. God Himself has marked you." Miss Paringham pointed with a bony finger.

Kate couldn't even reply. She raised her own trembling hand to her temple and traced the dramatic wine-colored birthmark splashed there.

She knew her birthmark made her an object of distaste, sometimes pity. In the most rural, uncultured of areas, it even caused some to view her with suspicion. For years, she'd tried to obscure the mark with wide-brimmed bonnets or artfully arranged ringlets of hair—to no avail. People always stared straight past them. Eventually, she'd decided not to hide it any longer. Amongst friends, Kate forgot the blotch entirely. But sometimes, it took a great deal of strength to hold her head high.

At the moment, she felt her chin sinking.

With her fingertips, she began to idly rub the mark, the same way she'd done as a young girl—as if she might erase it from her skin. Her whole life, she'd believed herself to be a loved child, whose parents had met an untimely demise. How horrid, to think that she'd been cast away, unwanted.

Her fingers stilled on her birthmark. Perhaps cast away because of *this*.

"You fool girl." The old woman's laugh was a caustic rasp. "Been dreaming of a fairy tale, have you? Thinking someday a messenger will knock on your door and declare you're a long-lost princess?"

Stay calm, Kate told herself. *She's a lonely, warped old woman who now lives to make others miserable. I will not give her the satisfaction of seeing me rattled.*

But she would not stay here a moment longer, either.

She reached to gather her wrapped parcel of music from the floor. "I'm sorry to have disturbed you, Miss Paringham. I will leave. You needn't say any more."

"Oh, I *will* say more. Ignorant thing that you are, you've reached the age of three-and-twenty without understanding this. I see I must take it upon myself to teach you one last lesson."

"Please, don't strain yourself." Rising from her chair, Kate curtseyed and gave the woman a defiant smile. "Thank you for the tea. I really must be going if I'm to catch the stage-coach. I'll see myself out."

"Impertinent girl!"

The old woman lashed out with her cane, striking Kate in the back of the knees.

Kate stumbled a bit, catching herself in the drawing room entryway. "You struck me. I can't believe you just struck me."

"Should have done it years ago. I might have knocked that smile straight from your face."

Kate braced her shoulder on the doorjamb. The sting of humiliation was far greater than the physical pain. Part of her wanted to just crumple into a tiny ball on the floor, but she knew she had to flee this place. More than that, she had to flee these *words*. These horrible, unthinkable notions that could leave her marked inside, as well as out.

"Good day, Miss Paringham." She placed weight on her smarting knee and drew a quick breath. The front door was just paces away.

"No one wanted you." Venom dripped from the old woman's voice. "No one wanted you then. Who on earth do you think will want you now?"

Someone, Kate's heart insisted. *Someone, somewhere.*

"No one." Malice twisted the old woman's face as she swung the cane again.

Kate heard its crisp *whack* against the doorjamb, but by that time, she was already wrestling open the front latch. She picked up her skirts and darted out of the garden, into the cobbled street. Her low-heeled boots were worn flat on the soles, and she slipped and stumbled a bit as she ran. The streets of Hastings were narrow and curved, lined with busy shops and inns. There was no possible way the sour-faced woman could have followed her.

Still, she ran.

She ran with hardly a care for which direction she was going, so long as it was away. Perhaps if she kept running fast enough, the truth would never catch up.

As she turned in the direction of the mews, the booming toll of a church bell struck dread in her gut.

One, two, three, four . . .

Oh no. Stop there. Please don't toll again.

Five.

Kate's heart flopped. Miss Paringham's clock must have been slow. She was too late. The coach would have already departed without her. There wouldn't be another until morning.

The summer had stretched daylight to its greatest length,

but in a few hours, night *would* fall. She'd spent most of her funds at the music shop, leaving only enough money for her passage back to Spindle Cove—no extra coin for an inn or a meal.

She came to a standstill in the crowded lane. People jostled and streamed about her on all sides. But she didn't belong to any of them. None of them would help her now. The despair she'd held at bay for so long crawled its way through her veins, cold and black.

She was alone. Not just tonight, but forever. Her own relations had abandoned her years ago. No one wanted her now. She would die alone, living in some cramped pensioner's apartment like Miss Paringham's, drinking thrice-washed tea and chewing on her own bitterness.

Be brave, my Katie.

Her whole life, she'd clung to the memory of those words. She'd held fast to the belief that they meant someone, somewhere cared. She wouldn't let that voice down.

She closed her eyes, drew a deep breath, and took a silent inventory. She had her wits. She had her talent. She had a young, healthy body. No one could take these things from her. Not even that cruel, shriveled wench with her cane and weak tea.

There had to be some solution. Did she have anything she could sell? Her pink muslin frock was rather fine—a handed-down gift from one of her pupils, trimmed with ribbon and lace—but she couldn't sell the clothes off her back. She'd left her best summer bonnet at Miss Paringham's, and she'd rather sleep in the streets than retrieve it.

If she hadn't cut it so short last summer, she might have tried to sell her hair. But the locks barely reached below her shoulders now, and they were an unremarkable shade of brown. No wigmaker would want it.

Her best chance was the music shop. Perhaps if she explained her predicament and asked very nicely, the proprietor would accept his music back and return Kate's money. She would promise to return next week and purchase all the same pieces again. That would afford her enough for a room at a somewhat respectable inn. Staying alone was never advisable, and she didn't even have her pistol. But she could prop a chair beneath her door and stay awake all night, clutching the fireplace poker and keeping her voice primed to scream.

There. She had a plan.

As she started to cross the street, an elbow knocked her off balance.

"Oy," its owner said. "Watch yerself, miss."

Kate whirled away, apologizing. The twine on her parcel snapped. White pages flapped and fluttered into the gusty summer afternoon, like a covey of startled doves.

"Oh no. The music."

She made wild sweeps with both hands. A few pages disappeared down the street and others fell to the cobblestones, quickly trampled by passersby. But the bulk of the parcel landed in the middle of the lane, still wrapped in brown paper.

She made a lunging grab for it, desperate to save what she could.

"Look sharp!" a man shouted.

Cartwheels creaked. Somewhere much too near, a horse bucked and whinnied. She looked up from where she'd crouched in the lane to see two windmilling, iron-shoed hooves, big as dinner plates, preparing to demolish her.

A woman screamed.

Kate threw her weight to one side. The horse's hooves landed just to her left. With a squalling hiss of the brake, a cartwheel screeched to a halt—inches from crushing her leg.

The parcel of sheet music landed some yards distant. Her "plan" was now a mud-stained, wheel-rutted smear on the street.

"Devil take you." The driver cursed her from the box, brandishing his horsewhip. "A fine little witch you are. Near overset my whole cart."

"I-I'm sorry, sir. It was an accident."

He cracked his whip against the cobblestones. "Out of my way then. You unnatural little—"

As he raised his whip for another strike, Kate flinched and ducked.

No blow came.

A man stepped between her and the cart. "Threaten her again," she heard him warn the driver in a low, inhuman growl, "and I will whip the flesh from your miserable bones."

Chilling, those words. But effective. The cart swiftly rolled away.

As strong arms pulled her to her feet, Kate's gaze climbed a veritable mountain of man. She saw black polished boots. Buff breeches stretched over granite thighs. A distinctive red wool officer's coat.

Her heart jumped. She *knew* this coat. She'd probably sewn the brass buttons on these cuffs. This was the uniform of the Spindle Cove militia. She was in familiar arms. She was saved. And when she lifted her head, she was guaranteed to find a friendly face, unless . . .

"Miss Taylor?"

Unless.

Unless it was *him*. The only soul in Spindle Cove she could not call a friend. They'd resided in the same village for almost a year now, and he'd made it abundantly clear he had no interest in friendship. He had no use for her company at all.

"Corporal Thorne," she whispered.

In all her life, she'd never known a man who could look so hard. His face was stony—composed of ruthless, chiseled angles and unyielding planes. Its stark terrain offered her no shelter, nowhere to hide. His mouth was a grim slash. His dark brows converged in disapproval. And his eyes . . . his eyes were the blue of river ice on the coldest, harshest winter night.

On another day, Kate could have laughed at the irony. Of all the people to come to her rescue, it *would* be this one—the man with no heart at all.

"Miss Taylor. What the devil are you doing here?"

At his rough tone, all her muscles pulled tight. "I . . . I came into town to purchase new sheet music and to . . ." She couldn't bring herself to mention calling on Miss Paringham. "But I dropped my parcel, and now I've missed the stage home. Silly me."

Silly, foolish, shame-marked, unwanted me.

"And now I'm truly stuck, I'm afraid. If only I'd brought a little more money, I could afford a room for the evening, then go back to Spindle Cove tomorrow."

"You've no money?"

She turned away, unable to bear the chastisement in his gaze.

"What were you thinking, traveling all this distance alone?"

"I hadn't any choice. I'm an unmarried woman with no parents, no siblings. No means to hire a companion." Her voice caught. "I am completely alone."

His grip firmed on her arms. "I'm here. You're not alone now."

Hardly poetry, those words. A simple statement of fact. They scarcely shared the same alphabet as kindness. If true comfort were a nourishing, wholemeal loaf, what he offered her were a few stale crumbs.

It didn't matter. It didn't matter. She was a starving girl, and she hadn't the dignity to refuse.

"I'm so sorry," she managed, choking back a sob. "You're not going to like this."

And with that, Kate fell into his immense, rigid, unwilling embrace—and wept.

Bloody hell.

She burst into tears. Right there in the street, for God's sake. Her lovely face screwed up. She bent forward until her forehead met his chest, then she heaved a loud, wrenching sob.

Then a second. And a third.

His gelding danced sideways, and Thorne shared the beast's unease. Given a choice between watching Miss Kate Taylor weep and offering his own liver to carrion birds, Thorne would have had his knife out and sharpened before the first tear rolled down her face.

He clucked his tongue softly, which did some good toward calming the horse. It had no effect on the girl. Her slender shoulders convulsed as she wept into his coat. His hands remained fixed on her arms.

In a desperate gesture, he slid them up. Then down.

No help.

What's happened? he wanted to ask. *Who's hurt you? Who can I maim or kill for distressing you this way?*

"I'm sorry," she said, pulling away after some minutes had passed.

"Why?"

"For weeping all over you. Forcing you to hold me. I know you must hate it." She fished a handkerchief from her sleeve and dabbed at her eyes. Her nose and eyes were red. "I mean, not that you don't like holding women. Everyone in Spindle Cove knows you like women. I've heard far more than I care to hear about your—"

She paled and stopped talking.

Just as well.

He took the horse's lead in one hand and laid the other hand to Miss Taylor's back, guiding her out of the street. Once they'd reached the side of the lane, he looped his horse's reins about a post and turned his sights toward making her comfortable. There wasn't anywhere for her to sit. No bench, no crate.

This disturbed him beyond reason.

His gaze went to a tavern across the street—the sort of establishment he'd never allow her to enter—but he was seriously considering crossing the lane, toppling the first available drunk off his seat, and dragging the vacated chair out for her. A woman shouldn't weep while standing. It just didn't seem right.

"Please, can't you just loan me a few shillings? I'll find an inn for the night, and I won't trouble you any further."

"Miss Taylor, I can't lend you money to pass the night alone in a coaching inn. It's not safe."

"I have no choice but to stay. There won't be another stage back to Spindle Cove until morning."

He looked at his gelding. "I'll hire you a horse, if you can ride."

She shook her head. "I never had any lessons."

Curse it. How was he going to remedy this situation? He easily had the money to hire another horse, but nowhere near enough coin in his pocket for a private carriage. Ten miles was an easy march for him, but too far to ask a lady to walk. He *could* put her up in an inn—but damned if he would let her stay alone.

A dangerous thought visited him, sinking talons into his mind.

He could stay *with* her.

Not in a tawdry way, he told himself. Just as her protector.

He could find a damned place for her to sit down as a start. He could see that she had food and drink and warm blankets. He could stand watch while she slept and make certain nothing disturbed her. He could be there when she woke.

After all these months of frustrated longing, maybe that would be enough.

Enough? Right.

"Good heavens." She took a sudden step back.

"What is it?"

Her gaze dropped and she swallowed hard. "Some part of you is *moving.*"

"No, it's not." Thorne conducted a quick, silent assessment of his personal equipment. He found all to be under regulation. On another occasion—one with fewer tears involved— this degree of closeness would have undoubtedly roused his lust. But today she was affecting him rather higher in his torso, tying his guts in knots and poking at whatever black, smoking cinder remained of his heart.

"Your satchel." She indicated the leather pouch slung crossways over his chest. "It's . . . wriggling."

Oh. That. In all the commotion, he'd nearly forgotten the creature.

He reached beneath the leather flap and withdrew the source of the wriggling, holding it up for her to see.

"It's just this."

And suddenly, everything was different. It was like the whole world took a knock and tilted at a fresh angle. In less time than it took a man's heart to skip, Miss Taylor's face transformed. The tears were gone. Her elegant, sweeping eyebrows arched in surprise. Her eyes candled to life— glowed, really, like two stars. Her lips fell apart in a delighted gasp.

"Oh." She pressed one hand to her cheek. "Oh, it's a *puppy.*"

She smiled. Lord, how she smiled. All because of this wriggling ball of snout and fur that was as likely to piss on her slippers as chew them to bits.

She tucked her parcel under one arm and reached forward. "May I?"

As if Thorne could refuse. He placed the pup in her arms.

She fawned and cooed over it like a baby. "Where did you come from, sweeting?"

"A farm nearby," Thorne answered. "Thought I'd take him back to the castle. Been needing a hound."

She cocked her head and peered at the pup. "*Is* he a hound?"

"Partly."

Her fingers traced a rust-colored patch over the pup's right eye. "I'd suppose he's partly many things, isn't he? Funny little dear."

She lifted the pup in both hands and looked at it nose-to-nose, puckering her lips to make a little chirping noise. The dog licked her face.

Lucky cur.

"Was that mean Corporal Thorne keeping you in a dark, nasty satchel?" She gave the pup a playful shake. "You like it so much better out here with me, don't you? Of course you do."

The dog yipped. She laughed and drew it close to her chest, bending over its furry neck.

"You are perfect," he heard her whisper. "You are just exactly what I needed today." She stroked the pup's fur. "Thank you."

Thorne felt a sharp twist in his chest. Like something rusted and bent, shaking loose. This girl had a way of doing that—making him *feel*. She always had, even years upon years in the past. That long-ago time seemed to fall beyond the reach of her earliest memories. A true mercy for her.

But Thorne remembered. He remembered it all.

He cleared his throat. "We'd best be on the road. It'll be near dark by the time we reach Spindle Cove."

She tore her attention from the dog and gave Thorne a curious glance. "But how?"

"You'll ride with me. The both of you. I'll take you up on my saddle. You'll carry the dog."

As if consulting all the concerned parties, she turned to the horse. Then to the dog. Lastly, she lifted her gaze to Thorne's. "You're certain we'll fit?"

"Just."

She bit her lip, looking unsure.

Her instinctive resistance to the idea was plain. And understandable. Thorne wasn't overeager to put his plan in action, either. Three hours astride a horse with Miss Kate Taylor nestled between his thighs? Torture of the keenest sort. But he could see no better way to have her swiftly and safely home.

He could do this. If he'd lasted a year with her in the same tiny village, he could withstand a few hours' closeness.

"I won't leave you here," he said. "It'll have to be done."

Her mouth quirked in a droll, self-conscious smile. It was reassuring to see, and at the same time, devastating.

"When you put it that way, I find myself unable to refuse."

For God's sake, don't say that.

"Thank you," she added. She laid a gentle touch to his sleeve.

For your own sake, don't do that.

He pulled away from her touch, and she looked hurt. Which made him want to soothe her, but he didn't dare try.

"Mind the pup," he said.

Thorne helped her into the saddle, boosting her at the knee, rather than the thigh, as might have been more efficient. He mounted the gelding, taking the reins in one hand

and keeping one arm about her waist. As he nudged the horse into a walk, she felt soft and warm against him. His thighs bracketed hers.

Her hair smelled of clover and lemon. The scent rushed all through his senses before he could stop it. Damn, damn, damn. He could discourage her from talking to him, touching him. He could keep her distracted with a dog. But how could he prevent her from being shaped like a woman and smelling like paradise?

Never mind the beatings, the lashings, the years of prison . . .

Thorne knew, without a doubt, the next three hours would be the harshest punishment of his life.